THE CAPONE CAPER

Borgo Press Books by S. Fowler Wright

Arresting Delia: An Inspector Cleveland Classic Crime Novel
*The Attic Murder: An Inspector Combridge and Mr. Jellipot Classic Crime
    Novel*
*The Bell Street Murders: An Inspector Combridge and Mr. Jellipot Classic
    Crime Novel*
Black Widow: A Classic Crime Novel
*The Capone Caper: Mr. Jellipot vs. the King of Crime: A Classic Crime
    Novel*
Crime & Co.: An Inspector Cleveland Classic Crime Novel
Dawn: A Novel of Global Warming
Dead by Saturday: An Inspector Cleveland Classic Crime Novel
The End of the Mildew Gang: An Inspector Cauldron Classic Crime Novel
    (Mildew Gang #3)
*Four Callers in Razor Street: An Inspector Combridge and Mr. Jellipot
    Classic Crime Novel*
*The Hanging of Constance Hillier: An Inspector Cleveland Classic Crime
    Novel*
*The Jordans Murder: An Inspector Combridge and Mr. Jellipot Classic
    Crime Novel*
The King Against Anne Bickerton: A Classic Crime Novel
The Mildew Gang: An Inspector Cauldron Classic Crime Novel (Mildew
    Gang #1)
*Murder in Bethnal Square: An Inspector Combridge and Mr. Jellipot
    Classic Crime Novel*
The Police and the Public
*Post-Mortem Evidence: An Inspector Combridge and Mr. Jellipot Classic
    Crime Novel*
*The Return of the Mildew Gang: An Inspector Cauldron Classic Crime
    Novel* (Mildew Gang #2)
*The Rissole Mystery: An Inspector Combridge and Mr. Jellipot Classic
    Crime Novel*
The Screaming Lake: A Lost Race Novel
*The Secret of the Screen: An Inspector Combridge and Mr. Jellipot Classic
    Crime Novel*
Three Witnesses: A Classic Crime Novel
*Too Much for Mr. Jellipot: An Inspector Combridge and Mr. Jellipot
    Classic Crime Novel*
The Vengeance of Gwa: A Fantasy of Prehistory
Was Murder Done? A Classic Crime Novel
Who Murdered Reynard? A Classic Crime Novel
*The Wills of Jane Kanwhistle: An Inspector Combridge and Mr. Jelli-
    pot Classic Crime Novel*
*With Cause Enough?: An Inspector Combridge and Mr. Jellipot Clas-
    sic Crime Novel*

THE CAPONE CAPER

MR. JELLIPOT VS. THE KING OF CRIME

A Classic Crime Novel

by

S. FOWLER WRIGHT

WRITING AS "SYDNEY FOWLER"

The Borgo Press
An Imprint of Wildside Press LLC

MMVIII

CONTENTS

PART THREE: DINNER IN NEW YORK

PART ONE

CONCERNING FIVE MILLION DOLLARS, AND SOME MURDERS APPERTAINING THERETO

▲

CHAPTER I.

MURDER AS A GOOD DEED

HENRY BRACKEN, Assistant Commissioner of Police for the Metropolitan area, a fussy man, looked at his host in some astonishment, having heard a sentiment from his lips which offended the ethics of his legal training, and seemed particularly outrageous from the chairman of the London and Northern Bank. But Sir Reginald Crowe had a reputation for saying things that no sensible man could take seriously. Paradoxical things, irritating to the settled mind: subversive things, which you were obliged to tell yourself that he could not mean. But this did not alter the fact that in spite, or perhaps because, of his unorthodox audacities, the London and Northern Bank, under his control, had advanced in the last six years from provincial obscurity to be a serious rival of the Big Five. Such men cannot be treated with disrespect, even when they say things that we are surprised to hear.

Henry controlled his lips to a deprecatory smile as he replied "Of course, I know that you don't mean that seriously."

As he spoke, he glanced across the table to Mr. Jellipot, but that circumspect lawyer, who had just cracked a walnut, and was now peeling its sections with particularity, showed no more than a mildly enquiring expression which a shrewder man than Sir Henry would not have found it easy to read.

"Mean it?" Sir Reginald replied. "Of course I mean it! There are cases where murder isn't a crime at all. The only criminal business is the fuss that's made when it's found out, and all the misery that the police and the lawyers make. Ask Jellipot if I'm not right about that."

Mr. Jellipot, now delicately inserting a section of walnut, completely skinned, into the little heap of salt at the rim of his plate, was deliberate in his reply: "I can't say that I entirely dissent from the generalisation which our host has propounded for our consideration, but I suppose—as must be the case with all, or almost all, generalisations—that there are few of such—shall I say incidents?—to which it would be exactly applicable."

The reply reduced the Assistant Commissioner to silence, he being no means clear as to what it meant, or whether Sir Reginald's subversive theory had been supported. But the banker laughed his appreciation. "Good for you, Jellipot! I never knew a man who could say less with more words than you.... But I don't mean that we all ought to go about knocking each other on the head whenever we've had a bad night, or don't like anyone eating asparagus with a knife. But just think of those American racketeers. When someone put a few ounces of lead into Jack Diamond—and he's said to be about the meanest rat that ever made the Creator wonder at His own works—the U.S. police began bustling about as though he were the President, or almost as though he were one of their own force. When those gangsters want to shoot each other they ought to have free ammunition served out, and a bonus on every corpse they bring in."

As the banker said this the expression of troubled wonder on Sir Henry's face lessened, though it did not disappear He would not have said that American lives and law are of less account than those of his own country, but he felt subconsciously relieved that the conversation had not been directed to really serious things."

Mr. Jellipot looked somewhat more alert than before. Sir Reginald, whose mental processes he knew well, had shown no previous interest in American gangsters, whose doings, even at the height of their 1929 activities, occupied no very great space in the London press. He was not surprised when Sir Reginald went on: "I had one of the dirty brutes in my own office this afternoon, and couldn't throw him out because of the credentials with which he came…. He'll be in again in the morning, and if I twist his neck you'll be making more trouble and spending more public money than if I'd killed a good dog."

"I am sure," Sir Henry replied uneasily, "that the position could not arise."

"No. I expect not. But that's not because I'm too good. It's because I prefer to come home at night."

Sir Reginald Crowe looked across the table as he spoke at a wife whose eyes gave a laughing response. The style of Sir Reginald's conversation held no difficulty, and his character was no secret, to her.

CHAPTER II.

A Redhead Calls to Collect

IT was the boast of Sir Reginald Crowe that he refused to see no one who had the temerity to ask for an interview with the chairman of the London and Northern Bank. If, he said, they had to wait, it could only be because someone had got in before them. It didn't work out quite like that, because he had an efficient secretary, and though he knew more of what went on around him than most men in such positions of authority do, there was still much of which he was not aware.

But however ready he might be to see those who should solicit an interview, he expected them to be preceded by their own names and his own consent, and when a young woman walked unannounced into his private room on the morning after the conversation related in the previous chapter, he looked up in a natural irritation from a letter he was in the act of sealing.

The young woman, who had a curly head of flaming red hair and blue eyes that were hard and bright, which contradicted the evidence of rather full lips, and a dented chin, got in the first word: "Say, you're Sir Reginald Crowe?"

The banker did not satisfy her curiosity or invite her to the comfort of the deep chair at his side. He said: "Perhaps you'll introduce yourself first and tell me how you got in here?"

"Me? I'm Moll Clancy. Redhead Clancy the boys call me, more times than not. I just came in. I don't need anyone to take care of me."

This was plain enough, though he was not familiar with its concluding idiom. He was still puzzled how she should have penetrated so far without being challenged, especially as she appeared to be a lover of primary colours, from the green scarf that was round her throat to the slacks that were cobalt blue. But he remembered that his name was on the outside of the door; and, anyway, what did it matter?

"Well," he said, "my name's Crowe, as you suppose. You'd better sit down and tell me what your business is."

"I've come over about Clancy's share. It's two hundred grand, and I won't take a cent less, so it's no use thinking they'll make a sucker out of Clancy or me."

"Over from where?"

"Chicago, of course."

"Well, Miss—Mrs. Clancy—"

"Mrs. to you."

"Well, Mrs. Clancy, if you or your husband has any money deposited with us, you should apply at the counter on the floor below, and you'll have attention at once."

"You think your tellers would pay out? I should say not. You can't put that over me. I've come to collect here."

"You know best what you've come to do, but if this is what you call a hold-up in your delightful country, I can assure you you've gone about it in the wrong way. There isn't any cash in this room, and I haven't even got a gun to prevent you going out by the way you came in, which I think you might find it wise to do."

"Oh, come off it! You know this is a share-out you've got to handle. I only want to know there's going to be a square deal, and you'll have no trouble from me."

"Whatever instructions we may have had in reference to any funds deposited here, you may be sure that they will be scrupulously carried out."

"You may be a peach for that, but I'd like to know a bit more about what those instructions are."

Sir Reginald did not profess to misunderstand her. What was puzzling him was that he could not remember the name Clancy occurring in the singular instructions which had come in by the last U.S. mail. Still, his memory was not infallible. There had certainly been Irish ones.

"Whatever instructions we may receive," he answered, "are of a strictly confidential character, excepting to those whom they immediately concern.... You have no doubt brought credentials with you?"

"I've brought this."

She handed over a letter. It had an ornately printed heading:

HOTEL ATLANTIS,
BROADWAY, U.S.A.

The bearer of this letter, Miss Mary O'Leary, represents me as well as herself. You can pay her anything due to me.

TIM CLANCY,

The London and Northern Bank, Ltd., London

Sir Reginald looked at it with puzzled eyes. "Miss O'Leary?" he asked.

"Yes. That's my passport name."

"Your legal name? Well, that's good enough. You have the passport with you?"

"I have that."

She passed it over. Sir Reginald looked at it with care. The photograph, which often has no more than a vague resemblance to its original, was unmistakably hers.

"Well, Mrs. Clancy," he said, "that seems plain enough. I'm not sure how far it gets us. Tell me—you're asking for a large sum—about forty thousand pounds—what exactly did you expect the procedure to be?"

"I don't know it in pounds. It's a thick wad. Two hundred thousand bucks. I want it paid over to me."

"Did you think it would be paid to you by the bank, or that you'd get it here from someone else who would draw it from us?"

"I don't care if I pick it up."

"That wasn't quite what I asked."

"I thought, of course, I'd have it from you."

"You are staying in London?"

"Yes."

"You could let me have your address?"

"I'm staying at an hotel in Oxford Street. I forget the name. It's a class joint. Near the top of Park Lane."

"Perhaps the Westmorland?"

"Yes. That's the name."

"Perhaps you could call again tomorrow morning? Or I could ring you there?"

"I'd rather clear this up now."

"I can't say more than this. There may be instructions already here which will lead to you being paid such a sum as you mention. I don't see any reason you shouldn't know that we have a sum in American currency in our hands which we are expecting to pay out. And I may add that, as soon as the necessary formalities are observed, I shall be very pleased to close a transaction into which we should never have entered if we'd known as much about it as we do now. But I'm sure those instructions don't authorise us to pay any sum out to you alone now. If you'll leave the matter till tomorrow morning I expect I shall know more."

The young woman heard this without rising. She sat in frowning hesitation.

"I'd say," she remarked at last, "you're a straight guy. I'll tell you there's those we don't trust, and if Ringan's here on the twist. I'd like to be close and handy when the payout's being done, if it's not meant to come to me first, as it ought to be."

"You think, so long as you're present, you'll be able to do your own collecting?"

"I reckon I'd have a try."

Sir Reginald looked at the speaker and did not doubt the truth of this confident assertion. Neither did he doubt that he was confronted by an associate of criminals, if not one who was herself an adept at crime. But he was disposed to think that, so far as right could be in such matters, she had come to assert a claim which was fairly hers and that of the man she represented. He was aware also that in anything he did, or declined to do, there might be legal difficulties of the gravest kind. Yet he was not over-much troubled by those aspects of the matter. He had some confidence in his own capacity to deal with an unusual circumstance, and he did not think that those for whom he was unwillingly acting would be quick to invoke the law. He suspected that it was from the menacing shadow of the law of another land that the huge sum which was now deposited with him had been removed.

It was a time at which the American racketeer was at the height of a power which was soon to fall, but he was less known to the English public than he afterwards became through the medium of the most realistic, and in some respects the most artistically satisfying, pictures that Hollywood was to make during the next ten years. Yet he had read enough to know that honour among thieves had no certain place in the code of these vultures in human form. That there would be attempts at double-crossing in the withdrawal of the money was a most probable thing, and the fear of it was actually indicated by the method he had been instructed to observe in its disbursement.

He looked speculatively at his visitor, who was regarding him with resolved but not hostile eyes. His own settled upon a narrow dead-white scar above her right temple, which the close-cut hair made no effort to hide. It was such as a bullet might have made, and most probably had. He considered that there was nothing furtive about her approach. She was one, in appearance and dress, whom no crowd would hide. It was also clear that she might become a dangerous nuisance if she were thwarted in what she considered her rights to be. He spoke with more frankness than a more orthodox banker might have been disposed to do.

"Mrs. Clancy, you're quite right when you call me a straight guy. If I weren't, it's not in the least likely that I should be sitting here. And I'm quite willing to do anything for you that I properly can. But we're talking about large sums. If I were to pay you two hundred thousand dollars, and then had a court order to pay it to someone else in a few weeks' time, my shareholders would have something nasty to say. But I don't think I shall be doing wrong in telling you how the matter stands. I don't suppose I shall be telling you much that you don't know.

"A few months ago we had a large sum transferred to our custody from a bank in your country. I can't be more particular than that, but—"

"It was the Dallas Sixth National Bank."

"Yes. It was the Sixth National Bank, Dallas, Texas. You evidently know. Coming to us in that way, there was no reason to decline the business nor to make any difficulty—"

"The boys bought it up. Al Capone had the idea. There's Detroit and the New York crowd in it, as well as us. Except Diamond. They wouldn't let Legs in."

"Well, we saw no reason to make any difficulty when further sums reached us in the same way, though we didn't like it because there were reasons, which I needn't go into, which made it little benefit to us.

"But by last Tuesday's mail we had instructions regarding the disposal of this money which I disliked, and yesterday one of your friends called whom I disliked—and what he told me—very much more."

"Who was he?"

"I don't think I can tell you that. But there's one thing I can do now. I can find out whether we have a specimen of Mr. Clancy's signature, and whether he's one of those to whom the money is to be paid. I suppose he hasn't got more than one name for such occasions as these?"

"No. Tim Clancy's the only name."

"I'm rather surprised that he didn't run over himself. The sum you ask for is worth some trouble in picking up."

"There might have been a bit of bother. You see, he was born in Liverpool."

"About landing? That should have made it easier."

"About landing here? Yep. But how about getting back?"

"I see. I have no doubt there were good reasons enough."

"You bet there were. For one thing, I know Ringan, and he doesn't. And, for another, this money's not to go back. It's to be salted here. And that's my job to do. He couldn't leave where he is, not for such a time as this needs."

"Well, we'll see what we can find out."

Sir Reginald took up his private telephone. He rang through to his secretary's office, and was surprised to get no reply. Miss Markham might be out. There was a reason why he should not be surprised at that. But, if so, Miss Glen should have been at the other end of the wire. At a second effort, and after a moment's delay, so she was.

"I'm so sorry," she said. "I was called away for a moment."

"Never mind that. Where's Miss Markham?"

"She's gone over to Mr. Jellipot's office. She ought to be back in ten minutes."

"Has she left her safe open? Or do you have the key when she's away?"

"No. It's always locked when she's out. She keeps the key on her own bunch."

"Yes. So she does."

He remembered having noticed previously Miss Markham's care regarding a safe of which there were only two keys, one being in his own pocket. He approved of that. He knew he need not ask whether the documents he required were on her table or would have been locked away as soon as she had made the copies which she was now taking to the lawyer's office. It seemed he must go himself.

He opened a drawer in the desk at which he sat, put into it the letter on which he had been engaged when Miss O'Leary entered, locked it with his usual precision, glanced over an otherwise vacant desk, and said: "I shall have to leave you a minute or two, but I shan't keep you long."

Sir Reginald's office was on the first floor. The passage outside it ran right and left—to the right to a private stairway only. This consisted of shallow, softly carpeted stairs, and to one of his active habits they were more attractive than the comparatively distant lift.

15

To the left, and on the left hand, was the boardroom door. The boardroom was spacious and lay lengthwise to the passage. At its further end the passage turned left, and anyone following its course would come first to the door of Miss Markham's room, then to that of one shared by Miss Glen and a junior typist, and then to an automatic lift which ran down to the ground floor and the vaults, and to the floor above, and was in general use by the staff. Further on, and still to the left, were the offices of Mr. Charles Adams, the head accountant of the bank, and other officials with whom we have no concern.

On the further side there were no doors, but windows only, the passage overlooking Lombard Street and a narrow adjoining thoroughfare.

Sir Reginald went straight to Miss Markham's room, where he unlocked the secretary's safe with his private key and found without difficulty the papers to which he wished to refer.

They consisted of instructions from the Sixth National Bank of Dallas to pay out five million dollars, deposited to their order, to three representatives of the bank (as they were described) who would present separate credentials, and of whose signatures specimens were enclosed. The money was only to be paid to the three men after they had separately presented their credentials and were all present together. It appeared to be assumed that it would be available at any moment in dollar currency.

Sir Reginald had already cabled concerning this and other points which he considered to require further elucidation, but which he understood better now that he had learned that Chicago gangsters had gained control of the bank. This morning he had instructed Miss Markham to take copies of the documents to Mr. Jellipot's office, and ask that astute lawyer to give his own, and to obtain counsel's, opinion thereon.

Now he inspected the originals, and it took little time to confirm his previous memory that Tim Clancy was not mentioned therein.

Sir Reginald subsequently professed that it was impossible for him to say, within ten or fifteen minutes, the time at which he left Miss O'Leary alone in his room, but it could be very nearly settled by other evidences, and was of the less importance, as the departure of that lady, who apparently became tired of waiting for his return, was observed by several, including a bank messenger, who was able to fix it exactly at 11:43 A.M.

It was also settled beyond dispute that it was after twelve—though how long after was less certain—when Sir Reginald telephoned Mr. Jellipot, having returned to his own room.

CHAPTER III.

A DEAD MAN ON THE MAT

MR. JELLIPOT, whose mind had been pleasantly occupied upon the interpretation of a loosely worded codicil which a client, recently deceased, had added to a lucid will of his own careful drafting, readily laid it aside for the consideration of the more urgent problem which Miss Markham had put before him.

He saw that it contained questions of fact and of banking practice on which he was less competent to advise than Sir Reginald would be to instruct him, but there were other issues such as are fascinating to the legal mind.

He was in doubt on the basic question of whether it would be a physical possibility to produce five million dollars in American currency in London in a shorter time than it would take to bring the bills from New York. He considered the operations of the Exchange Equalisation Fund, and admitted a degree of ignorance concerning the methods of its operations which it was annoying to recognise. But doubtless the Treasury or the Bank of England would know the answer to that, even if, as was improbable, Sir Reginald would need to enquire. But he supposed that the sudden demand for so large a sum in such a form would raise its value to a degree which might involve the bank in a serious margin of loss if the terms of the deposits should throw this obligation upon them. That was his and counsel's problem—to advise what the extent of the bank's obligation was. And, beyond that, as to any safeguards which could be used for their protection in regard to the highly peculiar manner in which the money was to be withdrawn.

"Doubtless," he thought, "it was one of these men who called in Lombard Street yesterday, of whom Sir Reginald said it would be justifiable homicide to make an end. It would certainly save a great deal of trouble, and probably some future crime, not to speak of a million pounds!"

He saw one or two points on which he would like some further information before drafting the case on which counsel's opinion was to be asked, and was just about to get through to the London and Northern Bank when he was informed that Sir Reginald was on the wire, wishing to speak to him.

"Jellipot," he heard, "you'd better come over here if you've got nothing more urgent to do. There's a dead man on the mat."

Mr. Jellipot, perhaps for the first time in his life, was startled out of his usual logical precision of speech. He echoed foolishly: "There's—there's a what?"

"You know you heard what I said. A dead man. I suppose you know what that is. There've been plenty before."

Mr. Jellipot recovered himself to ask: "You mean on the mat of your own office?"

"Yes. Outside the door."

"And you don't know who he is?"

"I didn't say that. It's the man I mentioned last night at dinner."

Mr. Jellipot was startled again. "I hope," he began, "you're not going to tell me—"

"Of course I'm not. If I *had* killed him I shouldn't be quite such a fool as that."

Mr. Jellipot, always liable to be led away by abstract considerations, felt bound to dissent. "It is usually best," he said, "to let your lawyer know what the facts are."

"That's what you lawyers say. But I'll give you a few, all the same. You can think them over while you're coming along. I left my own room for about half an hour, or perhaps a bit less, and when I came back I found this man outside the door."

"Was the door shut?"

"No, open."

"Was that how you left it?"

"Yes. I think it was. Yes, I'm quite sure. Well, he was lying face upwards. I said he was a dead man, but in fact he was twitching a bit then, though he was as plain a goner as you're ever likely to see. He was lying with a pool of blood spreading from under his back. I turned him over to see what the matter was, and found a knife stuck in it. I pulled it out, but that didn't do any good."

"Of course, you've called the police?"

"No. Not yet. I thought I'd let you know first."

"You can't be too quick in letting them know. They are sure to resent any delay."

"Oh, I expect you'll be able to deal with them."

"I hope you won't rely too much upon that. I'll come over at once. But there's the question of a doctor as well as the police. Doesn't anyone know at all except you?"

"Not yet. It didn't happen last year or the year before. And what good could a doctor do? The man's as dead as ditch water now, if he wasn't when I came on the scene. Pulling out the knife seemed to fetch the curtain down with a run."

"Well, I'm coming. But don't lose any more time in reporting the crime. It might be misunderstood in more ways than one."

The perturbation of Mr. Jellipot's mind, which had been shown in the unusual brevity of his conversational style, was further demonstrated by his attempt to insert his right arm into the left sleeve of his top-coat, and even more emphatically by the fact that he was already in the outer office before he became aware that the umbrella which it was his invariable custom to carry was still in its rack in his own room.

As he turned back to get it he pulled himself together with a visible effort, and it was with a return to his accustomed manner that he said mildly to a junior clerk: "Benson, get me a taxi quickly. I have a particular reason for avoiding delay."

Benson, being too familiar with his employer's manner to miss the significance of these quietly spoken words, was down the stairs with such speed that he not only beat the lift, but had the needed vehicle at the curb at the time of Mr. Jellipot's more sedate arrival.

For the four minutes of his short journey from Basinghall Street Mr. Jellipot sat back in a cogitation which was oblivious of outward things, but as he was roused by the stopping of the vehicle and the opening door, he muttered half aloud, in the tone of one who pronounces a final verdict: "It was a most foolish thing."

We may conclude that this remark was not unrelated to the event with which he had come to deal, but whether it were in reference to Sir Reginald's conversation of the previous evening, or his delay in informing the police of the homicide which had occurred, or of the unwisdom of stabbing a man in the back outside the private office of an important banker, is more than we are ever likely to know.

CHAPTER IV.

Sir Reginald's Own Account

MR. JELLIPOT arrived five or six minutes before the police, at which he was not entirely pleased.

He thought that Sir Reginald's action in summoning him first looked too much like the act of a guilty man, which it would, of course, be absurd to think him to be.

But, being on the scene, he was no less diligent to use those few minutes to learn as much as he could of the circumstances of the affair.

He was surprised on entering the bank to observe no evidence of excitement, or disturbance of its routine. Passing through the wide doors, which are at the street corner, he turned to the right and passed along the counter which is occupied by the disbursing cashiers, those who receive deposits being ranged along that which runs at right angles to it, left hand from the outer door. He passed behind the backs of customers who were fully occupying the attention of cashiers whose duties require that their minds and eyes be concentrated on what they do; and he considered how probably anyone walking quietly and confidently might pass unobserved to the swing door beyond the end of the counter, which gave access to a passage by which the automatic lift could be reached.

Though he was well known at the bank, he doubted whether anyone there, if questioned five minutes later, would be able to say that he had come in.

He encountered no one as he went up until he came to the angle of the passage on the first floor, where it turned towards Sir Reginald's private room, and here he found the bank porter standing on guard.

"I'm to let you through, sir, and the police, but no one else. That's Sir Reginald's orders."

"You mean no one except you knows what's happened?"

"Yes, sir. Sir Reginald doesn't want it to get about more than we can help."

"More than you *can't* help, Spooner," Mr. Jellipot smilingly corrected, his dislike of slovenly speech asserting itself in evidence that any perturbation he had felt on first hearing of this improbable murder had given place to his normal detachment and self-control.

Spooner did not show any interest in the correction he had received. He went on: "It isn't what you'd wish the young ladies to see. You'll find it's a nasty mess."

"Yes; you're quite right to keep them away."

Leaving the sentinel at his post, Mr. Jellipot went on toward a corpse which was already visible as it lay in an awkward sprawl outside Sir Reginald's door, which stood open. That which had been Tony Ringan an hour before lay in a pool of its own blood which the thick carpet had been inadequate to absorb. The knife which had been drawn from his back lay beside him. Stepping past it, Mr. Jellipot entered an empty room.

But as he did so Sir Reginald's voice sounded cheerfully from a bathroom to which there was no access from the passage, but which could be entered either from his or from the boardroom on its other side. "That you, Jellipot? Come in. I'm just trying to get cleaned up a bit before the cops come on the scene. I suppose it's too much a habit with these wops for them to give it up when they come over here; but I wish they'd choose somewhere else than my own mat."

Mr. Jellipot entered the bathroom. Sir Reginald was at the hand-basin, in which the water was a dull red. Reddened towels had been thrown into the bath. So had coat, collar and tie.

"Lucky for me," the banker went on, "that I keep a few clothes here, or I might have spent the next hour in a sticky mess."

Mr. Jellipot was deliberate in diction, but he came straight to his point: "I must conclude from what you have told me, and the observations I made as I came in, that there has been no attempt to arrest the criminal?"

"Right in one. He doesn't seem to have waited, as a good criminal should."

"I understand that you were away from the office when it occurred?"

"Right again. I was with Adams discussing some trouble that's come up at our Wigan branch."

"You had been away for a considerable time?"

"Oh, not so long! Couldn't say exactly. You see, I'd sent Miss Markham to office, and I went into her room for some papers I wanted, and when I was there the Wigan call came through—our manager at that branch has been trying to shoot himself, an didn't even do a simple little job like that thoroughly, and it's fifty-fifty whether it's domestic trouble or something short in our cash, and, anyway, it meant getting an inspector there at a run, and some other details that took a few minutes, more or less, so I may have been away any time between fifteen minutes and twice that long."

"Did you hear anyone come from the lift while you were in Miss Markham's room?"

"No. I can't say I did. I had my mind on what seemed to me to be more important matters."

"Naturally. But you and others would be passing from room to room. Someone would have been almost certain to see or hear anyone going up or down?"

"I don't know that they would. I was in Miss Markham's room telephoning most of the time. Then I just went along to speak to Adams, and came back here."

"Well, we must hope someone did.... You know who the dead man is?"

"I know what he told me about himself yesterday. I don't say how much I believe. Ringan he called himself, but I believe these beauties usually have more names than one.

"I'll tell you one proposal he made, and you'll understand that It wasn't a case where any doctor ought to have been hurried on to the scene, even if he hadn't been past help when I saw him first. He offered me what he called five grand—that's a bit over a thousand pounds—to help him to pick up his fellow-gangsters' money as well as his own."

"I don't see how you could do that without having to hand it out to them over again."

"Well, he thought he did. Our instructions are to pay it to the three together. He proposed that I should get them all to sign the receipt before I'd loose what he called the wad, and then lay it down so that he could pick it up, and he'd be near the door, and I was to have one or two porters placed so that they'd get in the way of the other men. He said half a minute would be enough for him, and they could seize the other men to stop them shooting, as they'd be sure to try, and if they did that, and stopped them altogether, he wouldn't mind paying another grand to them. Well, he's got just what he deserved, if you ask me. Though I dare say that the one who knifed him's a rat of the same breed."

Mr. Jellipot agreed that probabilities pointed in that direction, and would have asked further questions, for there were still many things which he would have liked to learn before the arrival of the

police, but there was the sound of a brisk voice in the passage—
"Yes, my man. I can see that"—which he recognised as belonging to
Dr. Corbett, a police surgeon whom he had met before, and next
moment he appeared, with Chief Detective-Inspector Ingram, strolling, with longer legs, in a more leisurely manner, behind him.

CHAPTER V.

The Friendliness of Inspector Ingram

INSPECTOR INGRAM was a tall thin man with a pleasant voice and a deceptively winning smile. His colleagues spoke of the "fatherly manner" in which he would deal with confused, frightened, or illiterate suspects while drawing from them the admissions or contradictions which would secure their convictions.

It was said of him also that he had never been seen to hurry or discompose himself under any circumstance. Yet he was of a lithe activity, and his leisurely movements might be as deceptive as the smile that came so easily to his questioning eyes.

It was Dr. Corbett who spoke first. "Who turned this man over?" he asked sharply.

Sir Reginald, coming out of the bathroom in Mr. Jellipot's rear, and pulling on his coat as he did so, answered readily: "I did. It was the only way to get the knife out of his back."

"You pulled the knife out?"

"Yes. It seemed the natural thing to do. But if I'd known what a mess I should get into…. The fact is, I've been cleaning up ever since, and I hardly feel decent now."

"It's always better to leave things as they are in a case like this."

"Well, it would have been better for me, and made precious little difference to him. But considering that he was lying on the knife so that his own weight must have been driving it further in—well, there was something to be said for a change of position, if nothing more."

Dr. Corbett made no reply. He turned to the inspector to say: "There's no hurry about anything I can do here. I'd better stand't back till you've got the pictures you'll want."

"So I was about to suggest. But Grey will be here any minute now," Ingram answered. He took a long stride over the corpse and the sodden carpet and glanced round the room. He saw that there were drops of blood scattered about, and his eyes paused for a second upon Sir Reginald's desk, where the white blotting-pad was discoloured, and there were other stains of an obvious kind. But he gave no sign of anything he may have thought, turning to Sir Reginald to enquire in his friendliest manner: "I take it you were not present when this happened?"

"No. I was probably in Mr. Adams' room at the further end of the passage."

"And you found him like this when you came back?"

"Yes. Lying on his back. Otherwise just about as he is now."

"Yes. That's how I understood. I expect you know who he is?"

"Yes. Ringan's the name. He was here yesterday afternoon."

"On private business with you?"

"No. Banking business. He wasn't the sort with whom I should have any personal business relations."

"He doesn't look a very choice specimen. But knowing what his business was, you may be able to make a good guess at who'd be likely to be here with him, or have a motive for doing this?"

"I expected him to come alone. But there were two others whom I was to arrange for him to meet. I haven't heard of them calling yet. I ought not to suggest that it was one of them. I know nothing about them at all, though I might guess. But I suppose it would be one of his fellow gangsters. There's certainly motive enough, judging by what I heard from him yesterday."

"Gangsters? Do you mean that literally? Do you mean he's an American?"

"Yes. What I believe they call a wop in New York."

"Well, there's evidently a lot more you can tell me, but it sounds as though it may be a simple job.... You'll excuse me a moment?"

Saying this, he turned to the camera-men, who had now arrived. "Get me some good pictures from all the usual angles. Be careful not to touch or disturb the knife. Get the room interior. It may be important that there's no sign of a struggle there.... Perhaps we'd better go into another room where we can talk quietly?"

"You can come into the boardroom. There's a way through here."

Sir Reginald led the way through the bathroom, and the detective followed. His eyes missed little, but he made no remark. Mr. Jellipot, who had remained silent and had not appeared to take much notice of the conversation, followed also.

The inspector, who knew him by sight and was well aware of his reputation, was not misled by this casual attitude, nor was he blind to the significance of his being there.

It was equally true that Mr. Jellipot was able to assess the exact value of the friendly warmth in his voice. They both knew each other, and each other's methods, for what they were.

More of habit than deliberation, the banker sat himself in the heavily carved armchair which he was accustomed to occupy when he presided at meetings of directors who did little beyond endorsing with their approval the forceful methods by which the bank had been advanced since it had come under his energetic control.

Inspector Ingram took a chair at his left hand, and Mr. Jellipot seated himself unobtrusively further down the table.

Inspector Ingram drew out his notebook. "Now," he said genially, "we'll get a few details straight. First, you might let me have the man's name and where he's been putting up."

"He gave his name as Antonio Ringan. I should call that an Italian name, and he looked Italian, and spoke English in the way that underbred Italians do, but that's the name on his passport. By the same evidence he was a citizen of the United States. I can't tell you more than that."

"Oh, but I expect you can! You'll have his London address if he's doing business with the bank."

"No. I haven't that. He introduced himself yesterday after. noon and said he would look in again this morning."

"But—"

"I think under the—somewhat unusual—circumstances I may tell you that his name had been sent to me, together with two others, by an American bank, with specimens of their signatures, and instructions to pay out a sum of money to them as soon as they should present themselves together to receive it."

"Have the others turned up?"

"Not to my knowledge. He was the first to arrive."

"Then why was he coming again this morning?"

"To enquire whether they had come."

"Wouldn't it have been more natural for him to have given you the address of his hotel so that you could advise him by telephone of their arrival?"

"Would it? Either course seems natural enough to me."

"It sounds extraordinary that they had not arranged to get in touch with one another on their arrival. That would surely have been the natural course to take."

"I'm not sure that they were in the habit of taking natural courses. If the other two are like this one, they have an extreme distrust of one another."

"It's a very interesting affair. I suppose you won't mind telling me what the amount of this money is?"

"I don't think I should mention that."

"You'll find it will have to come out."

"Possibly. What do you think, Mr. Jellipot?"

"I think that Inspector Ingram will agree that unless it is evident that such a disclosure will be of direct value in elucidating what has occurred, your duty of secrecy to your clients—who are not the men you have been discussing, but the bank which transferred the money to your control—must prevail. Of course, the position would be different if a court order should be obtained."

"Which it would be easy for us to get."

"Then there would be no objection whatever. It is solely a question of banking law."

"I suppose it is a large sum?"

"You may reasonably presume that. You will no doubt have observed that large sums of money, like diamonds of exceptional size, are often inciters of violent crime."

"But," the inspector objected, "if three men could only draw the money together, it is difficult to see any advantage one would gain by killing another. It looks too much like cooking his own goose."

"I confess," Mr. Jellipot replied, "that the same idea has occurred to my own mind. As an abstract proposition it would appear to be more probable that it would be the act of a fourth, who claims a share from which he had been excluded."

"Unless," Inspector Ingram added, "the money can be drawn by the remaining two."

Mr. Jellipot looked interrogation to the banker, who looked the same question at him. "That," Sir Reginald said, "is a question on which it may be necessary to take legal advice. But my own opinion is that we certainly could not pay it out to the remaining two. We must have the three signatures as our discharge."

"So," Inspector Ingram remarked, with his friendly smile, "the position actually is that this man's death removes the occasion for paying it out at all?"

"It may oblige us to hold it," Sir Reginald corrected, with some sharpness in his voice, "until we receive revised instructions from our American clients."

Inspector Ingram accepted the correction without appearing to notice the tone in which it was spoken. He changed the subject to ask: "Of course, you won't object to my questioning your staff as to who may have been seen coming up here or going out?"

"No. There can be no objection to that. Though I should have been glad if press publicity—I suppose some is inevitable—could be minimised. It would be possible to publish it in a way which would do no good to the bank, which I am naturally anxious to avoid.

"I'm afraid that you'll have a lot of that. As far as we are concerned, the slower the reporters are to get on the scent, the better pleased we shall be. But you'll find that it can't be done.... All the same, I don't mind questioning the staff in such a way that they don't know why I'm anxious to know. I may learn more that way than I otherwise should.... So if you'll let me have the names of those two other men, Sir Reginald, I won't trouble you further for the moment."

"I can tell you those. Joseph Ruscatti and Slick Maloon."

"Slick Maloon? That's a queer name."

"Well, we're dealing with a queer crowd."

Inspector Ingram went out to his job of questioning the bank staff, and Mr. Jellipot and Sir Reginald Crowe were left together.

"I wish, Jellipot, the banker commenced at once, "you hadn't said that about it not being likely that it was one of the other two."

Mr. Jellipot looked mildly surprised. "As a matter of fact," he said, "I believe that it was Inspector Ingram who remarked upon it in the first instance. Neither do I quite see—"

"But I do.... But it doesn't really matter. And I didn't mean to be rude.... I'll tell you what I wish you'd do. I wish you'd see that the press get hold of this in the right way. They're bound to have it, one way or other. The inspector was right about that. I suppose the next thing will be that Ingram's men will want to haul that example of Heaven's mistakes out through the street door.... But if you'll see to that I'll get home and into something that'll make me feel a bit cleaner than I do now, and let Evelyn know about this beastly affair before she reads of it in the evening papers."

CHAPTER VI.

THE CORONER MAY PROCEED

IT was during the following morning that Sir Henry Bracken sent for Chief Inspector Ingram. He saw him in his private room, and said that he wished to know what progress had been made with the Ringan case.

"It's a queer business," the inspector replied. "We've traced the other two men who were to pick up the money. They came over together, and landed at Southampton the night before last. They both stayed the night there. It couldn't have been either of them. We've learned that they expected to pick up over a million pounds, and to get it in American notes. Not an easy order, even for a bank like the London and Northern

"Beyond that, they're not much help. If they've any idea of who did it, they wouldn't tell us. They're the prosperous racketeer type, and even if they're taking each other for a ride they'll hold together against the law.

"They seem mad over the killing, which leaves them in doubt of how the money can be picked up. They've been sending cables to some of the big shots on the other side. Al Capone for one. They seem to take for granted that Crowe did it himself."

"What do you think, Ingram?"

"I don't know. It's a queer affair altogether, and not a very nice transaction for an English bank to be handling. Ringan was seen to by Crow private stairs. It seems that he'd come down that way the previous afternoon, so that was natural enough, and he was the sort of man who would be likely to announce himself. But no one else was seen to go up or down after him till we got on the scene. If it wasn't Crowe, we've got no clue at all. It seems a mad thing for anyone to have done in such a place, and marvellous that they got away—if they did. What happened isn't easy to reconstruct. Crowe's fingerprints are the only ones on the knife."

"He gave an explanation of that."

"Yes. Which may be true. But it's capable of another.... Suppose Crowe wouldn't agree to the kind of shell-out they'd come to get, and that led to a row? The puzzle is how he got hold of the knife."

"You've traced where that came from?"

"It was Ringan's. It has his initials on it, and there are the same ones, carved in the same way, on the sheath, which he was still wearing. It was on a belt under his jacket. The puzzle is how it could have got into Crowe's hands."

"Have you any theory as to that?"

"Well, suppose Ringan drew it and threatened Crowe. Crowe closed with him—he's a vigorous, athletic man—and wrenched it away. Ringan might turn to run—it was the only weapon he had—and then Crowe catches him up at the door and drives it into his back."

"You are inclined to think that's what happened?"

"I don't go quite that far. It's the best theory I've got. It's not strong enough to justify an arrest, without more evidence than we've got yet.... But there's one thing I've found out. Crowe's way of running the London and Northern isn't quite approved by the other banks. They think he takes too many risks, and they're never sure what he'll do next."

"He's very popular in social circles."

"Yes. And with the public. We should come a cropper if we were to act on what we've got on him now. Though, of course, if we arrest him, and he's really guilty, it would soon be a lot more. We know how it piles up when they're once under lock and key. Sir Henry hesitated. Chief Inspector Ingram, who knew him, well, wondered whether he were about to propose something foolish, from which it might take half an hour's diplomatic persuasion to turn him aside. But what came at last was of an unexpected kind.

"There's one thing I think I ought to tell you, Ingram, though I don't want it to influence you too much. I was at dinner with Sir Reginald on the evening before last, and he began talking about murdering people—he brought up the question himself—and saying that it was often more or less justifiable, and the pity was that the law is so active to interfere. Utter rot it was, but he was the host, and we had to listen with as much politeness as we could manage.

"Jellipot was there, and he tried to get his support, without much success. But it went beyond general talk. He actually mentioned Ringan having called upon him, and said it would be no loss if he were done in, or something that amounted to that. I got the impression that it was a subject on which he was a bit mad."

Chief Inspector Ingram looked thoughtful. "I wouldn't say, as an academic question, that there isn't something to be said for that point of view. But that's not our matter now. We're dealing with who killed Ringan, and I should say we could arrest him on that, and what we've got already, and feel pretty sure we're putting the bracelets on the right man."

"I don't know. I don't like it, Ingram," Sir Henry replied uncertainly. "We can't afford a mistake. He's a popular man, as we said before.... I'll tell you what we'll do. We'll leave Bryant to take it on. And you can give him the hint that you think Sir Reginald's his man and that he should try to get all the evidence he can in that direction. Tell him he can call me and I shan't mind."

Bryant—Dr. Rathbone Bryant—was the coroner. In earlier years he would have had an authority outside the interference of the police. So, in some respects, he had still. But as the powers of the police have increased and their activities extended during the past generation, there has been an overlapping of the old powers and the new which has led to compromise, a legalised custom by which the police notify the coroner of whether they wish him to act or to stand aside. In the latter case he may still summon his court to sit, but there will be an indefinite adjournment to give the police a clear field for their own methods. It is a matter of symbolic rather than primary importance, illustrating the shrinkage of English safeguards and liberties under the regimentation of bureaucracy.

Now the coroner was being told that the police preferred that he should proceed in his ancient way.

CHAPTER VII.

Where the Carcass Is

THE dingy courtroom was uncomfortably crowded even before the coroner took his seat. Duckworth Holmes, who had reported such enquiries for the last thirty years, and who knew everyone and everything that such a reporter should, was pointing out those whom he recognised to a younger colleague.

"That's Whatley-Cummings on the right. The man with the big fleshy face and the fringe of straw-coloured hair. You don't often see him without his gown. No, they're never worn in this court He'll be here for the police. I don't suppose anyone's representing the murdered man.... You don't suppose I know that redhead girl at the back? Well, it happens I do know something. Something we can't print, and we don't think the police are on the track of it yet. She's got a nerve to come here if I'm right. And she must have had some push to get in. There aren't many of the public who have.... But there's something queerer than that. There's the Assistant Commissioner here. That man on Whatley-Cummings' left who keeps on whispering to him. He's a fussy old fool. They say he gives them jitters at the Yard wondering what he'll try to do next. But it's funny him being here. They must be looking for something important to break.... That's Sir Reginald Crowe in the seat behind, further along with Lady Crowe on his right. Used to be Evelyn Merivale, and got kidnapped by a drug-smuggling gang, and shut up in a phoney jail while they blackmailed her brother. Of course, you remember that. She married Crowe after he helped get her out of the mess Looks as though the boot's on the other leg now, and she's here backing him up. Not that he seems to need any help from her.... And that's Jellipot on his other side. You know, the lawyer that made his name in the same case, and what happened after You wouldn't think he could say boo to a goose, but he's give one or two leading counsel a jolt before now, besides making the Yard look a bit silly. And the quiet way he does it always makes them a bit wild. Solicitor for the defence? No, you mustn't say that. There isn't any defence here. That would imply that there's some charge against Crowe, and your paper'd be scraping up money for damages that'd keep it poor for the next three years. This isn't a trial, it's an enquiry. But Crowe's a witness, and he can have a solicitor to watch his interests. Everything's a bit looser here than it is in a court of law. For one thing, the laws of evidence don't apply. And the jury always brings in a verdict, because a majority's all that's needed.

"Think they'll say Crowe did it? Haven't the foggiest. Coroners' juries mostly do what they're told. Now and then they get their teeth on the bit and give the court a surprise.... But I'll tell you one thing. If they say Crowe pushed in the knife there'll be a run on his bank. I know a fellow who's got an account at the London and Northern—the New Oxford Street branch. He drew out yesterday. Says he's left about three and four pence in. Didn't like to close it, but thought there was no harm in being on the safe side."

"Then the run's started already?"

"No. He said not. Everything seemed quiet. It's tomorrow the fun would start if Crowe found himself on the wrong side of the bars."

"He doesn't look as though anything's worrying him over-much."

"No. He wouldn't. I should say he's not often had anything in his hands that he hasn't been equal to pulling off.... That man on Bracken's other side? You mean— Hush! Here's the coroner coming in."

The murmur of voices ceased, and the crowded court rose respectfully to its feet as the coroner entered briskly.

CHAPTER VIII.

An Accusation of Murder

THE dull, inevitable preliminaries were over. The jury sworn. The explanatory statements made. The routine evidence given. The crowded court stirred to more animated expectation as Sir Reginald Crowe was called.

He gave his evidence confidently and clearly, and, till Whatley-Cummings, K.C., rose to cross-examine on behalf of the police, it is improbable that many of those who heard had any doubt that it was the simple truth of what he had seen and done. But it became evident, from the first question that the learned counsel asked, that that evidence was to be challenged from a surprising angle.

"You take, I believe, a rather unusual view of the conditions that would justify you in taking the life of a fellow man?"

If the question startled Sir Reginald, his self-control was sufficient to conceal it. He answered readily: "I hope I hold reasonable views, and I hope, therefore, that they are not unusual."

"Perhaps you will be good enough to tell the court what they are."

"If you really ask for a considered reply to a hypothetical—" But Mr. Jellipot, who had been considering the possibility of this line of attack since he had noticed the presence of Sir Henry Bracken, was on his feet.

"I submit," he said, "that the question is highly irregular and that the witness should not reply. He is not called as an expert, but as a witness of fact. His opinion on an abstract question of that kind can have no value at all."

Dr. Rathbone Bryant would not have admitted that he could be awed by Whatley-Cummings or any other eminent counsel in his own court, or influenced by the fact that that gentleman held an official brief; but now he temporised, where a stronger man would have allowed or denied the question. He said: "Unless the witness object to answer—"

"As his solicitor, I wish to make the strongest possible protest against a line of examination which is an abuse of the process of the court."

Whatley-Cummings did not wait for the coroner's decision. He said blandly: "I will withdraw a question to which such strong objection is taken. But I will ask this: Did you, or did you not, on the evening before this murder, which took place on the threshold of your own room, when no one else is known to have been present— did you or did you not say that to murder him would be a justifiable or venial act?"

Mr. Jellipot, hearing the question put thus, and recognising that it was now in a form to which he could not hope to object successfully, was in some doubt as to whether his interposition might not have done more harm than good, but he had gained some time for his client to adjust his mind to the attack which he had to meet, which it had been his first object to do, and he was satisfied with the result when he heard the quiet laconic denial: "No, I did not."

"Then will you repeat what you did say?"

"So far as I can recollect a casual after-dinner conversation, to which no importance could be attached at the time, what I argued was that murder varied very much in its gravity, and that there are actual instances where more harm and misery is caused by the investigation and punishment which follow than by the crime itself. It does not seem to me to be a proposition which reasonable men would dispute."

"No? Well, the court will hear what you did say from those— one or more—whose memories may be more exact than yours. But I suggest that you were far more specific than that—that you mentioned this man, who was to be found dead next morning at the door of your own office, as one whom it would be justifiable to destroy."

"Then you are suggesting something which is untrue. I am sure that I mentioned no one by name, and equally so that the expression 'justifiable to destroy' was not used by me. I will add freely that the man, whom I had first seen a few hours before, came to my mind, and was used by me as an illustration, as one of a criminal kind whose existence is of no benefit to the community."

"Why should you think that?"

"Because in the conversation I have mentioned he admitted, or rather boasted, to me that he was an American racketeer of what I suppose to be the worst kind."

"And your bank has business with such as he?"

"That is an imputation unwarranted by the facts. There is, of course, a sense in which a bank must have business relations with every class, and potentially with every member, of the community. We cannot enquire into the character of everyone to whom a customer may draw a cheque before we consent to pay it."

"But you do not receive them all in your private room?"

"I probably should if any one of them should ask to see me. You don't turn a man down or refuse his business before you know something about it."

The coroner, looking up from the notes he was making of this conversation, suggested doubtfully: "Aren't we getting somewhat wide of the actual subject of this enquiry, Mr. Whatley-Cummings?"

"I think not, sir. It may be important to ascertain the nature of the business which the witness had with this man on successive days in his private office."

"Very well; go on."

Sir Reginald did not wait for the question which would have followed. He said: "I can tell you that at once. He came with conditional authority to draw money from funds which had been placed with us by a United States bank. I had no business with him except to see that the conditions should be observed, and then to pay out the money. Had he proposed to open an account with my bank, I should have refused with emphasis."

"Perhaps he did?"

"He did not."

"Are you sure that on this his second visit, which was concluded—for he appears to have been going out when he was stabbed—*are you sure that money had not already been paid to him?*"

Sir Reginald laughed in what appeared to be genuine amusement at this question.

"You're trying to suggest that I paid him the money and then murdered him and got it back? You'll have to think of something better than that. It would be easy to prove that the money was never found. I don't keep the bank's cash in my private room, nor could I get access to it without others knowing and records being made."

"It is no occasion for levity. I was not suggesting—"

"No? It was an outrageous suggestion. But it was the absurdity of it that struck me first."

"I am suggesting nothing. I am merely—"

Mr. Jellipot rose. "The suggestion was made in the most pointed manner. It is one which cannot be supported by any evidence or probability, and which the witness should naturally resent—"

It was Mr. Whatley-Cummings' turn to interrupt with some effect: "But the witness did not resent it! He regards anything to do with homicide in too light a manner. If I may say so—"

At this point the coroner intruded into the legal skirmish: "Perhaps, Mr. Whatley-Cummings, it will be best to continue your examination "

"I must repeat that I am suggesting nothing. I am endeavouring only to elucidate what occurred during the last hour of the earthly life of this unfortunate man. The witness affects to ridicule the possibility of the money having been paid, on the ground that the bank's money is not kept in his own room. But are there not such things as documentary payments? Might not such a form of draft as would satisfy an alien wop (I think that was the word that the witness used to describe the man he—the murdered man) be readily available to one of his position?" He turned to Sir Reginald again. "I will ask you—" But Mr. Jellipot was on his feet.

"I am aware, Mr. Coroner, that in enquiries of this character there is a very wide latitude within your discretion, but I submit that this line of examination cannot be justified either in tone or substance, unless supported by other evidence, as I am sure that it cannot be."

The coroner temporised. "What do you say to that, Mr. Whatley-Cummings?"

"I submit that, in view of evidence which you will hear respecting the language used by the witness concerning the dead man on the previous evening, and the fact that he lay next morning at the door of Sir Reginald's vacant room, it becomes necessary to make the most searching enquiry into the transaction which was going on between these men—"

Sir Reginald interrupted in a sharper tone than he had yet used: "There was no transaction between us. It was as a customer of our banking correspondents that he came to me, and as representing the bank that I saw him."

"We may allow that. Now, as representing the bank, did no document pass on the morning of his death between him and you?"

"I have told you that I did not see him at all that morning until I found him lying with a knife in his back.... I may add that the sum which would, under certain circumstances, have become due to him was to have been paid in cash."

"It was a large sum?"

"Yes."

"Will you tell the court what it was?"

"I don't think I should do that."

"Why not? It may be no more than we know already. You see, we have the papers which were in Ringan's pockets."

"I have no objection to your knowing. It is a different matter to make a public statement."

"But Ringan is dead."

"I am not concerned about him. Our clients are the bank from whom we received the funds, and our duty of secrecy is to them."

The coroner asked: "Is it necessary to press the question?"

"I think it should be on the records of the court."

"Very well. I must direct you, Sir Reginald, to answer."

"The amount which would have become payable under certain circumstances to Ringan was approximately £337,000 at the normal rate of exchange."

"And that was part of a larger sum?"

"Yes. Of five million dollars."

"And the result of this man's death is that that huge sum will not need to be paid out?"

Sir Reginald was roused at last to a heated reply: "The suggestion is infamous and groundless. We hold the money at the disposal of our correspondents, whoever may be living or dead."

"But the *immediate* result of Ringan's death is that the conditions under which this huge sum would become payable do not arise?"

"The immediate result—yes."

"So that my infamous suggestion was exactly true?"

"I emphatically disagree. It contained an innuendo which was as poisonous as it was false."

"Well, it is for the jury to judge! I will ask you—"

The coroner, who had glanced at the clock more than once during the last ten minutes, interposed with: "If your examination is not very near its conclusion, I think it may be convenient to adjourn at this stage, Mr. Whatley-Cummings."

"I have a number of further questions to ask."

"Very well. We will adjourn for forty minutes. Gentlemen of the jury, you will be back in your places at one-fifty."

The coroner was out of his seat and through the door which opened behind his chair almost as the words died on his lips, and the crowded court waked to the murmur of many voices and the bustle of those who pushed their way out through its narrow doors.

CHAPTER IX.

A Consultation at Lunch

MR. JELLIPOT said: "There is a restaurant almost opposite where we may get a private room and lunch will be quickly served." He stood with Sir Reginald and Lady Crowe in the crowded vestibule of the court."

"Any phone there?"

"There's one in the room that I have in mind."

"Then we'd better hurry over, so that no one gets there before us."

"I have already reserved it."

"Good old Jellipot! Then we'll say no more till we're there and I the lunch is served."

This was a programme to which Mr. Jellipot was well content to adhere, and it was not until the soup plates had been removed and a more substantial course was before them that he began to discuss his client's position, with the words: "I had gathered earlier this morning that Whatley-Cummings would be inclined to be troublesome, but I didn't anticipate such a direct attack. It was unfortunate that we had that conversation the night before."

"It's unfortunate that Bracken's an ass."

"Yes. In combination with his holding the position he does. Anyway, we've got to face the fact that they mean to persuade the jury that you killed him, either to avoid paying out the money or for some reason unknown."

"Or just on general principles?"

"Yes. They may even try that."

"Funny, isn't it? And all because I said something that's obvious sense, and most men think, or would if they thought about the subject at all."

"It isn't merely that," Mr. Jellipot said, with his usual scrupulous equity. "The dead man is a fact. And it's another that he was on your mat, and that no one else was there."

"It's so absurd," Lady Crowe said, "that it's not easy to take it seriously."

"It will be serious if it causes a run on the London and Northern," her husband replied, in a more sober tone than his own peril had caused him to use.

"You're not really afraid of that?" There was more concern in r her own voice than it had held previously.

"Yes, I am. But, I say, Evelyn! Don't let that worry you. I didn't say we shan't be able to deal with it."

"I never knew of anything yet that you couldn't."

"Well, that's something to live up to! Jellipot, how should you like to have a wife who made you feel you daren't make a mess, even now and then?"

"I should think myself," Mr. Jellipot replied, "an exceptionally fortunate man."

"Well, I don't say you'd be wrong. But the question is what's the jury going to be persuaded to say?"

"I have never," Mr. Jellipot answered, "adopted the attitude of cynicism toward the British jury which is frequent in our profession. The average jury contains one cantankerous and two intelligent members, from whom much may be hoped. It is unfortunate that the one with which we have to deal—or perhaps I should say which will deal with us—shows no sign of including one of these.... I suppose what they say will depend entirely upon what Dr. Rathbone Bryant may say to them."

"And what will that be likely to be?"

"That, especially at this stage of proceedings, is difficult to forecast. He is what you may call a typically moderate man. Moderate in his ambitions, his sympathies and his intelligence Moderate in his conclusions also. I should say it would be "person unknown" unless he's influenced too much by the fact that the police are trying to fix it on to you. It is only fair to warn you of that."

"Sounds cheerful for me! I'll tell you what, Jellipot. Three months from now you and Evelyn will be searching for the real murderer, with a torch battery that's just going out, at the lower end of a London sewer, knowing that I'll be hanged in about three hours if you don't bring in the exhibit rather quicker than that.... And won't Evelyn lead you a life after if you re ten minutes late!"

Lady Crowe looked at her husband as he said this with more anxiety than she had shown previously. Knowing him as she did, she

saw that his mind entertained the possibility of troubles more seriously than his buoyant manner would indicate to a less intimate observation. Her eyes went to the lawyer in troubled query. Was it possible that Reggie, in whose fertility of resource she had learnt to
have such absolute confidence, was really in peril from this preposterous charge?

Mr. Jellipot, who understood them both, through the ordeal of
past experience, as few others would have been able to do, answered
the look in her eyes rather than the jesting words to which they had
listened.

"I should be sorry for any murderer whom Lady Crowe were
hunting under such circumstances, but there are several reasons why
I have some confidence that the position will not arise."

There was more ground for assurance to those who heard in the
quiet gravity of his voice than if he had spoken in the confident contempt of such charges being made or believed, which Lady Crowe,
if not her husband, needed to have. He went on: "I don't know that
we shall have so much difficulty in getting on the track of the man
we want. I got some information from Cross & Wardlaw this morning which I haven't had time to tell you till now—"

"Cross & Wardlaw being?"

"The lawyers from whom Whatley-Cummings has had his brief.
They let out that they've traced the two men who were to meet Ringan. They arrived at Southampton too late to make it possible that
they killed him, as it has never been sense to suppose they would.
But it's more than likely that they can put us on to whoever did, and
that they'll be glad to have their revenge on one who has upset their
own expectations of collecting their shares of the money."

"They won't give him away to us, however they feel," Sir
Reginald said. "They're more likely to run him down themselves."

"Which might be handled so that it would be equally good for
us."

"So it might. But I'd prefer to get out of this in another way. As
to who did it, I might make a good guess now, if I'd nothing more
decent to do."

Mr. Jellipot looked more interested than surprised. He said: "If
you can do that you have the position in your own hands."

"That's how it looks to you. Suppose the more I knew who it
was—which you mustn't think that I do—the more I should say
nothing at all?"

Mr. Jellipot made no effort to discuss this supposition. He
looked at his watch. He said: "We ought to be back in court in less

than six minutes. I remember that you made a point of having a telephone available here. I hope it was nothing important."

"Oh, I hadn't forgotten that! But I've left it as late as possible because I want to know what's happening at the bank after the midday papers were on the streets. If Bryant has to wait two or three minutes he'll get over that before he dies of old age or gets run down in the streets, as we mostly do. But we'll get back before he's in his chair, more likely than not.... Jellipot, you just finish lunch" (for Mr. Jellipot had given more attention to the conversation than to the excellent courses which the waiter had laid before him), "and if I'm not delayed getting through—"

Fortunately, there was no delay. In half a minute he was saying: "That you, Adams? Well, never mind anything else. What I want to know is how they're getting on at the counter since the papers got on the street. A bit busy? Well, so I expected to hear. Paying out, of course. We can stand that for today. But you've got to be ready for the morning, particularly with the country branches.... Any enquiries from—"

"Mr. Reed rang up half an hour ago."

"You mean the Capital & Counties? What did he say?"

"He said we could look to them to the limit of any cover we could put up."

"Good for him. Tell him we're all right yet. Five million dollars goes a long way, on the top of all we've got to throw on the counter besides that."

"I told him I'd go over to fix it up as soon as I'd taken this call from you."

"Well, perhaps you're right! We can't be too well prepared.... Anyone else?"

"There was an enquiry from the Bank of England a few minutes back."

"Any offer of help from them?"

"No. Just that they were anxious to know."

"Then if they have the cheek to come through again, tell them to go to hell."

"I'll make it clear that their assistance is not required."

"No, you won't. Don't make anything clear. I mean just what I say. Tell them to go to hell. If you add anything to that, just say that it's a message from me.... Anything else?"

"Lord Britleigh is anxious to be kept informed. I'm not sure whether he wants to help or to draw out."

"I don't suppose that he knows that himself. If you hear anything more, tell him to get in touch with Jellipot in the morning.

He'll trust him for the right advice, if he's not sure of me. But I can't go on talking now. You and Crofton will know how to carry on."

He cut off abruptly, turning to Lady Crowe to say: "There's that precious brother of yours getting a headache as to whether he'd be wiser to scuttle off or talk about offering his last crust. I've told Adams that Jellipot will make up his mind for him in the right way."

Evelyn laughed, perhaps for the first time that day. She said: "Poor Cyril! He will be in a stew. But if he were to—"

"He won't do that. But he'll lie awake all night wondering if he will."

"I think," Mr. Jellipot said gravely, "that Lord Britleigh's support is certain, though it is not one which we can suppose will be lightly given."

"Very well put, Jellipot. Well, there's the best part of a million there."

"I think we should be wise not to delay further."

"Well, who wants to? Come along, Evelyn. Let's hear what they've cooked up for us while we've been enjoying ourselves here."

They were two minutes (and twenty seconds, Mr. Jellipot would have added) late when they re-entered the court, but there was no trouble for that, the coroner being a full minute later than they.

It was a minute which Sir Reginald did not waste. He paused before the reporters' table to say: "Boys, I shouldn't wonder if you hear when you get back to Fleet Street that there's been a run on my bank. Well, if so, you can publish a message from me. There'll be an extra cashier tomorrow morning on every branch we've got where there's a counter long enough for him to stand, and an extra drawer for the cash. We'll pay out everyone who comes just as quickly as we can count the notes. But by this time next week I'll have a list on my desk of every customer who's been paid out, and everyone who's paid in, and they can be sure I shan't fail to turn it up when things change a bit, as they're always likely to do, and they're asking favours from me.

"They ought to know by now that I keep my word, and I'm not one to forget. And after I've said that, I don't know whether London will go on trying to knock us out, but I don't think Lancashire will."

With these confident words, upon which the reporters' pencils had not been idle, Sir Reginald passed on to his seat, as Dr. Rathbone Bryant settled himself in his loftier place and Whatley-Cummings rose.

CHAPTER X.

The Evidence of Sir Henry Bracken

IN legal actions or other processes, whether of civil or criminal character, the luncheon interval is no more than a deceptive pause, often filled with many hurried activities, and during which each side will take counsel upon the phases of battle already fought, and devise new tactics for those which are next to come Often it will be occasion for a flag of truce to pass the opposing barriers, and terms of settlement will be reached which would have been impracticable during the process of legal war.

For these and cognate reasons the interval may be welcomed by both contestants. The harried witness is glad of a respite which will give him time to consider the implications of the replies which have already been abstracted from him, and to decide how best he may avoid the pitfalls to which they lead. The counsel who has been conducting the examination may be glad of an interval to consider the same replies from an opposite angle. The watchful solicitors may have their own suggestions to make for his consideration. Their consultations may result in the adoption of different tactics from those which were interrupted by the rising of the court.

So it was now. Sir Reginald Crowe, expecting to be called back to the witness box, heard Mr. Whatley-Cummings say: "Before recalling the previous witness, I suggest that, if you approve, it may be well to take the evidence of Sir Henry Bracken, who has attended today at great inconvenience, and whose presence is now urgently required in connection with his public duties elsewhere."

The coroner said that this appeared to be a convenient course to adopt, and Sir Henry Bracken entered the box.

After the usual preliminaries, his examination proceeded in a court which had sunk to a silence of concentrated attention greater even than that which had been directed upon the previous witness.

"On the evening of Monday, the seventh instant—the evening before the murder—you had a conversation with Sir Reginald Crowe?"

"Yes. At dinner."

"Actually you were his guest?"

"Yes.

"Who else was present?"

"Lady Crowe and Mr. Jellipot."

"They must also have heard the conversation, in which, more or less, they took part?"

"Yes."

"No one else was there?"

"No one else. Mr. Jellipot and myself were the guests of Sir Reginald and Lady Crowe."

"Mr. Jellipot being Sir Reginald's lawyer, who is now representing him here?"

"Yes."

"What was the subject of the conversation?"

"Whether murder was a serious crime."

"Who started the subject?"

"Sir Reginald Crowe."

"What view did he take?"

"He said that many murders were justifiable. He seemed to think that they were a good thing rather than—"

Mr. Jellipot interposed. "Mr. Coroner, I object. If the witness will tell us what Sir Reginald Crowe said—or what he believes he remembers that he said in the course of an after-dinner conversation to which no importance could have been attached at the time—the court will be able to judge what he seemed to think, which is opinion only."

"I am sure, Mr. Jellipot," the coroner answered, "you may rely upon Sir Henry Bracken to give his evidence with scrupulous impartiality."

"I have no doubt of that. But my objection was on other grounds."

The coroner turned to the witness. "Perhaps, Sir Henry, you will tell us, as exactly as possible, what Sir Reginald said."

"He said too much for me to remember it all. Its general effect was that many murders would be good rather than bad if the murderer were not afterwards interfered with by the police."

The examination continued:

"Was this argument entirely of an abstract kind, or did he mention any example of those who, shall we say, required murdering for their own or the public good?"

"He mentioned no names that I recollect, but he said a man had called upon him that afternoon who would be no loss to the community."

"Did he describe him?"

"Yes."

"You have heard the descriptions of the murdered man which were given in court this morning?"

"Yes."

"Have you any doubt that it was to this man that Sir Reginald Crowe referred?"

"None whatever."

Mr. Jellipot, who had been engaged in a whispered conference with his client, rose again.

"I might easily show that the reference in question was of far too vague a character to admit of such identification, but my client wishes to treat the court with the utmost candour concerning a conversation the significance of which may be absurdly exaggerated in the light of events which subsequently occurred, and I will say at once that the reference was to Antonio Ringan."

Mr. Whatley-Cummings' glance swept the length of the jury box, as though to share with the gentlemen it contained the deadly implications of this admission. He turned back to the witness as he exclaimed: "That, if I may say so without unfairness, might have been difficult to deny.... Can you recall the nature of Sir Reginald Crowe's allusion to this unfortunate man, who was doomed to meet a violent and treacherous death at his door on the next day?"

"He said if he were to kill him he supposed there'd be more fuss than if he had killed a good dog."

This statement moved the court to an audible murmur, and caused the coroner to glance at Sir Reginald's solicitor as though to enquire whether that astonishing allegation were to pass unchallenged. But Mr. Jellipot gave no sign.

Mr. Whatley-Cummings, who had intended to put two or three further questions, was too good a tactician to do so. "I think," he said, as though he had demonstrated Sir Reginald's guilt to the satisfaction of every sensible mind, "that is all that I need ask," and sat down accordingly.

As he did so Mr. Jellipot rose. "With your permission, sir, there are one or two questions I should like to ask.... You have told us, Sir

Henry, your recollection of what Sir Reginald Crowe may have said. Do you recollect your own remarks on the subject in equal detail?"

"I don't think I said much. I was too astonished at what I heard."

"May I assist your recollection? Did you not say that you were sure that Sir Reginald's remarks were not seriously made?"

"I may have said something of that kind."

"Could you not be rather more explicit?"

"Yes, I think I did."

"You remember saying it?"

"Yes. Something to that effect."

"You are familiar with Sir Reginald Crowe's conversational style on such occasions? When his object will be to amuse and entertain his guests. It may often be of startling or paradoxical character?"

"Yes. I dare say it is."

"You know it is?"

"I am sure that I have no wish to misrepresent Sir Reginald in any way."

"I am equally sure of that; and I therefore press you for an explicit answer."

"I have heard Sir Reginald say things on other occasions which it is difficult to take seriously."

"I will accept that.... On this occasion it never entered your mind that the man to whom allusion had been made was in any danger at Sir Reginald's hands? It did not occur to you to warn him? Or to use the powers of the police whom you control for his protection?"

"No."

"And, because that power is in your hands, and the policing of the metropolitan area is a task in which you have so large a share of responsibility, you would be particularly likely—indeed, certain—to take such steps if any reasonable cause. should arise?"

"Yes. If I should see reasonable occasion to do so."

"And the fact that you hold that position would make it particularly unlikely that anyone of Sir Reginald's intelligence, having a homicidal intention, would mention it in your presence?"

"I was extremely surprised when I heard it said."

"That is not what I asked. But I think your inaction was the sufficient answer. You have said that you did not take the conversation seriously. I suppose, beyond that, you recognised the gulf which lies between academic theory and physical act?"

"I certainly didn't think it was a thing which Sir Reginald would be likely to do."

"I think that is all that I need ask you."

Mr. Jellipot sat down, and a moment later, with the coroner's permission, Sir Henry Bracken left the court, while Sir Reginald Crowe was recalled to the witness box.

CHAPTER XI.

SIR REGINALD DOES NOT DENY

"WHAT I said I meant, and I'm not going to soft-pedal now."

These words, spoken by Sir Reginald as he left his solicitor's side to submit himself once more to the examination of Mr, Whatley-Cummings, were not heard by Mr. Jellipot alone, but by a dozen of those who were closely round them. One, at least, of the reporters heard them and gave them a world-wide publicity. Faintly they reached the coroner's ears.

Mr. Jellipot looked his doubt, but did not repeat a protest already made "I was bound," he thought, "to advise an attitude of greater caution, which he was bound to reject. Were he less audacious or self-assured, he would not hold the position he now does. He must fight this in his own way, to which I must conform.... But for such a line it's about the worst jury I ever saw." He put his own thoughts aside to listen to a resumed examination on which he felt that Sir Reginald's immediate freedom, if not his ultimate fate, might depend.

"You have just heard, Sir Reginald, Sir Henry Bracken's account of some things you are alleged to have said regarding Antonio Ringan on the evening before his murder. Do you agree that they were substantially accurate?"

"It isn't likely, is it?"

"You mustn't ask me. Why isn't it likely?"

"Such after-dinner conversations are not likely to be remembered with accuracy."

"Well, do you happen to have a better memory?"

"Substantially, yes. I know what I meant, and I know I said it."

"Then perhaps you'll tell the court what your views are on the subject of private homicide, which were so startling that those who heard thought you couldn't possibly mean them seriously?"

"I'm quite willing to do that, though they have not the slightest relevance to this inquest."

"That is for the jury to judge."

"Naturally.... What I think, and may have said, is that there may be no crime that varies so greatly as murder, both in its criminality and in the evil of its results.

"Even when we put aside consideration of crimes of extreme provocation, or which arise from abnormal emotional disturbances, there are evident differences between the motives and impulses that lead to homicide, as there are also in the loss to the community or even to the individual most concerned. Life itself is of very varying value to those who possess it. An old man suffering from an incurable disease loses less than a young one in vigorous health, and if the young one be hanged for his murder he suffers a heavier penalty than would an old man if their rôles had been reversed.

"But it seems futile to occupy the time of the court in an abstract thesis with which, if it be carefully considered, I suppose few reasonable people would disagree."

"You may be wrong there. Most men may think *Thou shalt not kill* to be a commandment to which no specious qualifications should be applied.... But I must suggest that what you said went beyond such abstractions. Did you not actually mention the murdered man as one whom it would be a venial offence to kill?"

"No. I mentioned him as one whose death would be little loss to the community, which is a widely different matter."

"And next day he was dead. Will you tell the jury why you thought his life to be of so little value?"

"He was a criminal—a man who lived by violence and fraud—according to his own statement to me. He had actually proposed to me that afternoon that I should be a party to enabling him to defraud those who were to draw the money jointly with him."

"And after that you arranged to see him again next morning?"

"I had no option. When we are instructed to pay out, in any specified direction, funds which we hold, we cannot refuse to do so because we dislike the characters of the payees."

"Not if they are criminals?"

"Not even then, unless we have evidence of criminality relating to the funds in question, or the use to which they would be applied."

"And when you saw him you refused to be a party to this proposed fraud?"

"I certainly did."

"And this quarrel followed, with the fatal result which should not be taken too seriously?"

"That is an utterly false and groundless suggestion. I have told you that this proposal was made on the previous afternoon, and that on the following morning I did not see him at all until I found him dying at my office door."

"That is for the jury to say."

"That is surely for me to say, as I am the only one, except the murderer, who can possibly know."

The reply was given with more heat than Sir Reginald had previously shown, and drew a murmur of approval from some, though perhaps no more than a small minority, of those who heard. The sound ceased at a word of sharp rebuke from the coroner, and Whatley-Cummings, sensitive to the atmosphere of the court, as a good advocate always is, changed the tone, though not the direction, of his attack.

Sympathy for the witness was about the last emotion he would wish to arouse in those who listened to this rapid duel of words and wits. His tone became that of one who strives with patient kindness to draw reasonable admissions from a refractory and untruthful child.

"You ask us to believe that you came along the passage, your mind naturally occupied, and perhaps agitated, with the trouble at your Wigan branch, and you suddenly saw a dying man in a pool of his own blood, and—"

"I did not say that. There was comparatively little blood till I turned him over and pulled out the knife."

"Never mind that. Let us concentrate upon the essential fact that—"

"But it is essential that you should not put words into my mouth that I have not said."

The sharp interruption had disconcerted counsel in the smooth period which he had intended to reach. It was with a perceptible effort that he resumed his tone of persuasive reasoning, and went on: "I have no desire to put any words into your mouth, Sir Reginald, or to treat you with anything less than the most scrupulous fairness. But do you not see that your account is not one which any sensible person can be expected to believe? Would not any man, suddenly coming on such a sight, rouse an alarm, both to chase the assassin and to give help to a dying man?"

"I tried to give help myself."

"And that is all the explanation you propose to offer of the considerable interval which must have occurred between your finding the body and ringing up the police?"

"I telephoned my solicitor after I had ascertained that the man was beyond help."

"Was that the natural course to be taken by an innocent man?"

"It seemed natural to me."

"After the man was dead—by whatever hand—you turned him over, as you say, to draw out the knife. Was there any other more personal motive?"

"None whatever. What could there be?"

"You must not ask questions of me. Did you take nothing from him?"

"I did not. You appear to be suggesting that I am not only a murderer, but a common thief."

"I am not suggesting, but asking you a direct question. I do not I suppose that you robbed him of money. Indeed, from the large sum that was found upon him, it is highly unlikely that such a motive incited the crime or interested the criminal subsequently. But was there no document which, to your own knowledge, was in his possession, and which you would prefer to remove rather than it should be found upon him by the police?"

"No. I am aware of nothing which I could have the slightest interest in keeping from the observation of the police."

"Or taking from him in your own interests or that of your bank?"

"None whatever."

"You have told the court that when he called upon you on the previous afternoon he produced a document of great value—in fact, his authority to receive about £337,000."

"He did."

"He doubtless produced evidences of identification?"

"He did."

"His passport?"

"Yes."

"From which pocket did he abstract it?"

"I am not sure that I can recall that. It was not a thing which was likely to notice particularly. But I think—I may say I am sure—that it was from a hip-pocket. Yes. It was from his right hip-pocket. I remember that he moved his position on the chair as he drew the passport out."

"Do you think it likely that when he came to see you again in the morning he did not bring his passport with him, and also the document by which he hoped to draw £337,000?

"No. I think it improbable."

"Most improbable?"

"Yes. You may say that."

"And do you know that, though his passport and other documents, and a considerable sum of money, were found on him, the authority to collect that money was not among them?"

"I will accept your word for it. I did not know until now."

"And to reach that document, which you knew to be in his hip-pocket, it was necessary to turn him over?"

"No. You are wrong. As he lay, it would have been easy to reach his hip-pocket without moving him at all."

"You recall that precisely?"

"I remember how he lay."

"With special reference to his hip-pocket?"

"No. But I know where a hip-pocket is."

"It is a very awkward position for being got at when a man is lying on his back?"

"It is a point which I have never had occasion to consider. But I think you may be exaggerating the difficulty. A hip-pocket is at the side rather than the back."

"Anyway, you raised no alarm, you turned over the dying man, you then telephoned for your solicitor, and a document which could be of no value except to the man or your own bank has disappeared from his pocket. That is your own account of what occurred?"

"That is substantially correct, except that the disappearance of any document is outside my knowledge, and, if I accept your assurance, I must dissent from the statement that it could only be valuable to Ringan or the bank. Actually it could be of no value to us whatever, while I should suppose that it might be of much to the heirs or executors of the dead man."

"Well, I will not press you further on that. As I have said before, it is for the jury to judge. Let me ask you—"

But it would be wearisome to follow this examination in further detail. Whatley-Cummings pursued his favourite device of repeating questions in different forms and from various angles of approach, it being a method by which he would often lead a lying or bewildered witness into contradictions, real or apparent, from which he could draw deadly inferences when he subsequently addressed the jury. But from Sir Reginald Crowe he had no such profit. He had met an opponent here who could parry his swiftest thrusts. Sir Reginald Crowe's danger lay in the facts themselves as he asserted or admitted them to have been.

Mr. Jellipot, weighing them in a cautious mind, doubted the advantage that further questions would bring. He may have surprised the coroner, when at last the K.C. sat down and his opportunity came, by declining to take advantage of it. "I think," he said, "Sir Reginald Crowe has given the court all the assistance that is within his power. His evidence is quite clear, and there is nothing that requires further elucidation."

But if Dr. Bryant were surprised that Sir Reginald's solicitor should appear unperturbed by the peril in which his client appeared to stand, he was much more so when a rather strident voice from the back of the court enquired, "May I take the stand?" and he saw that a young woman whose bright red curls had little concealment under what may be described as a perfunctory hat had risen and was pushing her way resolutely forward.

CHAPTER XII.

The Redhead Has Something to Say

"DO you mean," the coroner asked, "that you know something about this murder?"

"I should say that. I was in the room."

"You mean you were in Sir Reginald Crowe's room when the murder occurred?"

"Nope. But I was there just before."

"You had better enter the box.... No, not this way. The steps to the right.... Wrightman, swear this lady."

The witness took the oath in the American manner, but with an ease suggestive of past experiences. She gave her name as Mary O'Leary, and her address as the Atlantis Hotel, Broadway, New York. The coroner asked: "That is your permanent address in your own country?"

"It's where I shall go back."

"You mean you have no other address in the United States?"

"You can say that."

"And your address here?"

"Hotel Westmorland."

"Westmorland Hotel. Very well. Tell the court, in your own way, what you know of this matter."

"I know Sir Crowe had gone out of the room."

"You mean you were there."

"I should say I was. He said he'd leave me a minute to get some dope, and he didn't come back, and I wasn't what you'd call sure what the racket was, and I got rattled and left But he wouldn't know I was gone till he got back into the room You might as well say it was me."

The coroner noticed that Mr. Whatley-Cummings, who had been observing the unexpected witness with intently speculative eyes, smiled broadly at this femininely illogical argument. But he let

55

it pass without comment. He went on: "How long were you in the room after Sir Reginald Crowe left?"

"Quite a time. I didn't check up on it. I didn't know any need. It was about half of eleven when I went out, or some time later than that."

"Did you see anything of Antonio Ringan or anyone else entering or approaching Sir Reginald's room?"

"I did not."

"How did you leave?"

"Down the stairs that I came up."

"It was stated in evidence this morning that Sir Reginald's visitors were usually taken up by a lift at the other end of the corridor."

"I wouldn't know."

"Was your business with Sir Reginald anything to do with that on which Ringan called?"

"I'd say it was."

"Then you probably knew him?"

"I did that. Not that I'd shout about it. He was just dirt."

"Is there anything further you can tell the court which would throw light on what happened?"

"He'd got it coming to him. I can say that."

"You mean you know of someone who intended to kill him?"

"I didn't say that."

"But you do?"

"That's a sort of talk I don't hear."

"You mean you know, but won't say?"

"I don't mean anything."

"I must direct you to answer the question."

"I've said all I can. I don't know who did it, and you wouldn't think I'd say if I did."

"I should certainly expect it. In the interests of justice it would be your duty to do so."

"Justice won't worry me.... You don't know what Tony was."

"I'm afraid, Miss O'Leary, you may hardly understand how serious your position is. Do you realise that if I direct you to answer a question, and you refuse, I have power to commit you to prison for contempt of court for an indefinite period?"

"Say, that's bully for you! But I'm not scared. I've been put wise that you've got no third degree here."

"But I suppose you would prefer to avoid imprisonment. I must ask you again, do you know of anyone who had threatened Ringan, or whom you have other reason to think may have committed the crime?"

"I'll say no to that."

The coroner gave it up. Perhaps the methods of Whatley-Cummings would be more successful! He glanced at the K.C., who rose at once.

"Now, Miss O'Leary," he began, "you say you know nothing about the murder of Antonio Ringan because you left Sir Reginald's room before he returned to it or Ringan arrived. Is that right?"

"Yep."

"Then what motive have you in offering to give evidence on a matter on which you know nothing?"

"Because, you poor boob, you were trying to make out that Sir Crowe stuck him, and I know that wasn't true."

"How do you know that?"

"I've told you he left me there. If you like making silly guesses, it might just as well have been me."

"No one is suggesting that. I have no doubt that, had you been present, you would have done everything possible to prevent the crime."

"You're telling me."

"I hope, by that cryptic remark, you don't mean—"

"I tried to stop one of the boys being bumped off once, and I got this."

Her hand went to the white scar on her temple.

"I see that you speak with some experience in these matters, which may be regarded more lightly in your own country than they are here."

"I wouldn't know."

"Perhaps not. But I can assure you that such crimes are not allowed to occur without such searching investigations as almost invariably end in the conviction and punishment of the criminal and of any others who may give him aid or concealment You may think us slow—we may be poor boobs to you—but you will find that we usually get there in our own way."

"Well, I only tipped you to lay off the wrong man."

"It is not for you or me to decide who is the wrong man. That is a matter for the jury alone."

Miss O'Leary showed no disposition to comment upon this obvious statement. Her eyes, hard, bright and alert, swept the double line of the jury box, but she gave no sign of her opinion of what she saw. Realising that she had allowed him the last word, Mr. Whatley-Cummings went on.

"You say you left the room before Sir Reginald returned or Ringan arrived. Why do you invite us to conclude from that fact—

which I am quite prepared to believe—that Sir Reginald had no part in what followed?"

"He'd have been a fast worker for that."

"I fail to see that he need have worked faster than whoever else it might be—and someone it certainly was—who struck the fatal blow."

"Well, if you can't see that I...."

"I must ask you, Miss O'Leary." the coroner interposed with some severity, "to confine yourself to answering questions and to treat the court and the learned counsel with greater respect."

"Well, if he can't help being a stupe!" Miss O'Leary replied, in what she evidently meant to be a tone of conciliation. "What I meant was that Tony wouldn't have been coming out of the room till they'd had their talk, and that would have taken more time than there was likely to be if you reckon up.

"I reckon whoever put that knife into Tony's back had gone in, with him, and they came out when they found Sir Crowe wasn't in, or else Tony didn't know he was there."

Mr. Jellipot, hearing this, was disposed to revise an opinion he had been forming that this confident witness, though she appeared to have come forward with contrary intentions, might be doing his client more harm than good. The point might be illogical in its assumptions, if not in itself, but to anyone who accepted Sir Reginald's account, and sought with an open mind to reconstruct what had occurred, there would be reason in what she said.

And next moment he saw further cause to reverse the doubt which had vexed his mind, for Whatley-Cummings, perhaps more deeply irritated by being called boob and stupe than his practised self-control allowed to appear, gave an opening which invited the devastating reply that it promptly had.

"It is an interesting speculation," he said, "which would be worthy of greater consideration if there were any evidence of a third party having been in the room at all."

There was amused contempt in the hard blue eyes that looked straight into his own as the reply came: "That's as good as saying if it wasn't Sir Crowe, it was me. But I can tell you that it's quite easy to go up those stairs without anyone giving you half a look if you just do it without loitering round, though I dare say it's what most people don't try. And Ringan did go up, whether or not; and if one, why not two?"

That, at least, was good logic. With Ringan, or behind him—if one, why not two? Whatley-Cummings, K.C., might ask himself, possibly for the first time in a life in which ambition had been largely fulfilled, had he been called by the right names?

Not that he had been blind to the possibility of Ringan having had a companion or a following foe. It was an obvious alternative to the theory that Sir Reginald had struck the blow, which he regarded as the greater probability. But that, by the most elementary laws of advocacy, was no excuse for having invited such a reply.

The coroner averted what might have been an awkward moment by saying briskly: "I think, Mr. Whatley-Cummings, this may be a convenient time to adjourn.... You will understand, Miss O'Leary, as will the jury, and the witnesses who have been summoned, that they must be here at ten tomorrow morning.... No, Mr. Whatley-Cummings, Sir Henry Bracken's attendance will be excused."

CHAPTER XIII.

Evelyn Does Not Go Home

SIR REGINALD paused in the crowded corridor of the court. He had pushed his way out with a minimum of consideration for others in a determined effort to reach Miss O'Leary's (or should we say Mrs. Clancy's?) side, followed as best they might by his wife and lawyer. Mr. Jellipot had surmised his purpose, which he did not approve, but, as he guessed correctly that it would fail, he had not been careful to intervene. If matters would go the right way of themselves, they would have no rash interference from him.

Mrs. Clancy had been much nearer the door. She had a muscular shoulder for such occasions, and her normal consideration for others was much less than that of Sir Reginald at particular need. He saw the flame of red hair beaconing him forward through its dark surrounding current of heads and hats, but he had been able to do little to shorten the separating distance when it disappeared into one of the waiting taxis which had drawn up at the pavement in anticipation of fares on the exodus of the court.

Recognising defeat, he now awaited his friends, and spoke when they reached his side with his usual decisive energy.

"Jellipot, I've got to have a few words with that young woman. I meant to catch her now, but she's slipped off. I must get to Lombard Street first, but after that I expect I can get her at her hotel. It makes it a bit uncertain what time I shall get home, and I should have liked a talk with you before we get here tomorrow. Would it be possible for you to take Evelyn home and put up for the night with us?"

"Yes," Mr. Jellipot agreed, after a moment of thoughtful hesitation. "I can telephone my housekeeper, and I must have a few words with Newman if I don't go back to the office; but I can do that.... What I don't like is you following Miss O'Leary. You're not the one to do that, for more reasons than one, especially as you'll be almost sure to meet Ingram there."

"I don't say I am. But someone must see the girl. What do you propose?"

"I had thought of looking her up myself."

Sir Reginald hesitated. What did Jellipot know—or rather what did he think he knew? What would his approach to Mrs. Clancy be?

Lady Crowe said: "If there's anything I can do—you know how glad I shall be."

"Yes, of course, Evelyn. I know that. But you've just got to stop worrying and leave this to Jellipot and to me."

Mr. Jellipot added, with more haste of speech than he was accustomed to use: "I think I can see how this can be handled best."

Evelyn, feeling that her vague offer of help had been doubly rejected, said: "Well, then, I think I'll go home now and expect you later. I'll send both cars to wait at the station. You're almost sure to come by different trains."

By this time Sir Reginald had resolved the doubt which disturbed his mind. He said: "Very well, I'll leave it to you, Jellipot, to deal with the girl. I can trust you not to do anything silly.... Goodbye, Evelyn, and don't worry. They haven't got me in Brixton yet."

With this cheerful observation he hurried away, and Mr. Jellipot's eyes turned to one of the benches that lined the sides of the now almost empty corridor. "If you wouldn't mind waiting a few minutes while I make two necessary calls—" he began, and was interrupted by: "Need I wait? I thought of catching the six-seven."

"When you said you would be glad to help if you could, were I you thinking of seeing Mrs. O'Leary yourself?"

"Yes. I did think of that. A woman will sometimes tell another what she won't tell a man.... And I thought she would be rather interesting to meet."

"Then if you will wait for a few minutes we will go together."

"But I thought you said—" Sudden comprehension, aided by the pleasure that the proposal gave, brought a light of laughter to Evelyn's eyes. "You must have meant this all the time, but you thought Reggie would object if you said it then!"

"That," Mr. Jellipot replied with gravity, "is an inference which it is legitimate to draw, but which it would be unwise of me either to confirm or deny.... If we proceed to that teashop which you favour in Oxford Street—"

"You mean Buzzard's?"

"I have no doubt that is the name—and get the tea which I have observed to be essential to your complacency of demeanour at this period of the day, we may still reach the Westmorland by about six-fifteen, having given the lady time for her own refreshment, and still—we may hope—being there before Chief Inspector Ingram will have arrived."

"You're sure he'll be on her track?"

"It is a reasonable assumption."

"But I thought he was trying all he knows to fix it on to Reggie. She didn't sound as though she'd given him much help

"I think you may be disposed to misunderstand a man of whose methods it is easy to disapprove. Chief Inspector Ingram may be one of those who will betray with a kiss or with smiling words, but he will betray to justice only. If he be led to think Sir Reginald innocent, you will have no more trouble from him."

"I've no doubt you're right...but all the same he's just poison to me.... I'll wait here while you phone."

CHAPTER XIV.

MISS O'LEARY WATCHES THE DOOR

MRS. CLANCY, as she preferred to be called, or Miss O'Leary, as her passport and the requirements of alien registration had obliged others to call her, was in the ground-floor lounge of the Westmorland, sitting with her back to the wall, an empty tray from which she had cleared the sandwiches with good appetite at her side, an American cigarette at her lips, and her eyes fixed on the entrance, so that she saw and recognised Lady Crowe and Mr. Jellipot as quickly as their own eyes were upon her.

She showed at once that she realised that it would be her they sought, and gave no sign that it was an unwelcome interview. She did not rise, but waved a hand of invitation, the cigarette which it contained pointing to two vacant chairs that stood near her own settee.

But when Mr. Jellipot took one of these chairs, mentioning Lady Crowe's name and his own as he did so with the formality which he considered the occasion required, she said affably: "Oh, cut it out! I didn't sit there all day without learning that. But you might turn that chair rather more to one side."

Seeing Mr. Jellipot's momentary hesitation, for he had drawn the chair from a position in which he would have sat at an awkward angle to both the ladies, and there was nothing of an aggressive or over-intimate character in the position he had given it, she added: "It's not that I should mind overmuch if you stopped a bullet that's meant for me, but I like to see who comes through the door."

"You mean," Mr. Jellipot enquired, without showing any sign of perturbation at this surprising explanation, and while giving his chair the minimum alteration that she required, "that you anticipate being the object of a homicidal attack?"

"I thought some of the boys might be bumping me off, if you mean that."

"I am sure we mean the same thing. May I suggest that, if you have serious ground for such a suspicion, you should waste no time in seeking the protection of the police."

"Squeal to the cops? And how long should you think I'd live when I'd done that?"

"You might be better protected than you suppose. The London police are a very efficient body of men."

"They'd need be that, and a bit more."

"It is a matter on which you should be the best judge. But I should suppose it must be unpleasant to remain in constant fear of an attack of that kind."

"Well, I'll soon know. They'd work fast in a case like this."

"Are we to understand that you put yourself in danger by the evidence you gave at the court today?"

"I don't see why I should. But I'd give a big pile to know. There's some of the boys might have got me wrong."

"But I should have supposed, even so, that you'd be in little danger at present. There cannot be many of your compatriots here who could be interested in what you said."

"Think not? They're as thick as flies. A thousand grand to be shared out is a big wad. It's bad luck that there aren't many friends of mine; but if I do get shot up there'll be some funerals Chicago way when they get back."

"Would you tell me," Mr. Jellipot asked, "exactly why you should anticipate that you are in danger through any evidence that you gave today?"

"It's not anything I said; it's if they thought I could say more and might let it slip."

"As to who killed Ringan?"

"Yep. What else could it be? But you didn't come along here to learn whether the boys were out looking for me. What is it you want to know?"

"I think," Mr. Jellipot answered, "you have told us already, and in more conclusive words than we could have expected to hear it."

There was a moment's pause as the girl mentally translated Mr. Jellipot's deliberate diction into what she supposed English to be, and then her quick underworld wit showed itself in the swift perception of the implication of what he said.

"You mean that you thought I'd done Ringan in myself when you came here, and you don't now?"

"It was," Mr. Jellipot admitted, "a most natural suspicion to have; and it was evidently a mistake, or you would have no reason to fear that you might be suspected of betraying whoever did."

"I can't do that, for I don't know. Though I won't say I'd be wrong in three guesses or even two. But you've put me wise to another thing. I reckon you're sure that it wasn't Sir Crowe, which I'd been getting to doubt. I should say he's not far short of being a real man."

Mr. Jellipot wondered whether her definition of a real man was one who would murder those who called upon him with their own knives, and might have investigated the subject further at a moment of greater leisure. Now the speculation reduced him to a moment's silence, during which Evelyn spoke for the first time.

"I wonder you offered to give evidence at all if you saw that it would be so risky for you."

"Well, I just reckoned I would. I like a man who shoots straight. And I liked what Sir Crowe said. And if you can make the cops look silly it's a chance that you shouldn't miss."

Evelyn heard these reasons with reflections which were best left in silence. The opportunity of making the police (or their legal representative) look silly would have been no temptation to her, but evidently had an aspect of compelling duty in Miss O'Leary's mind. She had no objection to Reggie being described as a straight shooter, but was dubious as to whether his abstract arguments regarding the relative guilt of different homicides was not being taken in a way which did much to support the wisdom of a more conventional attitude.

But these reflections did not reduce the cordiality of her feeling toward a girl who, she did not doubt, had been primarily actuated by a determination to support one who was being attacked by a hostile legal array, and whom she regarded with friendly eyes. What she said was: "Perhaps I ought to tell you that it is not usual to say Sir Crowe. Sir Reginald is how he is usually spoken of or addressed. But I can see that it is a very natural error to make."

"I didn't think to use his first name. I don't know him that well. But you're the one that should mind. What you say goes for—" She stopped abruptly. Her eyes hardened. She spoke again in a louder voice and a changed tone: "But if you think I'll be mixed up in it to save anyone's skin you're just making the wrong guess."

Mr. Jellipot heard, over his shoulder, the quiet, persuasive voice of Chief Inspector Ingram: "I'm sorry to hear you speak like that, Miss O'Leary. I think I may be able to show you that it will be worth while to help us, and that you may be helping yourself too. May I pull a chair into the little circle? I hope you won't feel that it's a case of three's company but four's none."

Evelyn, curious to see how the girl would react to this police intrusion, saw her whole face harden. There was no trace now of the softer lines of lips and chin which showed in her friendlier moods. Her eyes were murderous. It became easy to understand how formidable she could be, and how she would fit into the underworld to which she so clearly belonged.

Mr. Jellipot was the first to speak. It is improbable that he did not notice the girl's angry reluctance, but it did not influence what he said, though it may have made him a second quicker, lest something should be said of a different kind.

"Yes, of course. There is no one whom it could be more pleasure to see."

Miss O'Leary looked straight in the eyes of the detective as he drew up a chair on which his hand had been already laid. Her words, slow and loud, could be heard with startling clarity above the murmur of other voices that filled the lounge: "You lousy dog!" In a lower tone of concentrated bitterness she went on I suppose you don't give a thought to what it may mean to me?"

Ingram showed no sign of resentment, which he may not have felt. He answered affably: "Your expletive may explain yourself rather than define me. But, whatever I am, I'm sure you'll lose nothing by letting us talk things over quietly together."

"Cut it out! Have you got a gun?"

"No. I have not. I can assure you, Miss O'Leary, that the advantage of carrying one is much less in this country than in your own livelier land. I am probably safer here than—"

"*Safe?* Of course, you cops are. I wasn't thinking of you. But I suppose I'm in for it now. You'd better all come to my room. I'll go first, if you please. You"—to Ingram—"can come behind, and you may be more use than you often are."

With these words she led the way to the lift, her thoughts on the little deadly silver-mounted gun that her handbag held. She had concealed it successfully as she came through the customs at Southampton, and it would now have been nearer her hand had she not feared that the slightest indication of its existence would be noticed by the sharp eyes of the detective, and she would be deprived of the only means on which she could rely for protection in what to her was a lawless world.

When she reached the luxury of her own suite, which was the best that the hotel held, making it clear to her visitors that lack of dollars was no immediate trouble to her, she was in a mood to talk, though what she would say might not be what Chief Inspector Ingram would be most anxious to hear.

CHAPTER XV.

MISS O'LEARY EXPLAINS AMERICA

IN her own room Miss O'Leary did not allow the tension of the occasion to obliterate the duties of hospitality. She rang for drinks, for cigarettes and cigars. She instructed an obsequious page-boy to make up a fire with which (for the October evening was chilly) she had insisted on supplementing the central heating of the hotel, which did not reach the temperature of those of her own land.

But when the preliminaries had been arranged to her satisfaction she locked a door which she had not ceased to watch, and, having drawn her chair closer to the glowing fire than her visitors were disposed to do, she said abruptly: "Now, Inspector, what more do you want to know, and are we talking off the record or not? (Actually she said "re-cud," that being the mispronunciation that all Americans concur to use, from Detroit to Dallas, from the White House to a 'Frisco dive.)

"It's off the record, if you mean by that that it won't reach the press through me. I can't promise anything beyond that. I don't know what you may be going to say."

"Same here. But I shall when I've heard what you want to know."

"I should like to know whether you have any idea as to who may have committed the crime."

"I might make a guess."

"Then I'm sure you will not refuse to give us the name of the man you suspect. If it be suspicion only—if you did not see him anywhere near the scene of the crime and are still ignorant of what his movements may have been—we will ask you no more than that, and will proceed to our own enquiries, in which your name need not be used."

"You think you're a smart guy. Ever heard of Dorothy Keenan? I guess not. That baby had style. Rooms on 54th that might have made one of your duchesses turn green. Chloroformed she was. That was in '23.

"Then there was Lou Lawson. Film actress at Long Island when she couldn't get her dough quicker in other ways. Had a studio looking out over Central Park. Found strangled she was. That was in '24.

"Or Em Harrington? Beaten to death. Called herself an actress, but she got beaten up for another reason than that. Westside room in New York, like the rest. Christmas '27 that was.

"Or Doll Gables? So smart that the cops never caught up with her. In half the rackets going for four years, and never had to do as much as to hire bail. Fished out of Harlem River with a copper wire round her neck. That was a year last June.

"Or Viv Gordon? Oh, you *have* heard of her? Well, she's no dead yet, or wasn't when I left Broadway, but that's just her luck. She's got it coming to her."

"I can assure you that in this country you could have nothing to fear."

"Think not? You may have something to learn yet. But that wouldn't be any good to me. I'm going back to a country where you don't sneeze on the stairs."

"I suppose the murderers of these women are still at large?"

"You bet they are. Paul's doing time for Emma, but he wasn't one of the boys. He didn't know how these things are planned. But it all hangs on one thing. It's why those girls died, and why those who killed them don't need to worry. *Squealers don't live.*"

"There may be another reason," Ingram replied. "Any man who kills another in this country knows we *shall* get him, squealers or not, and that makes him think twice."

"And you don't third degree here? You must be real cute. How often do you get the right man? I should ask! It's the wrong one in our country, more often than not."

"Which suggests, if I may say so without disparagement to your very competent police, that third-degree methods may not be very reliable in their results."

"You're telling me! But I should say you make more mistakes than you ever know. It looks to me that you get the right man if you can, but you get someone whether or not. You're not all that smart if you're like the baldhead who questioned me.... And I'll tell you another thing. My country's bigger than yours. There are more places to lay up. If you tried your methods on our side there'd be some headaches coming to you."

"I am sure there would.... And we haven't got prohibition here."

"Nope. That's a bull point that the boys don't miss.... But I'll tell you this: if they were to come over here they'd give you the run-round till you'd got a pain in the legs. They were born wider awake than you're ever likely to be."

"But I believe there are more than a few of them over now."

Miss O'Leary gave a short laugh. "You think you've got me talking a lot, and I'll spill the beans. If you were a cat I should hear you purr. But if I talk all night I shan't tell you anything that you re itching to hear.

Chief Inspector Ingram heard this with no outward change in the glance of smiling appreciation which was fixed upon her. But he was inwardly disconcerted, for that was precisely what his attitude and expectation had been. *Get them to talk* had been his constant advice to younger officers. *Out of the fullness of the heart the mouth speaketh* was the one text in which he really believed. "Let him talk," he would say, "on whatever subject, and sooner or later the guilty man will let out something he didn't mean you to know." It was in the application of this theory that he had developed the friendly manner of approach to those whom he hoped to snare which had nicknamed him Judas among brother officers who admired his methods less than the results they brought. Miss O'Leary's danger lay in the fact that the warning she had given did not cause his purpose to change or relax. He said easily: "I wasn't asking you to give anyone away. But you can't suppose that about thirty of the worst gangsters of New York and Chicago can come here without our attention being aroused, or without your police letting us know what was on the way."

"Well, they haven't come for anything wrong. You know why they're here now, and you'll waste time interfering with them.

"That was not the deduction we were disposed to draw, and, if you are right as to your own innocence and. that of Sir Reginald Crowe, they've made a bad start by leaving a dead man on a banker's mat."

As Miss O'Leary met this opening with a discreet silence, he went on: "And if they were such innocent visitors it is difficult to see why they have come by so many indirect routes. To approach this country by way of Stockholm, Lisbon, or Genoa seems to be taking a needlessly expensive route."

"That's silly. They're not short of dough. It's less trouble to get than it is to spend."

Mr. Jellipot had taken no part in this conversation, but he had followed it no less closely for that. Now his mind wandered for a moment to consideration of the certain truth of that last remark:

More difficult to spend than to get. How largely it must apply to all money obtained by criminal means! Except as a source of power to do service to others, money in large sums is to all men of a very limited utility, though the lack of it may be a major curse. They cannot eat two meals, or wear two suits, or sleep in two beds at once. And when their records and associations are such that most doors worth opening are barred against them, that which money can still provide must be a poor return for the ceaseless hazards of their precarious lives.

And even when the easy money had been obtained it appeared that it might be by no means easy to keep, which was the origin of the trouble with which they were dealing now.

The gangsters of New York and Chicago must have developed an acute fear that the Federal Government of the United States would find some way, by income tax prosecutions or otherwise, to deprive them of it, and to provide against that threat they had first acquired control of a bank the funds of which had been transferred to London, and then, having perhaps had legal advice that the money might still be subject to seizure by the connivance of English law, had decided to draw it from its London deposit and scatter it beyond trace in continental investments.

And then the questions of how to divide and how to trust would become acute. For the main owners of this accumulated wealth to abandon their various rackets to visit Europe simultaneously would be to leave those unlawful enterprises to the mercy of lesser gangsters, who would be certain to shoot it out with the subordinates left in charge; and they would return to find their thrones usurped, and to the necessity of recovering them, if they could, by the desperate arguments of knife and bullet.

So they must have designed the threefold withdrawal, which was to be in untraceable currency, itself no simple matter in dealing with such a sum—and doubtless there were others sent over to watch the three, and probably others to watch the watchers; and with equal certainty there would be others with unrecognised claims to portions of the huge sums which would be passing about. And all of them outside the law or its protection, partly by their own acts and partly by their own code, so that they were controlled only by the fear of violence from those they wronged or any instincts of loyalty or fair-dealing which might still grow in unlikely ground....

"I still fail to see," Ingram had replied, why they should choose such indirect routes if they had no reason to wish that their coming should not be known."

"Well, you'd better ask them, not me," was Miss O'Leary's response, and the Chief Inspector, recognising finality in her tone, changed the subject abruptly. "I suppose," he suggested, with what he would have argued was a pardonable mendacity, "that you had no reason to wish Ringan dead?"

"What makes you suppose that?"

"It is a matter we are bound to consider. On your own evidence you were left in a room to which Sir Reginald Crowe says that he returned to find that you had gone, and there was a dead man there. If you could show us that you had no motive to wish him dead or even perhaps that it would have been to your advantage for him to remain alive—"

"Then there's nothing doing." She raised the little finger of her left hand as she spoke. "If I could bring Ringan back by bending that finger, I can tell you that he'd stay dead."

"Actually you had a strong motive for wishing him out of the way because it is likely to delay the distribution of this money, to part of which Clancy makes a claim which you fear may be ignored?"

"So you knew that all the time? You're the slimy sort, but I'll say you're not as dumb as you look.... Of course Tim wants his money. It's what's due to him for his share in selling out on the West Side. They may have given it to Crowley or not, but it didn't reach Tim, and that's what it had to do.... But I'll tell you this: I'm not a killer. You can ask the N'York cops, and they'll tell you that, and you can try all you know, but you won't fix it on me."

"Perhaps not. But if you want to make me feel sure you're innocent you'll have to think of a much better reason than that. Every murderer has to have a first go. And in this country the first is almost always the last, so they could all get off on that argument.... And you know, Miss O'Leary," he added, with his friendliest smile, "if you got a fair chance I'm not sure that you wouldn't feel very like killing me."

It was a suggestion to which the girl appeared indisposed to give a vehement denial. "Well," she conceded, "there's no cop like a dead cop. I'll give you that. But I'm no killer. And as to who stuck that bit of steel between Ringan's ribs, I don't say I know, but I wouldn't tell you if I did. You'll get no more from me, and you'd better go."

With these words Miss O'Leary rose and unlocked the door, which she held open until the Chief Inspector, recognising momentary defeat, had passed through it, when she locked it again and returned to her more welcome visitors, who had remained so discreetly silent during the exchanges which this chapter records.

CHAPTER XVI.

WE KNOW FOUR THINGS

As Miss O'Leary came back from the door she addressed her remaining guests with her usual directness: "I'll say your cops have me beat. I think they're too soft for their mothers to let them run out in the rain.... And then I'm not quite so sure. But what they'll take lying down! And now what more can I do for you?"

Mr. Jellipot looked silently at Lady Crowe, who understood that the fence was to be taken by her. She answered: "We don't want to ask you to tell us anything that would mean trouble for you, but you won't need me to say how anxious we are to clear it up, so that people will understand that Sir Reginald wasn't concerned in it in any way."

"And you think I can do that? Well, I'll tell you I can't. I didn't do it, though I won't say I'd be worse friends with the man who did. Not that that might not be friend at all. More likely the other way."

"Do you mind telling us," Mr. Jellipot asked, "how long you stayed in the room after Sir Reginald left you alone there?"

"It was quite a time. I'd say—and this is what I wouldn't think you'd want to have said in court—that there couldn't have been many minutes between when I left and when Sir Reginald came in.

"The cops might say that goes a long way to fix it on him, but I don't figure it that way. I reckon Ringan just looked into the room— I'd say I left the door wide—and turned round when he saw there was no one there, and someone stabbed him just then, but whether he knew he was there we can just guess."

"I confess," Mr. Jellipot replied, "I have had much the same theory, with less knowledge than you have now given me; but the scene is not easy to reconstruct. There is the little matter of it being his own knife—"

Mr. Jellipot paused, in the hope that she might have some suggestion to make on this puzzling feature of the crime, but his silence roused no response.

Her eyes had become blank. She remained standing in evident expectation that they would go.

Mr. Jellipot accepted the position readily. "We shall see you in court again tomorrow," he said, "but you may prefer that we should not speak to you there. We cannot go without thanking you again for the evidence you offered, which I trust may not involve you in any danger or trouble, for which, as I see it, no word of yours has given probable cause. But if you think differently—and you are in a far better position to judge—will you not permit me to make arrangements with the police to give you the protection which you require?"

Miss O'Leary laughed. "If there's anyone out gunning for me, I don't reckon your cops would be quick enough to do more than pick up the corpse. And I'll tell you this: if you see me walk into court tomorrow you can say there's been no cause to worry. That is, unless I've been quick on the draw, at which I'd be too easy to beat. But Sir Reginald did more than a bit for me, and I'd got to take the stand, whether or no."

With this, to Evelyn, rather cryptic statement, she gave a strong grip to a proffered hand and stood back warily from the. opening door.

It was when they were in the privacy of the taxi which was taking them to the station that Evelyn said: "We have been a time! I hope Reggie won't be home first. And we don't seem to have done anything. Though I dare say that girl was glad to have us there when Ingram was trying to draw her out.... Not that she wasn't equal to him!"

"I cannot," Mr. Jellipot replied, "call it a wasted visit. We have learnt four things, if not more.

"We know that Miss O'Leary did not commit the murder, of which I was almost sure before, but not quite.

"We know that Sir Reginald did not raise an alarm at once, because he either thought that she had committed the crime or that suspicion would be directed upon her if he should do so without delay.

"We know that she has an opinion approximating to certainty as to who the criminal is.

"And, finally, we know that, whatever opinion Ingram may have previously held, he is now convinced that Sir Reginald is not the murderer, though he may still doubt whether he is telling all and nothing but the truth, as the customary form of oath somewhat tauto-logically requires."

"Do we know all that! Then, if Inspector Ingram really knows Reggie didn't do it (no one but an ass could ever have thought he did), there isn't much we need bother about, unless there's a run on the bank tomorrow; and he says he can deal with that."

"I don't think that there is, or ever has been, great occasion for worry as to the ultimate issue of the affair," Mr. Jellipot replied gravely, "but I ought to tell you that the position is not quite as simple as you are now disposed to conclude.

"The immediate issue does not rest with Ingram, but with the jury, who appear to be rather a dull and perhaps mulish assembly of our fellow-citizens. And the police, who are very sensitive to the criticism which will follow a wrong arrest for which they are responsible, have no similar cause for apprehension if it be on a coroner's warrant, which is outside their responsibility."

"But," Evelyn replied with a recovered cheerfulness which declined to be overcast, "if the police know he didn't do it, they'll soon lay their hands on the man who did. It seems to me that it makes all the difference if they've made up their minds that it wasn't he."

Mr. Jellipot might have said that even that was much less than sure. If one man be arrested, on whatever warrant, and awaiting trial, it is not part of the routine duty of the C.I.D. to search for alternative criminals, on the assumption that a mistake has been made. But he felt that he had said enough. He left Evelyn to frown in silence over the mystery of the four points which had been demonstrated to him.

"I can't think," she said, "however you can deduce that that girl knows who did it. She only said that she wouldn't say if she did."

"She is in fear that she may be assassinated by someone who dreads that she may betray him to the police, but she knows that her fear will be groundless if he has made no attempt upon her during the next few hours. There are implications in that."

"I don't see quite as much as you seem to, but if you say so no doubt there are; and anyway, here's Charing Cross," she replied cheerfully as they drew up at the station curb.

CHAPTER XVII.

THE WORST QUESTION OF ALL

THE coroner's court reassembled next morning. Dr. Rathbone Bryant took his seat, and Miss O'Leary, who was still alive, and whose evidence had been interrupted by the adjournment of the previous day, returned to the box.

But it quickly became apparent that there was a different atmosphere from that of the previous afternoon. Mr. Whatley-Cummings, who had been in close conference with the instructing solicitors, announced to a surprised court that he had no more questions to ask. Mr. Jellipot, being given the same opportunity, showed the same indifference. The coroner, after a moment's hesitation and a glance over his notes, said she could leave the box.

It appeared that there were no further witnesses to call. Would Mr. Whatley-Cummings care to address the court? Mr. Whatley-Cummings would not.

"Looks as though half the stuffing had been knocked out of him," was the silent comment that passed through Miss O'Leary's lively and hostile mind.

Did Mr. Jellipot desire to say anything on his client's behalf? No. Mr. Jellipot was of the same reticent disposition.

Dr. Rathbone Bryant was somewhat puzzled and more seriously annoyed. It became his part to sum up at once, which he was not ready to do. Beyond that, he was left in doubt of the meaning of this sudden termination of an inquest which he had expected to last well into the afternoon, and perhaps longer than that. He felt that the police were letting him down, and that he had a right to expect more explicit signs of the judgement which they had formed.

But, in fact, that was the deliberate policy of an Assistant Commissioner who had become unsure of the wisdom of what he had already done, which he had since learnt that the Home Secretary did not entirely approve. The decision was made after an early morning conference with Inspector Ingram, whose suggestion it was. Let the coroner go his own way. If he should lead the jury to bring in a verdict of murder against Sir Reginald Crowe, and the charge should fail, the records of the inquest would be conclusive evidence that there had been no pressure in that direction from the police.

"And," Ingram had added to this contention, "I should say, if we can't get the kicks, it may be a good thing if they do. The man we want will be off his guard if he thinks that we're hanging Crowe."

"The man or woman," Sir Henry amended, and Ingram accepted the correction. "Though," he added, "I'm inclined to think that it wasn't she. Not that, if we gave her a sight of the cells, she wouldn't be in her right place."

So it had been agreed, and Mr. Whatley-Cummings, being so instructed, and very ill-content with the part he had been led to play, had replied that, if that were so, the less he said the better "I'm not going," he said aside to his clerk, "to blow hot and cold because Sir Henry Bracken's a wobbler born. I'd rather not blow at all." And no more he did.

Mr. Jellipot was surprised when he found that the K C. was throwing down his brief in all but the physical action of leaving his seat, for which he blamed himself afterwards, holding it to be a position for which he should have been better prepared.

He had expected to hear a speech which would tend to lead the jury's minds towards a verdict of wilful murder against Sir Reginald Crowe, and he had come prepared with many rebutting arguments, scaled to meet whatever ferocity or finesse there might be in the deployment of the attack. But was it wise to reply to a charge which had not been urged? Might not the coroner have had a hint that the attack against the banker must be called off? *The wicked fleeth when no man pursueth.* He had no mind to practise that foolish part. He was not easy in mind, for he disliked the look of the jury, whom he thought to be of a dangerous dullness, but he was in doubt, and, being in doubt, he remained silent, as his manner was.

Silence, during the minutes that followed, fell on the whole court as the coroner turned over his notes and considered a summing-up for which he was not fully prepared.

He looked up from this occupation to say with a recovered briskness: "There is one point which I consider has not yet been fully elucidated. I must recall Sir Reginald Crowe to the box."

Sir Reginald, who was never slow to face up to whatever came, rose as briskly as the coroner spoke, and was quickly in a position to reply to whatever additional battery might be turned upon him.

"It has been given in evidence that when you left your room, for whatever purpose, Miss O'Leary was there. Is that true?"

"Yes."

"You did not mention this?"

"I was not asked."

"It may naturally have been concluded, as you made no contrary statement, that you left the room vacant. Did you not appreciate that?"

"I may not have considered it at all. The evidence I was required to give was upon the murder, not upon my earlier visitors."

"Well, if that be the best reply you can make! Did you not expect to find the lady there when you returned?"

"I should not have been surprised. Nor can I say that I was surprised that she had not waited. I had been away a much longer time than I had told her I should."

"But, for all you knew, she might have been there when the murder occurred?"

"It does not appear to me to be a reasonable proposition."

"It was at least possible?"

"Possible. Yes. Almost anything is."

"And the police would naturally have desired to question her if they had known that you left her there?"

"Possibly. But I fail to see that they would have done anything better than waste their time."

"That should have been for them to judge.... Why did you leave her there?"

"I telephoned to my secretary, who was out of her room, and I. went there to refer to papers which were in her safe and might have been relevant to the business on which Miss O'Leary had called."

"And that business was?"

"It would be improper for me to say."

"Was it not the same business on which Ringan had seen you?"

"I can scarcely say yes to that."

"I must direct you to answer the question more clearly."

"It was in regard to another aspect of the same business."

"Had you no motive or purpose in omitting mention of Miss O'Leary's presence in the room?"

For the first time Sir Reginald paused in his reply. Then he said: "I wish to answer frankly. I may have been influenced by a natural desire not to involve a lady in an unpleasant enquiry respecting a matter with which, in my judgement, she had nothing to do. But, had I been asked, I should have mentioned the matter without reserve."

The coroner paused, and Mr. Jellipot, observing that the worst question had not been asked, hoped that the inquisition might be over, but then it came: "Was there any connection between your inclination to shield Miss O'Leary from the annoyance of such questioning and the delay which occurred in summoning the police?"

There was again a pause, slight but of significance, particularly to one familiar with Sir Reginald's conversational style, before the answer came: "I still wish to answer as accurately as possible, but motives are not always easy to analyse. I don't think there was any undue delay in calling in the police. I had to think of many things, including the interests of the bank. And, besides, the event was of a very unexpected and disconcerting kind. I have no doubt I should act more wisely after this rehearsal, if such a thing should happen again."

The coroner hesitated. He looked down at the notes he had made, and he had not the aspect of a satisfied man, but all he said was: "Well, if that's the best explanation you have to give I…. Any questions you would like to ask, Mr. Jellipot?"

But Mr. Jellipot said there was none. He would have liked to give the impression that he held the witness's reply to be so satisfactory that there was nothing further to say. But he was convinced that the whole truth had not been disclosed, and an equal conviction that Sir Reginald would not lie in the witness box made him feel that there would be a peril in every further question that might be asked. Reluctantly but resolutely he left bad alone, as few advocates may have the courage to do.

CHAPTER XVIII.

THE JURY THAT DID NOT KNOW

SIR REGINALD had returned to his seat, and the coroner was summing-up in the tone of impartiality which is universal in all English courts of today. The matter may be weighted on one side or other with deliberate deadly skill, but the tone of aloof impartial judgement is always there.

"The dead man," he was saying, "was not a citizen of this country. So far as we have been able to learn, he had no relatives here. No friends have come forward. He has not been legally represented. But English justice knows no distinction under such circumstances between those of British birth and the alien visitor to our shores. They enjoy the protection of the laws which, while with us, they are required to observe."

He went on to recapitulate the circumstances and topography of the crime. He dealt with and eliminated the possibilities of accident or self-destruction, dealing with facts with which we are familiar already, and there is no more need to record his survey than there was to linger over the police and technical evidence, or that of porter and clerk, with which the inquest began. The dull faces of the jury brightened when he directed that a plan of the first floor of the premises of the London and Northern Bank, which had been specially prepared for the occasion, and passed frequently between the coroner, witnesses, and legal gentlemen concerned during that phase of the inquest, should be submitted to their inspection. They gazed at it, two by two, with glances of real or assumed intelligence, as though feeling that they were at last being invited to take a real interest in the case. What they learnt from it, if anything, would be hard to guess.

Having dealt thus with the background of the crime, Dr. Rathbone Bryant went on: "You have heard Sir Reginald Crowe's account of his discovery of the murdered man and of his subsequent actions. You have also heard the evidence of Miss O'Leary, of whom it appears nothing would have been heard at all had she not herself, very properly, come forward to give her testimony of what she knew.

"If you accept the evidence of Sir Reginald Crowe, you must recognise the fact that he left Miss O'Leary in the room, and. that, when he came back after an interval which from his own and independent evidence can hardly have been less than twenty minutes, and may have been half an hour, he found that Miss O'Leary had gone, and that a dying man lay at the door. It is not reasonable to suppose that Miss O'Leary left without waiting for some minutes— we may say five, but ten or fifteen would be a more probable guess—and you will see that the interval between her departure and Sir Reginald's arrival must have been very short. It is during that short interval that the murder must have been committed and the murderer have left—unseen, as he must have come. That is, if you accept the evidence of the two witnesses I have named.

"You may, of course, decline to do so. Murders are seldom committed in public. It becomes necessary to look for the criminal among those who have substantial motive and to whom opportunity came.

"Here there is a suggestion of motive in both cases—inadequate motive, perhaps, but what motive could be adequate, to a normal mind, for this brutal and cowardly crime? The motive of Miss O'Leary might have been the simple, direct aim of preventing others from drawing money, to some part of which she had an unrecognised claim, or it might be an act of revenge against one of those who, she considered, had conspired to deprive her of what she claimed, or a combination of these impulses may have led to the fatal blow.

"In the case of Sir Reginald Crowe the suggested motive is weaker, or its existence is little more than plausible theory, to which the facts, if they were fully known, might give little support.

"There remains Sir Reginald's delay in ringing up the police, and you have to consider whether that was the act of an innocent man.

"It is fair to say that he gave his evidence on this, as on other points, in a tone of candour with which, speaking with the experience which my office brings, I was well impressed.

"I was impressed also with the apparent candour of the evidence of Miss O'Leary, though it was open, on other grounds, to criticism of the strongest kind. She appeared wanting in consciousness of the gravity of the occasion, or in respect to the court.

"But when I consider what I observed of the demeanour of Sir Reginald Crowe, I have to recognise that his apparent candour was of a restricted kind. He would have avoided, if not concealed, the presence of Miss O'Leary in his office, had she not herself volunteered to tell it.

"We are bound to ask ourselves what possible motive lay behind a reticence which you may think cannot be other than deliberate, and the more deliberate it was the more significance you may think it to have."

The coroner paused a moment at the end of this period, and in the short second of silence Mr. Jellipot heard a sound from the jury box—a little cough of approval he thought it to be—and his apprehension of what portentous folly might come from that double row of ill-chosen men was increased by the uncertain sound. It was an apprehension that was not lessened by the sound, low but audible, of a whisper from the bench behind him: "They'll hang each other more likely than not. It'll be the Bywater case over again."

At another time he would have dealt with careful analysis upon the subtler aspects of this unlikely comparison. Now he could do no more than recognise that there were others, besides those in the jury box of whom he had so low an opinion, who might conclude the guilt of one or other or both of the two who had been so contiguous to the crime. Had he failed in duty to his friend and client in not putting up a more aggressive defence? It was hard to say. But an inquest is not like a trial. There is no one on whom accusation has settled. It is poor advocacy that becomes active to fit the cap. And it was a case in which he had been less than fully instructed. Sir Reginald, always self-confident, had preferred to handle it in his own way. Well, he might prove to have been right. With a resolute effort of will Mr. Jellipot put these apprehensions aside, to listen to the summing-up, which was now concentrated upon his client again.

"There remains," the coroner was saying, "the evidence of Sir Henry Bracken. There seems to be little reason to doubt the substantial accuracy of his recollection of a conversation which is, in its essential particulars, admitted by Sir Reginald Crowe.

"Whatever view you may take of the opinions which he expressed, you may ask yourselves whether the murder that followed was a coincidence of a most extraordinary kind, or a deed which was already contemplated as possibility in an unbalanced mind. On the other hand, you may take the view that, had there been any serious thought of this dreadful crime in Sir Reginald's mind, it would have been unlikely that he would reveal it to others, and especially to one in the position occupied by Sir Henry Bracken. You will consider the force of the argument advanced by Sir Reginald Crowe's solicitor that there is a wide gulf between academic theory and violent action.

"But you are also bound to observe that the remarks on what I may perhaps not unfairly describe as the veniality of murder—or of particular murders—went beyond generalisation. He mentioned—so it is admitted—a particular man who might be eliminated, and who was, if you accept Sir Henry Bracken's recollection, of less account than a good dog. And it was this man whose blood was certainly on his hands on the next day.... Well, it is for you to decide."

The coroner went on for a further time, treating of other circumstances of the crime in a somewhat discursive manner. He touched on the mystery of the blow having been struck with the knife of the dead man. He pointed out the probability that it must have come from the hand of one whom Ringan had no cause to dread or, at least, whom he expected to be beside him.

He closed in his usual manner—stale to him by a hundred repetitions, but new to the different juries that he addressed—concerning the values and dangers of circumstantial evidence, the fact that probability is not proof, the degree of proof which they should require as being that which would decide them in their ordinary business affairs, the different verdicts which they might deliver, and the fact that the responsibility of decision was theirs.

A coroner has more freedom in the manner of his instructions to the jury than a high-court judge could allow himself, he having the shadow of the court of appeal over every word that he says or omits to say.

An incautious utterance may enable the worst murderer to escape the penalty of his crime. The coroner has no such fear. He is supreme in his own court, and there is not much, if he will that he may not say. But the summing-up which has been partially recorded here is less than a fair example of what these charges usually are, and inferior, particularly in constructive arrangement, to those which Dr. Rathbone Bryant would normally deliver. It had had less than his usual preparation, and came from a mind which was less than sure what verdict he would prefer. It would have been doubtful guidance to more intelligent men than were the majority of those whom he was addressing now.

When they filed out to the privacy of their own room, he did not rise, anticipating the possibility that they might have already consulted among themselves and agreed upon the verdict of "Some person unknown," which is that which is usually rendered with the minimum of delay.

But after a few minutes, when it became evident that there was no such immediate unanimity, he retired to his own room, giving the usher the usual instruction that he should be called whenever the jury should signify their readiness to return to court.

His withdrawal was a signal for a murmur of controlled voices to rise from the still crowded benches.

Sir Reginald turned to Mr. Jellipot, and there was actually a twinkle in his eye as he asked: "Well, what is it going to be?"

Mr. Jellipot, conscious of Evelyn's more anxious eyes on his other side, did not wish to cause deeper doubt than she already had, but he was too unsure to think it right to convey a confidence which he did not feel. "He would be a wise man who would answer that," he said. "There ought to be no doubt at all, but a jury's always a risk. A coroner's jury usually does what it's told, but what it's been told to do in this case isn't easy to say.... But there's the usher going to Bryant's room. I should think such a quick verdict is a good sign. Anyway, we shall soon know.... Miss O'Leary doesn't look very concerned."

Sir Reginald turned his head to observe the girl, who was not looking at him or at anything in particular. Her attention appeared to be concentrated on the peanuts which she was eating from a paper bag. Her aspect was that of one sure of her surroundings as of herself, having a conscience clear of offence and a mind at ease.

"Well," he said, "I'm glad they haven't kept us waiting long, whatever it is. I can bear anything but suspense, as the man said when he was about to be hanged.... Evelyn, don't look like that. They're making the mistake of their lives if they think they're going to hang me on the silliest charge that was ever talked into plausibility. It's about fifty to one that they won't try."

Evelyn forced the required smile as she answered: "Of course, I know that. I didn't—" and then her voice sank at the usher's call for silence as the coroner returned to his seat, and the court rose with the ceremonious politeness which the occasion traditionally requires.

The jury had filed back into the box, but it appeared that the expected verdict was not to come.

"Mr. Foreman," the coroner said, "I understand that you wish me to give you some advice on a point of law."

The foreman, who should normally have been occupied at this hour of the day in the distribution of sweets and tobacco from his counter in a side alley off Fenchurch Street, while his assistant would be at lunch, answered in a voice which held an echo of past disputation in its irritated accents: "No, sir, it isn't me. Most of us know well enough, but there's some who don't, and, who won't be told. The question is do they get tried again, or, if we say they're guilty, does it go through? We've told them there'll be a trial to come, but they'd rather hear it from you."

"It is your duty," the coroner answered, "to bring in your verdict in accordance with the evidence, without favour or fear, and without regard to what its consequences may be. But, as a matter of fact, if you should feel it to be your duty to bring in a verdict of a criminal kind against one or more individuals by name, it would then become my duty to issue a warrant or warrants for their arrest, and they would be fully and fairly tried by another jury sitting under a judge of the high court."

The jury, having received this instruction, retired again, contentious whispers of "I told you so" and "Making us look fools" being heard by those who were near their exit door.

"It seems to me," Sir Reginald said, with no abatement in his usual cheerfulness, "that I'd better ring up the bank while I've got time. It won't be long now before they've decided it was Miss O'Leary or I, and it's a good bet that I'm the first pick."

With these words he rose and made his way to a telephone booth in the outer corridor of the court, followed closely but unobtrusively by a plain-clothes man to whom Chief Inspector Ingram had signalled with a lifted finger. It was not likely that he would make a run for it, but it's always best to be on the safe side.

Disappointing this faint but attractive expectation, Sit Reginald came back to a court to which the jury had not returned, his looks still cheerful but rather grim.

"I hope," Mr. Jellipot asked, "that there's no serious trouble at Lombard Street?"

"No. Nothing we can't meet. But it's bad enough. We might be on the way down if we hadn't had this American money in hand; and Britleigh's thrown in all he can. He's been a big help, Evelyn, and we've got to thank him for that.... But it just shows what harm these dense pigs of policemen do. Making more fuss over a dead wop—but I said that once before, and that's more or less why we're here.... It looks as though those half-wits are coming back now."

CHAPTER XIX.

A Most Opportune Murder

THE coroner had taken his seat. The usher had placed a paper before him, at which he looked with eyebrows that were slightly raised. He exchanged whispered words with the officer. "It is a unanimous verdict?" he was heard by sharp ears at the reporters' table to say, less as one who asks a question than as accepting a fact. (The verdict of a coroner's jury need not be unanimous. A minority of less than three can be ignored, but they are not required to sign the inquisition from which they dissent.)

He looked up to the jury box, which was already filled by eleven men whose own eyes, ominously to Mr. Jellipot's experience, were inclined to look down. He addressed the foreman: "You are agreed on your verdict? And that is?"

The foreman read from a sheet he held: "We find Sir Reginald Crowe and Mary O'Leary guilty of the wilful murder of Antonio Ringan." Lady Crowe suppressed an exclamation of dismay, so that it did not penetrate beyond those immediately around her. She said more audibly: "What wicked nonsense!"

Sir Reginald, with unabated cheerfulness, said: "Hush, Evelyn! What's worth doing at all's worth doing well. If you think it may be one or other, isn't it the safest way to name both? Jellipot, what's the procedure now?"

Mr. Jellipot's reply was hindered by Miss O'Leary's high-toned voice: "Sounds batty. But I guess that's a message for me." She rose and pushed herself toward the front of a court in which the usher was vainly calling for silence, as though anxious to deliver herself to the bar of justice without delay. She reached the side of her companion in legal adversity with an explanation of her ready response to the accusation which had been made against her: "I reckon I shan't burn for this, but it lets me out of something I didn't like. They won't call me a squealer now."

Mr. Jellipot was explaining to Sir Reginald the position in which he now stood, but his words came in an absent-minded manner, as though his thoughts were on other things, as his eyes certainly were.

He said: "It will be the coroner's duty to issue a warrant for your detention, and another committing you for trial. There won't be anything much happening for some hours, though it wouldn't do for you to attempt to leave the court. There'll be the depositions of all the witnesses to be made out, and read over to and signed by them—that will include you—and they'll all have to be bound over to appear at the trial. They'll have to have Bracken here for that. And—oh, there's a good deal to be done.

"The coroner couldn't grant bail on a murder charge, though he could for manslaughter; but there's a way that we ought to get it. The high court has power to grant it if the committal is on a coroner's warrant. We can apply in chambers for that. And with a perverse verdict like this there oughtn't to be much difficulty. It seems almost lunatic Miss O'Leary's name being joined to yours."

"Oh, I don't know," Sir Reginald said, making a more accurate guess of what had gone on in the jury room than he may have seriously supposed. "I expect some of them said it was she, and some said it was I, and some weren't sure which, but wanted it to be one or other, and so they made what they called a compromise by putting us both down so that they could go home to tea. After all, it's quite a possible thing."

Miss O'Leary's voice broke in: "I'm not wanting you to do much for me, but if you'd tell me where I can buy bail when they run me in—"

"I am afraid," Mr. Jellipot replied with his usual punctiliousness of expression, but in the same absent-minded manner as before, "that you may find the procedure here somewhat different, in that and other particulars, from what you have been accustomed to in your own country. You cannot buy bail here under any circumstances."

"*Not buy bail*? Not on a phoney verdict like this? Well, you Britishers!" Miss O'Leary had learnt that even in God's own country there are some things that dollars are unable to do, but this—! Words failed on a fluent tongue.

Mr. Jellipot made no reply, for the coroner was now calling for order in a voice which no one could disregard. He had been oblivious for the last three or four minutes to the disordered state of a court which he was accustomed to rule with a firm hand, while he had been engaged in whispered colloquy with Mr. Mullins (Cross &

Wardlaw), the solicitor for the police, who had mounted his dais for the purpose of giving him some urgent information, and had now withdrawn to his own place. It was to be noticed also that Mr. Whatley-Cummings, who had left the court as the coroner started his summing-up, had surprisingly returned. Now he rose.

"Mr. Coroner," he said, "I am instructed to inform you that during the last few hours another murder has occurred on the premises of the London and Northern Bank, of such a character as to make it extremely probable that it was by the same hand as that by which Antonio Ringan met his death."

The coroner asked: "It is not known by whom this second murder was committed?"

"At present it is not known."

The coroner turned to the jury. "Having heard the statement of the learned counsel, which you may take it from me is a fact, although it may not have been formally proved under oath, you will, I am sure, recognise its bearing upon the verdict which you have Just delivered.

"Under these circumstances it has become one which I cannot accept, and one which, had this knowledge reached us earlier, I am sure you would not have brought in. I must direct you that the only proper verdict must be against some person or persons unknown, and I must have it in that form or adjourn the enquiry for your attendance on a later day."

PART TWO

BETWEEN TWO WORLDS

▲

CHAPTER XX.

SIR REGINALD MAKES A RASH BET

SIR REGINALD CROWE waked in something more than his normal good spirits on the Saturday morning which followed the sharp skirmish the destructive consequence of which he had so narrowly escaped, and that by caprice of fortune, and not at all by his own wisdom or skill.

Yet he was aware in a buoyant mind that the affair was not over and that there might be financial and other problems to be faced such as would have given the chairmen of his rival banks acute indigestion, even before coming down to the liberal breakfast over which Evelyn would already be prepared to preside on the floor below.

He looked out over the Elizabethan courtyard of the home which they had restored and beautified, and thanked that capricious fate that he was not gazing on such a view as may be gained from a Brixton cell, "though," he admitted to himself, with an acute realisation of how his enjoyment of life was based, "it would have been exciting enough; and I bet Jellipot would have got me out before I'd lost weight worrying.... I suppose I'd better tell him now what he'll say he ought to have known all along. Not that it would have done any good."

His mind wandered over the events of the past few days, with the result that the routine process of dressing lagged, so that he was three minutes late, and had only twenty-five instead of the twenty-eight he usually allowed for breakfast before the car would be at the door to take him to the station at Hither Dene.

When his coffee had been poured and he had selected from an ample dish the kidneys and bacon rashers he most approved, he said: "Don't come down to the station yourself tonight. I may be late. Send Blake down to meet the six-seven in, and tell him to wait till I turn up. There'll be a lot of clearing up to be done in more ways than one."

"But you haven't forgotten that we are going to Maidcote Manor for dinner?"

"Were we? Well, you'd better cry off as far as I am concerned. Mrs. Corder will understand."

"Oh yes. I can explain to Adeline. And if I go I shall be able to tell her most of what she'll be wanting to hear.... I suppose you can manage without me today?"

He answered the laughing query in its own tone. "Well, I'll have a good try.... Evelyn, you've been a brick! It would have been hell if you'd been as fussy as some wives are."

"I expect it would.... And perhaps now you won't mind telling me what all the fuss was about."

"Nothing much really. Just some dead wops. I thought you would have grasped that, more or less."

"You know I didn't mean that. I want to know why you didn't call up the police at once.... And about Miss O'Leary.... And whether I've got any real cause for divorce.... And—well, the whole tale."

"Divorce? There's no need for starting anything rash. I don't say I mightn't do worse, but there's a Tim Clancy waiting some-where on Broadway, who might object, and who counts with her. She started off by saying she was Mrs. Clancy to me."

"Prudent girl. Then what was it all about?"

"Well, it was just this. I got back to that room quite as quickly as the police think, and it might be sooner than that. Ringan lay as I said, and it's quite true that I pulled the knife out of his back. But that wasn't the first thing I did.

"I jumped over him and ran to look out of the window of my room. You know how easily you can see anyone who comes out of the door at the corner. Or perhaps you don't. Anyway, you can. I thought I might be in time to catch sight of the bounder who'd used the knife, but what I saw was this O'Leary girl—or Mrs. Clancy if she prefers—walking out at a good pace, and if she hadn't been there when Ringan got it, and didn't meet the murderer on the stairs, he must have used the lift, which I can tell you he didn't do.

"So I went back to the man, who was still making a bit of stir, as though he didn't like being snuffed out, and I saw he was half on his back, and lying so that he must have been driving the knife further in with his own weight, and it seemed sense to lift him enough to pull it out; but next minute, when I'd done it, I wasn't sure that it was. He rolled over, and out came the knife, and—well, if you've ever seen a pig killed—"

"I did once," Evelyn admitted. "When I was about eight. I think I rather enjoyed it. Anyway, you can take it that further details are not required.... And if you don't stop talking you'll have to go without breakfast or miss the train."

So admonished, Sir Reginald took a large mouthful, balanced a second on his fork, so that his plate appeared somewhat clearer than before, and almost immediately went on: "When I'd done that and made myself a dirtier mess than I've ever been, or am likely to be again, I began to think, and I'd no doubt then, and not such a lot now, that the girl was in it up to the neck, whether she'd been the operator or not, and that it would be a rather low thing to give her away.

"But I didn't exactly want to be found standing about doing nothing with the recently deceased, so I rang up Jellipot and talked to him as long as I could get him to listen, and then telephoned for the porter—I wasn't in a condition to go about calling him up—and showed him the mess, which he took without turning a hair—I don't say he's got over-many to turn—and posted him where he'd keep out the crowd, and then telephoned Scotland Yard, because I thought that would make it about two minutes slower than if I'd called up the local station.

"As it turned out, it made no difference at all, because no one thought of asking me if I'd left anyone in the office or seen them since, and I don't suppose they ever would if that girl had had the sense to keep a still tongue, which I shouldn't think she ever finds it easy to do."

"I think she was a very brave girl."

"Oh, she's got nerve I Though I should say it would be a job to wash all the dirt off her metaphorical hide.... All the same, if she *had* settled that lousy wop, I shouldn't have liked to have any hand in running her in. I meant what I said about that sort of thing. Of

course, I hadn't realised then what utter fools the police can be....
But as to some murders doing more good than harm—why, look at
this second one at the bank. If it hadn't been for that I'd like to know
where you think I should be now."

"Whoever it was," Evelyn conceded readily, "certainly did us a
good turn, but I suppose that wasn't why it was done, and we don't
owe them any particular thanks. But do you really think the police
are such fools?"

"Of course I don't. Not always, anyway. But I'll tell you one
thing: I mean to have this cleared up, and if the police fail I'll bet
you a new hat that I'll find out who did it within three months,
though whether I'll hand them on to the cops is more than I'd like to
say."

"Thanks. But I've got plenty of hats. If you'll bet me the bluebell wood that's along the side of Brook Meadow—"

"Yes. If you'll keep it quiet, so that the price doesn't rocket, I'll
bet you that.... No, I won't have another cup. There's no time. And I
can't risk being late today. For all I know, it's going to be a regular
custom to stick a man at my office door, and if it is I mean to be on
the spot and have something to say."

With these words Sir Reginald rose, put the remaining portion
of the buttered toast and marmalade on which he was now engaged
into his mouth, and hurried into the hall, where he kissed Evelyn
with rather more haste but no less warmth than usual, and departed
to a scene of action which he again felt to be under his firm control.

Evelyn, watching the car disappear rather more rapidly than
usual down the avenue which gave Trees its name, wondered: "Shall
I get the wood?"

Knowing her husband, she felt it to be much less than a certain
thing, but she was surer that the murderer of Antonio Ringan and
Joe Ruscatti (it was assumed that they had both died by the same
hand) was destined to a bad time.

CHAPTER XXI.

INGRAM DECIDES TO DEAL

JOE RUSCATTI had been found lying a few feet from the door of Sir Reginald's room in a pool of his own blood even more profuse than that which Antonio Ringan had contributed to the thick corridor carpet, with a throat that had been thoroughly slit. It was estimated that, when he was found, he had been dead for an hour, if not more.

There was nothing surprising in that. It would have been no less than likely that he would lie undiscovered for a longer time. Sir Reginald having the compulsory engagement elsewhere of which we already know, there was no occasion for anyone to enter his room or go along the corridor, on to which, until it made its left-hand turn, there was no other which opened, except the vacant boardroom.

Again, no one had been seen to go up or down the stairs or ascend the lift, other than the officials and clerks of the bank; but there was no wonder in that, for they had had their time and thoughts too fully occupied with their own business, or rather that of the bank they served, to have eyes for non-essential things. For whatever might be happening in Lancashire or the other northern counties in which it had its origin and its greatest strength, there had been a decided inclination on the part of its London customers to draw their money from a bank the chairman of which was under the shadow of accusation of the murder of an unsavoury American customer when he had called to discuss the withdrawal of a large sum of deposited money.

The kind of scandalous talk, whether spoken in jest or earnest, which was going about was evidenced by the frightened query of a girl who had been sent to cash a cheque on her employers' account. She asked the porter whether she would be able to get the money on the ground floor. "I shan't have to go upstairs, shall I?"

Nor did the position improve immediately upon the discovery of the body of Joe Ruscatti. To those who gave it cool thought it might show that, whoever might be the culprit, it was not the chairman of the bank. But that left a good deal to the imagination. However freely a bank may pay out money on the ground floor, it is unlikely to retain its popularity if it develop a habit of knifing its customers on the one above. Mr. Adams was a thankful man when he knew that they had closed their doors and weathered the storm of the second day.

Sir Reginald, having caught the train at which he aimed, rather by the courtesy of a station-master who had seen the approaching car than his own punctuality, arrived at the bank within the first half-hour of its opening.

On his way in he had looked at *The Times* and the *Morning Post* (which had not then been amalgamated with a rival publication), and from their reports he had concluded that the bank had little more to fear. But he saw at the first glance along the busy paying-out counter that the run was not over yet.

The fact that the bank had separate paying and receiving counters emphasised the prevailing tendency of its customers to withdraw their balances, the one row of cashiers being almost idle while the other dealt with waiting queues.

He passed along the back of these, and spoke with cheerful inconsequence to more than one of those who would have avoided his eye. One man, the clerk of a city house of world-wide reputation, called out as he passed: "I'm only drawing for petty cash, Sir Reginald. I've just paid in over two thousand pounds."

"It's a pity everyone hasn't that much sense. They'd save themselves needless trouble," he answered in a voice that overcame the murmur and bustle around him. He went up to the chief accountant's room with a renewed confidence. He had imagined a run as the jostling of an angry, frightened, excited crowd overflowing the bank and controlled with difficulty by the police in the outer street. If it were no more than this—

But the paying-out counter was long, and the cashiers, having no receiving to hinder them, worked with a smooth rapidity that passed much paper money out in a short time. He found that Adams looked grave.

"Not springing a leak yet?" he asked cheerfully.

"We look like lasting out, today being short," the Scot replied with his usual caution. "I'll tell more when I get some calls rough from the North. They're doing well enough at Rochdale and Blackburn. Darlington had to meet one or two rather big calls. Of course, Wigan—"

"Of course. It won't kill us if we have to settle up every Wigan account we've got. It's Sampson's done that, not I."

"It's the two things coming together," Adams replied with his usual scrupulous accuracy. "But of course we could stand that."

"There's nothing coming we can't stand, and there wouldn't have been if I'd been out of the way for the next month, as I nearly was."

"I don't say there would, not apart from that five million dollars. We shouldn't find it easy to raise that, if we should have proper instructions tomorrow, even as things are now. Of course, there are a lot of loans we can call in, but they'll take time. I've got the notices being typed out now, and a list for you to approve.

"I don't blame you for that, Adams. But you stop the girls wasting paper, and tear up the list. We're not going to call in anything.... As to that million, I'll get Jellipot on it, and after what's happened he'll find some way of hanging it up if they don't lie low, as it's more likely they will."

"We might have to pay it into court."

"Or we might not. I'll tell you what, Adams: you've not got to think of us for the rest of your natural life as though we've got a hole in our hull. The storm isn't rising, it's going down."

Mr. Adams did not dispute this confident prognostication, which had some reason for its support. He went on: "There's nothing else happened that need hinder you now. Tressick rang up and said he didn't want to bother you about the loan he'd asked for on his Middlesboro contract, as he could understand how things are, but he just wanted our formal reply, so that he could make arrangements elsewhere, as it couldn't wait. I told him he needn't wait for that. We should quite understand."

"You said *what*?" Sir Reginald broke out with one of his rare explosions into offensively intemperate speech. "Adams, of all the hidebound, purblind, blithering idiots that I've ever met, there wouldn't be one that would equal you. Do you *want* to spoil our credit from one end of the city to the other? You know how these things spread. And lose one of the best customers on our books to the L. and M.?

"I'll have him called up at once. Tell the operator to clear the line, whatever has to be cut off.... I didn't think anything could frighten me, but you've done it now."

A moment later he was on the telephone, saying: "Five thousand pounds? That's what I understood. Of course you can have it.

The security's good enough, and your name's better than that....
Yes, we've done some paying out, but we're not losing any sleep.
What's a bank for?"

"I'm sorry," the chastened Adams remarked, "but I thought—"

"Don't say that, Adams. It was just what you didn't. You only
felt, which is a very dangerous thing to do. But I'm sorry I spoke as
I did. You mustn't think I've got rattled. But someone's going to
pay for this, if I have to go over myself and turn Chicago into a
worse bear-garden than it is now."

"Chief Inspector Ingram is wanting to see you. I thought he
could wait till you'd dealt with our own matters."

"Yes. Or longer than that. But I'll see him now. I'll tell Miss
Markham to have him sent up to my room, if there's no one else being murdered there."

Sir Reginald went on to the scene of earlier bloodsheds, and
Chief Inspector Ingram was soon seated at the further side of his
desk.

"There'll be an inquest on Ruscatti on Monday," he said,
"unless we get the murderer first and call the coroner off. But I don't
think we shall need to trouble you, as you were not here at the time."

There was no friendliness in Sir Reginald's voice as he replied:
"No. You can't accuse me this time. If you hadn't been in such a
hurry, you might have been able to say I'd done ten murders instead
of one."

Ingram looked surprised. "I can understand," he said temper-
ately, "that you feel sore, but I can't agree that we accused you of
anything; and if you'd lost no time ringing us up I don't suppose the
jury would have gone off the rails as they did."

"We won't waste time arguing; but I'll just tell you that you
don't know how I feel, and I don't know that you ever will, and as to
when I rang up the police, I'd like to know what difference it would
have made if I'd done it ten minutes earlier."

"It might have made all the difference."

"Or it might not. And as to your not having accused me, I'd like
to know who instructed that clumsy bully whom Miss O'Leary
called by the right names, if it wasn't you? By the way, what a gift
of accurate language that young woman's got!"

"I should say," the detective replied, still without showing resentment, though the last remark must have recalled some epithets
that Miss O'Leary had directed upon him, "that she is a more dangerous criminal than may be easily recognised in this country. She
won't be far out of our sight till she's using her return ticket. But I

didn't come to say what we think of her. We mean to clear this up, and we look to you to give us any help you can.

"That sounds all right, but what do I do?"

"We thought you might know rather more than you told in court. We appreciate that you might have wished to avoid mentioning anything that might have been misinterpreted. But that reason for caution can no longer apply."

"What are you driving at now?"

"There is a question, among others, as to whether you may know more about, or from, Miss O'Leary than we should easily learn from her."

"Is there? Well, if there is I'm afraid you won't get it from me. You may be surprised to hear that killing people is not in my line, and if that young woman gets put on the spot, as I believe they call it in her interesting country, it's going to be your doing, not mine. I'm not sure that those thick-headed fools in the jury box didn't save her life."

"That," Ingram remarked, "is very interesting to know."

Sir Reginald, hearing this quiet remark, had an uneasy doubt of the wisdom of what he had said already, and characteristically he met the position by pushing further along the dangerous road.

"I'll tell you what, Ingram. I mean to get this cleared up just as much as you do, or a bit more. I expect, if you don't get your man in the next fortnight, more or less, you'll be thinking of other rascals you want to catch, and forgetting this, but I shan't. When I get a grip I'm not one to let go.

"And I'm quite prepared to play ball with you. If you'll tell me what you're doing now, and keep me posted in what develops, I'll not only give you any help that I see my way to, but when you tell me you're beat, if you ever do, I'll take it up, and when it's inside out you can have any credit that's going round."

"We're always glad of any help we can get," Ingram replied cautiously, "but we don't expect to fail, and, if we should, it isn't easy to see how you'd be likely to be able to clear it up, unless you know already—"

"Which I tell you freely I don't. But I see one thing. These crimes aren't England. They're U.S. And if you don't clear it up here I mean to run over and talk to some of what Mrs. Clancy calls the boys there till I've learnt all I want to know."

"You think you'd come back alive?"

"I'd have a good try.... I'll tell you this. It's only a few hours ago that I bet Lady Crowe a four-acre wood that I'd run the scoundrel down who's spoilt what I used to think was the best carpet in

Lombard Street. Now I don't mind telling you that I always pay that kind of bet. She'll get the bluebells she wants. They'll be no use to her. (I've told her not to call them that. They're wild hyacinths. But she never will.) They die in about two hours after they're plucked, and their looks'd turn a cat sick. I'll give her the wood. But I'll take precious good care that it's a gift, not a win. So if you have a fall here, it's got to be Chicago or me."

Ingram hesitated a moment. He knew that Sir Reginald Crowe, though he had the reputation of being adventurous at times, if not rash, so that his fellow-bankers wagged dubious heads, was a shrewd man. He saw that he might have a sound business reason for resolving that what might otherwise have the aspect of a scandal of obscure significance should be cleared up, and he knew that the destination of a large sum of American money was interwoven with it. He decided to accept the offer.

He said: "We'll call that a deal. And I'll hold off the girl as far as I can. I dare say you can get more out of her.... I'll tell you what we've done or are doing now.

"Our first trouble is that we've got no clue to why Ruscatti found his way here. He couldn't have thought he'd see you. We've questioned Slick Maloon, who was staying with him at the Rinaldo—they'd got the best suite there—and who seems quite willing to talk. But he makes out he understands it no more than we, and I'm not sure he isn't telling the truth.

"He says that they were waiting for fresh instructions from Chicago, and he'd no idea that Joe had gone to the city till he saw an afternoon paper and learnt that he was a dead man.

"He'd been playing snooker himself, and got enough alibis to fill a dock.

"It's a queer thing, and may be a pointer we shouldn't miss, that though Joe's wallet and other papers were untouched, his authority to draw the money here cannot be found—the two murders are alike in that—and it makes it about as certain as it can be that they were done under the same direction, if not by the same hand."

"Maloon didn't seem nervous?"

"No. He'd got an alibi that we can't break."

"I didn't mean that."

"Oh, I see! His warrant would complete the collection. He didn't seem to be thinking about that. But it wouldn't be easy to judge. Maloon's hard."

"Not a wop, by the name?"

"No. Not that type at all. He's just leather: hard leathery skin, hard jaw. Not a small man, nor thin, but with a lean look. Shouldn't say he'd be at all easy to knife. They'd be more likely to try a bullet."

"It mightn't be a bad idea to have him guarded, without him knowing what you were at. The murderer might tumble into the net."

"Yes. Having him watched won't do any harm, whether or no. We may learn things that you don't expect.... But I was telling you what we're doing now. We had a full list from the New York police of all the gangsters that they've been exporting here and there isn't one who hasn't been kept in sight or won't be when he gets off his boat.

"They've most of them landed, and when the first murder occurred we knew where to find them. I can tell you now that we had checked up on them all within a few hours, and at first we didn't doubt that they'd been quarrelling among themselves, and that we should find one or more whom our men had followed to Lombard Street, or who would have an hour or two about the time of the murder for which he couldn't account.

"Well, we drew a blank. We accounted for everyone, near and far, and they had about the most cast-iron set of alibis that you ever heard. There wasn't one except the O'Leary woman of whom, taken singly, we couldn't say with absolute certainty that he was innocent.

"We hadn't followed her up quite so closely, being a woman, and we fell down over her visit to Lombard Street. We might never have guessed it at all if she hadn't let it out in court as she did.

"You'll understand that this made me more inclined to listen to the idea that you—or Miss O'Leary when she'd spoken her piece— might have more to do with it than I was at first. You two were on the spot, and we seemed to have checked up on every other possible suspect.

"Of course, we can't have done that. We've been tricked, or there's someone we've overlooked, or there's some quite different solution to the crimes from anything that appears likely from what we now know—and the first guess seems the most likely to me.

"Now we're combing out all these beauties again, and if we find one of them who can't account for his movements quite as well as he did three days earlier we shall probably have our eyes on the right man."

"I expect you will; though the chance of pinning the crimes on to him would still look rather slim to me."

"It might not be an easy job. But he'd probably have gone a good way toward hanging himself. A man can't be made to explain where he was at any time we require. If he just says nothing, it's up to us to show what the fact was. But a false alibi goes a long way toward convicting himself, and two of them would get us halfway home, if not more."

"Well, I hope you succeed, in which case it will be no more trouble to me, or at least the murder won't. There'll still be the little question of the five million grand, as they call it in their vigorous use of our effete language."

"I don't see what trouble you need have about that. We recognise that you've got no option but to pay it out, if you get proper instructions from your American agents."

"No? I suppose you wouldn't, because you're only interested in criminal courts. But it's what civil courts may decide that cuts the ice in the banking world. Now you've put your cards face upward to me, I'll tell you something that you mayn't know.

"The Dallas bank, that we had no reason to regard differently from any other of the thousands that flourish (or perhaps don't) in the numerous American states, belongs to Al Capone and his gang. At least, that's what we're told, and the fact that they're handling this money makes it a likely thing. They've moved up in the world, and they've come to owning the banks they robbed. I suppose they've got to thank prohibition for that. You can use this how you please so long as you don't let out that it comes from me.

"I don't mind if you inform the U.S. police, though it would be a poor compliment to them to imply that they don't know."

"If they do they haven't told us, and they may be glad of the tip. It's a new one to me, but it's not surprising when you think what wealth these racketeers must control."

"Yes. And how small some of the U.S. banks are.... Anyway, you may take it that it's a fact; and, however I came to know it, I've no doubt it's a secret that's been well kept on that side."

"I can see how you feel. But you're being frank with us, and if we don't intervene I still don't see how there can be much worry for you if you act in strict accordance with banking law."

"No? Well, there's something else I'm going to tell you. You may know, or you may not. It's according to whether you've seen one of the three authorities to pay, of which two appear to have been taken from the murdered men, and the third is presumably in the pocket of Slick Maloon.

"When I was asked about these documents at the inquest I didn't say anything incorrect, and there wasn't anything I wished to conceal, but I may not have been explicit on a point which didn't directly arise.

"I said that the document could only be used if the other two were produced with it and the three men attended together That is so; but it may not have been clear that, even then, it didn't give us authority to pay Ringan £337,000 or any other amount. It gave us authority to pay the three men *jointly* five million dollars. And when you consider that the money was to be handed over in cash, and add that one of the three had asked us to act so that he'd pick up the lot, it may be clear that the problem isn't quite simple."

"I'll own that I hadn't looked at it in that way. But I suppose you'd take a joint receipt first and make yourselves safe that way."

"But could we? And do you think that it would? We know that some public officials and monopolists send out receipt which they require their creditors to sign before they issue cheques. It's unreasonable and almost certainly illegal. I've had more than one row over refusing to sign such documents. I've told them that what they are really doing is to make their receipts a heap of almost worthless paper. My point is that such receipt may be evidence, but it's not proof.

"Suppose we'd said to the three: 'Sign this receipt first,' and they'd refused, do you think we could have insisted on it? It's more than I know, but I think not.

"Or suppose they'd signed it and then one had picked up the money and bolted, while the other two sat there refusing to go till they were paid. I don't say we should be liable, but I don't think the fact that we'd taken a receipt would make much difference one way or other.

"I didn't like it, even before I'd met Ringan, and knew the kind of men with whom we should have to deal.

"I'd cabled Dallas for clearer instructions, which hadn't come, and I don't suppose they will now; and I'd asked Jellipot to advise us as to whether it would be payment within the terms of our instructions if we should open an account for the three men on which they could draw in their joint names, and we'd have taken very good care to hand the money, in one sum or more, to the one who actually handed us the cheques.

"I think that would have been legal and secured us, but I took advice all the same. And Jellipot said he must take counsel's opinion, as even the best lawyers will, because it lets them out of the cart, and counsel doesn't get in in the same way.

"I know that I've got a reputation for rashness, but it's not true. I take risks at times—it's very often the safest course—but I vet them in every way that I can. And I never take any risk that I can avoid, unless it's for a worth-while stake.... And now I'm afraid that we've got to part. It's Saturday, as you probably know, and that's the day when we're supposed to get off early, if we come down at all, though it won't work out quite like that today."

Chief Inspector Ingram got up to go. He had learnt much, particularly as to the character and business methods of the chairman of the London and Northern Bank. "If we draw a blank again," he thought, "it may be the best way to sit back and see what he can do. I wonder what Bracken would say to that."

CHAPTER XXII.

THE PROPOSALS OF SLICK MALOON

ADELINE CORDER, who will be known to most readers as the authoress of *Jam for Jane*, *Wantons Don't Starve*, and the inferior but even more popular *When Girls Rebel*, does not cross the threshold of this narrative, but the fact that Evelyn went to dinner on Saturday evening to Maidcote Manor, and that Sir Reginald did not accompany her, had a remote but critical consequence.

It led Fred Corder, when the subjects of doormat murders and the density of coroner's juries were at last exhausted, to excuse himself on a plea of urgent work, leaving the two women together, which led them to talk of clothes, as they would otherwise have been unlikely to do, and this culminated in Adeline describing a dress she had seen in Regent Street earlier in the week, which was not suited (she was too tactful to say that it would have been too ample) for her, but would be a perfect dream if draped round her friend's more substantial form. Evelyn, who had some confidence in Adeline's judgement, said that she would like to see it, and the final decision was that they would meet in London for lunch on Monday and inspect it together, Evelyn deferring a home appointment of little urgency for this purpose.

The result of this was that she went into the Lombard Street bank during the morning to cash a cheque at a counter which was less crowded than it had been at the end of the previous week, and over which notes were still being paid with cheerful celerity, and as she was stuffing thirty of these potent slips into a bag which was far from empty she said casually to the cashier: "The excitement seems to be dying down this morning."

"Yes," he replied, with the loyal confidence that their chief gained from his staff, however differently his opponents might speak and feel, "if they'd known Sir Reginald better they'd have saved themselves some trouble, drawing out money they must have had a job to know what to do with over the weekend."

"It's a silly world," she answered lightly. "Good morning."

"Good morning, Lady Crowe."

She turned as she spoke to look into the eyes of a man who, half behind and half beside her, had been regarding her with an admiration he had no care to conceal, and who had been alertly conscious of the name by which she had just been addressed.

Even in admiration the eyes into which she looked were hard, appraising coldly, and sinister in their exposure of the soul from which their animation came. There were women, doubtless, who would be fascinated by such a glance, admiring, possessive, threatening as it was; who would be led, as Mary O'Leary might have been, by such a union into an unrepentant life of danger and crime. But the fascination was not for Evelyn Crowe.

"All right, honey," the man said, with a smooth familiarity which was an insult in itself, and with an accent which left no doubt of the country from which he came, "you've no call to be scared of me."

She turned away without answering, and he took no step to follow. He addressed the cashier: "That baby the Crowe dame?"

"That was Lady Crowe."

The tone of the answer did not encourage further conversation, but the man appeared unconscious of offence: "Oh, she's a lady right enough. I know class. But to think of that!"

He did not explain what was worthy of thought in the identity of the lady he had so boldly admired, asking, with a change to a curter tone: "I want to see someone about this." He produced, without handing over, the third of the authorities to pay, of which he was the only holder remaining alive.

"I think," the cashier replied, "Sir Reginald Crowe will like to see you himself. What name shall I give?"

"That's O.K. by me. But not upstairs. My name's Patrick Maloon."

The cashier spoke to a clerk behind him. He said: "If you'd go to the end desk they will show you through."

A few minutes later Slick Maloon was led to the lift, which he declined to enter. "You're not going to take me up to that room," he said definitely.

"Sir Reginald will see you in Mr. Adams' room," was the suave reply. Slick Maloon, alertly conscious of his surroundings, and with his right hand in a jacket pocket which may have contained his handkerchief, but more probably a lethal precaution against anyone "pulling a fast one" on him, went up without further protest.

He was shown into a room where he faced a table on the other side of which sat Sir Reginald, Jellipot, and Adams, they having been engaged in conference upon the trouble at the Wigan branch, to which there was now leisure to attend. As the clerk who had guided him to the room withdrew, Maloon turned to the door, saw that it had a Yale lock, and dropped the catch.

"I don't like the things that are happening here," he said bluntly. "But if they're out to get me they'll land themselves in a bloody mess."

"You will, I believe," Sir Reginald said, "be absolutely safe while you are with us."

"You think that?" Doubt turned to contempt in the speaker's eyes. "If they wanted me, you'd be just extras to fill the bag."

"But not without an alarm being raised, which would be fatal to their escape."

"You can't do much of that with your hands up and when you know you'll get no more time than a bullet takes crossing the floor."

"One of us has his foot on a bell now."

"And you don't say which. You mayn't be that dumb after all."

With this moderate praise Maloon sat down and produced his document. "You'll know I've come about this."

Sir Reginald looked at Mr. Jellipot, who replied: "Of course, we understand that. But it is difficult to see what we can do in the circumstances which have arisen until we have fresh instructions from your Dallas bank, which may reach us at any moment."

"You mean you've cabled to them?"

"Naturally. It was our evident duty, although they will know the facts, we may reasonably surmise, from their own press."

"Yep. There'll be spreading it there. But I don't see that you need worry for them. There's two dead, and I take the bag. You don't need me to prove their deaths. That may be why they were done here."

"It is," Mr. Jellipot admitted, "an interesting speculation, and one which, I will confess, had not occurred to me. There is an enterprising freshness about the methods of your fellow countrymen which we may not always be quick to follow. But speaking as a lawyer—"

"I suppose," Maloon interrupted curtly, "you're not short of the cash?"

Sir Reginald answered quickly, being uncertain what effect Jellipot's cautious accuracy might have on the gangster's mind. "We are not only willing, we are most anxious, to pay out the money to the first one who can produce a sufficient authority, and to get the transaction off our books."

Maloon chewed upon this emphatic statement, which he appeared to accept. He had seen something of banks in financial difficulties, and of the methods which they adopted to defer ruin, in his own country. He had even assisted, in one instance, in relieving a bank of its most liquid assets, from which such a crisis came. "Well," he conceded, "things looked healthy with your tellers to me. But I'd like to collect. I don't say now. I'm not going to walk out with one gun and five million grand. I'd bring some of the boys along. And if you want to pay out—well, we feel the same, and we'll fix a deal."

"I'm afraid," Sir Reginald said, with as much emphasis as before, fearing that he had raised a hope which would have a violent reaction when Maloon should realise that it was vain, "that however anxious we may be to get rid of this money, we can do nothing till we hear from Dallas."

Maloon chewed again. "Oh, I wouldn't say that," he replied in the tone of one who would give new ideas to a dull mind. "There'll be ways to deal. Suppose we sign off with a bit less? I'm not mean. I'll give you a top bid. How about twenty-five grand? I can't go higher than that. It isn't my wad. Not more than part. There's a lot I must hand away."

Sir Reginald was too good a business man not to be tempted by this straightforward and generous offer, but he put it firmly aside. "It may sound to you as though you are making a tempting proposal, but it would be a very poor bargain for us if we should have to pay the whole sum again, as would be a very probable sequel."

Maloon, who, in his own way, was very far from a fool, recognised finality in this decision. He considered offering an assurance that no such dirty work would be attempted either by himself or his honourable colleagues, which might have had more truth in it than is reasonable to conclude, but he recognised that such an affirmation would be in vain. He had a better hope when he said: "We might fix a hold-up. No one'd blame you for that. We'd find what's needed to square the cops."

"I'm sorry. But it wouldn't work in more ways than one. You can't square the cops here."

"I've heard tell," Maloon admitted. "But you never know till you try."

Suddenly it became evident that he had accepted defeat. "Reckon," he said, "it's a case for a new deal. I'll be seeing you before long." He got up to go.

Sir Reginald said: "It will be best for someone to go down with you.... Adams, you might show Mr. Maloon to the lift."

He had a vision of another spoiled carpet, which he wished to avoid. Maloon evidently looked at it in the same way.

"I'll say it would," he remarked, in grim recollection of the fate which had fallen on the two who should have been with him then. He went out.

CHAPTER XXIII.

A COUNCIL OF WAR

IT was on Monday, October 28th, a full fortnight later, that Sir Reginald telephoned to Mr. Jellipot's Basinghall Street office and, learning that the lawyer was out, said: "Ask him when he comes in if he would care to lunch with me at Beverley's. Say it isn't business, and it doesn't matter if he's too busy. In fact, if he is, I'd rather he didn't come. But I shall be there, whether he's coming or not."

He had just finished his second course, and had given up expecting the company for which he had asked, when Mr. Jellipot walked in.

"I hope," Sir Reginald began at once, "they gave you my message straight. I want a good talk with nothing else on our minds, or I'd rather not begin."

"I have no reason to doubt," Mr. Jellipot replied, with his usual precision, "that your message was conveyed to me with substantial accuracy, and it was because I understood it in that way that I did not come earlier. I delayed to clear all essential business so that I can now give leisurely and undivided attention to whatever you may have to say."

"I can tell you what I want in a very few words. I want you to do two things. The first is to tell me what your fee would be for coming with me to the United States to clear up the murders—and, of course, the cash question as well."

Mr. Jellipot made no direct reply. He said: "I must conclude that the police have not made much progress in elucidating what occurred."

"Much? They've made none or a bit less. They've got a good conduct mark now for every gangster's killer who's come over here during the last few months. There isn't one of them, except the O'Leary girl, that they wouldn't provide witnesses for who'd *prove* he couldn't have been anywhere near when the murders occurred. I believe Ingram's halfway back to believing that it really was O'Leary or I, and I dare say Bracken tells his friends on the quiet that he never doubted it all along."

"You've had no fresh instructions about the money?"

"Not a word. And it's a queer thing that Ingram says that some of those who came over have already arranged their return passages, as though they know there's nothing left to stay for."

"Miss O'Leary gone?"

"No. She's still at the Westmorland. And Slick Maloon's still at the Rinaldo. He spends most of his time—so Ingram says—playing snooker, and never goes out without a bodyguard, or at I night. That's apart from what the police provide, of which he may not be aware.... But you haven't answered my first question yet."

"I don't think I should be tempted by any fee, of whatever amount."

"Oh, come, Jellipot! Anyone would. Suppose I were to say fifty thousand a week!"

"I might still not be tempted at all. I am a single man with an income sufficient for all my needs.... May I enquire: what is the second thing that you wish to ask?"

"I want you to tell Evelyn she ought not to come."

Mr. Jellipot looked genuinely surprised. "I am sure," he said, "that I should have no influence if she will not listen to you."

"Well, she won't. I mean she won't listen to me. And when she gets her teeth on the bit like that you're the only one for whose opinion she has any respect."

"I may be unable to help you there, even so, for I am disposed to think that she may be right. We have learnt before now that she is a particularly cool and sensible girl. I don't think she would get in the way of anything that it would be prudent to do; and if you leave her behind she may have a most anxious time."

"So she says, and I've told her it will be all to the good in keeping down her weight. Not that I should mind if it were a bit more than it is now. But you know how it is with her."

"Yes. I think I do. And I conclude, if that argument had no force, that there would be nothing that I could say which would help you at all."

"Well, she won't come."

"Then we shall be a duller party than if she should."

"You mean that you will?"

"Certainly. Have I said anything of a contrary application? I merely gave your direct question the only truthful reply. But I have been fascinated for many years by the differences which exist be-

tween our laws and those of the New World, which are derived almost entirely from them, and most particularly in their variations of
court procedure, and I should welcome the opportunity of observing
them in operation, which our expedition may well provide."

"You're not shy of the risk?"

"I am not a man of violence, as you have had previous occasion
to know, so that the question may not arise in an acute form."

Sir Reginald considered that Mr. Jellipot showed less than his
usual logical soundness in this reply, but as he had been plainly
warned, and it had been given with his usual placidity, it seemed
that there was no occasion for further words, and at that moment
they saw that Evelyn had entered the room and was approaching the
table at which they sat.

"I thought," she said, "that I should find you still here."

Mr. Jellipot, knowing the restaurant not to be one frequently patronised by Lady Crowe, whose business—or pleasure—occupied
her mainly in more western districts, suspected her husband of a deliberate plot to get them together there, that his influence might be
exerted without delay on an unruly wife; but, if that were so, the
purpose had been abandoned after he had expressed his reluctance to
take the desired side, and it was Evelyn, after announcing her willingness to join them in the coffee which was being served, who
brought up the subject.

"I suppose Reggie's told you," she said, "that he's grown so
fond of Miss O'Leary that he's taking her to Chicago instead of
me."

"No," Mr. Jellipot replied, with the smile of friendly understanding which Evelyn was accustomed to see take the place of his
normal gravity when he spoke directly to her, actually I hadn't heard
that Miss O'Leary would be one of the party" ("Neither had I," Sir
Reginald interpolated), "though I can suppose that her presence
would be an enlivening factor and increase the probability that it
would accomplish the purpose with which it starts."

"It's no use making eyes at Jellipot," Sir Reginald said, "first,
because he was on your side before you began, and, second, because
I've made up my mind for once, and you wouldn't change it if you
both talked for a week."

"Then," Mr. Jellipot replied, "it will be a waste of words to say
more."

"Oh, but it won't!" Evelyn exclaimed, "though it's nonsense to
say I make eyes at anyone. I don't even know how it's done. But
I've found out since we quarrelled at breakfast that you can't help
yourself. We're like the Siamese twins. There's only one passport

between us. It's a case of 'where thou goest' and all that. Ruth and Boaz over again."

Mr. Jellipot's mild ejaculation to the effect that it must be Ruth and Naomi with whom the comparison was intended went unheard beneath Sir Reginald's brisker reply: "You're quite wrong about that, Evelyn. The passport is equally available for me, whether I travel alone or take you with me."

"Then what about me?"

"If we were in the habit of travelling separately, separate passports would have been issued."

"You mean you were really mean enough to get a passport by which I couldn't travel alone, but you can? And we've been married nearly three years, and I've not understood your true character till today."

"You mustn't be too sure that you have now. There may be further depths to explore. But I didn't think when I took it out that—"

"Of course not. You were really fond of me then."

"I'm too fond of you now to take you with me when I visit the correspondents of Slick Maloon and his like."

"But you can't leave me without a passport. Suppose you *wanted* me to come out later on?"

"Under such a contingency the resources of international diplomacy might be equal to overcoming the difficulty."

"But suppose anything else. Suppose I might want to run over to Paris."

"If that's all the trouble, I'll get you a separate passport before leaving. If I do, will you promise not to worry me any more?"

Evelyn hesitated a moment and then said: "You mean about taking me with you? I know it's no use if you've made up your mind in your utterly piggish way. Yes, I'll promise."

Sir Reginald, who had a well-founded fear that further pressure might wear down a decision which he already found it difficult to maintain, accepted this unexpectedly easy victory with relief and an excess of kindness to the wife whom he was to leave behind which made life very pleasant for both during the brief period which remained.

Mr. Jellipot, who had listened silently to a skirmish into which he had not been asked to intrude, made no comment upon the terms of its conclusion, but was adroit to change the subject as quickly as possible. "You don't really mean," he asked, "to approach Miss O'Leary about coming with us?"

"I don't know that it would be wise to do so. If there were any terms on which we could gain her collaboration, it is evident that she and her pet gangster in New York might become potent allies. But, short of that, the only result might be to let the whole boiling of them know that we're going over before we start."

"I doubt very much whether you can make a secret of that."

"So do I. But, apart from that, should we gain anything? Wouldn't she be certain to turn us down?" Mr. Jellipot pondered his reply before answering: "I don't think that is certain. But isn't there an opposite possibility—that she might lead you into a trap? We may judge her without uncharitable severity and still conclude that her standard of ethics is not high."

"So she might. But I doubt it. Her methods seem to me to incline more to what she calls straight shooting. I don't say we shouldn't risk a bullet, but I don't think it would be likely to come from behind."

"We might judge better if we knew more about the pseudo-husband she represents."

"I can tell you something about him. To give the devil his due, we've got to thank Ingram for this. He got it from the New York police. Clancy isn't one of the beer-kings. He isn't a hijacker. There's quite a lot of things that he isn't. I'm not sure that we shouldn't risk an action for slander (if you can imagine such a thing in the States) if we should call him a racketeer. He first became interesting to the police in Montana, where he was a hold-up man who worked singly at first, and then with O'Leary as his right-hand girl. He specialised in robbing banks. As a large-scale operator he may be regarded as an important and respectable member of his profession. I needn't tell you that we've got plenty of that profession in this country, though they don't operate with revolvers, finding a quieter and more effectual weapon in dud bills.

"He shares with Slick Maloon the honour of being an unconvicted man. They've both been in the dock; so's O'Leary. But the police have never been able to get them further than that.

"Three years ago there was a bank hold-up in which someone lifted about thirty thousand dollars in one scoop. There was little doubt that it was one of Clancy's jobs, but the usual absence of proof.

"Then they thought they'd struck oil. A man came to them who said he'd got the proof they required. They agreed his price after some haggling, and he was to come and make his statement and pick up the dollars on the next day, but the appointment wasn't kept.

"The next day Mrs. Clancy (as she told me to call her) had had an accidental wound on the temple, and two months later the man's body was found in a gulley, with some reason to think that he'd been shot in the softer parts of his body, where bullets are particularly painful to have.

"By that time Mr. and Mrs. Clancy had come east to Chicago, where they associated with other gangsters, as such people would be likely to do; but there was no reason to think that Clancy was doing anything more in the hold-up line or mixing with the rackets there. He appeared to have retired from active business and the cops turned their minds to those who went on making more trouble for them.

"Now it seems that he can't have been quite as idle as they supposed, or what claim on the money here would he be likely to have? But that's guessing. I've told you all that we've learnt, and if you think it points to looking up Tim when we know more about what the Statue of Liberty looks like than we do now, I'll come with you to make the call."

"I think," Evelyn began eagerly, "if you'd agree to my having a talk with the girl...."—and then stopped as she saw the lack of support in Mr. Jellipot's eyes.

"I'm afraid," he said, "that any approach of that kind would fail and might do harm. If we ask them for any help in finding the murderer of Ringan or Ruscatti—whom they almost certainly know— they will refuse, and quite possibly pass the word to those who would start what I think they call gunning for us.

"But there's one obvious line of approach which they can't resent, because it's offering to help them to what they claim.

"If I write to her on the bank's behalf asking for any evidence she can submit regarding Clancy's claim, she can't refuse to reply, and no woman could talk as much as she does without mentioning something that it will be useful for us to know."

"Then, if you think that's the right line," Sir Reginald concluded, "the best thing we can do is to go back to our respective offices while there's time for you to get it off by tonight's post."

So the little council of war broke up with the outward amity common to such conferences, and with an inward disunity of purpose which may be no less frequent; and Mr. Jellipot, who had no wish to deviate either from the programme that Sir Reginald had openly announced or that which he believed Evelyn privately to intend, found that the wording of the letter required so much consideration that it was not posted until the morning of the next day.

CHAPTER XXIV.

Miss O'Leary Decides

80a Basinghall Street, London E.C.2
October 29th, 1929.

DEAR MISS O'LEARY,

Re Mr. T. Clancy.

When you called upon my clients, the London and Northern Bank, Ltd., at their Lombard Street office on the 8th instant you were understood to put forward a claim that there is an existing contract under which some part of a sum which my clients then held as agents for the Sixth National Bank of Dallas, U.S.A. (the existence of which sum has since become public knowledge, so that it may be admitted without derogation of trust), should be paid to you under an authority which you held.

The said sum still being in my clients' hands, they are anxious to examine your claim with a view to establishing its legality, or otherwise obtaining authority to deal with it on an equitable basis at any time when instructions for the allocation or transfer of the aforesaid sum may arrive.

I should be obliged if you could make it convenient to call upon me to discuss the matter. I shall be at liberty either tomorrow or Thursday afternoon at any time between 3:30 and 5:00 P.M. if you will kindly telephone to fix the appointment.

Yours faithfully,

E. E. JELLIPOT

Having drafted this letter to his satisfaction, Mr. Jellipot decided to withhold it from the post until evening, considering, in a mind which respected the details of negotiation, that Miss O'Leary would be less likely to respond affirmatively if she had the night hours in which to develop doubts than if the time to act should be quickly upon her.

"It is a letter," he said to himself, "to be received in a morning mood, and when (we may hope) she will be bored for lack of something more exciting than our effete civilisation can contrive diurnally to supply."

Mr. Jellipot's psychology may have been sound, and it is a fact that when Miss O'Leary read the letter (which was in her bedroom, for, like most of her kind, she preferred the late to the early hours) her inclination was to make the appointment at the earliest time which it proposed. But about twenty minutes later, when she was completing a toilet which had been undertaken with an alertness of movement for which the letter may have had its share of causation, she received two cables which she considered with frowning brows. Finally she locked them and the letter securely from prying eyes and went down to breakfast with a puzzled and doubtful mind.

Being somewhat earlier than usual, she found that Nina Atkins, a young lady with whom she had come to such intimacy as shared a table and exchanged such confidences as their occupations allowed, had not finished her earlier meal, and whatever worry may have been on Miss O'Leary's mind was not sufficient to abate the brightness of the greeting she gave or the conversation that followed.

Miss Atkins was private secretary to a diplomat of too much distinction to be named here, but she had never had the good fortune to do much travelling abroad, the gentleman having been in cold storage during the three months that she had occupied the position. There was a possibility that he might be sent to Washington, and she was too capable a secretary to miss the opportunity of learning from one of America's own citizens what she could of her probable destination.

Miss O'Leary obliged her with much vivid and some exciting detail, subject to inevitable reservations, due to the peculiar nature of her experiences, and limited by the fact that there was so much of Americans, if not of America, which she did not know.

Miss Atkins responded with such accounts of the habits and customs of her native land as came within her own duller but more respectable experiences and such confidences as a diplomat's private secretary may discreetly give.

115

They probably, in the course of the many conversations of the past three weeks, had both given themselves away beyond the exact limits of discretion or their own awareness.

Miss O'Leary, for instance, had not been entirely reticent concerning her preference for having her back to the wall and her eyes upon an opposite door, which still persisted, though she no longer felt the acute alarm which had followed the reading of the press reports of her evidence at the inquest, and consideration of what its implications to unfriendly "boys" might appear to be.

Her wariness had subsided now until it was little more than that which must be normal to those who live outside and beneath (or, as they might consider, above) the law, and may be assessed as one of the major penalties of anti-social activities, though exactness requires us to observe that her cautious dread was directed against those of her own kind and not the officers of the law, for whom, whether of New York or London, she had a measure of contempt which would be disapproved by a prudent mind.

She ate a very good breakfast, in the course of which she confided to Miss Atkins the authentic fact that, having been born in Texas and almost literally on a horse's back, she had not seen a tree till she went, at the age of twelve, to another state, where she had been frightened lest she should be crushed by the falling of the branches beneath which she saw others so boldly pass; and then gave an equally vivid and veracious account of a recent incident which had excited the emotions of a hundred million Americans, in which three school-teachers, touring their native land during their summer vacation, had parked their car by the roadside and wandered aside to explore its remoter beauties. Two days had passed before the derelict car, with its internal evidences of unintentional abandonment, had attracted attention, and three more before the hundreds of rescue parties which had gone out in vain were recalled by the news that the wanderers had been located, at the point of death, by a searching airplane.

Miss Atkins went to her morning work with an improved realisation of the variety and extent, if not of the inhabitants of the land to which she was likely to go? and Miss O'Leary went back to her own room to read again the cables the words of which she already knew, and to pace her room in a restless fury of in; decision, born of the fact that she could not probe the implications of words which might seem plain to a more ignorant mind. The cables, both addressed to Miss O'Leary, Hotel Westmorland, London, W.1, and both handed in at New York, read:

NO USE STAYING LONGER STOP RETURN
BALTIC STOP LOVE STOP TIM.

And:

CALL IT A DAY STOP COME BALTIC STOP
SWINE.

The first one appeared to have come from Tim Clancy, giving
plain instructions to return, and the second, of whatever origin, confirmed this programme, so that the occasion for the perturbation
which their recipient was showing was not clear, unless it arose
from the complication of Mr. Jellipot's letter, or the meaning of the
concluding word of the second cable. Actually the explanation was
quite different, and the reality of the cables was opposite from that
which appeared.

The first cable was not from Tim, and the second was. Miss
O'Leary had no doubt of this, for the possibility of her being misled
by faked cables had not been overlooked, and Tim Clancy had arranged a simple code which rendered it certain that she could not be
deluded in this manner. He had given her a sentence easy to remember, but not of a nature to be fully quoted here, "Al Capone and
every member of his gang is the...swine," of which he would use
one consecutive word signature for each cable he should have occasion to send, and it is evidence of the frequent communications
which had passed between them that he had now reached the last. It
was a code which could neither be interpreted nor forged, the key
sentence being known only to their two selves, and it made it absolutely certain that the call to return—and that by a boat which, not
being one of the luxury liners, was not usually patronised by the
racketeers—had come from him. But with what object had the
forged one been sent, and how should it be that they were identical
in intention, not only in requiring her to return, but in the selection
of the boat by which she should travel?

Reaching no solution to this conundrum, she took up Mr. Jellipot's letter again, but-found that she had done no more than to
change the subject of irresolution. In the end she threw into the
grate, with a gesture of decision, the end of the cigarette she had
been smoking, and exclaimed: "He seemed a wily old bird to me.
I'll see what he's got to say."

The next moment she was giving a number to the telephone operator, but the voice she called was not that of Mr. Jellipot, but the
more nasal accents of Slick Maloon.

"Slick," she said, with an apparent candour which made no mention of the cables that lay beside her, "I've had a letter from the bank's lawyer asking me to give him a call. What do you think I should do?"

"Why not go and hear what he's got to say?"

"I wasn't sure without asking Tim. But what you say goes with me."

"You won't do any harm, and you may hear something w ought to know. But you can please yourself. We're shuffling no for a new deal."

She talked for a few further minutes on unimportant topics, and gave a half-promise that she would meet him at a late-night party on Thursday. She had met him twice already during the previous week, which had been no more than a measure of prudent life insurance to her, as was the present call. She would have told Tim with truth that she liked Maloon as much as a bad smell.

But Maloon, for all his slickness, had understood her in a different way. He thought that she was growing restless for male companionship, which he was well able to provide. He reckoned that he had enough bucks to buy any dame that his eyes desired, but he would have had a special pleasure in trespassing upon Tim Clancy's property, especially as he was shrewd enough to know that it was not for sale on a cash basis. But if to the inclination which he supposed to exist should be added the argument that he could be of essential assistance to her in collecting Clancy's claim—well, would she not feel that she could please herself and earn Tim's praise at the same time?

"If Slick thinks he'll put me down, he's got another guess coming to him," she reflected, smiling at an imagination which we need not pursue. She was well content, especially at the, degree of confidence he had given her, though there might be little secret in that. Shuffling, were they, for a new deal? That might explain Tim's summons for her to return, though not the forged duplicate nor the chosen boat.

Secret or not, Slick was one who went through life with a close-shut mouth, and he would not have said it if he had been doubtful of her. It was with increased confidence in herself and her ability to handle the enigmatic position which confronted her, that she rang up Mr. Jellipot's office and said that she would be there at half-past three in the afternoon.

CHAPTER XXV.

MISS O'LEARY EXPLAINS

MR. JELLIPOT received Miss O'Leary with his usual quiet cordiality. He said: "I'm not asking you to tell me anything you know or suspect about the two murders that have occurred, which I understand that it might be dangerous to you to do. What we are anxious to know is what claim Mr. Clancy may have on any part of the money which is in our hands."

Miss O'Leary was not quick to reply. She said doubtfully: "That's telling a lot."

"Yet it may be very much to your advantage that we should know."

"Not if they thought you might have had it from me."

"I think I see what you mean." He had his own interval of silence before he went on, taking a deliberate gamble which instinct rather than habitual caution approved. "Suppose we trust each other to this extent: I will tell you what course we are proposing to take, which we do not wish your American acquaintances—I must hesitate to call them your friends—to know. And you shall tell me how this money became due to Mr. Clancy, and we will treat both confidences alike. They will be absolutely private between ourselves."

Miss O'Leary considered this and extended her hand. "Shake," she said. "I wouldn't say but I'll get more than I give, but it won't go further with me."

"Then I will tell you that the bank is resolved that the mystery of these murders shall be cleared up. And as nothing has been discovered by the police in this country, Sir Reginald Crowe has resolved to go over to yours to make enquiries which we hope may be more productive."

"He's riding high if he tries that."

"It seems the obvious thing for us to do."

"You mean you're going along?"

"That is what I am arranging to do."

"Then you'll be a wise guy if you bring your gun."

"On the contrary, I should be extremely foolish. I have no practice with such a weapon, and it is improbable, even if I should be confronted by a position such as would justify homicide to myself and your country's laws, that I should shoot with the straightness or expedition which must be requisite to such an emergency."

"There isn't many of the boys who can do that."

"You mean they cannot shoot straight?"

"Yep. They don't get practice enough. It's just boloney with most. They've got guns, but when they use them they hit the air.... Slick can shoot. So can Tim. It was he who gave me this." She touched the scar on her temple and smiled to herself at the recollection it brought.

"You mean," Mr. Jellipot asked, in some natural surprise, "that Mr. Clancy's shooting is so uncertain that you were nearly killed by a bullet from his own gun?"

"I didn't say that. I said Tim could shoot. It was near about what he meant to do. But that's all part of the tale.... Well, if you don't carry a gun, you'll need to be quick to put your hands where they ought to be."

"If you mean," Mr. Jellipot replied thoughtfully, "that I should be quick to raise my hands in an attitude of some indignity in response to the peremptory demands of others carrying lethal weapons, I am again inclined to disagree, even against the superior experience which you must be able to bring to bear upon a problem of conduct which I have only considered during the past forty-eight hours. It appears to me that the hold-ups which are practised so extensively by the more lawless of your citizens must depend almost entirely for their success (without which their popularity could not endure) upon the readiness of their fellows to respond with the gestures which they are invited to make."

"They like to keep their skins whole."

"Which, in the vast majority of cases, and to a net total exceeding that which they may attain by the method you recommend, suppose that they would be likely to do."

Miss O'Leary's opinion of Mr. Jellipot's English was not high. She thought that his use of words was excessive in relation to the burden of thought they bore, which was not simple true, and he vexed her by the use of some which she did not know. (So she did him, with a contrary result, for he admired her language, though it might not have occurred to him to call it English.) She may be excused that she did not follow the implications of his last remark, but she was in no doubt of the argument which it was designed to sustain. Less subtle, but as sharp-witted as he, she frowned over this heterodox view of one of the basic habits of her native land, and saw that there might be some reason in what he said.

But the question remained—was it quite fair? Was it playing the game? She imagined two hold-up men entering upon a scene of festivity and calling upon those present to put up their hands, so that they might be lined up against the wall and relieved of their rings and wads, without the distracting fear that one of them might suddenly snatch out a concealed weapon and start bloodshed, which it is always preferable to avoid. Suppose they should *all* refuse to make the required gesture? Were the hold-up men to walk along the rows of recalcitrant guests shooting the lot? It would be a necessity repugnant to every decent mind! There must be many occasions when an enterprising citizen will wish to cover another man and tell him to put up his hands, when it would be inconvenient to kill him. To decline to do so might create a most embarrassing situation. No, it would not be playing the game.

Yet she was fair enough to see that a foreigner might have some excuse for not looking at it in the same way. She said tolerantly: "Well, if they know you're a Britisher you might pull it off; but I should say it wouldn't be a fair thing for one of the boys to try." Mr. Jellipot understood her reaction, and it confirmed him in the opinion he had expressed. He said: "We must hope they will be generous enough to regard my deficiencies in that spirit. And in any case I should be no worse off than if I were to attempt the use of unfamiliar weapons. But I must not anticipate that such events will occur in your charming country."

"Nope. But it's best to be ready. Things happen quickly with us.... Are you going soon?"

"We shall probably sail on the *Baltic* in about a fortnight's time."

"Then we're likely to be on the same boat.... Say: wonder if that's why!"

"May I ask what?"

"Why I've had a cable from Tim telling me to get on that boat."

"That is, I can assure you, an impossible deduction. It is only during the last hour that I have telephoned to the White Star Line and arranged for the accommodation we require.... As a matter of fact, I left the selection of the boat to them, only asking for one which your friends would be unlikely to use."

"Well, you've got it. She's a wallowing old sow. One of the ten-day waddlers. Ties up at Boston first, more likely than not. Per-

THE CAPONE CAPER, BY S. FOWLER WRIGHT

haps that is why Tim—" But as she spoke she remembered the second cable. In view of what she was about to tell, might not this also be revealed, especially as they would be travelling together?

On an impulse which she had no later occasion to regret, she told Mr. Jellipot of the two cables and the confusion to which they had reduced her mind.

"It is," Mr. Jellipot remarked at the conclusion of this narrative, "a most interesting problem, and of more complexity than I had been disposed to think. It may be fortunate that we shall be on the same boat—and perhaps additionally so for you that it cannot be thought that you will have joined it for that reason."

"No," she said acutely, "but it might be reckoned up that you'd had the tip from me."

"It is possible," Mr. Jellipot admitted, "and must be accepted, unless you may think it sufficient reason for choosing another boat."

"I couldn't do that. Not after what Tim's said."

"Then we must leave it so. But you were to tell me another tale."

"Well, it's soon said. It was in Montana that I met Tim. He was good at cards, and he'd got plenty to spend, and I thought I knew how it came. So some of it did; but he got most from the banks, by the sort of loan that you don't have to repay. Everyone knows that now, including the cops, but they can't prove anything, because he worked alone. I don't say I was no use to him toward the end.

"He made his first mistake when he let Barker in. Barker would have sold him out to the cops, but he learnt that just in time, and we took him out for a ride, which was the only thing we could do. When he saw what was coming to him he started whining, and I got soft and tried to stop Tim using the gun, and he gave me this." (She touched the scar on her head.) "He didn't mean to hurt me more than he did, but he'd got to stop me squawking and show me where I got off."

"You mean," Mr. Jellipot said, in some mild surprise, though he was learning rapidly to understand the codes and customs of his new acquaintances, "that he gave you what was within an inch or two of a fatal wound because you asked him not to shoot Mr. Barker?"

"There wasn't that much risk. I told you Tim shoots straight. And I'd gotta learn. If he'd turned his eyes off Barker more than he did, it might have been worse for him than it was for me."

"I can believe," Mr. Jellipot conceded readily, "that there is reason in what you say. And, if it were satisfactory to yourselves, it is difficult to see why anyone should object.... But I interrupted you at an exciting moment."

"Well, that's how it was. We got Barker off our hands, and there was no loss in him, but Tim thought he'd done enough in the bank business, and we'd better call it a day.

"He'd got a big wad, and the only trouble was where to salt it. If he went into a bank to make a deposit, the tellers knew his face and didn't hold out their hands; they put them up or dived under the counter.

"They might just as likely have grabbed a gun and let off at him, and if he'd pulled his out the cops might have got him wrong, and he'd have felt the hot seat for something he didn't mean.

"So we came east to Chicago and got to know the boys there, but Tim kept out of the rackets. Some of them were that mean! And there was too much double-crossing for him. But he met Crowley, who'd muscled in on the West Side—in the beer racket, I mean. Crowley hadn't done anything wrong. There wasn't as much shooting then as there is now. And machine-guns weren't used. Fred Burke, in Detroit, began them.

"Crowley bought his pitch, but it left him short. Tim lent him two hundred grand, and was to have twice that back in two years. Before that time came Crowley had to sell out to Al Capone.

"Capone said he paid Crowley, but Crowley didn't pay Tim. Crowley said he sent the wad by Two-Gun Gordon, and Gordon said Jake Lingle took it from him. Jake said that was a lie, and if Gordon came within a hundred miles of N'York he'd be shot up, but that didn't pay us.

"Besides, Capone shouldn't have paid Crowley, because he knew about Tim's loan, and he'd been warned. But Tim couldn't go gunning Capone and Lingle and all the men who were passing the buck round. He wanted no more than his wad and a quiet life.

"So he had it out with Capone in a friendly way, and Capone said he'd pay again sooner than be bad friends with Tim, but he'd have to wait, owing to so much having been sent here, and expenses being high since.

"Now we were told we could have it in London, but Tim couldn't come. He's got another loan to collect of the same kind. We'd come to N'York a bit ago, and he lent some money to Larry Fay, which he isn't meaning to lose. Larry's in the taxicab racket. He runs the Fay Taxicab Company. There's nothing wrong about that. They've got the best cabs, and they ought to have the best fares. So they beat up any drivers who haven't got the sense to sit back. It's quite lively at times. But Larry's being run in more weeks than not, though the cops haven't put one across him yet, and with one thing and another Tim thought he'd better collect, and so he's on Broadway and I'm here.

"We thought you'd have orders to pay Tim or me; but, if not, Ringan would, and I meant to keep him in sight."

"Ringan not being a man whom you would trust, even if he had instructions to pay you?"

"You've said it. I wouldn't have trusted him with ten cents if he thought he could get away. But he had those watching him that would have handed him a warm time, and there'd have been Slick with something to say. I reckon whoever put the knife into Ringan did us out of that money, though I'd say we'll get it yet in another way."

"You think Mr. Maloon to be one on whom you could rely?"

"He's the meanest dirt that ever came out of Detroit, and if there's a worse devil with women he must be someone I don't know. But Slick's straight with money in his own way. He'll be straight with you if you're straight with him, and if you're on his side of the gate. I wouldn't say more than that."

"Well, you've told me a good deal, and you can rely upon it being treated with confidence. I must, of course, communicate it to Sir Reginald, but it need go no further than that."

"That's O.K. by me. And I don't mind Lady Crowe. Is she coming along?"

"Sir Reginald thinks that it will be safer for her to remain here."

"Oh, I don't know. The dames are safe enough if they keep out of the rain."

"Which Lady Crowe might not be certain to do."

"Then I'll bet she comes if she feels like that."

"It is a bet which I must decline to accept."

Miss O'Leary rose. "Well, so long. And thanks for hearing all that I'd got to say. See you on the *Baltic*, if not before."

Mr. Jellipot was slow to shake hands. He had a feeling, unusual with him, that there were other things which ought to be said, without being sure—or even certain of what they were.

He said hesitantly: "I have no doubt that we shall. It will, perhaps, be better for us to show no intimacy upon the train."

Miss O'Leary said that this also would be O.K. by her, and took a smiling departure.

When she got back to her own room she rang up Slick Maloon again and confided to him that the bank had asked her to explain the nature of her claim, and that she had said no more than that it was a business debt due from Crowley, and that Capone had kindly arranged for it to be paid.

When he had approved this commendable reticence she added a further confidence, over which she had been hesitating for the past hour. She said that she had had two cables from Tim telling her to return on the *Baltic*, and she had thought it best to tell the bank, so that they could communicate direct with New York after the boat should sail.

Slick said: "Two?"

She answered: "Yes. He must have meant to be sure I'd get it."

He did not blame her for telling the bank. Indeed, why should he?

It was a puzzling situation, and "puzzling" and "perilous" in her vocabulary were very similar words. She thought she had given him information which it was prudence that he should have, and avoided any dangerous excess.... Yes, she would see him on Thursday. She implied that she was looking forward to that.

CHAPTER XXVI.

A QUESTION OF CATCHING THE BOAT

THE *Baltic* sailed from Liverpool. It was not quite the "wallowing old sow" that it had been called by Miss O'Leary's contemptuous tongue, nor had she been quite accurate when she described it as a ten-day boat. It was a comfortable twenty-thousand-ton liner of mature but not ancient years, destined to premature condemnation and to be sold for breaking up by the Japanese in the racket which controlled and ruined the Atlantic ferry service of that day—a racket of competition in a controlled and most deadly form—not of prices, but of luxuries, so that, unless a passenger were prepared to be segregated to an inferior part of the ship, he must consent to pay exorbitantly for a swimming-pool and a palm court which he did not require, and even for a spacious superfluous restaurant where he could buy additional food if the five meals, unlimited in amount and bewildering in variety, which were freely provided should leave him with any possible need or desire for such refreshment.

The *Baltic*, not being one of these luxury liners, was not allowed to offer its best suites as first class, but only under the meaningless style of "cabin" accommodation; but the society which would be met there would be superior both in character and intellect to that which could be expected to be met on the larger boats. In the two years of slump that followed, and before the power of the gangsters was broken, this position reached a grotesque extreme, and there was one occasion when the *Majestic* sailed from New York with scarcely a passenger, except a few dozen bootleggers and other kings of the gangster world, to share the luxury of its first-class rooms.

Mr. Jellipot joined Sir Reginald Crowe on the boat-train at Euston, and found Evelyn there, she having announced her intention of accompanying them to the liner's side. They caught sight of Miss O'Leary's emphatic curls on the crowded platform, but afterwards saw her no more until they were out on the open sea, for while Mr. Jellipot, after joining the boat, remained at the rail to observe an unusual scene, Miss O'Leary, having a mind more fixed on her 'own affairs, retired at once to her cabin, where she summoned her steward, gave him a pound note, and told him that she did not wish to be disturbed till the boat had sailed. If he should see anyone try her door, would he be careful to probe his credentials and, if he should prove to be a passenger, report his identity later to her?

She had previously cabled to Tim acknowledging his *two* cables, both of which, she made it clear with no economy of words, had directed her to use the *Baltic* for her return; and having thus "put him wise" to the position, she felt that she had done all that prudence required until she should be on the boat and the passenger list should be issued for her to read.

While she remained in her cabin, waiting for the throb of the engines and the sight of a receding pier, and unpacking in a solitude which was not disturbed, Mr. Jellipot observed that which she would have been interested to know.

It was within half an hour of the time when the hawsers would be cast off and the gangway raised when Mr. Patrick Maloon drove up in a taxi, the driver of which had evidently been bribed to exceed the speed limit which was enforced—more or less—at that period in the urban areas. He was engaged next moment m a heated argument with the officer who was in charge of the gangway. He flourished a passport and other papers. He proffered bank-notes in a loose hand.

Whatever they might be, they were insufficient to secure his passage. The officer had been joined now by two others, who were urging the angry man to the custom-house on the other side of the pier. "The time's short enough now," Mr. Jellipot could hear one of the officers say. Maloon, abruptly accepting this advice, went the way he was directed, and disappeared from view.

Mr. Jellipot now watched the gangway with a double interest; Evelyn had said good-bye on the station platform. She had said truly that it would enable her to catch a return train to London and get home before midnight. With equal veracity she had added: "I made up my mind from the first that I wouldn't say good-bye to you on the boat." After that, and an affectionate leave-taking, she had gone to the refreshment-room, as it was reasonable to do.

Mr. Jellipot had concluded that he would see her again before dark, but the siren had given its final warning blast and the gangway was about to be hoisted in before she appeared, with no aspect of haste, and presented a newly issued passport and embarkation papers about which the officer made no trouble at all. After that he directed one final glance at a door from which Mr. Patrick Maloon did not emerge, and gave the signal to cast off.

Mr. Jellipot concluded that Maloon was not destined to be a fellow passenger of that voyage, and turned his eyes to the fussing tugs.

CHAPTER XXVII.

CONVERSATION AT DINNER

SIR REGINALD CROWE and his solicitor had been allocated by an experienced purser to the captain's table, at which they had both taken their seats while the remaining ones were still vacant, in a dining-room which was better filled on the first evening out than would be the case on the following day. The captain, they knew, would not be there. His place would be on the bridge until they had passed out into broader seas. But there were five other seats to be filled, and the pleasure and interest of the voyage would depend in no slight degree upon the congeniality of those who must assemble together for so many leisurely meals in the coming week. This allocation of places was the most delicate task that the purser must perform as each voyage commenced. Its result was more precarious at the captain's table than elsewhere because there was a slight social distinction involved, and congeniality was not the sole consideration he must observe.

Now Mrs. McClintock, a tall, mature lady with high cheekbones and an otherwise angular appearance, approached the table and would have seated herself between Sir Reginald and the captain's vacant chair had not an adroit steward interposed and guided her to its other side.

Following her, a Harvard lecturer on astronomy was seated absent-mindedly beside her, with a younger wife, more conscious of her environment, on his left. Mr. Jellipot, catching a glimpse of a red head at the doctor's table some distance away, was inclined to think that an exchange might have given them a livelier voyage. He concealed his surprise, but was in doubt of whether to revise his opinion, when Slick Maloon, immaculately garbed, sat down between the professor's wife and himself.

It was Sir Reginald's turn to be surprised when the steward drew the chair at his own left hand obsequiously backward and Evelyn sat down, with a glance toward him which a stranger might have thought cold.

Finding him silent—for he thought that there were things to be said which should not be for strangers' ears—she said casually, after she had given her order and put the menu aside: "I've come quite on my own. I shan't be any trouble to you."

"Oh, but that's nonsense, Evelyn! You ought not to have done it, and it's almost certain to mean trouble for me."

"Not if we go our own ways. That's what you got the new passport for, isn't it? I don't see why we should see much of each other till we get back. America's a large country."

She was smiling now, though she wasn't sure that she might not be in for a bad time with Reggie when—or if—he should get her alone. But why should he get her alone, if she didn't wish?

The few words they had had were too low to be overheard, Mr. Jellipot having engaged Mrs. McClintock in conversation on a much higher key, and the professor's wife being occupied in some playful exchanges with Slick Maloon, who would test any woman before deciding that she would be useless to him.

He had joined the ship when the pilot was taken off, and the price he had paid to secure that table seat was best known to himself and the head steward, who was still bemused by the size of the bribe which had induced him to guide the lady who should have occupied it to the table presided over by the chief engineer. "We are so sorry," he had said glibly, "but the captain had promised the seat to one of his own friends, and we only knew that a few minutes ago."

Slick Maloon looked round the dining-room, shining with silver and glass and white napery, and gay with the evening dresses that most of the lady passengers had already found time to unpack, and with flowers which would lessen and fade as the days passed, and his eyes were contemptuous, They came back to settle upon Mr. Jellipot, with the remark: "Fancy meeting you here!" He looked at Sir Reginald, whose attention was upon Evelyn, and who did not appear to have noticed his coming, and then at Evelyn, who looked back with recognition, though no friendliness, in her eyes. She said to her husband in a low voice: "There is a man at the table whom I saw in the bank last week. I don't know who he is."

Sir Reginald showed that he had been more observant than appeared. "That's Maloon," he said, without looking in his direction; "it's no chance that he's planked himself on to us. And this was the boat where Jellipot said we should find that those rats didn't come!"

"I shouldn't say," Evelyn replied, "that it's going to be such a dull voyage." For the moment they had forgotten that there was a quarrel of doubtful gravity to be resolved between them.

Meanwhile Mr. Jellipot had replied to Maloon's remark. "It is customary to observe on these occasions that it is a small world. But there may be times when such meetings may be less fortuitous than they appear."

Maloon made no reply, nor was it possible to judge whether he understood the implications of the remark. His habitual manner was that of one who expected to impress others with what he said, but who gave little regard to their reactions, even if he observed them at all. Mr. Jellipot wondered modestly whether he were destined to get more from Maloon than the gangster would get from him. It was like a contest between aliens bearing different weapons and with different training in the practice of arms. The issue was beyond prediction. But he thought Sir Reginald would not be easy to overreach He looked at Evelyn and had a doubt of whether he should not have said the word which would have left her in the pleasant woodlands of Hither Dene.

Maloon was speaking again: "I wonder whether it always makes that infernal row." He was alluding to the mast that rose through the centre of the room. It gave a long whining creak, as its habit was. So it had done for years, and would do perpetually till they should tie up for a few hours' stillness at Boston quay. It was the one sign of age that the *Baltic* had, and those who used the boat regularly noticed it less than they might have done the absence of a familiar sound.

Mr. Jellipot said tolerantly that there were many sounds of equal persistence that were more difficult to endure; but Maloon's attention had wandered again. He was looking across at where Miss O'Leary was telling some tale at the doctor's table which was exciting a general hilarity.

"Our young friend," Mr. Jellipot remarked, "appears to have made herself at home already."

"Redhead knows how to talk and how to keep mum," was the approving reply. "There isn't a gun-girl in Michigan I'd trust sooner than her.... Not that that's saying much. Most of those babies' necks need a good twist."

"You doubtless speak," Mr. Jellipot replied, "from a knowledge which I do not possess."

He reflected that Maloon had already told him that he trusted Molly O'Leary, which it might be useful to know. He observed also the free way in which these social outlaws had come to speak of each other and of the criminal courses which they pursued. He did not therefore consider that the United States would sink into a morass of crime. He judged that the reign of the gangster would not be long. He had not observed that a pendulum continues to swing in the same direction.

His reflection was interrupted by the voice of Mrs. McClintock, which sounded clearly across a table around which other voices had for a moment subsided. "But," she was saying to the mildly astonished astronomer and his more evidently resentful wife, "there aren't any gentlemen in America! You can see that from the films."

Sir Reginald, doubting whether the cause of international courtesy was well supported by the simple sincerity of this reflection, was quick to speak: "Just as there are no gentlemen in England. You can see that from the music-halls."

Mrs. McClintock was undisturbed by this curious form of corroboration. She said briefly: "Oh, the music-halls? But I never go."

The steward, standing alert and silent behind her chair, allowed a slight smile to appear on his well-disciplined lips. He was accustomed to stand thus at lunch and dinner (breakfast was a less gregarious meal) during periods of eight or ten days, listening to the conversations of half a dozen casually assembled people, observing their intimacies grow until the day of parting came and they would exchange addresses and promises of continued acquaintance, with varying degrees of momentary sincerity, and scatter to an almost instant forgetfulness.

About twenty-six times a year he would watch the comedy re-enacted with a new cast of performers. For the same number of times he would speculate as to the amounts which the affluence or generosity (or perhaps the timidity) of those upon whom he waited would slip into his hand or leave beside their plates on the final day.

These repeated episodes would constitute, according to his own intellectual receptivity, a monotony of a very varied, or a variety of a very monotonous, kind. He thought that the present table would be liberal in its benefactions; but that its intimacy would flower to the usual exuberance was less sure. Something was wrong with its composition. It was not merely that three gentlemen were seated together. The gentleman with the leathery complexion should not be there.

There, however, Maloon was; and there he remained, self-assured, polite in his own way, once or twice making a shrewd jest as the days passed, and the incongruous little assembly found common topics on which conversation could be safely made. He appeared to have nothing on his mind. His time between meals was largely spent at the card-table or the bar or in pacing the promenade deck with long, leisurely strides and a cigar in his mouth—or, more slowly with female companionship which was not always the same. He even found a bond of understanding with Mr. Jellipot, for they were both fastidious in what they smoked. He approved Mr. Jellipot's cigars, and Mr. Jellipot approved his.

So things went for six days, during which there was one of storm and another of slowly subsiding seas. The passengers who kept to their own cabins became more numerous than had been the case during the first day out. Miss O'Leary's red head was not seen, and there was a lunch at which Evelyn thought it prudent not to appear.

Then they came into a region of humid, foggy, and windless air. The prow cut through a level sea. The siren sounded at times as the fog closed. Games began to be played on a steady deck. To Jellipot, to the Crowes, even to Miss O'Leary, it had become evident that they would have no more than an eventless November voyage. Only Slick Maloon had other thoughts.

CHAPTER XXVIII.

THE FRANKNESS OF AL CAPONE

"I TOLD you," Al Capone said, "that you could bring your bodyguard with you, because I knew I was asking you more than a bit, and I was on a spot that I couldn't leave. All the same, there were things that I couldn't write that you ought to know."

"I'm not scared to trust you that bad," Clancy answered easily, though he was inwardly as wary as a fox in a farmer's barn, "and I'm not out after you. And I don't need any bodyguard better than I've got here." He made a gesture by which his hand went less than halfway to his hip-pocket, but it was enough to cause Capone's eyes to flicker uneasily, though he sat in his own palatial Chicago office and half a dozen of his most trusted killers were round his door.

Capone came to the point at once, as his way was. He would say that he was a business man first and last. It was no more than incidental that his business was outside the law, and required in consequence to be carried on in exceptional ways. He had merely studied the extraordinary position into which the beer trade had been thrown by legislation for which he had no responsibility, and taken such means as it required. It was not illegal to drink beer. It was only illegal to sell it. Men liked beer, for which they would pay more than its worth. His business was the logical—it might be said the inevitable—outcome of such partial and arbitrary legislation. Men might call him a gangster, but he thought of himself as a successful business man whose organisation must, through its outlawed status, be ruled by his own police. And in this new lawyers, judges, legislators of Chicago, more than half of its police force, and a large proportion of its private citizens fully concurred.

Now he said: "You want your wad, and you want to know that no harm's meant to your girl. And I've asked you here to tell you you'll get the bucks, and I reckon the girl's straight. We're meaning no harm to her.

"But I've asked you for more than that. We want your help. I'll put the cards face up, and you'll do the same when you've heard what I've got to say."

"If you're putting the cards like that," Clancy answered cautiously, "you'll tell me who cabled Moll to come back on the *Baltic*."

"If I knew that I shouldn't have needed to ask you here." Clancy's eyes were puzzled, if not incredulous. His voice was cold as he said: "I'm here to listen. I'll just tell you one thing. You put the wad first. I put Moll."

"Maloon's on the *Baltic*. He says she's straight. He'll look after her."

"He'll find she's too straight for him."

"You should know.... What I've got to tell you first, and what you've got to believe, is that we don't know who killed Ringan or Ruscatti. We wish we did. It made hell of our plans, and it shows there's something going on that we don't know."

"Why's Maloon on that boat?"

"Because the bank president and his lawyer are on it, and I want them talked to on their way over.... The girl thinks it was you who cabled her to use it, or so Maloon says."

"So I did. But she got another cable in my name that I didn't send."

"I might ask why you told her that boat."

"That's soon said. I wanted her to come on a boat the boys weren't using. I wanted her out of something I didn't understand and that looked hot to me. Whoever sent the other one must have had a different idea."

"Maloon knows the boys. He'll have combed the boat before now. You can leave that to him."

"And Moll? Well, I guess I can trust her. Can you trust him?"

"There aren't many I do. But if you've got an idea that he was in the killing you can start thinking again. He and Ruscatti were getting off the boat at Southampton when Ringan felt a pain in his back. And he could have got rid of Ruscatti going across any day with half a dozen of his boys on board if he'd crooked a finger that way. And if he'd sent a radio on ahead, don't you think the British cops would have tumbled to that? Maloon says they're not half as dumb as they look to us.

"You've got to take it that Maloon can't find out what happened, and we can't, and the British cops are in the same hole. You've got a mouthful to swallow there."

"You're that sure of Maloon?"

"You're sure of Redhead? She was a lot nearer the corpse."

"I know Moll. She's tough, but she's no killer. Not even when it needs to be done. If it had been Nelson's Helen or Puss Ribet! But, besides that, she'd no cause, and when Ruscatti was bumped off she was in court. You can't hang it on her."

"I know that. And you can say Maloon's in the same boat."

"Then we count him out. And you might say it was someone to whom a knife came more natural than a gun. That would rule out Burke and Marlo and most of Moran's gang. It might be one of the St. Louis bunch."

"There isn't one of Moran's boys we haven't traced. They add up to the full figure. And Burke didn't go over. And Marlo was getting off his boat at Cherbourg. It's nothing easy like that.... But there's one line for you to pull in. You say Redhead's straight, and I'm not thinking you're wrong. But she wasn't far off. And she knows most of the boys. She'll talk when she gets to you. If she saw anything that she reckons she mustn't say, you can tell her that it wasn't done on any orders from me.

"I don't mean she's to tell the cops. I'm not that low. But she needn't keep quieter than that."

"That's what I've been fearing. I mean that she might know something, and there'd be those who'd think it best for her to be put quiet. But if you're sure that Slick wasn't in it at all, he'll be likely to see her through.... If it's cards up, what's he going to say to the bank president?"

"He's going to offer him a new deal. But that won't matter to you." Capone drew his wallet out as he spoke. He took ten thousand-dollar bills from a fat wad. He went on as he passed them over: "You can take this on account. You'll get every cent that's to come your way. But I'm looking to you and Redhead to help us find out what happened. Ringan was my man, and if one of my men gets a knife in his back I want to know why.... Now I've said my piece, and you'll have some dinner before you go."

CHAPTER XXIX.

FENCING WITH SLICK MALOON

WHILE Capone and Clancy talked, dusk had gathered in the skies under which the *Baltic* pursued the sunset. The swirl of water against the ship's counter could be heard rather than seen as Maloon and Moll O'Leary leaned on the rail and exchanged low-voiced conversation.

It was a position which Maloon had selected with care in the daylight hours. There was no porthole below into which sound might capriciously drift. No boat so near that a listener might be concealed within it. The officer, pacing the bridge above, was too distant for the wind to bear even clearly spoken words.

"If you can tell us who did it," Slick was saying, "Capone will be glad to know."

"You must have used that telephone a long while."

"Capone did. He's wild to know who cooked his goose. He can't think who, and he can't think why. If you know you'll be a wise baby to tell."

"Slick, I don't! I didn't see anyone, and I can't think how it was. From when I went it must have been almost no time at all. He must have gone up the other way, though Sir Crowe says he's sure he didn't."

"I expect Crowe's been wrong before now."

"I expect he must have been this time. Anyway, I can't say what I don't know."

"Sure you can't."

"I shouldn't be so scared if I knew who might think I do."

"You've no call to be scared. You're not a squealer. The boys know that."

"But if it wasn't one of them?"

"Then you can say he's a long way back now.... Sure, gorgeous, you're too good for Tim to—"

She interrupted sharply, pushing off a hand the fingers of which were pressing into her neck beneath the heavy fold of the fur coat she had drawn round her shoulders to meet the damp chill of the wind: "Don't, Slick. I'm too scared."

He withdrew his hand at once. No woman should be allowed to think she meant much to him. They should be possessed, when the time allowed, with such measure of force as their natures chose, or made jealous of one another, as it was so easy to do.

"I've told you you've no cause for that. And I wouldn't say you're one that's easy to scare. If you find Tim's washed out any time, you can come to me. I don't say I'd not do more for you than for most. It's a good offer, baby, to keep in mind, in a world where there's more sugar than spoons. Now there's that Crowe dame—"

"She wouldn't look at you. She's class."

"Wouldn't look at me? She's done that.... I'll tell you what, honey, you leave the bolt off your door tonight—"

"I shouldn't dare that, even if—"

"You pull that bolt back when you hear four taps, and I'll see Tim gets that two hundred grand. You'll be all the same to him, and he'll think all the more of you."

"Why don't you offer me something that's not Tim's already?"

"Well, sugar, I might do that. I pay cash. But it would be a lot less than two hundred grand."

"Yes," she said, with a hard laugh, "I expect it would.... But there's the bugle. You can talk about that at some other time, if you're not too busy with Lady Crowe."

The bugle signal that it was time to dress for dinner had come opportunely for her. She hated Slick, and the idea of serious infidelity to her irregular union with Tim Clancy did not enter her mind. But to keep Slick's goodwill might be much to her. She might at any moment be in deadly peril—even if she were not so already—at which he would be the only one to whom to appeal with confidence that he would have the power and understanding, if only he should have the goodwill, which the position would need. It was true that she had not seen Ringan's murderer enter or leave the bank premises. But she had seen a face she knew in the Cheapside crowd less than a quarter of an hour after. She had been in a taxi then, and was confident that she had not been seen. But she had a reason—conclusive to her—for believing that she knew who Ringan's murderer was. But that was no explanation of why that, or Ruscatti's murder, should have occurred, and she had resolved that, even to Slick Maloon, she would give no hint of what she knew. Tim should hear it and decide what should be done. But when those of the underworld observed that which they did not understand they found silence best. Those who did not believe this were soon bumped off, so that the opportunity for further error did not arise.... Now she had seen that face again, earlier in the day, as she leaned over the games-deck rail and looked down on the second-class passengers exercising on their narrower space below. Again, she thought, he had not seen her. But that he did not know she was on the boat—? That there was no relation between his presence and that sinisterly mysterious cable? Probabilities were in the opposite scale.

She went down to her cabin feeling that she had fenced well. To have refused Slick on the mere ground that his proposals were distasteful might have offended him, as she could not afford to do. He might even be led to wonder why she had flirted with him, as, though to no intimate degree, she certainly had. He might even make a guess sufficiently near the truth to be a danger to her. But to bargain high—to demand more than he would be willing to pay—he would understand that. And she knew well that he cared nothing for her. He cared for women, and to select among them, in his own way. But it was not that in which a wolf cares for its mate, but for the deer that it tears apart.... Slick went to his own cabin well content also. He thought that he had roused her jealousy of Lady Crowe, who was also of the list of those whom it would be a pleasure to have, and whom he was not without expectation to get. But he could bargain as well as they, and meanwhile there was a young Jewess of uncertain nationality in B17, at whose cabin he would not tap in vain, and whose price would be easy to pay, even if she would look for any at all.

Apart from that, he had other things on his mind of more importance than any dame was ever likely to be.

CHAPTER XXX.

Mrs. McClintock Suggests a Doubt

DINNER was a cheerful if not a lively meal. The fog having cleared, the captain headed the table, and that meant that there would be two or three amusing stories from him. Every good liner captain has a store of these—which need not be numerous, especially on the short transatlantic run. The only trouble comes when a passenger makes frequent voyages on the same boat, as few do. Barring the nightmare of such a man who must be placed without variation at the captain's table, a couple of dozen stories and reminiscences would be sufficient to last from first appointment to pension age.

Tonight he had tales of vessels he had commanded before he reached the dignity of the White Star Line. There was the time when he had run cargoes of Californian wine from Los Angeles to Bordeaux—cargoes that went in casks and returned in bottles bearing labels that told truly of the (last) country from which they came.... There was the cargo that he had taken to Stockholm in another vessel in 1916—a cargo that had not been landed but transhipped in the midnight hours. On the way back, with the Shetlands on his port bow, he had had the misfortune (as he thought at first) to be signalled by a British destroyer, but its anxiety had not been to inspect the dubious documents on which he relied, but to warn him of enemy mines ahead and guide him to safer seas.

The conversation drifted to the vexed question of war debts, which must be treated with delicacy at that international table, with whatever assurance of ignorance, greater or less, everyone might be willing to speak at another time. It was a man's table rather than a woman's, though the three women there were sufficiently different to divert the conversation at times in surprising ways.

Now the astronomer, who had a vague idea that when his country's armies left France they had left great stores behind which their mean-minded allies had taken over on credit at bargain prices which they had subsequently refused to pay, observed tolerantly that most people will do things when they are hard-up of which they would otherwise be ashamed, and he supposed that nations were much the same.

Mr. Jellipot, in a mist of modifying words, was understood to suggest that the problem of pouring a quart from a pint pot, even in its simplest form, will always remain unsolved, and that its difficulty was increased when there was insistence upon its effluent consisting of something which was not there.

Mr. Maloon had no sympathy for his own country. Why had it not taken pledges (such as Jamaica) from its allies? It had been a sucker, and suckers deserve that which will certainly be coming to them.

Sir Reginald, who understood something of the subject, was tempted to speak, but had the wit to realise that he was faced by a chasm of prejudiced ignorance that no words could bridge. He said: "Well, America got her own back, anyway, and a bit more, when she jockeyed us into coming back to the gold standard."

That was hardly fair; for the responsibility for that callous error rested, as he well knew, with the heads of the Bank of England, who were to remain in sinister control of the nation's financial policy for many subsequent years. But it is hard to be fair when bitter feeling feathers the shaft, and to consider the stranglehold on British trade which the money magnates had imposed for their short-sighted gain was impossible without contempt and anger stirring equally in his lively mind.

The remark reduced the table to momentary silence. Most of those present knew as much of the gold standard as of the problem of war-debt payments, being precisely nothing in both cases, but the difference was that they were more aware of ignorance on the one topic than the other.

Captain Holder, who had learnt the virtue of silence when the word "war-debts" was spoken at that table (as it always was during the latter part of a voyage, if not earlier), now said: "Perhaps the fact that England and America are the countries most interested in gold production may have had something to do with that."

It seemed an innocent remark, suggesting a community of interest, and some reason for that for which reason was hard to see, but Mrs. McClintock looked puzzled and then broke out with: "But you wouldn't call America a *country*? Not a *country*, would you?"

It was an exclamation which no one was quick to answer. A nation newly born, which is of all nationalities, which consists of many semi-independent states, and occupies a large part of the earth's surface to which it has failed to Give a corporate name, so that it speaks of itself in that of the continent to which it belongs, whose very language is not its own—can it be classed with lands of ancient and clearly bounded cultures?

Professor Palfrey, who studied Mrs. McClintock as a particularly curious specimen of the species to which he himself belonged, regarded her with mild interest, but was not moved to speech. His wife, an intelligent and intensely patriotic Rhode Islander (a word which was already becoming associated less with the human race than a new mongrel breed of domestic poultry), flushed angrily. She could not trust herself to speech, or she would have dearly liked to tell that intolerable woman where she got off.

Maloon looked as indifferent as he felt. It was a land where witnesses were jailed and criminals could buy bail. It was God's own country for him. But of nationality he had next to none.

Mr. Jellipot was characteristically more interested in the subject itself than concerned with the reactions of those around him. It was only when in court that he would be conscious of these, which was a trained, not a natural, aptitude. He found that the lady's most imbecile gaucheries were productive of thought. There was nothing which she could have said in the English tongue which would have roused him to wrath with her.

Sir Reginald broke that pause of shocked or puzzled silence. He said something about a country that was in the vigour of a great youth, and not expecting it to have the qualities which only age can provide, and felt that it was awkwardly put.

Evelyn did better than that. Her eyes met those of the professor's wife as she said: "I don't care what you call it, but I know it's going to be wonderful. I think America's about the best hope that the world has."

Captain Holder saw a chance that he must not miss. He had a stock joke that was sometimes a frost and sometimes went off very well indeed.

"There's one thing," he said, "that the Americans don't have to worry about. They can walk round their country at night without having to take care that they don't fall over the edge."

The jest roused no more than the perfunctory laughter that politeness required, but it closed the episode, and in the next moment Evelyn had asked the professor's wife if she would care for a game at bridge, which she said she would be glad to have.

More than once before either she or Maloon had been asked to join Sir Reginald's little party, and these were opportunities she did not refuse, for, though the stakes were rather high (for her), she would be the banker's partner, and she played with New England soundness, and he with a lively audacity which would have more than seldom success, so that she was already nearly nine dollars in hand, and thinking how the extra money could best be spent when she would be strolling up Fifth Avenue next Monday, as he was planning to do.

Maloon cared nothing for such stakes as the Crowes preferred. They cut for partners when he played with them. If he should partner Evelyn he would win, even if he had to use some sleight-of-hand to supplement the favours that fortune gave. With other partners he would be careless to lose or win, sometimes even dealing himself a purposely poor hand, that he might have something to overcome.

He was not chatty, but he was prone to occasional anecdote, and Sir Reginald's conversational style had the quality of making other men talk. Maloon's bridge companions learnt several things from him concerning the customs and laws of the country to which they went, such as the fact that you can kill a man in Michigan without danger of being either electrocuted or hanged, which it may be very useful to know.

He was inwardly annoyed on this occasion, for he had expected the invitation to come to him (had it not hitherto been alternately given?), and he had intended, when the last rubber should be done, to turn the conversation to other things. But he was not lightly turned from any purpose on which his mind had become set. He said: "Perhaps we could have a talk later in the evening, before you turn in."

Sir Reginald was ready in his response: "Yes, about ten-thirty. That suit you, Jellipot?"

Mr. Jellipot said that it would be agreeable to him, and Maloon said it would suit him fine.

CHAPTER XXXI.

Maloon Offers a Friendly Deal

SIR REGINALD added the score. Mr. Jellipot paid him with ready precision. He was one who always had the correct change. Evelyn paid Mrs. Palfrey, after exploring her bag to its lowest corner for some odd cents that the occasion required. Mrs. Palfrey rose with the satisfactory knowledge that the nine dollars had become twelve-fifty and an odd dime. She said good-night.

Evelyn glanced at the clock. It was ten-twenty-five. She said: "I suppose you thinking I'd better go."

Sir Reginald said: "Nonsense, Evelyn. You don't need to go at this hour."

"I don't see," she said, "why you should mind. You can be as late as you like without fear of disturbing me."

She still kept to the separate cabin which she had selected as far from that which he occupied as the accommodation of the ship rendered it possible, without discomfort, to do. Had not Reggie shown his willingness, even his preference, for travelling alone? Is it not elementary diplomacy to show a sense of grievance towards those who may otherwise think that the boot is high up on the other leg? The trouble was that Reggie took it in such a casual manner. (Slick Maloon had observed it, and if his deduction was abysmal in its depth of error, he can hardly be blamed for that.)

Sir Reginald said: "Evelyn, don't be such an absolute pig. You can go to bed at any hour that you like, but you're either in this thing or you're not. If you are you'd better hear what Maloon's going to say."

"He mayn't want me here."

"Of course he will. He's got his eyes on you half the mealtimes more often than not. He'll probably sulk if you're not here."

"You know you're talking nonsense. Women and business are miles apart in his mind."

"You're talking nonsense yourself now. Women are in his business just as much as the men. Look at the O'Leary girl. And you heard him say that one of their worst killers—Baby-Face Nelson or something like that—has a wife who's a lot worse than he. If he won't talk with you here, he can shut up."

"I don't say he'd do that. But if he's interesting we shall want talk it over after, and it will make us so late—"

"We needn't stay up for that." Their eyes met, and which of them was the first to yield would be a dispute which would last for long years to come. But it was Evelyn who said: "Well, of course, if you're so keen on my being here"—and then hesitated again. She must give up her two-mile walk round the deck, and to a girl who had a tendency to put on weight, and who was resolved that she *would not* get fat, and who was now debarred from the horse exercise on which she relied, it was a sacrifice not to be lightly made. So she said; but Sir Reginald had an answer even for that.

"You're forgetting that every day's twenty-five hours long, and we don't get fed for that extra hour. The doctor tells me that the crews of these boats are two tons lighter at New York than their Liverpool weight, but they make up for it during the twenty-three-hour days on the way back. They go on all their lives taking off weight and putting it back again about once a month in that way, and when the time comes for them to retire he has to tell them to get off at Liverpool or New York according to what diseases they'd be more likely to get.... He says that if the boat went sailing west without turning, by when it had been seven times round the world they would have disappeared altogether. That's a mathematical certainty, not a joke."

Evelyn laughed. "I believe you've made it all up. He doesn't look at all the kind of doctor who would talk nonsense like that. But if it's true we'd better go back the Pacific way; and if you'll promise that, I don't mind—"

"We'll talk about that another time. Here's Maloon coming now.

Evelyn sat down, and Mr. Jellipot's cigar pointed Slick to the vacant chair at her side.

If he were surprised at her continued presence, he gave no sign. He said, with the directness of approach which, whether it were used to guide aright or to lead astray, appeared to be common among these lawless, blood-guilty men: "I don't want you to get me wrong, but we want a seat in your show. We've bought a few shares."

Sir Reginald gave no sign of his thoughts. He said evenly: "Everyone has a right to do that, so long as there are any to be had on the market. How many have you got?"

"Up to yesterday noon—I haven't heard anything today— they'd got twenty-seven thousand in London. I don't know what they've done in N'York."

"May I ask the average price you have paid?"

"About thirty-six or a bit more."

"Dollars?"

"Yep. I can't think in pounds."

"It is a substantial investment."

"It's not much to what we're laid out to do. Seventy-five million bucks wouldn't buy Capone's business alone. You don't need to talk chicken feed when you do business with us."

"What business exactly, do you wish to do with me?"

"We want a bank in your country. One with more class than the one-horse show in Texas that's been dealing with you. And we want you to run it. You know the ropes, and we don't. And you've got more go than most Britishers have."

"It is an interesting Proposition. Would there be anything in the proposed policy of the bank that I ought to know before going further in its discussion?"

"There'd be no call to shy.... We don't want you to get us wrong. We know there've been two of our men bumped off on your mat, and you may owe us a grudge for that. But it was no doing of ours. We don't say that we don't have to take someone for a ride now and then. It's the only law that we've got. But we don't kill anyone who's worth keeping alive. It's like Uncle Sam giving someone the hot seat, as he often does."

"It is an arguable proposition. But you would not propose to introduce the bumping-off policy into the operations of the bank in our country?"

Slick took the question seriously, but was brusque in its dismissal. "Nope. We're business men. There's nothing loony about this. It's been thought out. We want law where out money lies. And your country's too small to move. There's no room to run. There's not a hide-out the cops couldn't find in something under a week."

"It is a very reasonable view to take. And you would like me to continue to manage the bank which you would control?"

"Sure we should. We've got to stay put. And Capone says you're the man. He liked what you said about killings. You've got sense, and you've got class, and you've got go. And a Britisher's what we've got to have. We can see that."

"There are American banks which have branches in London which are controlled by citizens of your country."

"Sure there are. But Al wants something better than that."

"Yes. He may have good reasons.... You know why I am on the way to New York and perhaps to Chicago now?"

"You mean to show that it wasn't your bank that bumped Ringan off"

"I mean to find out who did, and hand him over to the police. Would you help me in that?"

"We don't work with the cops. And Al says it wasn't on his orders, and he can't find who did it. That's something fresh on him. There isn't much that they won't bring to him. If you can put him wise he'll leave that to you. You can't ask more than that."

"Perhaps not. Nor less.... Jellipot, what do you think of this?"

To this point neither Evelyn nor Mr. Jellipot had spoken, being content to listen to the quick duel of words between the banker of the old and the gangster of the younger world, neither of whom may have been entirely typical of their country or class; but, for that matter, who is?

Mr. Jellipot was not unready but deliberate in his reply: "It is a proposal of a most interesting and, I may add, to me, of a most unexpected nature. It deserves—I may say it requires—consideration from several angles. May I suggest that we should adjourn the discussion at this point, to be resumed here tomorrow night?"

"That's O.K. by me. Have a drink on it?"

The invitation being declined on the double grounds of the lateness of the hour and refreshments already taken, Mr. Maloon went off to the bar alone, and Evelyn rose with the words: "Well, you can't say he hasn't given you what he'd call a mouthful now! You'd better come to my cabin talk it over where you won't be overheard."

"I think," Sir Reginald replied, "that my cabin will be much better for that, if Jellipot will be good enough to join us there."

This was reasonable, as Evelyn had sufficient sense to see without further words, for her cabin was such that there were times when she could hear voices from either side, and Sir Reginald had a private bathroom on one side and Mr. Jellipot's cabin on the other. She said: "Then I'll be with you in three minutes." And it is simple justice to her to record that she was scarcely more than fifteen.

CHAPTER XXXII.

IN SIR REGINALD'S CABIN

EVELYN entered the cabin with a suitcase in her hand which did not appear to be essential to the discussion to which she came, but Reggie, whatever he may have observed, took no notice of that.

The best of the *Baltic* cabins were not very large, but two-thirds of them were unoccupied during the autumns of that period, and Mr. Jellipot had had no difficulty in securing the exclusive use of the two best that the boat contained. Had he been more conversant with the conditions that then controlled North Atlantic traffic, or of a hard-bargaining kind, he would have taken the cheapest cabins in that section of the ship, complained to the purser that they were unsuitable on going aboard, and given him a pound note to transfer them to better accommodation without further payment. Such bargains were made at that time on every voyage on every boat, and the owners winked at them, preferring that they should have their best cabins occupied. They were the logical consequence of an international racket which held up fares and cultivated competition in other forms; and should the ring be reconstructed under any future circumstances, they will doubtless happen again.

Now Sir Reginald and Mr. Jellipot sat at a small table to which a third chair had been brought from the next cabin, and Evelyn had scarcely settled herself into its moderate comfort before Sir Reginald, who may have desired her presence there for other reasons rather than to assist at the financial discussion to which she came, brought her directly into the conversation.

"Look here, Evelyn, we're in a jam. How long do you think Cyril could hold out if he were offered more than his shares are worth?"

"How much more do you mean?"

"I don't know. On what Maloon said, they've risen more than twenty percent since we left England. I don't say they're not good shares, but they're not worth that, and I expect they've rocketed up further today."

"You'd better radio him not to sell."

"I did that before I came down. But it's asking a lot. And I daren't say much. The way Maloon tips, there isn't much that isn't open to him."

"You think he'll learn you've sent the message?"

"The way it's worded I don't care if he does. But Britleigh isn't an ass. He'll see what I mean, knowing all he already does."

"No. Cyril isn't an ass. Not in business matters. But you do give him some headaches! I believe I've said that before.... I thought you controlled enough shares to vote yourself what you like."

"I do if I have your brother's support. I've always counted on that. I do without him—just about—if he stands aside. If his shares could be used against me I'd have to dance to Capone's tune or stop dancing in Lombard Street till I'd got hold of another bank."

"I don't think Cyril will let you down."

"He won't if he knows. The proper game is to sell them every share we can without losing control, at the highest price we can make them pay.... But we'd need to be in England to handle that properly. Jellipot thinks we're in the soup. He says Maloon wouldn't have let anything out till he felt safe."

"It is a reasonable supposition," Mr. Jellipot said, "though we must hope it may be wrong.

"Oh, I don't know!" Evelyn said more hopefully. "They want you as well as the bank, and they think they can buy both. People often go wrong when they're too sure."

"Well, we can't risk anything more, whether Maloon tumbles to it or not. It must be four-thirty in London now. I'll tell you what, Evelyn, you'd better radio Menzies to buy for you. There may be some stray shares knocking about yet, and the more brokers we get on the job the better. Tell him to pay cash or do anything short of murder to get the scrip. There'll be some selling short for a sure guess, and that wouldn't be much good to us. "I think you'd better write that."

"So I will. It can go in a code which it's about forty to one that Maloon won't be slick enough to read if he should get a sight. And you might do the same, Jellipot, with your broker, and when we get them off our minds we'll all get some sleep and then think out what to do with Maloon tomorrow."

He spoke with his usual decisive energy, but when the radiograms had been despatched, and Mr. Jellipot had retired to his own cabin, he muttered something which caused Evelyn to say: "Reggie, you seem a lot more worried about this than when heaps of people thought you'd be lucky if you got off with fifteen years' hard. Is that how you really feel?"

"How should you feel if you thought you might have to go to bed with a rattlesnake or lie out on the cold floor?"

"A lot worse than I do now," Evelyn replied truthfully; and after that their conversation was of more importance to themselves than it is ever likely to be to us.

CHAPTER XXXIII.

FRIENDS?

"HULLO, Tim," Miss O'Leary's shrill voice sounded cheerfully over the hubbub as Clancy pushed his way across the gangway to the deck of the *Baltic* that lay in the closing dusk along Boston pier.

"Hullo to you," came back, with equal cheerfulness, from the stocky figure of the retired bank robber. Next minute he was at her side, and with no further greeting, but a measure of understanding and mutual confidence which many married couples of exemplary respectability will never reach, she led him to the smoking-room, found a corner which, at a time when most of the passengers were on deck, was sufficiently deserted for privacy, ordered drinks, and was quickly exchanging ideas and information upon the subject which occupied both their minds. "You're coming on to N'York?"

"Yep. Or we'll go by train if you say the word. You'd have about two hours to get off the boat."

"Not for me. Not without you've got more reason than I should know. What set you to come here?"

"I flew from Chicago this morning. Capone called me there."

"He'd a nerve. And so'd you to go. How'd you get on with him?"

"Swell, if it's a straight deal."

"And you're not that sure? Tim, there's something queer going on that I don't like."

"You know something you're scared to say?"

"I do that.... I've told no one yet.... But it doesn't make sense.... I thought I'd wait and tell you."

"Sure you can."

"Tim, you remember Cassidy? Him that was at Toscatti's the night that—"

"You don't mean that Boston cop?"

"That's him. He got off this boat when it tied up today."

"So he would."

"Yep. But what's he been doing? When I left the bank I saw him in the street near. It wasn't half an hour after the time Ringan must have been knifed."

"He saw you?"

"I'd say not. I was in a car."

"Then I don't see—"

"Tim, think! You remember that faro game? And how Ringan lost, and Jake Flannigan had his knife, and how he said it was lost when the cops came, and we know Cassidy picked it up? And then that cable to me to come on this boat, and there's Cassidy too?"

"Yep. It adds up. Cassidy said much to you?"

"Nope. He came second. I saw him once, and I saw him get off the boat. But I don't say that he saw me."

"Anyway, you've come safe."

"I have that. Would you say something changed their plans?"

"There's been some changing of plans. Capone's told me that. He wants us to pull in with him. He says he knows no more than we, and he won't lie down till he does. You've got something we might sell, but I'm not that sure.... Here's Maloon coming.... Been friendly with him?"

"Till he tried getting fresh. But we haven't split. He's in with— I'll tell you another time."

Tim had barely time to say, "Don't let on you know anything now," before Maloon saw him and approached with an aspect of as much affability as his countenance was adapted to show.

"Brought her back safe," he said, as though he might have earned personal thanks for that, as perhaps he had. "How's it with you?"

"Fine. Sit down and have one with us."

"Coming on to N'York?"

"Yep."

"Seen Capone?"

"Yep."

"All set for a new deal?"

"Yep."

"Know what we're doing to get a hold on the British bank?"

"Nope. Al said you'd put me wise about that."

"Got a guess who bumped Ringan off?"

"Nope. But I told Al I'd have a look round. Only left Chicago today."

"I've got Crowe and his dame on the hook. You'd better sit in with us."

Tim looked at Miss O'Leary in doubt of exactly what this proposition was, or how it should be received. She, knowing that Professor Palfrey and his wife had left the boat, and that there would be two places vacant at the captain's table, was quick-witted enough to see what was proposed, but in no greater certainty of how it should be received.

"Slick," she explained, "is at the captain's table, and two of those who were there have gone off. You couldn't sit with me unless I change somewhere. My table's still full. Lady Crowe and Sir Reginald and his attorney are at the same table as Slick."

"I wouldn't ask that," Tim said doubtfully.

"You won't need," Slick answered; "you'll find it's fixed." He was not averse from showing them how easily such things could be arranged now that they were understood to be in the same boat as the major gangsters. He knew that it might have been impossible on one of the luxury boats, where there might be men and women of artistic, social, or political eminence too numerous for the seats of honour which a harassed purser must distribute as best he could.... But even in them, during these days of gathering financial clouds, had there not been one recent voyage of the *Berengaria* from New York when there had been only a few dozen first-class passengers, and among these bootleggers, hijackers, and other species of racketeers in so large a majority that a frightened lady with a small child had asked to be transferred to the second class?

Slick strolled off to see the dining-room steward, and found no difficulty in arranging that which might have been done without the five-dollar bill which he considered the occasion required. There was little formality during the last twenty-four hours of the nine-day voyage.

Some had gone ashore. Others had joined the boat for the last lap of the voyage. The captain would not come down again, his place being on the bridge till he should see the hawsers cast and the *Baltic* docked at Manhattan pier. There would be the bustle of packing, the thronged rails of the upper decks as people watched the low line of Long Island shore—the crowded shipping—the long, slow channel approach—Ellis Island—the Statue of Liberty—the world-famous skyline of the capital city, though not the capital, of the first power of the Western world. Even the stewards' minds would be divided between the prospect of getting ashore and the tips which they hoped to receive. In the dining-room people might sit very much where they would, providing that it were an unclaimed place.

Miss O'Leary watched Slick stroll off with uncertain eyes. "He means it friendly to us," she said, "but I don't know. I hope he won't slip, thinking that I'm Miss O'Leary on this boat. That goes for you, Tim, as well."

She remembered, as she spoke, that she had told Sir Reginald that he should call her by a different name. Curse passports! And which of her sufficiently numerous and expensive dresses would it be best to wear? But Tim was speaking.

"What say? Oh, the banker! They're class, Lady Crowe and he. He's a swell guy. Wouldn't tell the cops I'd been round when Tony was bumped off. We owe him something for that."

"Sure we do. But what kind of a guy is he? Will he sell out to Capone or go in with him?"

"Search me, Tim! These Britishers have me beat. You think they're asleep, and then you find that they've got hold, and they won't let go. Not that Sir Crowe's asleep. He's a live wire...in with Al? He'd just call him dirt. But he's come over to find who had the nerve to kill men in his bank, and if that's what Capone wants to know, they're after the same thing."

"And you're the one that can put them wise? It sounds bully for us."

"It sounds more like bullets to me. I don't like what I can't figure out. Tim, I'm scared. More scared than I was when Barker tried to sell us out to the cops."

"Take it easy, kid. If there are bullets going about, there'll be some coming out of my gun. But we'll sit in with these guys tonight and get wise. If I don't open out, you'll keep mum."

CHAPTER XXXIV.

MR. JELLIPOT IS TO TALK TONIGHT

SIR REGINALD CROWE did not disguise the fact that he was a worried man.

A number of years earlier he had gained control of the London and Northern Bank by a bold and unexpected Stock Exchange operation, in which he had had the essential assistance of Lord Britleigh's substantial wealth. That was before he married Evelyn Merivale, and their association had been entirely a business one. It had been satisfactory to Lord Britleigh (who put business before most, if not all, the activities and relations of earthly life), as had been the continued and closer bonds, both business and social, of later years. Evelyn's brother was a man of good reputation and unquestioned honour. He had stood by the bank during the past month when some would have hesitated or refused. Sir Reginald recognised this, but he knew Lord Britleigh to be one who took the less or risking of money very seriously indeed. And he was one who hesitated—and fussed. When Evelyn said that Sir Reginald's methods gave headaches to her less audacious brother she had not overstated the case.

Sir Reginald's first motive for gaining control of the voting power of the bank had been no more than to have the satisfaction of dismissing a bank manager whose conduct had caused him annoyance; its result had been to move him from Lancashire to London, from the commercial to the financial world.

Now he was threatened with the weapon he had used, and to a somewhat similar purpose, and his security depended upon Lord Britleigh's action—or rather inaction—under circumstances which he would not fully understand, and without either Mr. Jellipot or himself being on the scene to give guiding counsel.

To gain voting control of a large bank or insurance company, with all that it might imply, may not be easy—may, indeed, in the majority of cases be impossible—but that is not because the amount involved is beyond the wealth which will be in the hands of a few or one. Many such corporations have an original share capital grotesquely small in proportion to their resources and operations, and the bulk of that capital may be uncalled, so that it will not figure in the purchase price of the shares. A mere fraction of the wealth of the racketeers of Chicago and New York—say nothing of other centres of operation, such as St. Louis or Maloon's native Detroit—judiciously applied would be sufficient to acquire a majority of the shares of the London and Northern at the price at which they had been quietly and occasionally changing hands on the London Exchange—if they were there to be had. What would happen now that unrestricted buying orders had sent their price skyward to twenty or thirty percent beyond their normal value? What would Lord Britleigh have done?

There was an end to Sir Reginald's doubts, though not to his anxiety, when he received and decoded this radiogram:

MARKET WENT MAD STOP HAVE SOLD JUDI-
CIOUSLY STOP SHALL BUY BACK ON INEVI-
TABLE RELAPSE STOP BRITLEIGH.

"It was," Mr. Jellipot conceded, "a natural course for him to take."

"Think so?" Sir Reginald retorted, with less than his habitual self-control. "Then perhaps you'll say what it's natural for him to be doing today."

Mr. Jellipot, being unused to giving unconsidered opinions, pondered this problem in silence, and Sir Reginald broke out again: "I don't suppose it'll do any good now, but I've got to send him something he'll understand. How will this do? 'You won't get them back. Capone's buying. What price licking his boots?'"

"I think," Mr. Jellipot replied, "it may not be easy to codify."

"I'll do that, or I'll send it plain."

"Then we must see what the code will do."

The difficulty of "licking his boots" in a phrase code which did not include that picturesque metaphor having been partially overcome, and there being nothing more to do on the London arena but to await the result of a battle they could not share, Sir Reginald's thoughts turned to the more local issue of what was to be said to Maloon, and his decision went no further than to recognise the advantages of maintaining a neutral attitude till he knew more of what was happening in both hemispheres.

"I'm going to leave the talking to you tonight, Jellipot. I can't do it without telling lies or saying something I mean. I never knew anyone who could say more than you without anyone being able to tell whether it means anything, or what it is if it does."

Mr. Jellipot showed no resentment at this dubious appraisement of his conversational powers, though his reply did not accept it without demur.

"The theory of—was it Talleyrand? I am unsure—that the use of language is to conceal thought is not one that I admire or have sought to practise at any time. But it is a fact which I have had occasion to observe, while it is one over which I have, of course, no control, that the more precisely a statement be made, the more vaguely it will be received, and it is at least equally so that when the truth is stated with the most scrupulous accuracy it is most open to misconstruction or unbelief."

"Good old Jellipot! That's the stuff to give him," Sir Reginald returned, with some recovery of his normal buoyancy. "We're not dead yet. And I wouldn't say that whoever killed Ringan has got much longer to live. He doesn't seem to have many friends."

At this point Mr. Jellipot excused himself on the ground that his own simple packing required attention, and it was at the dinner-table that they next met. In the interval he had devoted much thought, though he would readily have allowed that it was of a fruitless kind, to Sir Reginald's last words. *He doesn't seem to have many friends.* He recalled Miss O'Leary's boast—or at least assertion—of the immunity enjoyed by the gangster killers of the country to which they came. They had behind them the resources, the organisation, above all the invincible silence of the gangs. That was against the constituted authority of the law. But the killer of Ringan and Ruscatti had—or seemed to have—no such protection. No one would own him. No one would admit knowledge of who he was. That might mean little if it went no further. But they professed to be anxious and active to hunt him down. Capone, in Chicago, was marshalling his forces for discovery of the man who had upset his plans and brought them into disastrous publicity. Maloon, understood to be the leading gangster of Detroit, was leagued with him on that issue. Miss O'Leary, so far as she could be considered to represent the criminal elements of New York (on which point he had little competence to judge), was emphatic that the man was no friend of hers. If she knew him (as he thought she did) she did not recognise him as one whom Capone or Maloon had instigated or would befriend, though he might, on other grounds, be a danger to her.

Outcast from or unrecognised by the criminal world, sought by the police of two continents, and with Sir Reginald as an impetuous but persistent amateur on his track, he might indeed be considered a risk which no life office would be prudent to take. But Mr. Jellipot was least interested in that aspect of the matter. He felt that, if the man could be identified and his motives probed, it might be an explosive event which would free them from a net he was unsure that they would otherwise have the strength to break.

It was in vain theorising, born of such thoughts as these, that he spent the short time that still remained before the second dinner bugle sounded along the gangways. He went to the dining room with no thought that there would be any immediate call upon his smoke-screen of words, for he had correctly understood Sir Reginald to refer to the later appointment with Maloon alone, but when he saw that Miss O'Leary and a stranger were at the table he became aware of the possible imminence of the part which he would be expected to play.

CHAPTER XXXV.

LAST NIGHT ON THE *BALTIC*

MRS. McCLINTOCK was the last to sit down at a table which became full on her arrival, excepting only the captain's chair. She looked sideways at the stranger at her left hand, and then across to Evelyn, and it was clear that she did not approve. Evelyn's eyes were irresponsive. She liked Miss O'Leary (with reservations) and was interested in her irregular partner in semi-matrimony and crime. Mrs. McClintock had met Redhead in the drawing-room and on deck, and had heard language from her which she did not approve.

Clancy said, "Good evening, ma'am," as good Montana manners required, and received an icy response. Maloon had already introduced the newcomer to Mr. Jellipot and the Crowes. Regarding Mrs. McClintock as negligible, he looked round upon his five dinner companions as at a team he would assemble and direct. He was sure of himself, being the only one of the six who had, or represented, constructive plans which he had no cause to conceal. The others were warily alert, on defensives they did not wish to betray.

English people in such an atmosphere, even though of some established familiarity, have one topic on which their first exchanges will invariably be made. Evelyn, looking across at Miss O'Leary, remarked on the bleakness of the wind that had met them on Boston pier and the fine powder of early snow that had whitened the roofs of the custom-house sheds.

Miss O'Leary said: "Guess it seemed cold to you. It wouldn't cut much ice with us here."

They were now moving again, and would soon be clear of the harbour mouth and heading eastward for open sea, with Cape Cod on the weather bow, but the brief call at Boston had given the Americans a sense of being at home again, and of the English that they had become visitors, though they were still on an English boat.

Miss O'Leary's remark, by a simple association of ideas, reminded Clancy of some episode of earlier days. "I've known us," he said, "to have to cut the ice with a pick before we could get any water into the coffee-pot.... That was the Montana way. There's real cold there that follows the fall."

Mr. Jellipot was not so deeply intrigued by the weird pronunciation of water, or a momentary misconception that the Montana cold had resulted from the deplorable conduct of Adam's wife, as to fail to observe the haste with which Miss O'Leary interrupted. Evidently she distrusted the direction in which the ex-banker-robber's recollections might wander, in their association with crime or her. She said quickly: "I guess you Britishers might feel the cold less if you got your rooms warmer.... Tim, they like to freeze all the year through.... Not that England's cold. It wasn't the days I've been there. I'd say they don't know what cold is. It's just green and wet."

Here was a safe and natural direction for the conversation to take! Mr. Jellipot asked: "You consider the American climate to be better than ours?"

"The English climate," Mrs. McClintock interposed, in a tone of decision, "is the best in the world. Everyone knows that."

"You don't say!" Miss O'Leary responded, not as contradicting, but as one informed of a surprising fact. "Now, I wouldn't have known."

"America's a large country," Sir Reginald said obviously. "There must be a great variety in its climatic conditions."

It was a subject on which the three Americans present were particularly competent witnesses. They knew it, one or other, from Florida to Oregon, from Michigan to Texas. But it seemed that a perfect climate was as hard to find as a perfect wife. At chosen moments you might flirt with any and find it fair. It was a case of—

> Light love stands clear of thunder,
> And safe from storms at sea.

But to dwell with them all the year was to learn that they could not be always or completely kind. Even California of the clear sunshine and the cool nights had its coastline mists. (Fogs in the American tongue.) Miss O'Leary admitted that the summer heat of Texas was at times excessive. She said to Sir Reginald: "You'll be going Texas way?"

It was a natural presumption. Would he not be likely to visit the bankers who had placed in his hands the huge fund from which all this trouble came? But Sir Reginald was aware that Maloon had become watchful for his reply.

"I don't know," he said vaguely, "how much I shall have time to do. I would go over the whole country if there were time."

Miss O'Leary seemed unconscious of his reply. Her eyes had become distant and hard. The question had taken her thoughts back to her own home—a ranch not a hundred miles from Dallas, where there lived a father who would have no welcome for her. She remembered his last letter, stern and sad, with references to Hebrew texts which she had not looked up, expecting that they would not be complimentary either to Tim or herself, or their highly probable ends. Well, you must do as your nature leads! She had longed to go places from the earliest childhood years as she had gazed at the treeless horizon of her upland world, and the longing had led her here. She had had some fun. She would not whine at the price. And she was loyal to Tim, as he to her. There was some honour in that, in a life in which honour was not otherwise easy to see.

She felt this, rather than thought. Subjective thought rarely troubled her mind. And the feeling did not obscure her consciousness of Slick's remark: "You'll be for Chicago first?"

It was not an order. That would have been an absurd construction to place upon it. Neither was it a question. Neither was it a mere mentioning of something already known. But it was compounded of all the three. Subtly it conveyed the impression of an understanding between Sir Reginald and himself, and one in which he was a controlling partner. She became curious and alert. She was aware, without word or sign, that Tim recognised it in the same way.

So did Sir Reginald. It would be too much to say that Maloon had flicked the whip. He had merely drawn the lash through his finger in a casual gesture. Sir Reginald turned his eyes directly upon him. His voice was level and pleasant as he answered have not yet decided what I shall do." But it had been an encounter of which all, unless it were Mrs. McClintock, whose eyes were on the pear she was peeling, had been conscious. It was as though Sir Reginald had placed his hand on a weapon that was still sheathed.

And after that there was silence while the words "and all talk died" came with a haunting threat into Evelyn's mind. Where did they come from? Oh, she remembered now!

> And all talk died, as in a grove all song
> Beneath the shadow of a bird of prey.

They were inopportune words to remember now. And it v as the second time today! In the afternoon, as she had looked out from the rail of the docked ship, she had thought idly:

Oh, once we ha' met at Baltimore, and twice on Boston pier,

and had driven the line fretfully from her mind because of the ill omen of the one that followed. Damn all poetry! "Yes, it's always strawberry for me. You never forget anything," she smiled at the gratified steward.... "I suppose," she said to Miss O'Leary, "you'll be able to get plenty of ices now?"

Miss O'Leary said she sure would, and she'd be that glad! But the table fell to silence again....

It may have been merely because Mrs. Palfrey had ceased to be a possible alternative that Maloon assumed that there would be a place at the bridge table for him, but he went further than that when he said to Tim and his companion, as the long, leisurely meal concluded and they rose to leave a fast-emptying room: "We'll be having bridge in the lounge. How'd one of you like to be cutting in?"

Tim said: "Suit me fine." And as Miss O'Leary, who had a better knowledge of the position, ignored the invitation, Evelyn addressed her directly: "Yes, please do, if you'd like it. It's another girl that we really need."

Out of the hearing of others, Sir Reginald said: "Good for you, Evelyn. We don't need to make the Clancys stand off because that foul swine's pushing his snout into the game."

"Well, we've asked him some other nights," Evelyn said equably.

"That's the difference. We didn't ask him tonight. He needs drowning, if any water could be found dirty enough for the job. I hope he comes to a quick end, and that the man who bumps him off gets what he deserves. I couldn't wish him anything better than that."

"In fact," she agreed, "you couldn't have a better illustration of the theory which brought us into this mess. Why not do a lecture tour, with him in a cage as an exhibit? 'Murders That Save the State,' or something like that?"

"That's a sound idea, and one that ought to please everybody, including the cops. But I can't joke about this till I know how big a mess Britleigh's made."

"I'm sorry. What do you want me to do tonight?"

"I asked Jellipot to cover everything up in one of his best fogs. But I've altered my mind. I want to draw Maloon out and see how far the other two back him up.... Suppose you ask him a few straight questions. Let's hear about murders from his angle instead of mine. It'll come best from you."

"Very well. That sounds easy enough."

CHAPTER XXXVI.

LAST NIGHT ON THE *BALTIC* II

IT was half an hour later that the Crowes caught up Mr. Jellipot as they made their way to the lounge. Sir Reginald said: "There'll be no need for you to let off your guns tonight. I've given Evelyn the deck. She's to draw Maloon out as to what his business ethics and practices really are, and we'll be better able to judge what the next chairman of the London and Northern will be likely to be expected to do."

Mr. Jellipot looked dubious. There was more than one ground on which he thought it to be inexpedient, but there was no opportunity for discussion, and Evelyn was on the stair above. He said: "I am sure that Lady Crowe will handle Maloon." His doubts did not arise from any lack of confidence in her coolness or verbal skill....

They cut for partners, and Evelyn found that Slick was opposite to her. She found herself winner of the first rubber in two hands, the first of which was played by Slick and was fairly fought. The second was on Slick's deal. He passed, as did Jellipot on his left. Evelyn gazed at her hand in wonder and bid three spades. Sir Reginald had a moment of consideration and said: "Four diamonds." Slick passed again. Mr. Jellipot, without hesitation, said: "Six diamonds." Evelyn, having had no support from her partner, might well have declined to go further, but after a mere ten seconds of reflection she said: "Seven no trumps."

Mr. Jellipot led the king of diamonds. Slick laid down his hand. It contained no diamonds, and there was no card of any suit over an eight. Evelyn took from it the first card that came. There would be no leading into that hand. Sir Reginald played the two, and she put down the ace. It was the only diamond she had.

But there was no cause for worry in that. She took the next five tricks in spades, and then three in hearts, and four in clubs from her own hand.

After that Miss O'Leary cut in, taking Mr. Jellipot's place. The rubber was longer, but the winners were the same as before. Again, when Slick dealt, Evelyn had all the cards. Mr. Jellipot, watching with quiet intentness, owned to himself that he was baffled by Slick's careless-seeming skill. But there was no doubt that Slick was playing with his opponents in more senses than one.

At the end of that rubber Slick said: "Had enough? We shan't want to be late tonight."

Miss O'Leary, who had paid her loss without showing consciousness of the kind of game it had been, said "Enough for me. I'm getting low in small bills."

Maloon said genially: "Never mind, kid. You'll get it another day. The drinks are on me."

What he had won could have meant nothing to him. It was a demonstration of the experiences which his partners or opponents could expect to have.

Sir Reginald said: "Would you like a game, Mr. Clancy?"

Tim said he wasn't all that keen.

Sir Reginald said: "I believe Mr. Maloon is anxious for a talk before we turn in."

Tim said that was O.K. by him. Miss O'Leary, a refilled glass in her hand, rose to go, and Tim followed her cue.

Maloon waved them down. "We're all friends here," he said. "Let's see where we can get."

Sir Reginald had certainly changed his mind since he had suggested the smoke-screen tactics which he thought that Jellipot was most competent to conduct. His naturally combative nature was asserting itself against the provocation he had received. He said: "Mr. Maloon and his friends are buying up the London and Northern Bank, I expect he's going to tell us how it's going to be conducted in future."

Miss O'Leary looked an incredulous query at Maloon.

Clancy said: "Say, that's a big bite!" His eyes moved between Crowe and Maloon, wondering whether Sir Reginald had been bought. Had he been induced to sell out to Capone? Perhaps to betray his own shareholders? Or was there hostility under his level voice? He was inclined to the latter conclusion, though these Britishers were not easy to read. Anyway, what was the game?

Sir Reginald thought he had learnt one thing already—that Clancy and the girl had not previously been in Maloon's confidence. There might be little in that.

Evelyn, watching for her opportunity to break into the conversation, said: "I wish you'd tell us, Mr. Maloon, just how your friends make such piles of dollars; and how we could start doing it on our side?"

Maloon had no intention of being rude to her. When he had made her husband a sucker, or when—as was likely enough in the next week—he had been bumped off, there was something interesting to be said to her. Yet his reply was short: "You've not got prohibition there."

"Yes, I understand that," she answered, with innocently enquiring eyes, "but it isn't only the drink I mean. I've heard you have all sorts of good rackets. About taxi-cabs and trade protections and on the docks—I don't understand that at all—and—and in all sorts of ways."

"It's organisation," he said briefly.

"I understand that. But couldn't we do the same?"

Maloon looked at her doubtfully. From one of the others he would have taken the questions differently, but from her—for all his slickness he was unsure. And was it, in itself, a serious proposition? England was a rich country. And English people are thick-witted. Everyone knows that. Honestly, he was unsure.

"It's a big thing to start," he said cautiously. "It's not safe in a small way. You've got to have enough money to square the cops and some of the judges, and if you can get the district attorney it saves a lot of trouble all round."

"I'm sure it must. But why should the police want to interfere?"

"They want to get bought *off*, don't they? I wouldn't blame them if they stopped there." He looked round at the little audience who were listening in silent intentness, and he became serious in explanation.

"Take the cabs. Larry Fay in N'York. He's made a good business of that. He's got the best cabs, and he ought to have the best stands, oughtn't he?"

"It sounds reasonable. And I suppose, if other drivers come on to the best stands, they have to be beaten up or something like that?"

"There oughtn't to be any call for that. Larry's reasonable enough. They've only got to pay his commission to him."

Clancy interposed a comparative testimonial. "There's a fat lot in N'York that are worse than Fay."[1]

---

[1] Larry Fay, one of the most astute and successful of the racketeers, escaped being sent to Sing-Sing, taken for a ride, or otherwise bumped off until January 2, 1933, when he was ignominiously shot by one of his own drivers, whom he was putting on to short-time, which the man, being drunk, resented in this too emphatic manner. Larry was arrested forty-nine times, but never convicted on

Maloon did not dispute that. Being fairly started, he went on to expound the ethics of racketeering, its business possibilities, and the difficulties of conducting it in sensible, peaceful ways. It was the one subject which, from his own angle, he understood, and he exemplified the truth of the text that Ingram approved. It appeared that racketeering was carried on under two great difficulties, both of which arose from the bullying or blundering follies of the police.

In illustration of the first he instanced the orderly levies which were made upon the consignments of fruit which came to New York by rail from Florida. The gentleman who controlled that racket levied the moderate tariff of one cent per pound, and, to save the merchants from the dishonourable and dangerous temptation of making inaccurate returns to him, he had reliable men posted at the arrival platforms to check the incoming traffic. From this levy the cops had an agreed rake-off, and, to avert similar errors on the part of the racketeer, they posted their own men to check the work of his checkers. Here was order and method, and all went well; and it had the further advantage that if any other racketeer should attempt to muscle in, either asking extra or perhaps extortionate dues, or to drive out the man already in peaceful possession, the police would act firmly, and if any regrettable shooting should occur it would have the support of the law.

The second difficulty arose from the unwillingness of the law to enforce the discipline or collect the debts of the racketeers. Disputes were sure to arise, instances of bad faith to occur, which could only be dealt with by violent methods, when the cops—though, as reasonable men, they might see their necessity—became active to interfere. Even a simple question such as a request for a rise in salary might lead to serious trouble. There must be a limit to the granting of such requests. Anyone could see that. Yet a discontented man could not be allowed to resign. He would be a potential danger in more ways than one. If it should end in some shooting up, surely the police should enquire who had been reasonable and who wrong, rather than merely who had shot who, by which justice might not be done.

Then—whatever care might be taken—there was always the possibility of a man of bad character getting into one of the rackets, in which case something drastic had to be done. To take him for a ride would become a necessity all should see.

---

any serious charge. He was one of the last of the racketeers to die, after gaining international notoriety as a financier of nightclub vice.

The trouble that lack of discipline caused was illustrated by the homicides which had occurred in Harlem last June. Then the younger men—youths of from fifteen to twenty—had revolted against the big shots—five or ten years older than themselves—who, they said, took most of the swag, while they did almost all of the dirty work. They got the liquor ashore—they fought the hijackers— they delivered it to the speak-easies—and they claimed higher wages and a percentage on the profits, which Foxy Rosa, a veteran of twenty-four, had refused to consider. Had the dispute been brought before a magistrate, as it should have been, he would have declined to hear it; and it was in consequence of this cynical attitude that Foxy Rosa had died (it had taken nine bullets which hit the mark to settle him) and that it had culminated in two carloads of gangsters shooting it out in a crowded New York street, where the casualty list had naturally included some who had not been interested in the dispute.

Such were the two texts of Maloon's discourse, leading to the comfortable conclusion that these evils, however great, were not beyond control when confronted by the genius of such men (he was too modest to say much of his own Detroit exploits) as Al Capone.

Chicago, under his sagacious rule, had been brought to a point of order and discipline which should be a guide to the present and an inspiration to new generations of racketeers.

This enlightened city had voted six to one against prohibition, which it had been consistently determined not to endure. Capone had found that the larger half of the population, including most of its leading citizens, were prepared to be his customers if he could supply their demand. He had come to terms with the magistrates, with the judicature, with the municipal officials, even with the police. And he had found it possible to enforce order and discipline among the large number of assistants that his large business required.

Maloon had probably never spoken of Al Capone with such approval (for there was no real friendship and far more rivalry than community of business interests between them) as now that he was expounding the gangsters' creed to these interested and intelligent aliens, who might become graduates in the same school.

To this point he had been uninterrupted, except by Evelyn's occasional questions, which were directed to lead him on. Mr. Jellipot had been learning too much to interpose any word which might dam or divert a current that flowed so well. And Sir Reginald was content to leave Evelyn to her own success.

Clancy, to whom Maloon had appealed at one point for confirmation of improbable fact, had declined to be drawn in. "I wouldn't know," had been his non-committal response. A retired bank robber is not necessarily familiar with all the ways of the racketeer. Miss O'Leary, perhaps because she had a better acquaintance with Maloon's auditors, was nearest to understanding the position. She had previously admired the cuteness of the Crowe dame, but she had not supposed that she could make a sucker of Slick Maloon.

But at this point Mr. Jellipot spoke. He was genuinely puzzled by Maloon's account of conditions in Chicago, in view of some things which he had recently read.

"I suppose," he suggested mildly, "that your newspapers sometimes print things which are not true?"

"Sure," Maloon replied heartily, for his respect for the American newspaper reporter was not great, and his love less. "They'll give you ten lies for a true word, and that'll be put in by mistake."

"Because," Mr, Jellipot said, "I read very recently that seven gentlemen of the profession which we are discussing were taken into a garage by the members of a more numerous—or it may be merely a bolder or more enterprising—organisation and were there placed in a row against the wall and shot down by machine-gun fire. And unless my memory is more at fault than I have often found it to be, it was in Chicago that these murders—or should I say these executions?—occurred."

Maloon did not dispute the accuracy of this report, but he gave long and what was doubtless to him a convincing reply. He said (which was true) that there were many others besides the beer racket in Chicago, in some of which Capone had no interest, and did not attempt control. Their rivalries and conflicts, he argued, might be contrasted to Capone's more orderly organisation. He did not even deny that there had been times when Capone's authority had been seriously challenged, and invasion upon his territory, or rebellion within it, had not been overcome without sanguinary violence. But he said that Capone had always preferred the pacific course. He would always rather buy out opposition than resort to gunning. Yet, if that latter operation should become necessary, the more drastic method was the more merciful, and almost certainly the more economical in the final total of lives which must be taken before order would be restored. The sawn-off shotgun was good, but the machine-gun was much better. And the honour of first using the machine-gun belonged to his own Detroit. He did not claim personal credit for this. He gave praise where it belonged. It was Fred Burke who had started that.

As to the seven men who had been shot in the garage, the open way in which it had been done, and the fact that no one had been

punished, showed that a great city had recognised that it had probably been no more than a necessary if regrettable incident in the conduct of a huge business which it approved. Personally, he had not
been concerned. It was an incident of which he knew little; but, if
reports were true, the seven men had been a particularly lousy lot.

To demonstrate Capone's fitness for the high position he held,
and his preference for peaceful and generous rather than brutal
methods, he gave two illustrations.

When Capone's trusted lieutenant, Jack Zuta, had fled from
Chicago to escape arrest for murder, Capone had discussed the matter with the police in a spirit of reasonable adjustment, and had actually paid them $12,000 to secure his unmolested return. It was due
to the cops to say that they had honourably observed the bargain and
that Zuta's subsequent assassination was not at their instigation.

Even more remarkable was the step which Capone was now
taking to end a difficult situation between himself and the Frank
Diamond gang (with which Jack Diamond must not be ignorantly
confused). Capone had offered his sister Mafalda in marriage to the
brother of the head of the rival dynasty, and though those most concerned, with the perversity of youth, were said to object, there was
no doubt that the blessing of the Catholic Church would shortly be
given (as in fact it was) to this momentous union.

The hour had become late when Maloon brought his exposition
to this romantic climax, and Sir Reginald felt that the time had come
to break up the party.

"You've given me," he said, "a lot to think over, and we must
all thank you for putting the case so clearly. Your friend Capone—
Scarface, as we are told in the English press that he is commonly
called, but I suppose you would not address him by that name—will
be most interesting to meet.... But I am inclined to think that the
difficulty of introducing these features of Western civilisation into
England might be too formidable to be overcome."

"You're the one to know," Maloon conceded readily, "and I
wouldn't say you're far wrong." He had already observed the British
to be a stiff and difficult race. Let them stay put. And a programme
of opening rackets in that country was not one to which Capone
would be likely to give consent. He wanted a quiet place where their
accumulating wealth could be safely cached. So did they all. It
might be a fatal error to make themselves a nuisance to Scotland
Yard. Maloon's design was to place himself permanently in charge
of financial operations in London. It would be a position of immense
power, and with opportunities for peculation on which it was most
attractive to dwell. It would be far safer for him than any part of the

States, where he had numerous unscrupulous foes; and that safety would be increased if there were an understanding in gangster circles that no disturbances were to be allowed in the land where their wealth would lie.

Beyond that, he saw, in an agile mind, the possibility of a bargain that he did not think any intelligent cops—even the most stiff-necked and prejudiced—could refuse. Cash, of course, must be tendered first. No gentlemen could omit the offer to pay fairly for the protection they wished to have. But, if that should be declined, there could still be a gentleman's agreement that, if there should be no obstruction by the British police to their transatlantic crossings, or the financial operations for which they came. There should be no homicides in the land of hospitality, nor other serious breaches of English law. Even smuggling might have to be discouraged on the eastern voyages. And such a programme would, he thought, be likely to win the approval of Sir Reginald Crowe, whose willing cooperation he was shrewd enough to see it was important to gain.

Control of the London and Northern Bank—the present chairman retained as their willing tool—the friendly benevolence of the police—himself in control in London of an accumulating reservoir of wealth which was increasingly menaced by Federal action in the country where it was made—it was a dream of affluence, security, and continued power which it was pleasant to have. It transcended even that of bumping off Sir Reginald and taking at least temporary possession of his attractive dame, who had been showing such intelligent interest in the subject next to his own heart. But that plan was capable of many variations of a roseate character, such as a nimble mind will contrive when opportunities come. (But no dame, however easy on the eyes, is worth the wreckage of business plans. There is no shortage of them.)

He rose in good humour. He had still another favour to offer, being that which, apart from Sir Reginald's preferences. He had agreed with Capone to do.

"You won't want the newspaper boys buzzing round?" he asked casually.

"I certainly don't want to give any interviews to the press," Sir Reginald replied, "if you mean that."

Mr. Jellipot remained silent, being unsure. He had thought that press publicity would be impossible to escape, and he had regarded it as likely to gain for them a measure of security, while militating against the easy success of the enquiry on which they came. But it appeared that even this was not entirely beyond the gangsters' control.

"It'll be cheap," Maloon said, "if I get it done for a grand, but. we won't talk of that between friends. And I shall have to give them some sort of dope. I'll say there's a story to break before long, and we'll let them in on the ground floor.... You can dodge them better when you're off the boat.... Do you know where you'll put up?"

"I have already radio'd for reservations at the Hotel Atlantis," Sir Reginald replied, to Mr. Jellipot's surprise, for it was a point which they had not discussed, and he saw it to be one on which the banker had resolved that he would not be turned from his own way.

Maloon looked surprised, but not dissatisfied. "You'll come on to Chicago," he said, but in the tone of one who knew the answer before it came.

"Yes. We shall just have a day or two to look round in New York first."

"Suit me. I've got one or two things to do first."

"Shall we have the pleasure of seeing you at the Atlantis?"

"I'm not staying there. I'll put up with Joe Masseria. He may give us what you're wanting to know."

"It will shorten my visit very much if he can."

Maloon did not discuss that. He said good-night with as much affability as it was natural for him to show, and strolled off as steadily as was possible on a boat that was moving at its maximum speed against a head sea.

Clancy and his companion still kept their places, finishing hitherto neglected drinks.

Sir Reginald asked: "We shall probably see you at the hotel?"

Miss O'Leary started to speak: "You wouldn't think—" Her voice broke off abruptly.

Mr. Jellipot thought she had intended to warn them, and then seen reason to change her mind.

Tim said noncommittally, "We'll be there," which was what Sir Reginald had wanted to know.

Evelyn gave them her friendliest smile. "We have been hoping that you would be able to help us."

"I might—or I might not," Tim answered, still in the reserved though not unfriendly voice he had used before. "I'm not in with Maloon.... And I've no truck with the cops."

"Neither have we," Evelyn answered readily, "and we're not in with Maloon. We want to do this off our own bat."

Clancy looked puzzled, perhaps by the concluding idiom. He made no reply.

Miss O'Leary said: "We might help you more ways than one."

They also rose and retired.

Sir Reginald said: "It was a bit risky, Evelyn, to say that we're not in with Maloon."

"Was it? I thought it was a bit safer than not. They don't trust Maloon."

"I shouldn't say Clancy trusts anyone but himself."

"Oh yes, he does. He trusts the girl."

"Clancy," Mr. Jellipot observed, "can keep a shut mouth."

"Yes, we must hope he will," Sir Reginald agreed. "If he doesn't trust Maloon, Maloon thinks that he's in with him."

"Maloon may think he can buy him, as he does us."

"And Maloon may be right in that.... Apart from that, Evelyn, it was hardly right to say we're not in with the cops. I've got a deal with Ingram I've got to keep."

"Oh, you make me tired! I'm not in with the cops, anyway. And I *am* in with that girl, whether or no. And you're going to be glad about it before we've done."

PART THREE

DINNER IN NEW YORK

▲

CHAPTER XXXVII.

A Bargain with Tim Clancy

IT was early on Tuesday morning when Mr. Jellipot sat in the breakfast-room of the Hotel Atlantis, awaiting the coming of Tim Clancy, whom he had arranged on the previous evening to meet at their morning meal.

He was in no hurry for Tim to arrive, having already gathered much material for reflection since they had come down the *Baltic* gangway less than twenty-four hours before.

He knew that in entering that hotel they had penetrated to the citadel of gangland, that it was gangster owned and gangster occupied, and he supposed, quite wrongly, that it was a place where murders might at any moment occur. Anyway, it was one in which it was very interesting to be.

And it was extremely comfortable. The blight of depression which was understood to have fallen upon America had not penetrated the rotating door of the Hotel Atlantis. What the bill for all this luxury would be they had still to discover, but it was not likely that it would seriously affect the resources of the London and Northern Bank, on whose business they came.

He had seen signs of the depression last afternoon, which had been astonishing to his English mind. He had explored the untidy length of Broadway, which was a thoroughfare before the city was designed in orderly blocks, so that it runs from southeast to northwest of Manhattan, cutting obliquely through the straight and regularly spaced "avenues" of a later date. He had discovered, as all who visit New York will be likely to do, that the European idea of Broadway has little factual basis. One small portion north and south of Times Square has numerous places of entertainment, as have the surrounding streets. Beyond that its aspect varies, as that of a very long street will, but the impression left most strongly upon Mr. Jellipot's mind was of dinginess and of third-rate shops.

Not that there had been lack of interest or novelty in what he had seen. In the lower part of Broadway he had come upon the establishments of many tailors and outfitters who appeared to be feeling the depression, but to be meeting it in a resilient spirit.

One enterprising Hebrew, considering that customers might hope that he would sell cheaply if short of cash, had decorated his premises with a huge blazon: CREDITORS PRESSING HARD. Competitors, seeing the success of this curious method of attracting trade, had emulated each other in the production of signs which would announce their even deeper descent into the abyss of insolvency, until one genius had arranged with a friend to sue him for a small sum and levy a distress for the amount of the judgement debt, whereon he had triumphantly displayed the unbeatable slogan: SHERIFF ACTUALLY IN.

From these observations Mr. Jellipot had wandered into a popular restaurant in Forty-Second Street, the temperature of which had helped him to an understanding of why Americans drink iced water in winter months, and had there been drawn into conversation with a gentleman who recognised his nationality and invited him to admire the height of the surrounding buildings.

Mr. Jellipot, enjoying a liberal supply of strawberries and cream, and recognising with suitable gratitude that they would have been beyond the winter resources of his own country, was very willing to do so. "But," he had added diffidently, "I have been told—I am probably wrong; it is a subject on which I have no knowledge at all—but I have been told that the effect of your excellent sea air upon the steel structures of these buildings is such that they may become unsafe within forty years."

"Well," had been the devastating reply, "who wants a building to last forty years?"

Mr. Jellipot had to admit that he did not know. "There is much," he said to himself, as he reflected upon these experiences, "there is much which we English have still to learn."

Now he sat in a large, low-ceiled, rose-coloured room, into which little daylight came, but with a sufficiency of red-shaded lights for those who had no occasion to see clearly far beyond their own tables, and waited for Clancy to appear, as he soon did.

The room would be full at a later hour, but those who patronised the Hotel Atlantis were not early risers, and the majority breakfasted in their own apartments. Tim knew what he was doing when he made this appointment, which might have the appearance of casuality and was unlikely to be observed. He had heard Moll's opinion of these invading Britishers, but he was anxious to form, or perhaps to confirm, his own.

He sat down opposite Mr. Jellipot with no further greeting than a muttered "I wouldn't talk while the boy's about," and he had finished his grapefruit and a plate of wheat flakes that followed before he expanded to further words.

Having been served with coffee and fried eggs (for he was one who breakfasted well), he said abruptly: "What did that banker's dame mean when she said she'd be looking for help from us?"

"Lady Crowe may have had in mind that we are seeking the murderer of Ringan and Ruscatti."

"What's that matter to you?"

"Sir Reginald strongly objects to Americans killing each other on his mat."

"You can come clean with me. There's more to it than that."

"You may have heard that he was himself accused of the first murder."

"I heard they dropped that like a hot spud."

"And he has money placed with his bank, of which he is anxious to rid it in a legal manner."

"It sounds batty to me. You'd say he's not in with Maloon?"

"I'm trusting you more than you trust me when I assure you that he is not and is never likely to be."

"That's what Moll says.... I might trust you a whole pile yet.... Why do you think she could help you?"

"We think she knows—or at least guesses—who the murderer is."

"Told Maloon that?"

"No."

"Sure?"

"Absolutely. Maloon is one whom we have had no inducement to trust. And I may add that we have come to gather information, not to give it away."

"Moll said Slick was the sucker. But who'd have thought it of that dame! You've got a nerve coming here."

"Our purpose in coming here was to have some conversation with Miss O'Leary—"

"You can say Mrs. Clancy now."

"With Mrs. Clancy after she had had an opportunity of talking with you."

"Yep. But I didn't mean coming to this joint. You're safe here. Birds don't foul their own nests. I reckon you'll have heard that. I meant coming to this country at all."

"It seemed to us a most natural thing to do."

"And, if you're not in with Maloon, what made you think you could get in here?"

"It may not have occurred to Sir Reginald that there would be any difficulty."

"Nope? They don't let anyone in who comes to the desk. It might get lousy with cops if they did that. I reckon Maloon passed the word, and that means that, if you're not in with him, he counts himself in with you."

"I suppose," Mr. Jellipot replied with deliberate frankness, "that that is just what the position is."

"Then I'll try a deal. It's more Moll's matter than mine, though you can bet that I'll make it mine if anything happens to her, and it's what she wants me to do.... I'll tell you this. Moll thinks she knows who it is. Someone thought the same, and meant to have her bumped off on the *Baltic*, and then altered his mind. That's a sure thing. And that means it's one of the big shots. Capone says he doesn't know who it is. Maloon says the same. But they mean to find out. I'm not in the rackets. I like something a bit cleaner than them. But when the big shots fall out I know it's best to keep indoors till the sky clears. If it gets talked that Moll knows, I'd reckon she'd be another dead girl, and I don't mean it to be.... If you'll give us your words that you won't let Maloon or Capone—that you won't let *anyone* know that you think she could spot the man, we'll let you know what we find out when we safely can, and if you get in a jam—and the devil knows whether you're heading for that—you can count us pals."

"It is a bargain which we shall be most willing to make," Mr. Jellipot replied. "And I may add that you could have had our promise if there had been no bargain at all. It would have been enough for

THE CAPONE CAPER, BY S. FOWLER WRIGHT

us to know that it would endanger Mrs. Clancy's safety, and it would not have been mentioned."

"Well, I'd say you're white. I'm tickled thinking how you'll get on with Al.

"I'm looking forward to the meeting with considerable interest."

"Well, I've said you've got nerve. There isn't much that Scarface won't do if his business calls. There's not many things, but there are some. He's not Maloon. Know where Maloon is now?"

"Not precisely. He did mention a friend who—"

"He's with Joe Masseria—Joe the Boss. Joe's in the White Slave business. He's in big. Maloon's in with him. They're meeting for one of their settlings up.... Well, so long."

Clancy, satisfied that he had done that which Moll wished, and his own judgement had come to approve, strolled off to the billiard-room, and Mr. Jellipot went upstairs to acquaint his friends with the knowledge he had obtained and the bargain which he had made.

CHAPTER XXXVIII.

WHO KILLED RINGAN?

MR. JELLIPOT found his friends having a rather later meal in their own suite, where Sir Reginald had been occupied with matters more vital to him even than the identity of the slayer of Ringan and Ruscatti.

London cables lay on the table. The time of day in London being much later than in New York, he had already had telephone conversations with Adams, with Lord Britleigh, and with his brokers there, so that he knew the position with which he would have to deal, so far as they were able to explain or foretell it.

"The fact is," he said, "that these rats have bought more than half the shares in the L. and M. Their brokers, Rosbach & Grotz, made no secret of this when they called to inspect our register yesterday afternoon—at least, that's what they told Adams they'd called for, which they've got a legal right to do, but I should say they had other reasons—and Britleigh says he's got good cause to think it's true.

"But that isn't all the tale. If they've got more than half the shares, so have we. There's been a lot of selling short as the price rose, and it won't be till the next settling day that either of us will know where we are. "Britleigh's done well since he knew what the position is. He was just in time to get a big block of shares back from one of Rosbach's agents who couldn't resist the take-it-or-leave-it-now offer he made, without allowing him time to refer to Rosbach. That cost him over three thousand pounds, besides losing the profit he would have made. And he's bought from more than one shareholder who was on the point of selling to them. Maloon may be slick, but he let out what they were doing a bit too soon."

"He probably underestimated what you could do—or would be likely to try to do—from this distance," Mr. Jellipot agreed, "and he may have been oversure that he could come to deal with you on his own terms. But whether he was really too soon seems to be a question that won't be answered for a few days. Well, we've got that time during which they'll think they own the bank, and if it should turn out to be wrong it may have produced a very interesting position."

"I don't call it interesting," Sir Reginald replied irritably. "I call it damnable. But we're not beaten yet. I want to make one or two more phone calls, and then we'll go down to Wall Street together and see if our brokers have been able to do anything—it couldn't be much—there. Evelyn says she'll look after herself till we get back."

"You don't think," Mr. Jellipot asked doubtfully, "that you're being indiscreet 'phoning from here?"

"No, I don't. I don't say any of Capone's friends wouldn't like to listen in, but I'm told it's not done at this hotel, and it sounds sense. All the big shots, as they call the master criminals, come here, and they're not all friendly with each other or him. It's a kind of neutral ground, and the man who runs it has made it the success it is on those lines. Nothing's ever done that could bring the cops over the front step, and even if they want to put each other on the spot, or give them the works, or go riding together, they won't start it from this address."

Mr. Jellipot recognised the plausibility of this view, which increased the significance of their reception at a hotel where casual strangers would certainly have been told that no rooms were available. He went on to recount his conversation and bargain with Clancy.

"Of course," Sir Reginald agreed, "we shouldn't have mentioned that. We don't want to get the girl in the soup more than she is now."

"I'm not sure," Evelyn said, "that we can help doing that if we do anything to find out who the man is. If we succeed, won they be likely to think we had the right tip from her?"

"I have thought," Mr. Jellipot said, "that we might leave that part of our investigation for the present, in some reasonable anticipation that some of our new acquaintances may make a discovery on which they appear to be resolved, and for which they may have better facilities than ourselves."

"So we will," Sir Reginald agreed, "with the qualification that I don't intend to go back without clearing it up, and I can't afford to be long here."

Having said this, he turned his thoughts to the financial matters with which he should deal that morning, and Evelyn, left alone, determined to explore the city beyond Broadway and the adjacent Seventh Avenue slums.

Having dressed suitably for this project, she descended to the lounge, and found Miss O'Leary (who may have been intending to waylay her) sitting there with a bulky New York newspaper before her, on the front page of which a recent bank robbery in Arizona was boldly featured, in the details of which her professional interest may be reasonably presumed.

She rose as Evelyn approached, and moved toward the door, being already dressed for the street. If she wished to talk to Evelyn, they were of the same mind.

Evelyn said: "I'm going to do some shopping and looking round. I want to get to Fifth Avenue first. I suppose a taxi's the best way?

"It depends on what part you want. Fifth is no distance from here. You'll see more if you walk."

"I'd rather walk really."

"I'm going that way. I'll show you, if you like.... I don't want to push in."

"You're not doing that. I shall be very glad to be shown, if I'm not a nuisance to you."

So they went out together, and it was dusk when Evelyn returned alone and went up to find that the two men had come in earlier and were engaged in a consultation which she had no scruple in interrupting for the news she brought.

"I've had all day with Miss O'Leary, but we've got to remember to say Mrs. Clancy here. She's Moll now to me. She only left me a few minutes ago to meet Clancy somewhere. I don't think she wanted us to come in together.

"But I know the name of the man who did the murders now. And I can tell you as long as you don't use the knowledge until it comes to you another way. That mayn't sound so much, but it'll save no end of trouble looking in the wrong places for someone who isn't there. I'd better tell you the whole tale. I haven't Moll's gift of speech, but I'll do it as well as our inferior language permits.

"Perhaps the knife's the best point at which to begin. You know the puzzle it's been to think of how anyone could get hold of it without Ringan knowing what he was at. Well, the explanation's simply that, though it was his knife, it had been out of his possession since before he sailed for England.

"Clancy says it happened like this. It's not hearsay, it's what he saw. Ringan was fond of gambling, but he was a bad loser. If he lost all he had with him, he wanted to go on, and if he lost more it mightn't be easy to get it from him another time. He wasn't short of money, but just mean. Anyway, no one liked to play with him unless the money was there.

"One night, less than three months ago, Clancy was in a speak-easy in Thirty-Eighth Street—I can't remember the name, it doesn't matter—where faro was being played. Ringan was losing to a man named Flannigan. There was a Boston cop there named Cassidy. He comes here when he gets leave, because it's where his family live. Ringan got cleared out and offered to stake his knife for twenty-four dollars, on condition that, if he lost it, he could redeem it next day for that amount. Flannigan didn't mind agreeing to that, because they all knew that Ringan wouldn't part with his knife, about which he had some superstitious idea.

"Well, Ringan lost the knife, and after that there was a police raid. The lights went out and there was some confusion. It was soon over, because the cops didn't want to be really nasty. Not to the customers, anyway. They were just giving the owner a shake-up because he hadn't been square with them. And when the lights went up the knife was gone. There was a great row. Ringan said Flannigan had got it, and Flannigan said Ringan must have snatched it back in the dark. Ringan couldn't be as nasty as he'd have liked because he hadn't got the knife to be nasty with. Tim doesn't know how they settled it up, but Ringan must have gone on wearing the sheath, perhaps hoping to get it back.

"It wasn't any mystery to Tim because he'd seen Cassidy pick up the knife just as the lights went out, and while most people's eyes were on the cops pushing in at the door. But he didn't say anything. He didn't like Ringan, and he didn't see that it was any business of his.

"It was just after that that Cassidy said he'd got leave, and he was going over to Ireland to see his old grandmother there. He may have landed at Cobh, and perhaps gone there on a United States Line boat. The London police wouldn't think of him in connection with the murder, even if they checked up on everyone landing there, he being a cop like themselves. But Moll says it was he she saw in Cheapside, and again on the *Baltic*, and she saw him leave at Boston. So you'll see how it adds up.

"She says no one, as far as she knows, has ever suspected him of being anything worse than a dirty cop, but he must act as a gunman for one of the big shots, and the question is which?

"As he gambles, he probably gets to need the money he earns in that way, and while no one's guessed what he's at, it's been easy to get away with it.

"There was a gunman named Brice shot in Boston after dark some months ago, and Cassidy was on the spot. There were a lot of shots, and when some more police came up Cassidy said that he'd seen the murder, and then emptied his revolver at two men who fired back, and he was sure that he'd hit one in the leg.

"Of course, they were never found, but Cassidy was commended for what he'd done. Moll says that she expects he did the killing, and all the other shots came out of his gun."

"There would be a question of ballistics there," Mr. Jellipot suggested; "the police might—"

"Moll said something about that. She said the cops wouldn't be likely to test whether the bullet came out of a cop's gun, and he might have used two—and, anyway, that's what she thinks happened.

"Now you can see what a jam she's in. If the murders had been done—but it seems to be bad manners in her circle to call them murders; they're bumpings-off—if they had been done by one of the boys she knows, and all open and regular as you might say, it wouldn't matter much what she'd seen as long as they could feel sure that she wouldn't squeal to the cops.

"But if one of the big shots—she thinks Joe the Boss is the most likely, unless it's Jack Diamond, which she told me a lot of reasons for not thinking it is, one of them being that she's almost sure he's in jail—working against Capone and those who are in with him, he won't let her live long if he suspects she could spill the beans—"

"If she could—" Mr. Jellipot interrupted in a momentarily puzzled tone, which changed as he went on: "Yes, I see. The metaphor is not without force. Miss O'Leary's, we may presume?"

"Yes. It sounds plain to me. I wish you'd both try to understand what a mess it is. She might get killed any minute, it seems to me. The fact that it's been such a secret that Cassidy's a gunman at all that even the other gangsters haven't suspected it makes it a lot worse. Moll says the big shot might do almost anything to prevent that getting known, and it's a point on which Cassidy's almost sure to feel the same."

"We all want to do anything in our power for Mrs. Clancy," Sir Reginald said, "though I hope your affection for her won't go so far as to lead you to join the gang. But I fail to see how we can relieve the position beyond keeping silent, as we have already undertaken to do."

"I don't know what gang you mean. Moll doesn't belong to any that I've heard of.... But as to doing nothing, she says that Tim tried giving her the same advice. He said if they'd meant to do her any harm on the *Baltic* they'd changed their plans. They must have decided she isn't dangerous, and he said if he made a big dust looking in the wrong places they'd feel surer than ever."

"Yes, I think I see what you mean. But—"

"But I haven't finished. She'd kept mum till she'd told Tim, but she made up her mind that she doesn't want any more suspense now. She seems to think he can do anything, and she's given him orders to do it quick. He didn't say much, except that she should have it her way, but she thinks he's gone gunning after someone now."

"Then I should think," Mr. Jellipot reflected, "someone will be having a bad time."

"You can bet that," Evelyn agreed, with an enthusiasm evidently borrowed from her recent companion. "Moll says that he's that quick on the draw! And he's always cool, and most of the boys get flurried when they're in a tight spot. And there aren't many who can shoot straight, whether or no."

"I can recall," Mr. Jellipot replied, "some supporting evidence in the incidents of a motion picture which I had the pleasure of seeing, in the course of which about half a dozen of these gentlemen exchanged about forty shots with a larger number of police in a room of quite moderate size, of which two only reached their destinations, and the remaining thirty-eight damaged the furniture.

"I was led to conclude that plausibility was sacrificed to prolong the dramatic interest of the clash, but I may have been largely wrong."

"Well, Moll ought to know.... But what a dream New York is! And the people! In the shops, or anywhere, you couldn't meet a nicer, kinder, more decent lot. Why, they changed a fifty-dollar bill for me at one place without looking at it twice. If you asked a London shop to change a ten-pound note, they'd look at you as though you'd stolen it, and ask you to write your name on the back.... I asked one lady where we had lunch how they came to tolerate all these shootings-up and the rackets that go on, and she said decent people don't go in for politics. I should have asked her why not, and a lot more, but Moll looked as though the conversation wasn't quite what it should be, and I shut up."

"It's beginning to look as though I shall have to turn bank-robber," Sir Reginald said, "or forfeit such small respect for me as my wife ever had.

"I shouldn't hurry about that," Evelyn said lightly. "It's more important to order dinner just now; and I'll go and change while they bring it up."

CHAPTER XXXIX.

He Only Wants Twenty Grand

CLANCY dropped his gun into his right-hand jacket pocket and some small, bright tools into the left. He had never been a habitual picklock, preferring more direct methods of approach, but it does no harm to know how. The manipulation he had in mind was not difficult. He had inspected the door already. and knew that he could have done it with one hand in the dark. But it might be important that it should be done neatly and leave no mark.

He knew that Cassidy rented an apartment in a rooming house in the Bronx. He could not often need it, and the fact that he had it at all seemed confirmatory evidence—of which there was little need—that he had other associations than those of his Boston police station,

It was an apartment on the top floor, to which Tim ascended without meeting anyone. The one opposite to it was untenanted and unfurnished. Its door stood wide.

So far, so good. He manipulated the lock without difficulty and, having entered, locked it, though this was more troublesome from the inside.

The apartment consisted of two rooms and a kitchenette. It was untidy and appeared to have been carelessly, though not recently, left. Fragments of bread on the kitchen dresser were green with mould. An empty scent-bottle, a broken cigarette-holder, and a single shoe, from which the high heel had been torn away, lay by the stove. It was a sordid place, and its general appearance did not encourage hope that he would find what he had come to seek.

He searched with slight anticipation of finding anything which would either disclose that which it was so urgent to know, or which might give him a hold on Cassidy in some other way.

He opened drawers which were empty, littered with table cutlery of doubtful cleanliness, or stuffed with unwashed linen. He searched for a concealed safe which was not there. He was disposed to admit failure and withdraw when the telephone rang.

He took up the receiver and answered in as toneless a voice as he could produce, "Hullo," and was answered: "That you, Cassidy? This is Gill. I'll be with you in twenty minutes."

He said, "You've got the wrong number, Buddy. This is Thomson and Cross," and hung up.

He left it unanswered when the ring was repeated, and it soon ceased.

He saw the need for quick decision. The man Gill might come, or might not, having failed to connect. But he had evidently expected that his call would be answered, which made it likely that Cassidy might arrive at any moment. Not certain, but a likely thing.

He decided to stay, if he could conceal himself effectually, on which point fate appeared kind.

One of the two uncurtained windows of the living-room faced a similar one not more than ten feet away, and it was evidently to secure privacy for himself that Cassidy had placed a screen between it and the interior of the room. Clancy moved a chair into the window and sat down. It was unlikely that its absence would be noticed in that untidy room. He could be seen by any one who should look out at the opposite window, but he cared little for that. Indeed, he cared little if he should be discovered, having a cool confidence in his own ability to handle the situation. But, if he were, he intended to be entirely ready, and he did not wish to make the slightest sound after anyone should enter the flat. His finger was now at the trigger of a gun that lay on his knee.

He had sat thus for fifteen minutes or more, and was beginning to question the use of a longer vigil, when he heard the sound of a key in the outer door. He made a correct guess that the owner of the flat had arrived, and he resolved at once that there should be a showdown before either of them should leave. But he would overhear first, if he could, what the man Gill (a name that was strange to him) might have to say. He saw that the risk of discovery was great while Cassidy was alone. If Gill would only come! As he wished it, the bell rang, and Cassidy went to the door.

The words of the conversation that followed were as plain as though the two men were speaking to him. They were, in fact, not more than three yards away.

It was Cassidy's voice, almost surly in tone, that asked: "You'll be Fred Gill?"

"Yep."

"You've brought it?"

"Yep."

"How much?"

"Two grand. That's one for each. The Chief says you had your expenses before you sailed."

The voice seemed to be that of an older man than Cassidy. There was nothing formidable in its sound. Clancy's confidence increased. But he had no inclination to interrupt. There was a short silence while Cassidy checked the money that had been handed over to him. Then he said: "Have a drink?"

"No, thanks. I must be getting back. The last train's an hour from now."

Clancy noticed that neither of the men had sat down. Evidently Gill was a mere messenger. It would be best to let him go, with nothing to tell his boss when he got back, and then talk to Cassidy alone.

Gill went on: "If you'll give me the papers, I'll be getting along."

"What papers?"

"The authorities to collect the money in London, of course."

"I'm not being paid for them. There was to be a grand each for the bumpings-off."

"But the Chief said I was to take them back."

"If he wants them they're worth paying for."

"You don't mean me to tell him that?"

"If you don't somebody else will."

"You mean you'll hold out for a price?"

"Yes. And you can say what it is. I want twenty grand."

"You won't get it. It isn't that I care. I'll tell him anything that you say. But you'll be cat's meat in a week's time if I tell that to the Chief."

"That's what you think. He's more likely to send a bodyguard to see that I don't slip.... You can tell him that I've salted those bits of paper away where they can't be found. But if anything happens to me they go to Capone, with the whole tale; and who took Jap-eyed Pete for a ride, and what for, as well."

"Then I'll tell him that. It's your funeral if it goes off the rails. The Chief wants those papers out of the way. He'd say it's good for you too. If the cops get them it comes mighty near being the hot seat for you."

"I'll take care of that.... And there's another thing. What's he going to do with Clancy's sugar? He told me to put her out, and then not. But you can tell him now that if he doesn't I will."

"He says she doesn't know anything."

"And I know she does. She saw me as plain as I see you now. And Clancy knows—other things. I tell you it won't do."

"You think she might squeal?"

"Not to us cops. Clancy'd twist her neck himself if she did that. But she'll tell Capone when he gets her there. It's the natural thing to do."

"And Clancy may, if she's told him."

"That's just why she should have been put away on the boat. I'd got it all figured out when I got the word to go slow. Now Clancy may. You can tell the Chief he should think hard, and think quickly. And come across with the twenty grand. And then he can go ahead in his own way, and he'll hear no more from me."

Well, if you think he'll skip when you call the tune! I'll just tell him.... So long."

Mr. Fred Gill could be heard to go, and Cassidy, coming back from the door, looked into the muzzle of Clancy's gun.

CHAPTER XL.

CLANCY TALKS WITH A GUN

CASSIDY'S hands went up. For one moment he had the look of a frightened, as he was surely a startled, man. Then he said smoothly: "Don't be a boob, Clancy. You've heard all that's been said, and you won't shoot after that."

"I'll shoot you plenty if you don't give me the name of the man who's paid you those two thousand bucks."

"And what'll happen to me if I do?"

"That's not my worry. But I'll promise you, by when he knows he's been sold out, he'll be too busy to think of you."

"But I've got something to collect before he blows up."

"That's too bad. You won't want to collect much after you've been drilled by one or two of the bullets that I've got waiting here.

"And when you've shot me you won't know his name, and he won't lose much time before his boys start gunning for Redhead, even if he doesn't put this down to you, and say he'll have two in the bag. Clancy, we've just got to sit down and figure a way out."

"I don't want to shoot you. I want the name of that man. But it's going to be one or other. I'll have the name, or I'll shoot you for the dirty double crossing gutter cop that you are.... You'd better give me your gun. And hold it the right way. You don't know how quick I can let off."

"You'll give it back? It's a police gun. I can't go back to the station without it."

"Yep. I'll give it back. But whether you'll be alive to know of it's up to you."

"That's O.K. by me. There'll be no shooting tonight. We've both got too much sense for that." Saying this, Cassidy handed over his gun, with a natural care that it should not point toward Clancy and tempt a bullet that would he quicker than his.

He sat down at the table, but Clancy pushed it aside.

"I know all the tricks," he said, "and all the answers from A to Z. I've seen tables tipped up before now."

"You may know the tricks, but you don't seem to know how to get on the car. Don't you see you've got something to sell?"

"You'd better talk straighter than that."

"So I will. You heard what I said to Fred?"

"Yep."

"Then you know I want twenty grand, which they won't dare refuse. But I've got to figure out how to collect and how to stay alive after that."

"They're your headaches, not mine. If you think I'm going to be bodyguard to a rat like you—"

"I don't want you for that. I shouldn't feel safe with a dozen guns. You'll see that when you know who the Chief is.... And as to getting the money, I've got a plan, but it means waiting a week or so. There's a dinner being given to Al Vitale. You wouldn't know which day it'll be?"

"Yep. I know that. I've seen an invite. It's December seventh. That's Saturday week."

"Well, it's Tuesday now—that's twelve days—and I shan't care then how quick you let Capone know. You come to the dinner, and as soon as I've handed over the papers and got the money I'll let you know who the Chief is; and if you've got some of Capone's boys handy to give him the works it'll be all the better for me. And, of course, I'll tell Fred that they've got to hold off Redhead till then."

"And suppose they don't? It sounds swell for me. I hang round saying nothing and doing nothing for twelve days; and if Moll gets a bullet, or a bit of wire round her neck, or if I get shot up, it'll be just too bad! You've got to think of something a lot better than that."

"Can't you see I shall *want* you to stay alive, and Moll too? If she got bumped off I shouldn't be looking for you to help me."

Clancy saw the shrewdness of the plan and the probability that it would be carried out. But he was not sure. Anyone who trusted Cassidy would be a bigger fool than Tim Clancy. He said: "You keep still for a bit. I've got to think about this."

"You've got Moll at the Atlantis, haven't you? Well, keep her inside. No one's ever bumped off there."

"She might be coaxed out. I've told you I know all the tricks. And I've told you to keep quiet. I don't want to get riled."

Having secured the silence he required, Tim considered the problem on the correct solving of which his life and that of Redhead, about which he was more worried, might so probably depend.

He saw that Cassidy's position, as against the unknown Big Shot for whom he had worked, was very strong so long as the documents were in his possession, the place of their deposit unknown, and the conditions under which they would be put into circulation beyond control.

Cassidy's difficulty was how to exchange them safely for the price which he required. His danger must become acute from the moment that he should hand them over and have the money in his pocket. This difficulty was increased by the fact that he had worked alone. He had no supporting gang, and was yet attempting such a coup as only a big shot, having many gunmen at his call, should expect to handle.

In this difficulty the idea had come to him of making the exchange at a public dinner, which, owing to its nature, could hardly be made the scene of violent crime.

He had thought a way through his first difficulty, but his second—how to escape the vengeance of the employer he had held up in this way—remained; and the plan which he now proposed would get over that.

Clancy saw here the principle of mutuality which must be the basis of all satisfactory business deals. He was inclined to agree.

But that did not alter the fact that he would not trust Cassidy a yard; and he was being asked to do nothing for the next ten days on a mere promise that he would then hear a whispered name. It was not good enough. And suppose that, in the meantime, Cassidy should make some new deal with the unknown racketeer whom he was now blackmailing? Suppose a name should be whispered that was not the right one, so that Capone could be used to get rid of a personal enemy of the true culprit? No, it was not good enough. If Cassidy thought he could make a sucker of him, he must guess again.

"I'm going to agree," he said, "but it's got to be done in my own way. Got a pen?"

"Nope. And I won't write anything. I'm not that green."

"That's where you're wrong. You'll write just what I say. And if you do that, and play straight, you'll get the money and get safe away to wherever you want to go. I'd say another ticket for Ireland wouldn't be a bad spend."

"Maybe not. But I've figured out where I want to go. I won't write anything. You won't bounce me to that."

"No? Then it's growing daisies for you. Got any paper about here?"

"There may be some in that desk."

"Yep. I remember there is."

Clancy rose and got out two sheets. He wrote slowly on one, often stopping to think, his eyes on Cassidy sitting clear of the table the while, and the two guns ready to his hand. He passed the two sheets over, saying: "You'd better read it and then copy it. It's got to be in your writing, not mine. It's got to be the same, word for word, only that where I've put the Chief you've got to put the right name. I won't argue. If you're a wise guy you'll just write and sign. And so long as Moll's safe I'll keep it quiet long enough for you to collect at Vitale's dinner.... If you haven't got a pen you can use mine."

Cassidy read:

> "I hereby declare that I killed Tony Ringan and Joe Ruscatti at the Chief's orders, for which he paid me two thousand bucks, which Fred Gill brought to me at 58, Bevis Street, Bronx, on Tuesday, November 26th, 1929.
>
> "I took the authorities they held to collect the money from the London bank from them, which I have offered to sell to the Chief for twenty thousand bucks, and if he agrees I shall have them at the Vitale dinner on December 7th, to be exchanged for the money there."

"I shan't write that," Cassidy said curtly. Clancy fingered his gun.

"You can't scare me with that. You've got too much to lose."

"If I can't scare you it'll be just too bad for you. If I can't scare I shall shoot. I shall shoot you first in the right leg. You won't have much cause to howl about that.

"If you're still stiff I shall shoot you in the left leg. That'll be a bit worse. You'll lose quite a lot of blood that time.

"After that you'll have one in the left arm. That'll break the bone.

"I shan't shoot you in the right arm. You'll be wanting to write with that. But if you get to the dinner on your own feet it'll mean you've found a good nurse."

The hesitation was plain in Cassidy's face, and Clancy, who saw he was near to win, put in the decisive word: "I'll tell you this. If you sign that I'll play straight. I may be dirt, but it's not dirt of your kind. That won't go to the cops. It won't go anywhere where it would mean a bullet for you. I'll let you do the deal at Vitale's, and I'll let you get away with the wad.

"I'll do more than that. There's Crowe come over here gunning for you, and I'll call him off if I can.

"And when I tell Capone I'll make it part of the deal that you're to go free, and I call this about the dirtiest thing that I ever did."

Cassidy said: "Give me the pen."

He thought: "If I get in a jam, I can say he made me write and it's all lies." But he knew that there would be too much confirmatory evidence for this to be easily believed. He must trust Clancy. And, after all, he might be taking the only road to security, though it was a perilous path.

CHAPTER XLI.

CLANCY CALLS IT A SUCCESS

CLANCY went back to the Hotel Atlantis with the document in his wallet, his eyes warily searching the shadows, his hand round the butt of the gun in his jacket pocket, and his mind busy upon the bargain he had made, which reason told him was good, but which he still did not entirely like.

He was glad when he left the half-lighted street behind and passed through the revolving door at the hotel entrance, for, in addition to the normal fear of a gangster's bullet, which had not left him since he had learnt of the bogus cablegram which had been sent in his name, he had been wary of any contact with the cops, which was always possible for such as he. Even the gun he carried, as he had no licence, could be made a pretext for running him in, or he might be wanted for questioning on any charge, new or old, which might be on the books—perhaps a bank hold-up that day within the city limits of which he might not even have heard.

These were no more than natural incidents to such a life as his, and would not normally have disturbed his mind. They were remote possibilities now that he had retired from the activities of a life of crime, which, having worked on his own or only with Moll, it had been possible for him to do, as the gangster rarely could. If he were run in, he knew the ropes. There was bail, which it would be easy for him to buy. There was the Habeas Corpus, which can be even more potent in the country which has inherited its blessings than as it is operated by English law. There was more than one big shot who would pass a word to the cops that would be likely to set him free.

At the worst, more than half the magistrates of New York, if report did them no injustice, could be bought on most moderate terms. A rota system had been introduced by zealous reformers to check the effects of this venality. No courts could now be mentioned as places where justice was habitually sold; no districts where it could be said that a girl could never walk alone with safety lest she should be arrested by the police on a faked charge, and have to pay for a bail-bond before she could go home, and return to court in the morning to pay a fine which would be heavily increased if she should make a scene by protesting that the evidence was an utter preposterous lie.... Now the magistrates took turns at each court, changing from week to week, but the result of this had been forecast in a too sanguine spirit. There were some magistrates who were beyond corruption and they could be recognised by the number of cases called before them in which the police would ask for adjournments, saying that they would not be ready to proceed till the next week....

Clancy knew that he was in no serious danger from anything the cops would be likely to do, but even for them to give him the once-over while that confession was in his pocket would have consequences difficult to foresee, but very unlikely to spell permanent safety for either Moll or himself.

But he reached his apartment without incident, and found Moll combing out her red hair in preparation for a night's rest, for which even her bright vitality was disposed, and with relief from anxiety at his return which she had learned that he would not thank her to show.

"Any luck?" she asked, without turning her head, as she saw his entrance through the mirror at which she stood.

"I'd say I have." He crossed the room, throwing hat and gun on to the wide expanse of the double bed as he passed it, and laid the document he had obtained open before her.

Her eyes fell on it without changing her position, and she was instant in understanding.

"Gee!" she said. "To think that! You wouldn't say it's not true?"

"Nope. It explains quite a lot."

"He's alive?"

"Was when he left me."

"Did he kick hard?"

"Not to matter. I've had to promise we'll lie low till his deal's through."

"You mean if he sells out at Vitale's feed?"

"You've got it in one. I don't wait longer than that."

"Think it's safe?"

"It ought to be, if that bit of paper's put where it can't be got at. I thought we'd ask Crowe to take care of that."

"But if you tell him—"

"I meant sealed up, of course. I've thought out how much I must say to him. We'll go up now if you'll put something on."

"Maloon's there."

"Then tomorrow morning will have to do."

"Suit me. I'm that tired! I've been out with Evelyn all day, saying the piece you told me to, and—well, showing her round. She's a peach.... Say, Tim, they're afraid Capone's really bought their bank."

"Sure? Those Britishers aren't that easy to tie up, if you ask me."

"I'd say not. But I don't know. They have me guessing at times. Evelyn says—"

"You mean Lady Crowe?"

"Yes. She told me to call her that. I've gone up to her floor. She says she was kidnapped once. Something about a drug racket. But Sir Crowe got her clear when she was going to be done in, and while all the cops in England were running around after their own tails."

"Then they have some rackets there? He'll need to be wide awake if he means downing Capone.... But I don't know that I'd bet much either way. We've got to see what he'll make of this."

"He won't like it. That's a sure thing. But we'll leave that till tomorrow now."

The bedroom doors of the Hotel Atlantis are fitted with good bolts. Clancy looked at his with care. He inserted wedges, which would increase the difficulty of manipulation. He resorted to the primitive but effective device of the chair-back under the door-handle.

"We don't need to," he said. "We know the rule here. But there's nothing wrong about being extra sure.... Kid, you owe me a good night."

Moll said: "Oh, yeah!" And then: "Reckon I do?"

CHAPTER XLII.

AN AGREEMENT WITH TIM CLANCY

THEY were all breakfasting together next morning when Tim told his tale, with the reservations that his own sense of expediency and his bargain with Cassidy required. He had rung up Sir Reginald's room at an early hour to make the arrangement, which had been agreed all the more readily because of a bargain which had been made with Maloon the night before.

Now Mr. Jellipot listened with intent but otherwise expressionless eyes, and Sir Reginald looked doubtful and discontent. He had no reason to distrust Tim or the veracity of what he told. On the other hand, his reasons for trusting him were less than conclusive, and he thought that he was being asked much in return for an equivocal gain and a tale of a confession he was not to see.

"There's one weak point," he said, "about the whole thing. The Chief, as you call him, mayn't agree to pay out."

"That's not a weak point for us. If he doesn't we can do what we like about him after the day of the dinner."

"That's what I mean. It isn't easy to see how Cassidy should be content with a bargain that all depends on that chance."

"I didn't say he was. It isn't what he'd have signed if he'd thought there were no bullets in my gun.... But I'd say the Chief will pay out. He's got too much to lose if he ducks, and he'll plan to get the papers first, and then the money back on the next day.

"Besides, we're giving Cassidy quite a lot. He gets a promise that we shan't set the cops on to him, and the Chief's to find Capone on his back just as Cassidy's making his getaway."

"It's well put; and there's more than a little reason in what you say." Sir Reginald's eyes moved from Clancy to the silent girl at his side. 'I suppose Mrs. Clancy has seen the confession? You'll have been more confidential to her than you feel able to be with us?"

"I don't keep much back from Moll, if you mean that. But she won't talk."

"I didn't suppose she would. I only want to know that she's as sure as you that this is the right course to take."

"I think," she said, speaking for the first time since she had entered the room, "Tim's giving you the right dope, and you might be a bit more pleased than you are. He's found out what you'd got to know, and it wouldn't have come any other way."

Sir Reginald gave her a smiling response. "I'm more pleased already now you've said that. You've been straight with me, and I've learnt to have a great respect for your opinion on these matters, with which you have been so much more conversant than ourselves."

Redhead, on her side, might have looked more pleased than she did. She said: "Tim's done more for you than I'd be likely to think I could. You'll know that if you wait."

Tim said: "Shut up, Moll. I told you to leave this to me.... I knew it wouldn't sound much, and if you're a bit sore I'm not taking it wrong."

"I'm not sore," Sir Reginald replied, with some apology in his voice, "and I can see that you have been successful in a difficult enterprise, which must have had danger for you. But it needs some thinking out, all the same.

"I came here to find the man who'd been making a bloody mess (that isn't swearing, Evelyn, so don't look like that) of my carpet, and to find out what it all meant, and now you say I'm to know who the murderer was if I let him go free."

Mr. Jellipot spoke at last. "I don't think that is quite accurate. The real murderer was not the hired man, who has had a bit of trouble already and may have more ahead, but the one who paid him two thousand dollars for what he did.

"Mr. Clancy is arranging for us to know who he is and for the information to be passed on to Capone, who seems to be the sort of gentleman who will deal with him in a most chastening manner. It appears to me that, with Mr. Clancy's consent, the information may be given to Capone in a way which will make him grateful to us on what may be a most opportune day."

This emphatic support, which had reminded Sir Reginald of that which had been for a moment out of his mind, appeared to remove all cloud of remaining doubt.

"You've hit the right nail on the head, Jellipot," he said, "as you always do.... Mr. Clancy, we'll be franker with you than you feel able to be with us.

"Capone thinks he's bought my bank, and he's going to use it to salt away the dirty money that he and his brother vermin collect here. He feels sure he's bought it, and he thinks he can buy me. You know that, more or less. You don't know that Maloon was here last night telling us that it's all over and they've got the bank in the bag. They feel sure; but we're not. We shan't give up hope till we hear what happens on next settling day on the London Exchange. That's Friday, next week.

"Now, if he's right, this may be a big enough thing to be some use, or it may not. I can't say. And if he's wrong—you know him, and you may guess how he'll take it better than I can. But there'll be no harm in having something else for him to think of that comes from us.

Redhead said dryly, "You'll be surprised," and Tim said again sharply: "Shut up, Moll."

Evelyn saw that Tim felt that Moll had been indiscreet, though it was hard to see how. She interposed with: "I suppose Cassidy didn't tell you how he managed to do his murders and disappear without being seen in rather less time than none. That's the point I've hoped we should be able to clear up before we go home."

"Yes, ma'am, he did say something about that. We had a few general words after business was put away and he'd had his gun back with the bullets drawn. He said there was a bathroom a with a way through another room. When Sir Reginald came he wouldn't have had time to get away. He just backed in there.... He saw you look out of the window, though you didn't see him, and then you went back to Ringan, and he went through a big empty room and got to a lift without meeting anyone."

"And to think," Sir Reginald said, with natural irritation, "that if I'd had the sense to open that door I should have saved all the trouble of coming here!"

"It's most likely you'd have got shot if you had. He'd got his tale ready. He was a cop from over here who'd followed Ringan, but too late to save you. He's fly enough to have got away with it too.

"And it sounds as though he's fly enough to get away with it now, and with a much bigger haul than he was intended to have.... And now we've got something else to be saying to you.

"Maloon was here last night. He was just starting for Detroit for some dirty business—it's sure to be dirty—that he's got there. He'll be back on Sunday, and he wants us all to go to Chicago together then.

"He was very anxious we should give Dallas a miss, and I agreed to that. If Capone owns the bank there we shouldn't do much good talking to whoever he's got in charge.

"He wants you and Mrs. Clancy to come along with us. He says it'll be safest for her, and, with all the enquiries that he and Capone are making, he reckons that they'll comb out who ordered the killings—as, of course, they may yet, without your help—if you'd found out nothing by that day."

Clancy spoke with decision: "I'll come along, if you like. I've got something to collect, and I mean to be on the spot at the right time. But Moll stays here."

"You think she'll be safer here than with you?"

"I do that. And I mean *here*. She won't go outside the street door. Not if she's told that I've sent her a dying prayer. And you'll leave Lady Crowe too, if you'll hear sense from me."

Evelyn looked her annoyance. She was about to speak, but saw that Moll was looking at her with anxious eyes. Why settle that now?

Sir Reginald said: "You can be sure that anything you advise will have serious consideration. Do we understand that Maloon is included among those who must have no hint of what you have told us?"

"Yep. But not him in particular. No *one's* to have a word till it comes from me."

"That is a bargain that cannot be misunderstood and that you can be sure that we shall not break."

Clancy hesitated a moment, and then said: "There's just one thing more. If Cassidy tells the Chief what he's given me there'll be hell to pay, and no time lost with the bill. I don't say he will—I'm sure he won't—but if there's any try to get that bit of paper he's signed back out of my pocket—well, I'd rather it's not there."

"You mean," Mr. Jellipot suggested, "that you would like us to arrange for its deposit in a secure place?"

"You've said it. If it's not asking too much."

"It seems to me to be no more than a prudent precaution.... You will, of course, deliver it to Sir Reginald in a sealed envelope?"

"I'll stick it down, if you mean that. But I'm not thinking you'd take a look-see. I reckon you could get it put where even Capone couldn't get his foot through the door."

"You can rely on that."

"And if anything happens to Moll or me, that'll mean you can read it just as quick as you like."

"And communicate its contents to Maloon or Capone?"

"You can please yourselves. It'll be yours to use any way you will.... We'll bring it up to you now."

CHAPTER XLIII.

Mr. Jellipot Learns Much

BREAKFAST and its discussions over, Evelyn, whose purchases of American goods were already sufficient to ensure substantial increment to the English Customs on her return, said that she was going shopping again. She looked uncertainly at Moll, who looked dutifully at Tim.

Evelyn, who had understood that Moll's voluntary incarceration was to begin when they would go to Chicago and leave her alone, had a sudden fear that he might consent to Moll coming now if he should make a third. She felt that would be just a little too much. Feeling mean, she looked away.

At that the Clancys withdrew, Tim returning in a few minutes with an envelope which he handed over to the banker's charge.

Sir Reginald had already spoken of appointments with brother bankers, from whom he was familiarising himself with the weirder features of his profession as it was then carried on in the New World—or, at least, such as could be observed in the comparatively conservative atmosphere of New York. It was a time when all values were falling, though their ultimate levels were in an abyss which was still to come, and the word "depression" was on every tongue; even those who professed expertness in economic laws speaking of it as though it were an inscrutable act of God rather than the logical consequence of their own defaults.

Mr. Jellipot, whose interests were of law and sociology rather than finance, said that he had an appointment with the highly respected firm of attorneys who had been his agents for many years. He was struggling with a scrupulous conscience to justify, and a cautious temperament to allow himself to make, such enquiries concerning the coming dinner to the New York magistrate as would enable him to visualise better the background of the projected blackmailing settlement of which he had heard.

So they went out to the crude vitality of this new, strange city their different ways, and Mr. Jellipot, when the courtesies of initial contact with Messrs. Infrey and Rostor had been observed, found that he was in no danger of indiscretions with them, for they knew nothing of local criminal courts, and the existence of racketeers was something of which they were only vaguely aware. Irishmen—politicians—Italians—even Jews—their existence must be allowed. They formed a large part of the population of the greatest city in the New World. That was indisputable statistic fact. But it was not one on which it was necessary to dwell. People of culture and settled wealth turned their thoughts and their eyes elsewhere. No doubt the prices of many commodities were increased by the operations of racketeers. But they could afford o pay them, even during this mysterious depression, which could not last. And if these men shot each other at times they were no loss to lament, and it was only what it was of the nature of such vermin to do.

Finding that Mr. Jellipot was really interested in the low life of the city (which included the operations of the magistrates' courts to them), they very courteously recommended him to lawyers of different practice, Messrs. Tozer, Battle & Young, who would tell him all he might wish to know....

Mr. Herbert A. Battle was rapidly polite for three minutes, and regretted that his brother Charles, who would have been delighted to take care of Mr. Jellipot, was not in. But Mr. Young would do so, he had no doubt.

Mr. Young had, unfortunately, a client in urgent difficulties a bail-bond runner on whose activities the spotlight had fallen at an unfortunate moment. He passed Mr. Jellipot over to Mr. Whalen, who, after explaining modestly that he was no relation of the Police Commissioner, but claiming some connection by marriage with Jimmy Walker, the mayor, proved to be a young man of much peculiar knowledge and a cheerfully cynical wit

When Mr. Jellipot returned to the Atlantis to join his friends at their dinner, he had acquired a knowledge of social conditions and of the administration of Justice in New York at which he was appalled and amazed, and which he judged, with riper wisdom than that of his livelier young guide, would not be tolerated permanently in a civilised city.

It was true that Mr. Whalen had mentioned various and energetic efforts by individual citizens, by committees and police commissioners, to improve the practices of the courts. These had the young man's entire sympathy, but he regarded their eventual failure as an operation of natural law. It was like clearing a cistern into which fresh dirt would be continually poured. And though in a spirit of generous indignation citizens of influence and reputation might explore the political slough, it was not likely that they would endure its contaminations long.

Mr. Jellipot was led to mention that there was a good priest in Italy in the Middle Ages who had been elected to the Pontifical Chair, but who had refused the position because he disliked the corrupt political atmosphere of the Papacy of that day, for which refusal Dante placed him in hell.

Mr. Whalen exclaimed, "You don't say!" with suitable surprise at this anecdote, but whether he appreciated its implications may be left in doubt.

By interesting himself in accounts of others, whose names were nothing to him, Mr. Jellipot was able to obtain a vivid though possibly inaccurate picture of Magistrate Vitale, and an idea of what the atmosphere of a dinner given in his honour was likely to be.

Mr. Whalen had heard of the dinner. He knew of the pseudo-political society, The Tepecano Democratic Club, by which it would be given. It was knowledge that an alert young lawyer, practising in the criminal courts, would be sure to have.

He was careful to say that the magistrate was not known to be in any rackets himself. But the society which honoured him included notorious criminal members, and entertained criminals at its feasts; and it was said that he could be seen at times in public places in company with leading racketeers, such as Cito Terranova. Mr. Jellipot had not heard of him? Mr. Whalen showed as much surprise as politeness allowed. He was the Artichoke King. Harlem was his business stronghold. His private residence was a palatial $50,000 structure in Pelham Manor. His bodyguard was the best in the well-gunned ranks of the racketeers. His bullet-proof car was an example of luxury and security which Capone himself had been glad to copy.

Mr. Jellipot avoided further exposure of his deplorable ignorance by enquiring how transactions in artichokes could require such protection or bring such wealth. He asked: "I suppose that Magistrate Vitale's headquarters may be in Harlem also?"

But that, it appeared, was not so. His stronghold was the Bronx. It was at the Bronx Roman Gardens Restaurant that the ceremonial dinner in his honour would be held. As a magistrate he was on a rota, going from court to court. Of course, much that was said about him might not be true. But Whalen had been in court recently when he had made everyone happy by acquitting a thief against whom there was overwhelming evidence, and ordering the money he had stolen to be returned to its owner. He believed that this remarkable magistrate had explained his action by saying that, if he had heard all the evidence which the press subsequently published as having been given before him, he should have sent the man to jail; but he was taking notes at the time, and it must have escaped his attention.... And the record of the trial had not afterwards been easy to find. Mr. Whalen also mentioned that the magistrate had been seen with Jack Diamond, which he seemed to think required no interpretation.

Mr. Jellipot was anxious to show that his ignorance of American celebrities was not absolute. He said: "I believe I have heard of that gentleman, as one who is familiarly nicknamed Legs."

Mr. Whalen said that was so. He gave some details of Diamond's career. He had started as a professional gunner—a bodyguard for those able to hire such protection. His high mission in life had been to protect life, not to take it.

But he had not been altogether fortunate in the fulfilment of these offices. He had been bodyguard to Little Augie, an east-side gangster of some notoriety, when he had been shot. He had been bodyguard also to the more famous Rothstein, acknowledged prince of gamblers and gambling-dens, when he had been shot under circumstances that the police knew but were unable to prove.

After that two men had been shot in Broadway at the Hotsy Totsy Club, and the police wanted to prosecute Charles Entratta and Diamond for their murder. Diamond had not, on this occasion, been the bodyguard of either of the dead men. He was the proprietor, more or less, of the Hotsy Totsy. Entratta had been arrested three or four months ago, but there had been no trial, as Diamond could not be found. It was said that he had been seen with Vitale since then at Joe Ward's Club, but that might be no more than a tale.

Mr. Jellipot said that Vitale would be very interesting to meet, and was told that there would be no difficulty about that. Whalen described him as of Neapolitan type, with black hair plastered flat and rather Napoleonic features. A pleasant-mannered, accessible man. Being a barrister also, he was one with whom a murderer, avoiding justice, would naturally be glad to confer.

After this the talk became more recondite, Mr. Jellipot learning much of the interactions of Federal and State laws and the mutual jealousies which hindered their operations and became profitable to the astuter members of the criminal population. He came to understand, though he could not palliate, the monstrous system which gave bail to criminals but imprisoned innocent witnesses of their crimes.

Mr. Whalen came to recognise both the acuteness of his questions and the friendly attitude of his mind. They parted with mutual liking, Mr. Jellipot saying truly that he had learned much.

CHAPTER XLIV.

TERRANOVA CAN ALSO PLOT

"IT is an aspect of the matter," Mr. Jellipot said, "which I could not propound for Mr. Whalen's consideration, but it appears to me that Cassidy has chosen his opportunity with great astuteness. A dinner to a magistrate appears to be one at which a detective officer may be present without risk of incurring the censure of his superiors, and, though it is a singular circumstance that this one appears to be given by men of a peculiarly criminal type, it is that contradictory circumstance which should procure for him the immunity he requires. For these men, whom Vitale appears to use his magisterial office to serve, would give him a poor requital if they should allow the complimentary dinner to become the scene of a violent crime, such as must bring it to the probing notice of the police.... I should suppose it to be a place of even greater safety than this hotel."

He was at dinner with the Crowes when he said this, they having returned from their several ways, and Sir Reginald answered: "I don't suppose you're far wrong. It shows what a wily fox this Cassidy is, and I only hope Clancy isn't the one that he means to leave in the soup. But, all the same, you might have put it a better way. I've just been telling Evelyn to stay here, and saying there isn't a safer place in the world, and you sit down and tell her that it's worse than one that no decent woman would enter."

This remark reduced Mr. Jellipot to silence. It was not merely that the retort contained the species of inexactitudes to which he preferred to render precise reply, such as would require choice of deliberate words, but the fact was that he was by no means sure of the expediency of leaving Lady Crowe for several days in the Atlantis, with no company but Moll, and it was this doubt which must be resolved before he could reply in the right way.

Evelyn said: "Reggie tried to leave me at Hither Dene, and now he's at the same game again. I'm told there aren't more than four states in the Union where I couldn't get a divorce for desertion for such conduct as that."

"That's nonsense, Evelyn. I don't suppose there are four where you could; even if such a divorce could be worth what it costs to get.... But this time you've got to see reason, whether you like it or not.

"Look here, Jellipot, you've got brains, and you know what we've got to face. As I see it, we've got to go to Chicago on Monday and then talk friendly without meaning anything till Friday comes—that's four days, if not five—and we know where we are. We can't quit stalling till then, and we've got to pretend we're friends, more or less, with this mucky crew, without pledging ourselves to anything that we shouldn't mean, and then be ready to use this information that Clancy's got according to how things will have gone on the London Exchange, and at this dinner, which we shan't know till two days later.

"When you get in a jam like that, the fewer mouths there are to talk at all, the less trouble there's likely to be. And that's only one reason; I could tell you of forty-nine more, if necessary, without stopping to think."

"That," Evelyn retorted, "is just how you've told us that. It's more likely I should help you off the topics you want to miss. I should go for the young bride-to-be and make friends with her."

"You think that? When you see that she-wop (I don't suppose she's young at all—Al's over thirty), I expect you'll just go away to be sick."

"No, I shouldn't. I'm too interested in strange beasts. I know you think, after the way I vamped Maloon yesterday, that we're best apart, but I can tell you it's about the biggest mistake that you ever made. There's a little Hebrew with well-oiled hair and the most beautiful eyes that you ever saw who comes in and out of this hotel—I've heard him called Slinker—and the way he keeps looking over his shoulder and fingering the bulge on his left hip is what Moll would call just too cute for words. He'd only have to crook his finger to me, and I'd follow him to the South Pole. So you'll know what to expect if you leave us together here."

"Evelyn, don't be an ass—though I don't say I wouldn't be more inclined to let you come if Maloon were staying here. I've got a feeling that there'd be more trouble where that man is than is likely anywhere else. But I'll tell you what we'll do.

"We'll ask Clancy whether he thinks it's best for you to come with us or to stay here. He knows how the land lies, and I think we'll get a straight answer from him."

"He'll want me to stay with Moll."

"Will he? I shouldn't say you'd be much protection to her."

"He wouldn't look at it like that." But Sir Reginald held to the idea, and, when she found that it had Mr. Jellipot's support, Evelyn gave in.

Clancy, being found and asked, had no hesitation in his reply. When you went to see Capone on business you didn't take dames along. Not if you were a wise guy.

It was a final verdict, and Evelyn saw that she was destined to stay behind.

While this conversation had been proceeding, another, which would have at least equal influence upon the dramatic events of the next ten days, was proceeding in a private room at the Tepecano Club, where Vitale and Terranova conferred together.

"There's a bit of business," Terranova began, "I could do at that dinner, but it's for you to say. I don't want you to get me wrong."

Vitale recognised the voice as that in which proposals were made such as would end in a wad of untraceable bills passing from another pocket into his, but the fact that the Artichoke King should preface it in this diffident manner warned him that something unusual or potentially perilous to himself was to be proposed.

"You can depend upon me to do anything I can. You know that. Anything that won't end in my being disbarred. I don't want to make a mistake that would put me out of a position to help the boys when they get run in. You'd better tell me first what the trouble is, and we'll see what can be done."

"That's soon said. You know that Frankie Yale and Frank Marlow got bumped off, and there's been no arrest, and the cops couldn't guess who did it or even why it was done."

"Yes. That was months back. Whoever's in it can reckon that's dead. Even the P.C. will be thinking of something else now."

"I bet he is. But I can't. You see, I had to order the bumpings-off.... I had Burke from Chicago for them. He's a good man, and he works alone. But he put his price high. He wanted twenty thousand bucks. You know I pay well. But if every bumping-off is to cost ten grand, I might as well retire while I've got a few dollars left.

"He wanted me to pay in advance, which I wouldn't do. Not beyond his expenses in coming here, and a week to hang round, picking his chance.

"So he said if I'd give him a written promise he'd be content. I didn't like doing that, but I thought it over and it seemed safe enough. He wouldn't leave the paper lying about. He'd be too scared for his own skin. And if he got shot up himself and the cops got it, it would be evidence against me, but not proof, and I might have to shell out to the cops—or perhaps to you—but I shouldn't have to pay him.

"So in the end I gave him the note he wanted.

"Well, he knocked Yale and Marlow off, as you know. They were neat jobs, though it was a long while before he got Marlow; and after he got back to Chicago that time I sent him five grand, and I thought he'd shut his mouth.

"But he's been on me ever since for fifteen more, and he won't quit. Now he's written that unless he gets them within a week he'll send the contract to the police."

"He wouldn't dare to do that."

"Think not? I'm not that sure. He'd know I'd have to buy the cops off, and I couldn't do that without covering him."

"I wouldn't stake you could do that. The P.C.'s too active just now.

"Well, I reckon I could. They'd say the note might be phoney, and they'd better take the money and not risk a jury throwing them out by the ears. But I should have to pay big, and I've thought of something a lot better than that."

"How can I help you?"

"It isn't anything that I want you to do. It's just to stand by and understand that the trouble's not meant for you. I'm going to tell him I'll pay that fifteen grand, but he's got to let me have the paper back at the same time. He can't kick at that."

"He'll want to make himself safe."

"Sure he will. That's where you come in. I'll tell him to bring it to your dinner, and he'll feel sure there'll be no upset there. The boys wouldn't stand for that."

"I don't mind if it's all done quietly. You'll need to send him a ticket. I don't want too many who've got their names in the cops' books."

"There won't be that. But I'd got a better idea. I'll say again that I don't want you to get me wrong. But I don't mean to give him that fifteen grand, and I do mean to get that paper into a good fire. And I reckon a hold-up'll do the trick."

"You don't mean at the dinner?"

"I don't mean a real hold-up. We'd have to make it look real to him. We'd have to frisk the guests, and not only him. But we'll give back what we take. We shouldn't want to do anything dirty to them."

The magistrate laid down his cigar. He got up and paced the length of the room several times. He saw the value of the idea. It would avert what would otherwise almost certainly be one of those murderous feuds in which killing followed killing, as each death gave a fresh impetus to vengeance from alternate sides. If the man could not produce the document, he could not complain that he were not paid. But to bring him to the right frame of mind he must have no doubt that the hold-up had been genuine, and that Terranova had suffered as well as himself. He must believe that Terranova had come in a mood of willingness to pay, from which only the absence of the document held him back.

Vitale liked to persuade himself that the semi-criminal courses which he pursued, while enriching himself, were beneficial to others. He was adroit in manœuvring such positions, as when he had set the thief free (for a sufficient bribe) on condition that the stolen money were restored. Was there anything wrong in the bribe? Was it not fair payment for the risk he took? But he disliked risks.

He spoke at last: "You can't tell all the guests."

"Nope. There'd be too many'd give us away. But they can have their properties back if they're some you wouldn't want to feel sore."

"There's some that might shoot it out if they don't know. I can't have that."

"We wouldn't risk it. I wouldn't trust to two men. I'd have six or more. There'd be no one'd try shooting it out then."

Vitale thought again. There would be two score guests, more or less. Ladies among them. And some of them could be put wise. It ought to be safe enough. He wouldn't refuse if Terranova had set his heart on it being done this way. They did too much business together. And Terranova had a name for pulling off what he took in hand.

"I don't like it," he said. "But I won't refuse, if you're that keen. But you must take care that it means no scandal for me."

"Sure I will. I want it to go quiet. That's how I'll shape it to be."

So he planned, without thought of the possibility that there might be others who thought to use the same occasion, more or less—to a point—in the same way.

And Clancy planned in an equal ignorance, and the event moved on to an end that no astuteness would be able to guess.

CHAPTER XLV.

WHAT CAN BE WRONG ABOUT THAT?

IT was Sunday afternoon when Maloon came back to the Atlantis. Whatever he had been doing in the meantime had not improved his temper, and there was no pretence of courtesy in the tone or manner of his response when Sir Reginald told him that he was not intending to arrive in Chicago before Wednesday.

"Reckon," he said, "that it was fixed that we'd go tomorrow."

"Scarcely that," Sir Reginald replied smoothly. "It was mentioned, and perhaps anticipated, but I have matters that I can attend to here, and our visit to Chicago is not of such urgency that forty-eight hours—"

"You'll make Capone raw."

"You need have no concern for that. I have had him on the phone and ascertained that Wednesday will be a convenient day for us to arrive.... Of course, if tomorrow be preferable for you, we have no claim upon you to delay for our convenience."

Maloon recognised finality in this, but was reduced to obvious indecision. "I've no call," he said, "to see Capone before you. I don't say but—no, we'll go Wednesday, We'll go by plane.... Found out anything yet?"

"Nothing whatever."

"Tim been luckier?"

Sir Reginald smiled. "I'm afraid you must ask him that. We have seen little of him. And if he has found out who the murderer was, he has certainly not confided his name to us." Maloon got up to go. "See you Wednesday," he said to Evelyn as he shook hands. The tone might have implied that it would be a certain pleasure to her.

"I'm not coming to Chicago, if you mean that."

He looked black again at this, and then the cloud passed. "Well, so long," he said abruptly, and went out.

"I should say," Sir Reginald remarked with satisfaction rather than sympathy, "that business has been going badly with him."

But Moll, when Evelyn afterwards told her of what had occurred, reduced its significance by saying: "You just don't know Slick. He always hustles. He thinks all Britishers too darned slow to live. Besides, he likes to have things go the way he fixes them up."

Sir Reginald had telephoned to Capone after the doubt which had been in his own mind had been supported by Evelyn's question: "If you've got to stall, why not stall here?" It was common sense to reduce the time of abortive talk, if it could be peacefully done, and, though he guessed that Maloon would resent any change of plan, he felt that that was not of the first importance if Capone were content.

As to that, the great man, whose telephone voice had an agreeable softness, made no trouble at all. He probably knew nothing of the tentative arrangement made with Maloon, and certainly nothing of the subsequent events which made next Saturday a critical date. He had no doubt that he controlled the London and Northern Bank, and was shrewd enough to see the importance of retaining a chairman of whose versatile activities he was fully informed. He said that Wednesday would be O.K. by him. But for some business difficulties he would have come to New York. Of course, Lady Crowe would come? No? He was sorry for that. He hoped people hadn't been talking to her about Chicago in the wrong way.

Sir Reginald, as he hung up, recognised the wisdom of what he had done. He thought that he knew Capone better by that short conversation than he had done before. Deadly as a snake he might be. But he was not one who would he hasty to use his fangs.

He had learned already the reason that barred Capone from the journey to New York, whether or not he would otherwise have undertaken it. He was already treating the Federal Court with contempt, having ignored an order to appear before it, with consequences difficult to foresee. To serve any process on Capone in his Chicago stronghold according to the requirements of Federal law was not easy, but to travel to New York with the bodyguard that his safety required, and the consequent publicity of his movements, was to ask for more trouble than he had yet had.

So they had two more days in New York which, even for those who had cut themselves off from its normal hospitalities by putting up at the Hotel Atlantis and other eccentricities of approach, were very easy to fill; and then Sir Reginald, Jellipot, and Maloon departed together, and the two women were left to their own devices and such anxieties as the positions in which they stood and their own natures gave them.

For the first two days they remained in their own apartment—it had been arranged for Moll to migrate to the banker's suite—or descended to the public rooms together. But they attracted little attention in a hotel where their status was settled by the fact that they had been allowed to register there, and it was not good manners to show curiosity concerning the identity of others or the business they had to do.

Evelyn learned much from Moll, both of the life and the personalities of the underworld, some of whom she was able to point out as they passed through lounge or bar, or dined liberally in that citadel of wealthy, successful crime. Incidentally, she learned that Slinker, whom she had described so appreciatively to a husband who could not be roused to any jealous reaction, was a gun man with some reputation for stealthy homicides. He was not known to be attached to one of the big shots, but to be open to entertain business from any direction if it were of sufficient secrecy and would bring a sufficient fee.

Each evening Tim, and each noon Sir Reginald, rang up to enquire for the well-being of those they left. As to what they were doing themselves, Tim was laconic. He said no more than that he was O.K., and that he would tell his baby everything when he got back.

Moll said that meant nothing. He would have talked just the same if he had just shot Maloon and were going to treat Capone in the same way within the hour.

Sir Reginald was also guarded in what he said. He generalised fluently. He talked deliberate or unconscious American. He said Chicago was a swell city and that he was feeling fine. Evelyn formed the opinion that he thought someone was listening m, which could not be considered improbable. She was equally vague and guarded in her replies.

But on Friday there was, to her practised ear, a note of suppressed excitement in his voice as he had said he should soon be back. He expected to arrive in New York some time on Monday. Everything was being fixed up "fine." Evelyn was left wondering whether this were sincere or intended for other ears. She was conscious of vague disquiet, which she suppressed with a firm will.

It was in the middle afternoon that the post came in. Letters at the Hotel Atlantis were not left for guests to collect from the counter. They were distributed at once by the porter's staff. This post brought nothing for Evelyn, but an official envelope for Moll, at the contents of which she barely glanced before saying what a pest it all was!

Evelyn asked, "More trouble now?" and Moll said: "I meant it's a pest that I've promised not to go out. Look at this."

She handed over a meagre slip of thin paper which informed her that a parcel from England awaited her at the post office, where it was held for assessment of customs dues. She said: "Won't they send it here?"

"No. You have to open them there. It's something I bought in England. They couldn't give me the colour I wanted, and I paid them to get it and send it on.... Anyone could see this isn't a trap."

"No. I suppose not."

"It isn't 'suppose.' It's a sure thing. Even if they could, no one's going to monkey with the Federal mails."

Evelyn already knew enough of the complications of American law and the growing dread the gangsters had of conflict with the Federal Government, which was to be their ruin at last, to see the force of this argument. If Moll should go to the post office to collect this parcel, there could be no fear that she was being lured out by a faked call.

But her promise to Tim was absolute, and, though she wanted the parcel, it was one which she would not break.

Evelyn was not held by a similar pledge, though she had preferred to remain in during the last two days. She said: "Could I go for you? If I take a taxi I can be back in an hour. Would they let me have it?"

"I expect they would if you take this. They'll charge you twice what they ought, but I shan't die. I'll be real glad if you do."

"I'll be glad to get out. Is the post office far?"

"About six blocks."

"Then I'll go now."

A few minutes later she descended to the street, where a row of cars was always await for the affluent patrons of the hotel. Most of them were the primrose-yellow of the Fay Company, but it was one of darker colour that moved up as she came down the steps. The driver had the door open and was waiting for her instructions as she reached the curb. She entered without hesitation, and was too ignorant of the locality to know that they did not head for the post office, but for the New Jersey subway.

It was only when they pulled up at a red light, and the door opened just as they were moving again, and Slinker got in beside her, that she had a sudden fear that something was gravely wrong.

CHAPTER XLVI.

A Bargain with Al Capone

SIR REGINALD looked into the large, smooth face of a man who was grossly fat. He received a firm grip from a flabby hand.

"Glad to meet you, Sir Reginald." The voice had an Italian softness. The eyes were large and liquid and of a lively intelligence. Sir Reginald judged his host to be highly capable, sentimental, ruthless where his own safety or profit were at stake, liable to crack if he were faced by too hard a test. One with intelligence and driving force that made him a natural leader of men of his own race. One, if caught by extremes of fate, who might either bully or whine.

The little party had been met at the airport by Capone's own well-armoured car and driven, not to his down-town office, but to the high-walled home, which was palace, fortress, and park in one. People had not lined up and cheered as the car passed, but they had been aware of glances from many eyes, and that the cops were disposed to hold up other traffic to pass them through....

Capone had not always been of the ungainly figure that they now saw. Associates of his earlier Chicago days could remember him when he was of athletic build, vigorous of movement, and hard-hitting with his fists as well as quick with a gun. And he was only thirty-one now. But he was experiencing the failure of success, as few men have the misfortune to do.

Tradition, going a few years further back, said that he had been a youth of exemplary character and reputation in his home town until he had been deluded into believing that he had killed a man in a quarrel which had been forced upon him, in which fear he had fled to Chicago, and, before he knew the truth, had become too closely associated with a criminal gang there to be allowed to withdraw. As he could not withdraw, he had resolved to lead, and so, twelve years later, he sat in his steel-shuttered stronghold, the Napoleon of the beer racket, controlling a business which, had it produced a proper

216

balance-sheet, might have disclosed capitalised profits of not less than ten million pounds.

He met his visitors now with the careful gradations of manner that a monarch must learn to practise.

To Maloon there was no cordiality, but there was the formal courtesy due to an important ally. To Clancy there was a hint of condescension, tempered by a slightly more friendly tone, as to one not of his lofty rank, but with whom an amicable understanding prevailed. To Sir Reginald Crowe there was a fuller elaboration of diplomatic courtesy than Maloon had received, and to Mr. Jellipot there was a noncommittal affability, as to one whose status wag not defined. His voice had a tone of attractive sincerity as he regretted that Lady Crowe had not found it convenient to come. He turned next moment to say to Clancy, in a less formal manner: "And I thought you'd have been bringing Redhead along."

Clancy was blunt. "Redhead's scared."

Capone looked both hurt and surprised. "She's no call to be scared of me. You'd tell her that?"

"Not of you. Scared of being about till this muddle's cleared."

"I don't see," Slick said, "that she's that much cause. If she knows nothing she can't give much away."

"It's not what she knows. It's what might be thought. She might get a bit of wire round her neck, and it wouldn't do her much good for anyone to come to me next week to say that they were so sorry for the mistake.... It wouldn't do them any good either."

"You'd like a bodyguard for her till this is cleared up?" Capone asked.

"Nope. You might say I'm good for that. She's in the Atlantis now. I reckon she's safe there."

Capone agreed. He turned to Sir Reginald to say: "We'll have a little informal dinner together as soon as you've settled in. You'll like to see your rooms first. Eat first and talk after's the way I like. There'll be just ourselves for tonight."

When they were assembled at a well-served meal he talked shop, for it was the only subject he had, but he kept his word. He avoided finance. He avoided the recent events in which his visitors were concerned. But he was eloquent on the magnitude and profits of the beer business which he controlled, and how impregnably it was established in supplying a universal need. Only the repeal of prohibition could shake his throne, and even then a huge legitimate trade should be his.

Sir Reginald, quietly responding, and judging the man with whom so heavy a skirmish was soon to come, modified, if he did not reverse, the plan of "stalling" on which he had previously resolved. He saw Capone as a man who did not hesitate to control his organisation by means of criminal violence of the most ruthless nature. But he judged that he was one of the Italian type to whom craft was preferable to the violent courses which, he would say, had been thrust upon him. Primarily he was a business man. One who would be most difficult to hoodwink, but quick to see the folly of attempting to hold an untenable position. It was at least probable that the idea of getting his own way by illegal methods had never entered his mind—which it was not very easy to see how even his ingenuity could contrive.

He saw that if he should adopt evasive tactics they would afterwards be recognised, almost certainly, for what they would have been, which might be of actual disadvantage to him in the critical negotiations which might lie ahead. Mr. Jellipot's disposition was to delay action when in doubt, but Sir Reginald was of a contrary habit. When the meal had been concluded and they had with drawn to a lounge furnished with the lavish counterpart of noble living natural to the gangster world, he did not wait for Capone to open the subject, but, to Mr. Jellipot's momentary surprise—a feeling which quickly died as he observed that the banker was only acting with his usual opportunist versatility—he began: "Before we start talking business I ought to thank you for your kindness in putting us up. I didn't expect it, and had actually made a reservation at the Bilton. But it places an additional obligation upon me to speak freely."

"Shoot straight, and we'll get on fine."

"So I hope we may. Mr. Maloon has already told us of the step you have taken to get control of the London and Northern Bank."

"I reckoned he would. But you've no call to fret. We don't mean it to be any funeral to you."

"You will agree that most men in my position would prefer to retain control of their own banks?"

"Sure they would. But I'd say there's not one in ten that has that. Not if all the others should line up on the wrong side. I'd say you didn't for one, or we shouldn't be sitting pretty the way we do."

"You mean that I did not hold a majority of the bank's shares in my own control? That is true. But they were held by those on whose support I could entirely rely."

"And that's just how it is now. It's that easy to get us wrong! We've heard you're the best banker in London, and that's like saying the best there is, and we want you where you are now. Maloon, you'd have said that?"

Maloon had sat silent during these exchanges, his long legs stretched out before a fire that added to the temperature of an otherwise heated room (for a bleak gale from Lake Michigan blew round the outer walls), a cigar between his teeth, and his eyes fixed on the coals, as though taking little notice of what went on. Now he said, "Sure," without altering his attitude. It was clear that he meant to leave the conversation in Capone's hands.

Mr. Jellipot, on the other side of the fire, and drawing equal satisfaction from another of Maloon's cigars, was of the same mind. Sir Reginald had the bit in his teeth. He would have little interference from him.

Clancy, being outside the discussion, had been guided to a drawing-room, where he would find the ladies of Capone's family, with whom he had had some acquaintance before.

But now Mr. Jellipot saw an opening which he felt that he should not miss.

"I think," he said, "that Mr. Capone makes a sound point. It would be most exceptional for the chairman of a large bank to hold control of a majority of its shares. Actually it would be far more exceptional in England than I suppose it to be in this country. In the majority of cases, owing to our system of using banks as nominees, he would not even know by whom they are held. It would be unreasonable for him to make a difficulty of that so long as his own policies were not opposed."

Sir Reginald showed little appreciation of the way in which his solicitor attempted to switch the points. He said: "That's true enough. But Mr. Capone hasn't gone to the trouble of buying all these shares so that I can carry out my own policies. He could have relied on my doing that without paying a cent."

Capone showed the subtlety of his Italian brain and his anxiety to secure Sir Reginald's support in his reply: "Oh, but I might! We want you there; but you might sell out. Changes come. We want to be sure that there won't be one there without our having something to say."

"I appreciate your confidence, of course. But what I was going to ask you was whether it might not be best to put off this discussion until you are quite sure what the position is?"

"Meaning just what?"

"Meaning that neither of us can know that until next settling day, when our brokers should get delivery of the stock we bought."

Capone could scarcely have been too ignorant of the methods of the 1929 stock market to fail to understand the significance of this suggestion, but his face showed nothing of this as he replied: "We know we've bought more than half the stock."

"So do we."

"Then it's O.K. for—"

"I mean we know that we have more than half the stock."

Capone's face flushed and darkened as he replied: "You mean you've pulled a fast one? I don't see how—"

"I don't mean anything of the kind. I don't know that anyone has. I suppose you know the meaning of selling short?"

"I'll know what you mean if you say you Britishers have been making suckers of us.

"Or perhaps you of us. But I haven't said what I don't know. I say we must wait and see."

"Wait till when?"

"Friday ought to make the position clear."

"That's not long." Capone's expression became difficult to read—a dangerous signal to those who knew what he could be in his worst moods. "Know," he asked, "what we've put into this?"

"No. But it must be a large sum."

"We'd lose if we gold out?"

"Yes. I should say you would."

"Reckon how much?"

"It might be anything up to twenty or thirty thousand pounds, if I make a guess. It would depend upon the discretion of your retreat. And whether you could make the penalties of those who should fail to deliver stock sufficiently high.... It would be a position in which we might give you substantial help."

"We're not there yet."

"No. I am not attempting to forecast what may result. I am only saying that it is not yet certain.... But I should like you to tell me what you propose to do if you obtain control."

"We don't want anything done wrong. We just want a bank we can use and that we can be sure won't sell us out. I can't be there, but Maloon will. We've got to have one we can trust, and Slick fits the part. No one monkeys with him, and he keeps his cash straight. That's between friends, of course."

Mr. Jellipot spoke to confirm that definite though limited praise. "Mrs. Clancy," he said, "told me the same thing. She said that Mr. Maloon could be relied upon in monetary matters—she meant between friends, no doubt."

Maloon said, "You're just saying I'm not a fool," and his words had a sincerity which was not invariable to his discourse.

It was true that he had a reputation for straight dealing in money matters, the absence of which was among the commonest causes for the bumpings-off which made the gangster's life seem so precarious to those who observed the incidence of racketeering. But he did not claim or desire any reputation for virtue. It was what he could well afford, and it greatly reduced the risk which most gangsters feared far more than any legal prosecution—that of a charge from a sawn-off shotgun being emptied into the back of his head, or the abdominal regions, where its operation, though less rapid, is no less sure.

How he would act in the comparative security of a European environment was a question which intrigued Mr. Jellipot's mind, but which it would have been obviously impolitic to raise.

Capone also had reputation for a similar degree of financial integrity, which, though he made many implacable enemies by the ruthlessness of his business methods, is the probable explanation of the fact that he is almost the only gangster there has been occasion to mention (except Fred Burke, who received a life sentence for murdering a cop in a state which has no death penalty) who survived the fierce gang warfare of the next two years, to reach the comparative security of a Federal penitentiary.

"Well," Sir Reginald said in a noncommittal way that did not bang a half-open door, "I think I see what you mean. For my part, I came over here without expecting such a development, and with two purposes only: to teach someone here that if he wants to put his friends on the spot it's a mistake to make it the first floor of my bank, and—"

"We've told you we'll take care of him. We're bound to find out—"

"I've no doubt you can. The other thing is to deal with that five million dollars you've put into our till. What's to become of that?"

"Our attorneys say that it can be transferred into other names and passed about so that no Government can follow it round. They just want you to play the game."

"You mean London lawyers?"

"That's it. But they tell me there's no nationality in finance."

Sir Reginald knew that to be largely true. So far as there were no violent interference by tyrannical rulers, high finance was controlled by those who considered its interests to be superior even to the well-being of their own countries—or those which were their adopted homes. The deliberate disaster of England's return to the gold standard, and the false basis on which it had been arranged, had been too recent and glaring an illustration of this for any banker of Sir Reginald's lively intelligence to misread.

"There may be no nationality," he said, "but there's banking law, which we are bound to observe. If your lawyers arrange matters so that Mr. Jellipot advises us that we're bound to act on the instructions we receive, you'll get what you want, and the less we know what it is, the easier it may be for you."

Capone said: "That's straight talk.... How soon shall we know which cock's going to crow?"

"About two o'clock on Friday, by your time here, we ought to have the whole tale. Perhaps an hour or so before that."

"Well, we'll lay off till then. But whichever way it turns up I reckon we're business men, and we'll make a deal."

Sir Reginald said nothing to that, and Capone rose and led his guests to the drawing-room. He said they'd get some good music there, which was no more than the truth.

CHAPTER XLVII.

The Unexpected from London

CAPONE kept his word. Until Friday came he made no further attempt to discuss business with his English guests. He had a conference with Clancy, the nature of which was not revealed, but it may be supposed that Clancy, who was no waster of words, gave him to understand that any help he was to give must be at his own time and in his own way.

On these terms he may have felt free to indicate the probability that there might be something to come from him. Capone was away all day at his downtown offices, to which he did not invite Sir Reginald or Mr. Jellipot, though Maloon went with him. He placed a car at their disposal, with a driver who had instructions to be their guide to any places they might wish to see, within the limits of the four states which surround Lake Michigan, and which, from Chicago, can be easily reached. He provided what he called a bodyguard of two silent saturnine men, who sat in the back of the car. It may have been no more than what he would regard as a normal courtesy, or he may have had a genuine concern for the safety of valued guests, but whether they were guards or warders was hard to tell.

Maloon did not return that evening. Capone said he had run over to Detroit to attend to his business interests there. He would be back by midday tomorrow.

On Friday morning Capone met his guests at breakfast and said that he would be going down-town, but would be back with Maloon at midday. Meanwhile, need he say that the telephone was at Sir Reginald's disposal for long-distance calls? Sir Reginald thanked him for that. It appeared to both of them that they were near the hour of bargain or open war, but it was still unsure on what terms it would be. There was a battle behind them which had already been lost and won, but which was victor or vanquished, they did not know.

It was eleven-thirty when Sir Reginald heard his brother-in-law's voice on the telephone. He expected to be overheard—wrongly, for Capone's phones (or at least some of them) were so installed that they could not be tapped by anyone in the house at any time or under whatever circumstances; and this precaution now became the security of his guests—though he thought little of that, for he was seeking facts which, he supposed, could not be long concealed. But there was an item of news he had not expected to hear, about which Lord Britleigh felt differently. Against Sir Reginald's impatience he opposed a determination to talk in code or not at all, and the code message was long.

When it concluded the banker said: "If you won't tell me anything in plain words, there's nothing I can reply. I'm no wiser than when we began."

"There's no need to say anything more."

"You might at least tell me in three words whether we're underneath or on top. They're bound to know as much as we in the next hour."

"When you've decoded my message you'll understand."

"I don't know that I can. I didn't bring all my papers here."

"Jellipot might help."

"Or he might not."

"Well, try."

With an exclamation of impatience, Sir Reginald put the receiver back.

He turned to Mr. Jellipot, who had sat beside him writing down the unmeaning words as they came over the wire. "Well, there we are. I suppose the best we can do is to take that round to a Western Union office and try all the codes they have. If they can help us they can do the same for anyone who's been listening in, and Britleigh might as well have said something we could understand without all this fuss; and if they can't I've nothing here that will help us. We might as well not have phoned at all."

"It may not be as bad as that," the lawyer replied. "Perhaps I ought to have told you before that I arranged with Lord Britleigh that he should use a code in any extreme need which is of an arbitrary character, so that it could only be decoded by ourselves under any circumstances."

"Meaning by you?"

"Yes. By myself, as I had not taken the precaution of communicating it to you, as you have some right to say that I should. But actually I regarded it as a most remote contingency that he would have occasion to use it at all, in preference to our usual codes. As it is—"

"We'd better get to work and see what it says."

"So I will. But I was about to say that it will not be a short or easy matter. It was intended to be used for a few words at most. I shall be surprised if I can decipher a message of that length in less than two or three hours. It is evident that some matter of particular importance and secrecy has arisen, for the coding of it would be an even longer task than it will be to turn it back into plain language."

"Then we'd better both get to work and see what we can do. I'm not going to meet Capone till I know what Britleigh's been up to."

Mr. Jellipot began, 'I don't think I should say—" and then stopped. What was the use of discussion before they knew? He added: "But we shall need an Old Testament. It may not be possible to get without sending out to buy one."

"Think not? I'd bet Capone sleeps with one under his pillow, if there's room for it between the guns."

This might not be precisely true, but it was a fact that Miss Capone not merely supplied the required book, without showing surprise or curiosity at such a demand being made upon her, but sent a second copy a few minutes later, with a message to say that it might be preferred, being printed in larger type.

It was a point on which Sir Reginald had shown his psychological insight to be superior to that of Mr. Jellipot, who was not usually deficient in that direction. Many gangsters were frequenters of Christian churches, with which their womenfolk showed even more active sympathy.

Joe the Boss—white-slaver, blackmailer, racketeer, owner of twenty gambling-dens and speak-easies within the limits of New York City—had a highly respectable family mansion west of Central Park, where one of his four children was studying for Holy Orders....

It was two hours later, and word had already been received that Capone was waiting for them in his own room, before the complete message lay in plain English before them:

> "Neither side has clear majority. Grice refuses all offers, and could tip the scale either way. Should he retain his holding, but not vote, we should be in a minority of seven shares. He may not know, but he certainly suspects this position. Capone's agents may think they are beaten. I have offered fantastic price, but Grice only laughs."

"Well, that's that," Sir Reginald said, with his usual briskness.... "A lot seems to depend upon how much Capone knows.... I can't altogether blame Grice.... I might have been tempted to do the same."

Grice held no more than two hundred shares. But he had been chairman of the London and Northern Bank before Sir Reginald had gained voting control and claimed that position as his own right.

Grice might have retained a seat on the board, but he had refused any compromise.... He had resigned, and looked on, waiting, perhaps, for such a moment as this. He might not sell out to Capone, but the price of his support might be very high. It might end in the alternatives of letting the bank pass into the hands of American racketeers or giving the chairmanship back to Grice. Sir Reginald should have felt depressed, but his spirits would always rise when the moment for action came.

"Come on," he said, "and let's see what the bounders have got to say."

Cool and wary of mind, and with more gravity than his client showed, Mr. Jellipot accompanied him to the room where the two leaders of organised and successful crime waited for them with no friendliness in their eyes.

Capone was the first to speak: "So you reckon you're one up on us?" The voice was smooth. Capone justified his character as a business man. He would not quarrel or threaten until all prospects of bargaining had gone.

"If you mean that you have not succeeded in purchasing a majority of the shares of the London and Northern, it agrees with information which I received this morning."

"I mean that. You've jockeyed us out so far. The question is what price you'll ask for the shares we've still got to have."

"I see how you feel. But you'll admit that I was not consulted when you decided to try to buy up the bank. Had you asked me, I might have told you that it would be a very risky thing to attempt."

"Risk be damned!" Maloon interjected. He was in a worse temper than Capone, or less disposed to conceal the anger he felt. "We've gone too far to back down. What we want to know is how much you'll stick us for now."

"I don't think I should dispose of any of my shares, if you I mean that. I might help you by taking some off your hands. And I expect there's been a good deal of selling short. That was almost sure to follow a rise of value such as your buying caused. If we act together we can make something of that."

"I have been wondering," Mr. Jellipot interposed, "whether we might not meet at Sir Reginald's brokers in New York on Monday and thresh out the whole position. I have some expectation that we might be able to relieve you financially without serious loss to ourselves."

"I should not leave Chicago. I do my business here," Capone said curtly. He had had a fresh reminder that morning that all the precautions he used to keep the Federal process-servers away might not avail much longer.

"But perhaps," Mr. Jellipot suggested, "Mr. Maloon might?"

Maloon gave the proposal no better response. "Reckon we'll settle this now," he said, with scowling eyes that gazed into the fire. It was plain that, unless directly addressed, he meant Capone to handle the situation, as his way was. It was equally plain how he intended than it should end. And though he might not speak, his attitude must have influence on the more moderate-tempered man.

Capone said: "You want us to think that there's no price at which you would come to our terms, but you don't know yet what we might be prepared to agree. We want to feel that our money's safe in your country, and that the bank will look after our interests properly. We don't ask more than that. We don't ask you to take an active part in our finance. Maloon will do that. It's what he's to sell out his Detroit business to me for, so that he can settle in London and be someone that the boys know they can trust there.... And you don't even know that we shan't come out on top. There may be some shares floating about that neither of us has got yet."

"We're not worrying about that," Sir Reginald replied quickly, feeling it to be a remark with which he could deal better than Mr. Jellipot would be certain to do. "And if you want to settle everything now, we've got to do it on how things are today. I've offered to leave it till Monday and go into it in New York then."

"I'm not leaving Chicago. But I'll offer you a deal on rather different lines. Whether we've got a majority of the shares or not, we've got a bigger block than are in any other single hand, and we must deserve some consideration for that. If you'll let the bank make an agreement, one that our London attorneys will O.K., to handle our financial interests there—it needn't be with us, it can be with the Dallas bank—we'll shake hands on that now and call it a day."

Sir Reginald was face was inscrutable as he replied: "Will you give me till after dinner to think that over?"

"Sure I will. We want this to be done in a friendly way. If some fool hadn't given Ringan and Ruscatti the works on your mat, we'd have had no trouble at all.... And Slick thinks he's on the track of that rat, and you can bet we're going to make him pay. We don't hold with telling the cops, but it won't make any odds to him if you do. They'd have to be that quick to be in front of us!"

Back in his own room, Sir Reginald said: "I made up my mind that I wouldn't stall, but I've done it now. And to get no more than a few hours! It would ruin the bank for it to be known that these vermin held about half the shares, even without such an agreement as that.... I tell you, Jellipot, I'm going to get those shares back before I sail for London if I stay here for a year. But how I'm going to do it I don't know."

CHAPTER XLVIII.

The Capitulation of Sir Reginald Crowe

MANY bitter and contemptuous things have been said about Scarface Capone, but no one has ever suggested that he was not a good business man. He had judged correctly that his English guests would not be well impressed by the atmosphere and personnel of his down-town offices, and had taken them straight to his own home. Like many criminals of Latin extraction, he appeared best against a background of domesticity, and he had been careful on this occasion not to entertain any of such associates as would have exposed the darker side of his illicit business.

But for good or evil, and in spite of the darkening shadow of Federal law, he was still a great power in Chicago, and many of its most influential men were anxious to call him friend.

On this occasion he had invited a few prominent citizens and their wives, of carefully chosen types, such as would feel it an honour to meet the London banker, and whom he could hardly object to know. They were such as would be favourably influenced by the fact that Capone had such guests, and, as he watched even the finest points of the difficult game he played, he was not indifferent to that.

They were such also as could be relied upon not to give publicity to what they might hear or see. Capone's influence on the local press was far from absolute, but he had been able to prevent any reference to Sir Reginald's visit appearing. Publicity—so inopportunely given by the London murders—it had become essential to him to avoid. Maloon saw this as clearly as he, and it was a restraining influence upon the starker methods which it was his nature to use.

The dinner went well. There was all the luxury and some of the beauty which wealth, however gained, will be able to give. There was even a superficial tone of culture among the guests.

Mr. Jellipot had a lively, birdlike lady at his right hand, whose knowledge of ceramics certainly passed his own, and who could talk on other subjects without exposing abysmal ignorance, though her knowledge might not be much. Sir Reginald found himself beside the massive wife of a city magnate who spent most of her summers in the Old World. She was so tactful that it was in less than half her sentences that she abused British institutions or expressed her preference for continental Europe. Sir Reginald saw much reason in what she said. He played her like a trout on a thin line, and she thought him a charming man.

Clancy did not come in till the meal was half over. He had not left the house since his talk with Capone, but he had kept much to himself and his own room. He was waiting for Saturday night to come, and may have thought that meanwhile he was safer within those walls than he would have been anywhere else in the States, unless it were the Atlantis or a Federal jail. He was late, having had delay in getting his long-distance call through to Moll, and had found that there was more than usual to say, including that which was disquieting to hear.

When he came to the table he was more preoccupied than usual. Mafalda Capone, who was at his side, would have noticed this more particularly had she not known that he was not one who talked freely at any time, but she was surprised when he answered a light remark by wondering where any of those present would be in a year's time. It was the sort of thing which, in such circles, it is bad manners to say.

He followed Capone as they rose. "I want a word with you alone." The voice was urgent, and the request was one which Capone was accustomed to hear.

"I've got Slick and the Britishers coming to my room," he said. "Is it something they shouldn't know?"

"They've got to know. But you may like to know first. Someone's kidnapped Lady Crowe."

Capone stared. Clancy had no doubt that it was news, and most unwelcome to him. He asked: "Sure?"

"Yep. She went out to the Customs—the post office—for Moll. She took a phoney car, and Slinker followed in another. She didn't reach the post office, and she didn't get back."

"Come into the smoking-room."

Having reached that solitude, Capone locked the door. "Cops on it?" he asked anxiously.

"Nope. No one knows but Moll, if she's got the facts right. I've told her to do nothing till I call her again."

Capone looked his relief. "You've done right. Someone must have gone mad, unless they're so hot on ruining us that they don't care what's coming to them.... We've got to get her back quietly if it costs anything that they like to ask. Who'd have thought anyone'd be such a fool.... We'd better have Maloon here."

Maloon came, heard, and swore. He agreed with Capone that the Crowe dame must be recovered quickly and in such a way that the cops—or the press—would never know what had occurred. He agreed also that whoever was wrecking their plans by these repeated, inopportune crimes must be liquidated (he did not use that word, which originated with the ruling gangsters who dominated most of Europe during the decade following that in which their American prototypes perished beneath the slow, inexorable pressure of Federal law), even though it were Terra-Nova or Larry Fay, though neither of them—nor Joe Masseria—was a likely bet. But he had a new suggestion as to how they should put the matter to Sir Reginald.

Capone was for instant action through all the underworld channels which they controlled for the recovery of the kidnapped girl. He was unsure of the wisdom of telling Sir Reginald. They had till midday tomorrow before he would be likely to try to call her again. If they could find her before then—

Maloon agreed as to the need for urgent and secret search, but he said tell Sir Reginald, and stipulate for payment from him in the coin they desired to have.

Capone pulled his lip doubtfully. At that moment, if he could have cancelled the whole business by sacrificing his own interest in the five million grand with which the trouble had commenced, it would have been quickly done. He said: "Have it your own way. But we've got to hustle." They went to the room where Sir Reginald and Mr. Jellipot were already waiting.

Clancy told his tale once again. Sir Reginald took it with more self-control than those who watched had expected him to show. But he said: "You mean you've known this for the last hour and done nothing at all? We'd better get through to Mrs. Clancy at once and tell her to inform the police, and—"

"She won't do that," Clancy replied sharply, "and she'd be a fool if she did."

"We want you to understand," Maloon said, "that this is no doing of ours. But we'll get her back if we turn every hiding-hole from here to Albany upside down. That is, if you'll play ball with us."

"*If?*" Sir Reginald interjected sharply. "I'd like to know what you mean by that. Of course I shall get her back, whether you help or not, and it'll be God help anyone by whom any harm comes to her."

"Slick," Capone said, "you'd better leave this to me. Sir Reginald, I want you to understand that we're not to be blamed for this. It's like those London murders. It's aimed at us rather than you, though what the motive is, is more than we've been able to guess.

"But Slick's right about one thing, and you can see that Clancy looks at it in the same way. It wouldn't do to call in the cops. While they lie quiet you needn't have much fear of what's happening to Lady Crowe. But if those who've got her think that they're near being run down there's no knowing what they might do.

"We mean to get her back for you safe and quick, and we've got ways of doing it that are about a thousand times surer than any the cops would try. If you tell the cops you'll have it in the papers in half-an hour, and—well, if they're cornered they'll kill her more likely than not, so that she can't talk against them. It's better to put it plain. They're depending on us not to be fools enough to call out, and if they mean to make us pay—well, we'll do it without asking you, whatever party we set up for them on the next day. And all Slick meant was that if we do this—I don't say just if we try, but if we get her back safely—you won't stand out from a fair deal, such as we were going to ask if this hadn't happened at all."

Sir Reginald hesitated. What he would have said if he had not caught Clancy's eye at that moment will never be known. But Clancy was standing somewhat behind the two racketeers, and he nodded slightly. It was an urgent hint of the wisdom of giving way from one in whose friendship Sir Reginald had found reason to trust, and who, being partly in either camp, was in an exceptional position to judge. He said: "If you play fair, I'll do that."

It was a vague promise, but Capone accepted it readily. "Your word's good for me," he said, and picked up the telephone to give orders which would stir the underworld from Long Island to the Pacific coast.

CHAPTER XLIX.

The Redhead in Pursuit

THERE was a switchboard in Capone's house, controlling several lines, but Clancy, who, saying little, observed much, approved the fact that there were several others which operated without that intervention. One of these was in Sir Reginald's room, and it was this which they both had used in ringing up the Atlantis, and it was its separate number which Evelyn and her companion had.

Now Clancy said: "I'd better get through to Moll again. She may have a bit more to tell. I'll use your phone if I may."

Sir Reginald said yes to that. It was a natural proposal, apart from precedent, for Capone's henchmen, leaping to life, as it seemed from every corner, were accepting curt, incisive orders with a quick understanding and economy of words which showed their training and went far to explain the perilous eminence which Capone had gained. A line would doubtless have been made available for the purpose which Clancy had, but it was natural to turn to one which was not already in urgent use.

The phone was ringing when they reached the room, and Sir Reginald picked up the receiver quickly. "It's long distance," he said. "They say they've been trying to get us for half an hour for an urgent call. Perhaps she's got back after all." But the next moment the hopeful note died from his voice. "It's for you, Clancy. It's your friend Fay. He's in a deuce of a stew, if you ask me."

Clancy said: "I wonder he'd get me here." And then: "That you, Larry? What's broken now?"

"You're sure you're not being overheard?"

"Yes. Shoot." It was a risk that must be taken, and it was not much!

"Redhead's been on to me. She wants to hire the best car I've got for a week, with a bodyguard of my two best men. Men who'll shoot and no questions asked. I said you must O.K. that, and she gave me your number; but she's like a bear with a sore head now because I'm not up to her schedule. She said she wouldn't call you herself, so's to leave the line clear, but she'll want you to call her up."

Clancy was instant in his reply. "O.K., Larry. What Redhead says goes. Charge it to me. Send Paul if you can. And tell them to shoot first and think after. They'll find it'll iron out. And if they bring her back safe there'll be two hundred bucks extra for them to split. So long, Larry."

He hung up and instantly put in a call for Moll.

"Redhead's gone off the rails," he said angrily as he waited for it to come through. "She's getting a car to follow your dame. It's a risk for her, and it's what she's not needed to do. If she knows where to look she should tell me, and I'd take care of that. But I'd not say that to Fay."

Ten minutes later he heard Moll's voice. "I thought you'd never get through.... No, I've no time to explain. Larry's car's at the door now.... Well, I've got to. She went out for me.... But I wanted you to know, and Larry was sticky unless you did.... Yes, I knew you'd say the right thing to him.... Yes, I'm sure.... No, I won't say it. You never know who may hear. Remember when we had to chop ice for the kettle? What you talked about once at dinner.... Tim, *think*.... Yes. I thought you would"

"You've got it, baby.... Go ahead, but don't rush the fence.... And take a bend south. Give Chicago a miss. Come Sunday we'll have it all right as rain.... What about the street?" Tim, I don't *want* to get shot. Larry's men are giving the once-over to every loiterer within fifty yards of the door. And you know I'll be safe enough in a Fay car.... Yes, I've thought of that, too. I asked for a car with some steel in the back panels—and one that can go a bit quicker than anything that's likely to be coming behind. But I can't stop now. You'll hear from me soon. So long."

Abruptly she rang off. He turned to Sir Reginald and Mr. Jellipot to say: "Moll's made a guess where Lady Crowe's likely to be tied up. It sounds good to me.... Anyhow she'll have a look-see; and I'm not saying there'll be much danger for her. If they see her go, and where she's heading, they'll think she's coming here to report. It's Montana she's for, but I don't reckon they'd guess that. If they try cutting her out, it'll be at this end, or somewhere between here and Detroit. That's why I put her wise to give Chicago a miss. She'll be fly enough to see what I meant by that.... And she's right that she'll be safe in a Fay car. Larry owes me more than he's wanting to pay just now, and he'll be glad to do something to pull it down."

"Of course," Sir Reginald said, "whatever it costs must be charged to me."

"I wouldn't say no to that.... Larry'll charge big.... But I don't say we won't collect.... I'm figuring to do that, and to pull out while the going's good."

Mr. Jellipot, a silent auditor of these exchanges, thought that if what was happening now represented good going, when it was bad things must be lively indeed. But he did not deny to himself that there was stimulation in unexpected events, and that he was not sorry that he had come.

"I hope," Sir Reginald said, "that it may be possible for me to join Mrs. Clancy, as she will, I suppose, be passing not far south of this city within a few hours from now. If you have reason to think you know where Lady Crowe is, I am sure you will see that I should be there."

Clancy hesitated. "Yep. I see that. But it won't do. You'll be needed here. And if you go off with Moll.... No, it won't work. If she's made the right guess—no, it would just blow the fuse. And if she hasn't, you'd be off the scene just when you'd be needed here.... And Moll will phone here. She won't get out of touch with us."

Sir Reginald saw that, for the moment he must accept this decision. And it was true that Mrs. Clancy might have made a wrong guess. Any moment the wide enquiries which Capone and Maloon were busily sending out might result in information which would enable him to set off in another direction. Or, if the pointer should be toward Montana, it would be something which Clancy could not obstruct.

"We'll leave it like that," he said, "anyway, till tomorrow. And I'd better know your room, for if Mrs. Clancy should call you during the night."

"I wouldn't say she'd do that," Clancy replied, and proved to be right. The night passed without further incident or any news of the kidnappers coming in.

In the morning the post brought an unexpected letter for Mr. Jellipot, which had been forwarded from the Hotel Atlantis. It was from Mr. Whalan, enclosing a card of invitation for the Vitale dinner that evening.

"I got it for myself," the young man wrote, "but I meant it for you. There's no name on it, except our firm's, so if any question's asked you've only got to say you've had it from me. They'll take darned good care not to quarrel with us. You needn't use it unless you want, but you seemed so interested that I thought you might like to be there."

Mr. Jellipot was disposed to go. He thought that, with the preliminary knowledge he had, there might be things of interest to observe, though he was inadequate in his preconception of what those things were destined to be.

He consulted with his friends, who were of the same mind, though it was agreed that a generous interpretation of Clancy's promise to Cassidy might require that he should not mention to Capone or others the purpose for which he would be returning to New York.

Sir Reginald told Capone at breakfast that Jellipot would be leaving, and Capone showed an interest in the matter.

He was searching the morning papers with anxious eyes, fearing that the news of the kidnapping might have broken, with consequences difficult to foresee, but most likely to be detrimental to the business deal he was trying to make. Relieved of this fear, he said that there was little doubt that they'd have Lady Crowe back, safe and well, before many hours were passed. "I'm not afraid," he said, "if we can keep the cops out of this."

So Mr. Jellipot returned to New York on a train which charged him more than the full ordinary fare, on a bargain that unless it should arrive punctually the extra money would be returned.

"It is," he thought, "as though my grocer were to say to me: 'This sugar is two pence a pound, but I am asking you to pay two pence halfpenny on condition that, if you should find it to be under weight, the extra halfpenny will be refunded.' It is a weird world." But he was broadminded enough to see that some things which happened in his own country might seem equally weird to an American visitor.

CHAPTER L.

CLANCY GIVES THE NAME

IN Chicago, Saturday passed without more than negative news being received.

Sir Reginald's impatience grew, and Capone had the look of a worried man. With this worry there were disturbing elements both of bewilderment and wrath. He would have said yesterday that it would be impossible for the kidnappers to elude the widespread search which he instituted, and m which the aid of so many big shots, allied to him by interest if not by friendship, and easily made to realise the disturbance which was threatened to their underworld activities if Evelyn should not be found without the intervention of the police and the world-wide publicity it would involve, had been supplemented to his. His vanity was concerned that Sir Reginald should see evidence of his power, and his judgement told him that the success of the negotiations he had on hand might depend entirely upon his ability to recover the missing girl. He would have been even more disturbed had not his guests accepted the delay with something less than the extreme impatience that he would have expected them to show.

Maloon remained confident that Evelyn would be found. His one complaint was that the bargain with Sir Reginald had not been more explicitly worded, and particularly that Capone had not required that it should be written. Capone defended himself on that. He was never one who would snap a thin line. He trusted much to Sir Reginald's honour. The hour of Evelyn's return, as the result of a rescue by his own gunmen, would be the time to claim interpretation of the promise on liberal terms.

As to Sir Reginald and Clancy, he would not guess that they were counting the hours to the evening—the one with fuller knowledge than the other of what its revelations would be likely to mean.

Dinner was a meal of tension and gloom until, toward its conclusion, Clancy said, rather to Maloon than Capone: "I've got an idea of something more we might do. Perhaps after dinner we'll talk it out."

Capone said: "Any idea's worth hearing now. You'd better all come with me."

They were soon seated around the fire in Capone's room. Drinks, cigars, and cigarettes were served to the satisfaction of each, and the obsequious manservant faded away. Maloon sat on the extreme left, his long legs stretched out, as his habit was. His attitude was relaxed, but the eyes were alert in his inscrutable brown-mahogany face.

Clancy sat opposite to him on the further side, with Capone on his left and Sir Reginald nearer Maloon. Clancy began at once: "How I figure it out is that they must have taken her for a long ride, or she'd have been found before now. She's not been put where there's many moving about. And Slinker's gone too. The way all the city hide-outs have been combed, and the—well, it all points to that. The puzzle is how did they get through?"

"I don't see that quite so plain," Capone interposed. "We've got to reckon there's a new hand in this, and he'll have hideouts we don't know."

"Yep. If there's a new hand. But I don't say there is. It's hard to make out how any guy'd get a mob together that could work in London as well as here and do this kidnapping act without us getting wise to what's going on."

"It cuts no ice saying that when the thing's done. What do you mean we should do now?"

"I'd go west and look for places where she could be put away."

Maloon said: "There's an idea. I wouldn't say you were far wrong."

"How many million square miles," Capone asked, "will you rake over for that?" His tone had a faintly sarcastic note. Had they come together to hear nothing better than this?

But Clancy went on in his stubborn way: "It mightn't be so bad if you knew where to look."

"Meaning?"

"Well, there's a little shack up beyond Ashlands, on the Tongue river—"

Maloon sat up suddenly. Then he relaxed again and said curtly: "If you've found out something, cut the fooling and let us know.

"I haven't found out anything yet. I'm just figuring. What has me beat is how they'd get her there and the boys let them through. But if they'd gone north through Michigan and ferried over—"

"They'd not have done that," Capone said, looking at Clancy with puzzled eyes. "That's Slick's own ground. He had every road covered for us in the first hour."

Clancy made no direct reply. He said, as though thinking aloud: "It's a long way round. They'd hardly be there yet. There'd be no sense finding them there while they were still on the way. *Put your hands up, Slick, or you're a dead guy.*"

Moll had boasted that Tim was "that quick" on the draw, but he was so slow now that he gave the warning before his gun showed in his hand. It was a chance which a less alert man than Slick Maloon would have been tempted to take. The two shots had less than half a dividing second between them, but Maloon's came from a hand that sagged on a broken wrist, which was exactly how Clancy had meant it to be.

Capone had his gun out, but Clancy took no notice of that. He kept Maloon covered, but did not fire again. He said: "Now we know where we are. Shall I tell Capone what I've learned, or will you do it in your own way?"

Maloon looked at Capone. "I don't know what this is about, or what quarrel Clancy's got with me, but I shouldn't reckon you'll thank him for starting here. Suppose I get this tied up"—he raised his right arm from which the blood dripped, and the hand hung limply—"and we talk it over and find out what it's all about."

"I'll hear what Clancy's got to say first," Capone answered. "It shouldn't take that long."

"Oh, it's quite a piece," Clancy answered, "but there'll be no more shooting from me. It'll be up to you then. Sir Reginald, you might pick up that gun and just frisk him over to make sure there's nothing that might come out from the other side, and he'll hear all he wants from me."

Capone asked, without turning his eyes from Clancy: "You in this, Sir Reginald?"

"No more than we all are. But I'll be glad to do anything which will prevent any more bloodshed here. I can assure you that the carpets suffer more than a good carpet should."

With this pacific assurance he stooped down and picked up the gun which had fallen from Maloon's hand. He put it on to a table behind them, in sufficient evidence that he anticipated no further use for such weapons. He added, "It's always best to make sure," and bent over Maloon so that he was between him and the watchful

Clancy. It was a moment which Maloon had anticipated, and which gave him the last chance of life that he might be likely to have.

He had another gun in his left-hand pocket, and it was out before Sir Reginald had had time to feel it. In another second it would have been discharging its contents at Clancy, who would have had little at which to aim in return, but before its muzzle could be raised, Sir Reginald's fingers were round Maloon's wrist.

There was a moment of desperate struggle, during which the gun was twice discharged into the floor, but it was over even before the other two men, who had risen quickly, could give their aid.

"Don't shoot, Clancy. I give in," Maloon said as he sank back baffled and exhausted from the brief effort he had made, while Sir Reginald placed the gun on the table beside the other.

"That was good work," Capone said, observing his English guest from an unexpected angle.

"He hadn't much chance with one hand."

Capone looked at Slick. "You must have been scared of what Tim would say to try that."

"I'll have my say when he's done. You won't shoot if I have a drink?"

"Nope."

The glass was op a little stool at Maloon's left hand. He raised and drained it, and lay back again, the injured hand on his knees. He was clearly in need of medical aid, but there was no mercy in the eyes of the man who accused him or of the watchful Capone.

"I'll tell you what I know," Clancy said, "and if I'm wrong it's for you to say. But there's not much guessing for me to do.

"You've been hiring a Boston cop, Cassidy, to do gunning for you, outside your own gang, so that no one'd guess who put the bullets into his gun, and, he being a cop, no one even suspected him. There's nothing new about that. It was he bumped off Jap-eyed Pete.... Oh, you didn't think I knew that? I know quite a lot.... You sent him over to Europe to knock off Ringan and Ruscatti. I don't know whether you thought you could collect without them—Sir Reginald will know whether you tried that—but, if so, you found it wouldn't work, and you got on the phone with Al here and sold him the idea of buying the bank, so that you could be in London to look after the money. You'd have been sitting pretty, clear of all the risk of the rackets, and handling all the cash for the boys here. And you thought you could shoot the way to this, and no one'd figure out where it was from that the killings came.

"You thought Moll might have seen Cassidy, and you meant him to bump her off on the *Baltic*, and then you thought she hadn't and you'd better not have any trouble on that boat, Sir Reginald being there, and you having gone on board to see him. Well, that was where you went wrong.

"And you've kidnapped Lady Crowe now, so that you could find her as soon as you'd had time to get her put away where you'd got the stage set, and it's all been done so that it couldn't be traced to you. And, of course, Sir Reginald was to be so grateful that he'd come across just as you want him to do. Or, if he hadn't given the promise he did, you might have worked it with her another way. You know best about that.

"You've had Cassidy blackmailing you, and I reckon he's got the wad in his pocket an hour or two before this; but you didn't know that he's signed a confession that Sir Reginald's put in a safe place."

"That it, Sir Reginald?" Capone asked.

"It is a sealed envelope the contents of which I have not seen. I had no previous knowledge that Maloon was the man we were out to find. But I have no doubt it is true."

Capone looked at Maloon, who lay back as though little conscious of what was said, which may have been half-genuine, half-assumed. "I reckon, Slick, you'll say this is all lies. But there'll be ways—"

"I won't say either way. Cassidy tried blackmailing me. You're right there. But I reckon he's dead by now. He might write anything that he thought he could sell. But I'll tell you this. I know something about Lady Crowe, and if you try holding me she'll be a dead Jane."

There was a discreet knock on the door and the butler entered. "Beg pardon, sir, but Miss Mafalda wanted to know if you might need anything?"

"I hope nothing disturbed her," Capone answered.

"She did say she thought she heard some shots. And there's a fruit-dish smashed in the dining-room."

"Tell her there was an accident with Mr. Maloon's gun. Nothing that mattered, unless it's a good dish. I'll get another, if there's any trouble about that.... And—oh, Miles, tell Muller to come to me in about five minutes, and to bring two of the boys.... And *nothing's* to be said about this, inside or out. *Nothing.* You'll see that that's understood?"

Miles said yes to that, and retired in his noiseless way.

Capone said: "Now what's this about Lady Crowe?"

"You think I'll tell you, and then you'll give me the works? I reckon we'll make a different bargain from that."

Capone answered in his most reasonable business tone: "I can't let you live, Slick. You wouldn't figure on that. But there's ways and ways.... There's ways that I don't like and don't try. But I've heard that a red-hot poker can do a lot."

"It couldn't save that dame's life."

"You just put the end of it to the right spot—the breastbone might be a good pick—and let it burn itself in. I've heard say that it won't go half an inch deep, let alone do any real harm, before you'll learn what you want to know."

"You might learn a lot, but that wouldn't save her. The boys have their orders from me, and even without them they'll twist her neck if they get scared. You can't blame them for that."

There was another knock at the door, and the three gunmen entered.

"Muller," Capone said, "I expect you'll have to take Mr. Maloon for a ride, but there's a bit of business to clear up first. You'll take him to his room now, and you can put his hand as straight as you know how—he's had an accident with a gun—and you'll keep him safe. There'll be one of you on each side of his bed, and if they're wise guys they won't nod. Never less than two. And there's not a word of this to get outside the gates."

Muller, a bull-necked man of the more brutal German type, gave a sound of assent. With his two companions he approached his charge.

Maloon rose to go with them without protest. He said only: "Well, I've told you. You can have her dead or alive. It's for you to say."

CHAPTER LI.

THE REDHEAD MAKES A GOOD GUESS

THE most comfortable hotel may soon become boring if you let the days pass without leaving it, and this is particularly true when the cause of seclusion is not indolence or lassitude, but a compulsion of circumstance reluctantly obeyed.

Under such a condition it is natural to spend time in gazing from windows which give a view of the outside world, and was especially so to one of Moll Clancy's disposition, with the activities of Broadway beneath her eyes—eyes which had learned alertness in a hard school, and to which that which they saw had fuller meanings than would have been apparent to more orthodox members of the community.

During the two previous days she had sat for hours, either with Evelyn or alone, at a window of the lounge, which gave a side view of the entrance to the hotel, and it was more by habit than any conscious intention that when Evelyn went down the lift on Friday afternoon she strolled toward the position from which she would be able to see her as she gained the street.

Actually, Evelyn's downward progress was so brisk, and the approach of the waiting car so prompt, that Moll's more leisurely movements would have entirely missed what passed in the street below had she not been roused to sudden alertness as she entered the lounge by seeing two of the pageboys gazing from the window with gloating eyes, and caught the words: "Slinker's at it again."

She was just in time to see Slinker disappear into a car. It moved off rapidly, following another which had become familiar to her during the idle gazing of the last two days.

The boys had separated. She called to the nearer one, who came readily enough, but when she asked, "Who was in the first car?" his expression became blank. He had seen nothing at all. She gave him a five-dollar bill, and told him to fetch her some cigarettes. "If you

243

can think of who it was while you're fetching them there won't be any change."

When he came back with the cigarettes he said: "I can't find Lady Crowe, ma'am. I think she must have gone out."

She saw that those who were employed in the Hotel Atlantis acquired discretion in early years.

She had learned enough to cause anxiety, but was in doubt as to what it might mean. She knew that Evelyn had not gone in a taxi. It was a car which she had noticed hanging about for the last two days. It was not one belonging to the Fay Company, which was saying that it was not a taxi at all. Many cars came and went, or waited round the hotel, which were the private property of its affluent clients, but none plying for public hire were permitted by the Fay Company to approach the block.

She saw that the car which Evelyn had entered might have been await there to trap her whenever she should come out, as she would be expected to do; and, with the knowledge she had of the name in Cassidy's confession, she had no difficulty in guessing what would be the meaning of that.

But there might be other explanations, especially as to the fact that Slinker had followed. The car—it was possible but improbable—might have been stationed there by Sir Reginald himself for Evelyn's use, to avoid the risk of her entering a strange one outside that metropolis of crime. And—or—Slinker might have been engaged by him as a bodyguard for her, should she leave the hotel. He might have taken these precautions without wishing her to know the full measure of the anxiety he felt. Or Slinker might have instructions from Capone. as a mere safe-guard against any harm coming to the wife of the man with whom he was attempting to establish friendly relations.

It might even be that the waiting car had been intended for herself—there was surely nothing improbable in that!—and that Evelyn had been picked up by a mere error or exaggeration of the orders which had been given.

Vexing her mind with these possibilities, she decided that she could do nothing until the time had passed during which Evelyn should return, which should be less than an hour, even allowing for more delay at the post office than there was likely to be.

For that hour she waited, and then telephoned the post office to enquire concerning the parcel. She asked whether the name of the sender was on it. The reply made it clear that it had not been collected. On learning that, she telephoned Tim, and, having thus relieved her mind, she began to think out the problem in her own way.

She had, at first, no thought of active intervention. Having told Tim, she had passed the matter into more capable hands. She did not doubt that he would tell Capone, and that there would be resulting activities far beyond anything which it would be in her power to do. But she naturally speculated as to what Maloon's method of operation would be. Pondering this, she remembered the first time that she had seen the Detroit gangster, who was not one whom it would be easy to forget or mistake.

It was nearly four years before, when she had been hiding with Tim in the Montana hills. There had been a wide valley below them, and on the further side they had observed smoke rising from a narrow gorge. They had not been seeking to overlook others, but to escape notice themselves.

It was for their own security that they had made cautious approach to a little cabin hidden in an abrupt hollow, where they had seen Maloon, who, they had been sure, had not seen and was not looking for them.

He had lived there alone for six weeks, and had then gone, leaving the cabin strongly locked, though it appeared to contain little to tempt a thief. A year later he had been there again for a shorter time, when he had had a single companion with him. After that they had left the district themselves.

It was a simple guess that it was a place which he kept as a last retreat if he should have occasion to hide from the law's pursuit or the more dangerous enmity of his associates in crime.

Would it not be a likely place to use now? It would be fatal to employ his usual resorts, or those who were known as his own retinue. For he must not only hold his hostage securely until he had obtained whatever his purpose might be. He must be able to arrange for her discovery and rescue, so that it should not appear that the abduction had been his doing.

It was less than a logical deduction. Intuition might be a better word. But as her mind settled upon it the idea grew till it had the force of certainty. And with the idea the sense of Evelyn's peril increased. She did not doubt that, if Sir Reginald could be brought to do what Maloon required, Evelyn would be safely returned. She knew that business came first with him. But what if the negotiations with Capone should be ending in final quarrel? What if Sir Reginald should even now be insisting on the intervention of the police, and a situation should develop in which Evelyn could not be safely returned? She knew that Maloon would not hesitate for a moment at any crime which could turn suspicion from his own door.

Would it be possible to follow and stop the car while it was still within districts too thickly populated for abduction or murder to be safely practised, especially without the co-operation of the underworld organisations? It was Maloon's weakness that he was operating with what could be no more than a small group of agents, outside his own powerful gang, and unrecognised by others which—against the police, at least—might have given him invaluable support.

As she thought of the possibility of successful pursuit, Moll's mind naturally turned to Larry Fay. He was friendly. He owed them money. No one in New York—certainly not the police—had such power where questions of transport were concerned.

It was now nearly two hours since Evelyn had gone, but, if her guess were right, her destination was two or three thousand miles away, and for such a distance a start of two or three hours was not much. She had promised Tim that she would do nothing till he called her again. Well, she would keep that promise.

She would not leave the hotel. She would await his call. But in a matter of such urgency she need not interpret her promise in such a way that no arrangements for action should be made. She rang up Larry Fay.

Larry Fay, who admired efficiency in any form, approved of Redhead. "Clancy's Luck," he had been heard to call her. He was entirely willing to help. But she asked much, and he said that, while he would make preparations at once, he must have Tim's assent. He suggested that that need entail no real delay. Probably it did not mean much, though the connection was slow.

While he waited he talked to her on another line. She described the car which she wished to pursue, and made it clear that the help for which she asked was to be given to her and Tim, and that, if he should disregard anything he should hear subsequently from other directions, it would be a favour to them. It followed that, when a request came from Capone a few minutes later that there should be a lookout for Evelyn and her abductors, he stirred great activity in every direction but that in which he knew that the car had gone.

It is possible to doubt the wisdom of her request, but she acted with a knowledge of Maloon's treachery, a profound distrust of Capone, and the thought that Fay's help would be given at any moment should it be Tim's voice that asked it.

As to the car, she learned at once how potent Larry's help could be. His men who were accustomed to wait for fares outside the Hotel Atlantis had keen eyes for what went on around them, and especially for cars which hung round the hotel. They gave a description of the one Evelyn had entered, even to its number, which was to be of vital assistance.... So the time passed until she heard Tim's voice calling her again, and was able to set out with the cheering knowledge that she had gained some measure of approval from him. "I expect he thought," she reflected shrewdly, "that if I'm not in the hotel I couldn't be in a much safer place than one of Larry's best cars."

"Paul," she said, as she stepped into the front seat, "they're heading for Montana, unless I've guessed wrong. They've got five hours' start, and they'll step on the gas. Can we catch them this side Chicago?"

The tall, one-eyed Swede she addressed answered non-committally: "Not if they know how to drive."

"Well," she said, "you'll catch them, if anyone can."

That was mere fact. Before the accident which had left him with only one eye and a hand from which two fingers were missing, Paul had been the best racing motorist in the United States, and some would have said in Europe also. Now he could not obtain a licence to drive a taxi, but his skill remained, as did his love of the road. Larry Fay had shown shrewdness in engaging him for the driving of cars which were not licensed for public hire. His one eye was more use to him than three would have been to another man. He was no gangster, but would be a good man to have on the right side if there should be trouble to face.

A gunman whose acquaintance Moll had still to make sat silently in the back of the car. His selection arose from the fact that he had a bitter grudge against Slinker which Fay had, until now, refused to allow him to square in his own way.

They drew up for the moment for the red light as they came to Eighth Avenue, and, as they did so, a yellow car pulled up beside them. A man leaned out to say: "Slinker's car's come back, but he wasn't in it. It was back four hours ago."

Paul said: "He'll be in her car." Moll sat silent. It was too obvious to need a reply. She watched Paul drive, and thought she could have gone faster herself, in which she was wrong. There was deception in the smooth running of a car which was perfectly adjusted, and had an ultra-powerful engine. But Paul was too good a driver to use his speed till he got to a clear road, which would not be for many miles yet.

It was three hours later, and they had been running fast on a frosty moonlit road through the wooded Pennsylvanian hills, when Paul slackened speed abruptly and ran into one of those white-painted wooden combined filling stations and cafes which the long-distance American road travelling renders it profitable to keep open both night and day.

"You're not short of gas already?" Moll asked.

"Nope, I've gotta phone. You'd better eat."

"How long shall we be?"

"Maybe half an hour. Maybe less."

He moved off to talk to a man who was at the petrol pumps, and she went on to push open the swing door of the refreshment-room and blink at its well-lighted interior. It was spacious and clean. A bar faced her, with a row of revolving stools. At her right hand was a store of fruit and groceries.

As she went forward and took one of the stools, ordering coffee and a hamburger, the gunman who had been on the rear seat came in behind her, and the barman's glance went past her, and looked with no favour at what he saw.

The man paused at the door as though he were of too cautious a habit to enter a lighted place without a previous survey. He was an undersized, weedy type of the underworld of New York, black-eyed, swarthy, with a rat's bright restless eyes.

"Toughs," the barman thought, with a downward glance at the gun that lay ready on the shelf beneath his hand, but he gave no sign of his thoughts as he sent the sugar-castor sliding the length of the counter, to stop within two inches of Moll's cup, being an act which he repeated scores of times every day, and of the precision of which he was justly proud.

There were few types of American citizen, respectable or criminal, high or low, who were not seen on those revolving stools, either by day or night. Few whom he could not judge at the first glance, and take such precautions as their appearance required. There was a bell which would summon help from the garage, on which he sometimes had occasion to tread, but he did not do that now. "Toughs," he thought, "but I'd say there'll be no trouble from them." Anyway, there was not much in the till.

Moll looked at the man who had taken a place two stools away—a distance which she approved.

"Name?" she asked.

"Cæsar to you," the man said, with what he meant to be an ingratiating smile.

"Know Slinker?"

"Happen I do."

"Get his hands up, and I'll tell you what to do next."

"Reckon I'll know that."

"Reckon you'll ask me."

"Sure. That's what the boss said."

"Then we both know."

Moll gave him no more attention, finishing her hamburger and ordering custard pie, liberal cut portions of which were displayed with other edibles on shelves behind the bar.

As she did so Paul came in. The barman knew him, and his manner thawed as he took his order.

Moll looked at Paul, but did not speak. She was impatient to be gone, but saw that he must have time to eat.

He answered the look in her eyes. "I've gotta wait. There's a call coming through. We'll be off in five minutes now."

"Heard anything of them?"

"I'd say we have. They're going fast. I'm just hearing which way they take, at a place where they might turn. We'll have the spot-light on them from now."

"We'll catch them?"

"Sure thing."

The man to whom Paul had first spoken came in. He said: "They went straight ahead."

Paul looked surprised. "Reckoned," he said to Moll, "they'd give Chicago a miss."

"Tim said we'd better do that."

"So we can. We shan't catch them this side."

He said no more, but he looked puzzled.

They returned to the car.

"You'll get in at the back," Paul said. "Cæsar's coming with me."

"I'd rather watch the road."

"You'll do better sleeping than that."

It was plain sense, and she gave way.

She waked twice during the night, when they pulled up at way-side stations, in each case to receive reports of the position of those they pursued. Moll saw how complete and far-reaching was the watch which had been set on the road. She did not know how much was due to the orders of Larry Fay, or how much to Paul's personal popularity, but she knew it was more than the police would have been able to do or would have got done for them, if at all, without much of threats and bribes, of talk and delay.

But the flying car must be fast approaching ground where Fay's influence would decline and that of Capone's would be potent on every side. A wide detour to the south seemed an elementary pru-dence. To go through Chicago itself was to ask for trouble with a loud voice....

But at the second stop there was different news. The trail, which had seemed so plain and obvious, had abruptly failed. Hearing this, Paul got out of the car. He went with the garage owner to the telephone, discussing with him who could be safely approached and how enquiries could most safely be made. He did not telephone himself now, but prompted the man. He could trust him, but he did not forget that he was on Capone's ground. Chicago was less than two hundred miles away.

After half an hour had produced nothing but blank replies, Moll, who had been walking restlessly on the edge of a frozen road, interposed. "Paul," she said, "we're just wasting time. They went north."

"Why," he asked, "should they do that?"

"Because it's Maloon's ground. He'll have given orders to pass them through. They'll get over Mackinaw and have a clear run, where there'd be no one looking for them at all."

"Guess you're right," he said. "It adds up. But I can't ask. Not round Detroit way."

"But you've asked every other and drawn blank. We've got to guess that. Say it's right, what's best to do now?"

Paul said, as though talking to himself rather than her: "We gained eighty miles—or say ninety—to here. They've been going well. But we could. I've not been there since twenty-five. There's three roads they might take till—but after that.... Yes, it's a long run, but I'd say we should get them sure."

"You're not meaning to follow the same way?"

"No.... We'll do better. We'll cut them off if it's the right guess."

"You'll go south Chicago? I promised Tim."

"We'll do that."

They went back to the car. Paul asked Cæsar, who had dozed beside him most of the night, if he knew the Logansport road, and, receiving an affirmative reply, gave him the driver's seat.

It was six o'clock in the evening, and Capone's territory was far behind, when Moll telephoned to Tim and gave him her idea of what had happened, which he was to use so effectively with Maloon at a later hour.

It was at the same time that Paul rang up an old acquaintance in North Dakota and asked that the road should be watched for the car they sought. There would be fifty dollars for any information concerning it which could be given when he should phone on the next day.

CHAPTER LII.

AN IDEA TOO LOW FOR CAPONE

AS Maloon left the room Sir Reginald said "There's only one thing I really care about now, and that's knowing that Lady Crowe's safe, but it won't hinder anything if we understand one another on business matters. I don't suppose you'll want to go further with your London plans after this?"

Capone was explicit in reply: "I want to pull out first thing I do."

"Then I may be able to give you substantial help. We shall probably be able to relieve you of the shares without serious loss if our brokers co-operate with yours, and the matter be dealt with gradually—say, within three months from now.

"I anticipate that some of those who have sold short will be customers of the right kind. And the five million dollars we hold on deposit can be dealt with in accordance with instructions which I am sure that we shall receive from your Dallas bank in a regular form.... I would only stipulate, if I may, that Clancy's claim shall be dealt with, and also the charges which Mrs. Clancy has incurred with the New York Cab Company—"

"You've no cause to get warm about that," Capone said. "You'll know I'm not mean when you get me right, and what Clancy's done for me adds up more than you'd be likely to think. He's given me the Detroit ground, and most of Maloon's boys'll come over to me. When this breaks they'll be in that much hurry to scramble over the fence before the guns might begin! And there's Maloon's share of that thousand grand.... No, I've no call to be mean with Clancy or you.

"We've got to get the dames back, and we'll say things might have gone worse by a whole lot."

"Well, if you feel like that, we'll forget it now; and when I'm back in London we'll soon have it balanced up. The question is what

251

are we going to do now?" He turned to Clancy to ask: "This Montana shack—what is there in that?"

"It was Moll thought of that first. It was just a might-be, but the way Slick rose to it makes it a sure guess. When we came east and first met Maloon, Moll and I both said we'd seen him in Montana before. He used to live by himself for weeks in a mountain shack which no one'd find in a year if they didn't get shown the way. He must have kept it as a place he could lie low and it's odds but he has it still."

"But it was no secret from you?"

"It was our business to know who was round, and for them not to know that much of us."

"I see. And you think Mrs. Clancy's on the way there now?"

"I know she is. Larry gave her the right men and the right car."

"And we could be there ourselves in twenty-four hours, more or less?"

"We could. But I won't say—"

They were interrupted by the telephone ringing. Clancy looked up sharply. Moll again? But the hope faded as he heard Capone's reply: "No, he said he wouldn't be speaking to anyone more tonight. He's a bit sick. No, not slick—*sick*.... No, not after what he said when he turned in. But I'll take a message. Or is it what I can do? Anything that a pal could.... Well, I'll tell him. And you can call him again tomorrow? Reckon he'll be about then."

Capone said, as he put back the receiver: "We can't keep this in long. We've got to move quick."

Sir Reginald said: "If I start tonight—"

"You'd be late for the show. And Redhead's covering that. We've got to work this out here."

"Well, you can do that in the next hour. If you'd give up the idea of bumping Maloon off, he'd soon have Lady Crowe back if he knew he'd be let out when she arrived."

"I couldn't let him go now."

"It wouldn't do him much good. Not if Clancy lets me up on my promise not to give Cassidy's signature to the police."

The suggestion brought exclamations of protest from both Sir Reginald's auditors. "I couldn't do it that low," Capone said. "Egan's rats wouldn't do that." (Egan's rats were a St. Louis gang which even Chicago gangsters regarded as loathsome dirt.)

Sir Reginald saw that he had proposed that which seemed as monstrous to Capone as it would be to a punctilious Home Secretary in his own country to suggest that a murderer, against whom legal proof was incomplete, should be given up for illegal destruction to the friends of the murdered man. There are some things which, even for the vindication of abstract justice, we do not do!

Clancy made a more logical protest. "There isn't only him. There's Cassidy."

"No, we can't break your word to him. But Maloon said that Cassidy would be dead by now."

Capone said, not as one who wavered in his decision, but as dismissing the idea of an amateur mind: "Maloon wouldn't believe. He's too slick."

Sir Reginald saw that there might be real difficulty there. If it should be agreed to let Maloon go in exchange for Evelyn's safety, he would want it to be done in such a way that his release would depend on something better than Capone's word. As the position was it might be extremely difficult to arrange the exchange on terms that both sides would accept. But, even so, he saw hope. He said boldly: "He might believe me. But I should have to tell him if I intended to give him away to the police."

Capone dismissed that difficulty at once. "He wouldn't get hot about that. Not the way you think. He knows what the cops are."

"You mean they'd give him time to get away?"

"They would that. I wouldn't say they'd move at all on what Cassidy's signed. Anyway, they'd be that slow! But I've told you we won't have it that way."

"Then it seems to me that the only way is to let Maloon go if we get Lady Crowe safely back. He might take my word for that—or let him think of a way. With his life at stake, he'd think hard." He added, seeing the look of stubborn dissent on Capone's face: "He'd be a ruined man, and you'd have the Detroit trade."

"You think I'd let him loose to come gunning for me?"

"You can let me tell him that I'll set the police on him if he doesn't clear. If he does, and Cassidy's dead, we'd leave it at that. We can let the tale break that Cassidy knocked Ringan and Ruscatti off, and let it end there. We'll all have got what we want, and you'll have Detroit."

Clancy asked: "You wouldn't let it break if Cassidy isn't dead?"

"No. You've my word on that."

Capone was still frowning, but he said at last: "You can talk to him your own way. I wouldn't say but I owe you that. I'll give him six hours if you get your dame, but then he'll be on the run."

"Then I'll see him now."

Capone picked up the house telephone and said that he wanted Muller.

CHAPTER LIII.

A BARGAIN WITH MALOON

MALOON lay in bed on his back, somewhat propped up. His right hand had been dressed and bandaged by men who, though they might have had no professional training, were not without experience in such matters. He had a writing-pad before him, on which he had been endeavouring to figure with his left hand.

He looked up as Sir Reginald entered. "I reckoned," he said, "you'd soon be here."

Muller, standing at the door, called to the two men who sat at either side of the bed to come out. The door closed, and Sir Reginald and Maloon were alone together.

"You made a good guess," Sir Reginald said. "Perhaps you know what I've come to say."

"I'm not going to guess that."

"Well, it's soon said. If I get Lady Crowe back safely, Capone lets you go."

Maloon looked his contempt. "And how far would that be?"

"As far as you could get in six hours. He wouldn't promise a minute more."

"I wouldn't trust him, not if—"

"You don't trust him. You trust me."

"How do you figure that?"

"It is part of a bargain with Capone which covers the financial and other issues involved. Besides, if he should break faith with me, I could make the whole of the facts public, which he is anxious to avoid."

"You'd do that if he tried any trick on me?"

"I certainly should. He'll give you six hours' start. I don't promise anything beyond that." Maloon was slow to reply. The offer had a fair sound. But he saw snags. He assumed that Capone was already planning to take over his Detroit ground and his organisation with it. Suppose Al should give a hint to men who would be on his pay-roll next week that

Maloon would be less trouble dead than alive? Things might happen which could not be laid at Capone's door. His mind went beyond that. He was already planning revenge and recovery of the position which, for the moment, was lost. Was there anyone whom he could trust to be his bodyguard in so radically altered a position? The occupation of the six hours must include a visit to his Detroit bank.... But it was hard to think that Capone would take the risk of letting him live. His own plans of revenge, already taking shape, confirmed the wisdom of the code which they both knew.... Bumping-off was the only way.

"I'll have to think this over till morning. Lady Crowe'll be quite safe so long as no one's been on the phone for me."

"Someone has. But he was told to ring up again tomorrow. Capone said you were sick."

Maloon sat up sharply. "He said that? I'd better get through at once. If I don't there'll be hell to pay."

"I doubt whether Capone will agree to that."

"Sure he will. Won't he see that I've got to get your dame safe? It's no use giving any message. If they don't hear my voice they'll know something's wrong, and what'll be done next—"

"I'll tell him what you say."

Sir Reginald went back to Capone and related the conversation. Capone had had time for thought, and it had raised a fresh difficulty in his mind. He might say with sincerity that he would have no part in setting the law on Maloon's track, but it did not alter the fact that the prudence—it might be said the sanity—of letting him free depended upon Sir Reginald's ability and inclination to do so, or, at least, upon Maloon's belief that he would. Apart from that, Maloon, once released, would have no occasion for flight. He would rally his own forces, and there would be another of those bitter gang wars by which the racketeers reduced their own ranks more rapidly than the police, at this point, appeared able to do.

It would be a war in which there would be many murderous clashes, which might end in the death of one or other of the rival leaders, but in which their underlings would take greater risks and suffer more certain casualties than their well-guarded selves. To let Maloon go, after what had been disclosed, to take such action would be an impossible folly. It was gangsters' law, and, though the ethical standards involved were low, the reasoning was hard to refute.

Against this development he had the presumption that Maloon would not be able to wage such a war upon him while the police were seeking him as the instigator of the London murders. He would be in hiding or under arrest. In fact, he would be likely to be too slick to attempt the double struggle. He would collect such funds as he quickly could and disappear while his movements would be unnoticed by the police.

But suppose he should linger, lengthening the chance to the last minute he dare, and Sir Reginald did not act? And Sir Reginald had given Clancy his word that he would do nothing while Cassidy lived.

That was what he had been discussing with Clancy, who had not denied, though he had minimised, the risk.

"I promised Cassidy," he said, "and I'm not going back on that, and I had to get Sir Reginald's promise, which Slick needn't know. And Slick says Cassidy'd be a dead man by about now. I shouldn't say there's much risk in that.... And we've got to get the dame back, or where the hell should we all be?"

That was a generous way of putting it, for it was a matter in which he had little direct concern, apart from the fact that fresh trouble might complicate the prospect of getting back the money he claimed.

Capone admitted the force of the argument, but frowned over a position he did not like, till he reassured himself with the thought that Cassidy need not live. Whatever bargains others had made, he did not consider that they were binding to him.

Having reached this satisfactory conclusion, he was ready to hear what Sir Reginald had to say, to whose surprise he made no difficulty of Maloon's request.

"Wants to phone, does he? Sure he can do that. Tell him to open out. We'll hear what he says, and maybe we'll learn some, and a bit. There's no private line from the room where they've put him. You didn't think I'd kick, did you? You wouldn't figure I'm that green?"

Sir Reginald said that, if he had, the stupidity had been his.

It was, indeed, certain that, with his own freedom at stake, Maloon would do nothing to jeopardise Evelyn's safety. It was equally certain that, should he intend to accept the six-hours offer, he would not wish any advance knowledge of the position to reach those on whose loyalty his security would, in the first instance, depend. Capone could make an easy guess that his use of that brief period of immunity would be to visit his own home and his own bank. Would he prefer to do these things surrounded by those who did not question his continued authority, or such as would be already trimming their sails to a new wind, and might think that opportunities of present plunder or future favour with Capone would be secured by his own destruction? Even if he were plotting to defy both Capone's enmity and the later threat of police action, he would not wish to say anything that would cause unrest among his own followers till he were free once more and at their head.

So he was allowed to phone as he would, and, if he guessed he were overheard, he had no cause for worry in that, for his conversations were mainly directed to the details of his own bootlegging business. As to Evelyn, it appeared that the only important consequence of the earlier call not having reached him was that a simple opportunity of intercepting the flying car had been lost. Now she had passed beyond the district over which he had firm control. The wooded Wisconsin country, which was, in a later year, to be the favourite hideout of the Dillinger gang, was beyond his range.

Speaking with fuller knowledge than others could have, and a stake which could not be less than theirs, he said that the surest way of avoiding any adverse development would now be to let events follow the course he had originally planned. That was that the car should take a road which ran near the Yellowstone, where, at the crossing of Beaver Creek, a man of his would report its passage and would be instructed to trail it. Thus by the vigilance and gallantry of one of his own gunmen—for the man was to rescue Evelyn after a mock combat, in which many bullets would go astray—he would have restored to Sir Reginald his abducted wife, whose gratitude to Capone, but most particularly to himself, must have created an obligation that could not be lightly ignored. Now his instructions could be so far varied that he would stop the car and direct it to turn back and come to Chicago by the shortest road.

As he had had a separate plan, which included the recovery of the papers that Cassidy held, to be promptly followed by the death of the gunman-cop, he had decided that the identity of one who could no longer speak might be safely disclosed as that of the perpetrator of the London murders. He had seen no direction from which Sir Reginald would not be satisfied, or from which suspicion could point to himself. And all these plans, he thought, with a natural bitterness, had come to wreck because he had failed to bump off the girl who had seen Cassidy and been clever enough to conceal her knowledge until she could communicate it to Clancy's more dangerous mind! He reflected that most of life's major troubles come, not from bumping-off those whose conduct requires it, but from omissions to do it at the first warning that prudence gives. It was a mistake which—he had some reason to hope—Capone might be making now.

"Will it not be wise to stop Mrs. Clancy now?" Sir Reginald asked. He felt a diminished anxiety, but it was acute, and he was restless at the inaction which the course of events had thrust upon him. What would Evelyn think when she should learn that for two days, more or less, he had known of her abduction and remained idle here?

So he said. But Clancy was cool in reply: "I wouldn't say I don't see how it feels to you, but there's no cause to get hot. We can't stop Redhead unless she calls up again, as I hope she may. If there's any risk, it's from what she may do, and more for her than your dame. But I'd say she'll come through.... We couldn't catch up with them now, and I reckon we'd best let it break its own way. We're sitting pretty while we've got Slick in the bag."

Sir Reginald saw that he could do nothing but wait, which it was temperamentally difficult for him to do. Of course, it all showed that Evelyn should not have come I She should have been content to leave it to him and to the hope of getting the bluebell wood. But— while he did not know she was safe—there was no consolation in that.

CHAPTER LIV.

Dinner in New York

THE train from Chicago was three minutes late, but Mr. Jellipot, finding that no one came forward to refund any part of his fare, and observing no look of pleasant expectancy on the faces of his fellow-passengers, concluded correctly that this margin of time was insufficient to win the prize. Anyway, it made no difference to him. The Tepecano Democratic Club honoured its magistrate guest at a late hour, and he had time to reach the Bronx, even though he had to discover a way which he did not know.

The first direction he received led him to the underground railway, at that time probably the cheapest, the most ill-lit, and the dingiest in the civilised world. He was puzzled by the absence of escalators, having been led to believe (not without reason) that the United States led the way in the use of mechanical power. He observed with interest the different conduct of a New York from that of a London crowd when boarding or leaving a crowded train. The New Yorker would push with a more highly developed individualism, but he would also receive pushes with a good humour which a Londoner would have been unlikely to show.

Leaving the train, he was intrigued to read a notice on the grimy wall of the station threatening that anyone spitting therein would incur a penalty of six months' imprisonment *and* a fine of five hundred dollars. "Spitting in these murky regions," he reflected, "appears to be regarded more seriously than bumping-off Probably if I should use a word here which Mr. Hays would not approve I should be hurried to the electric chair."

He was glad to leave the dim inferno for the Elevated Railway. He could not observe that it was much cleaner or that its rolling stock was of higher type, but he had the advantage of wider views and of the keen, cold, health-giving New York air....

His taxi deposited him at the Tepecano Club off Southern Boulevard, the night being too dark to enable him to judge the nature of the neighbourhood to which he came, but the coming and going of affluent private cars gave him assurance that he was not conspicuously late, nor too early, which he would have more acutely disliked.

He showed his card of invitation to a negro attendant at the brilliantly lighted entrance, which he did not observe that other of the entering guests were required to do, but he saw that that was natural enough, for most of them must have been well known, both to one another and to the service of the club. He heard familiar greetings called and returned, sometimes in Italian, but more often in the language of the New World, as it is spoken by men of a Latin race. He felt that he was conspicuously alien there, but could not observe that anyone took much notice of him.

It was a cheerful, chattering crowd among whom he was relieved by a brown-skinned mulatto of hat and coat and umbrella, and then guided to an upper room, where an Italian waiter, whose English was of elementary monosyllables, drew back a chair for him at the larger of two long tables laid for between fifty and sixty people, which were rapidly filling up.

Mr. Jellipot settled himself to observe and enjoy. The dinner was very good. His fellow-guests had a general aspect of well-being, and most of them were obviously in carefree mood. The majority were of evident Italian origin. It was an assembly in which men predominated, but dark-eyed bejewelled women of youthful slimness or mature voluptuousness were also present.

Mr. Jellipot looked round with a natural curiosity, seeking to distinguish Cassidy, and with some hope that he might observe something of the transaction which was expected to take place under the unconscious protection of the assembled guests. He could not see him, because he was seated on the same side as himself, and was obscured by the intervening bulk of a particularly massive feminine guest. His ideas settled doubtfully on a man seated nearly opposite, of particularly brutal aspect, with a thin, cruel, tight-lipped mouth and cunning, restless eyes. He was Irish enough, and had the aspect of one who had come on other than a festive errand. But Mr. Jellipot found it hard to believe that he could be a Boston cop—even such a one as could be hired by Slick Maloon to do murders for the relief of his gambling-debts.

Seeking information, Mr. Jellipot turned to his companions on either side. He was seated about halfway down the table, with the door by which he had entered almost directly behind him. He had a lady on his right whom he had heard addressed as Mrs. Savino, whose shrill, impudent backchat to some of the further guests did not suggest that there would be any exceptional reticence in her conversational exchanges. But when he began to ask her as to the identity of those who headed the table, she gave him a sharp interrogative glance, half hostile and half afraid, and met him with a blank wall of denial: "I wouldn't know."

Giving her up, Mr. Jellipot turned with patient persistence to his left-hand neighbour, and found a better response. He learned that he was a medical practitioner, Dr. Joseph Martoccio, and when he had disclosed his own identity with an equal frankness the doctor was very willing to point out the local celebrities of the Italian colony to an English visitor. Not that he spoke of them as Italians. It was to be disclosed, in the course of public enquiries that were to follow, that every man and woman there (except Mr. Jellipot) was a citizen of the United States. But most of them were of common origin, and Italian was still the tongue in which they thought, and in which they would most frequently speak together.

The chairman? That was ex-magistrate Delagi. Magistrate Vitale, in whose honour the dinner was being given, on his return from a vacation in Virginia, was on Delagi's right. The gentleman three seats away (whom eighteen of the guests were to take public oath a few weeks later that they had not seen) was Morello, or some called him Terranova. Dr. Martoccio's voice was reserved as he spoke of him. But he was appreciative as he reverted quickly to the chairman and Vitale. They were active in the ward for the cause of the Democratic Party, combating Al Smith's deplorable popularity They collected funds for the poor. Magistrate Vitale, in his judicial functions, had proved himself to be a friend on whom good citizens could rely. Mr. Jellipot recognised sincerity. He remembered having noticed before that good doctors are not always well informed nor sound in judgement in matters outside their own exacting profession. He learned that the members present included other medical men, three or four lawyers, an assistant boxing commissioner, and others prominent in the professional or business interests of the Bronx—an assembly where almost anyone might be proud to be.

Mr. Jellipot enquired concerning the man whom he had half thought to be Cassidy, and was told at once that he was Fred Burke. Dr. Martoccio frowned over him. He was not a member. He did not know how he came to be there. Not a man, Mr. Jellipot understood, with whom to associate, nor with whom to quarrel. One who was too quick with a gun.

Mr. Jellipot gave up looking for Cassidy. There was a second table, where the guests were less easy to see. He might be there. Or he might not yet have come. It was an informal gathering. The places were not named or numbered. There were still vacant seats. There was one on Dr. Martoccio's left....

It was easy to talk without being overheard, for a band was playing at the end of the room, and the noise of many voices contended with it. There was shouting at times to attract the attention of those a few seats away.... The music, like the dinner, was good. Neither fact was surprising at an Italian club.

Mrs. Savino was looking over her left shoulder, and Mr. Jellipot turned his eyes in the same direction. A man whom he easily placed as a member of the detective force stood rather uncertainly at the door. Was he Cassidy? Mr. Jellipot thought not. He was over forty, with a square, blunt-featured face. Not an Irish type. Perhaps he had come to interrupt the festivities? To investigate something which would interrupt the growing hilarity? It was not an improbable guess. The wine which was on the table (which Dr. Martoccio was to frankly admit on a later day, but which Magistrate Vitale was to swear that he had not seen) was alone sufficient legal reason for breaking up the gathering.

Mrs. Savino (if such she were, but the whole event became a nightmare concerning which nothing could be stated which someone would not deny. "Listen, you fellows," Savino said to the reporters a few weeks later, when the lady had been arrested pleaded guilty to "vagrancy," and been immediately released without penalty, to the astonishment of all who read of this remarkable police activity, "I want you to get this straight. That woman is not my wife.... I have never been married." Well he was the one to know).... Mrs. Savino called out: "Hullo, Arthur."

The detective responded cordially: "Hullo, Grace."

Several voices were now inviting him to sit down. He took the vacant chair on Dr. Martoccio's left.

Cassidy's name was not Arthur. Mr. Jellipot had learnt that names in some New York circles were more numerous than their owners, but a detective would be unlikely to indulge in such plurality. Clearly, Cassidy must still be looked for elsewhere.

Whoever he might be, Arthur had not entered with any intention of spoiling the evening He had come to eat, which everyone appeared very willing for him to do.

Terranova rose and strolled down the room. He bent over the back of Burke's chair and whispered to him. Mr. Jellipot observed this, but did not attach importance to it, not knowing what kind of entertainment Terranova was proposing to give, though he was curious to know what the Artichoke King could have to say to one of whom he had heard so sinister an account.

The conversation—drowned in a final blare of the band, which was now approaching a period of silence to allow of speeches being made—was short and pointed.

"Brought the paper along?"

"Yep. Got the fifteen grand?"

"Yes. We'll settle this up now. Come into Vitale's room after he's made his speech, and he'll see it through."

"Nothing doing."

"Say, you get me wrong. I want to give you a square deal, and all friends. Delagi'll be there as well."

"We'll all go together?"

"Sure we will. You'll have no cause to be sore at me."

Burke nodded grimly. There were twenty notches on his gun, each of which meant a dead enemy or someone he had been hired to slay. He made no secret of that. And those deaths were only a fraction of the homicides in which he had been directly concerned. And the police knew, and had always failed to find the legal proof which a prosecution requires. He did not think that anyone would be quick to monkey with him.... And when he left it would be in an armoured car, and there would be bodyguards on each side of the door into the street. They were due to arrive in an hour's time. There was no hurry yet.

The band ceased, and all eyes turned to the top of the table, where the chairman and Vitale were seen to be whispering together. Vitale, who had been wearing a rather mechanical smile during the dinner, looked nervous and worried. To return thanks for such a reception might be an ordeal to a less experienced man, but Vitale was used to such exercises. He was a barrister, trained in advocacy; a magistrate, used to preside, a politician, accustomed to facing unruly audiences. And here he was among friends.

But he was not worrying about what he would have to reply. He spoke in Italian, too low to be audible two seats away, till the band ceased. He was saying: "It's a curse Johnson dropping in I didn't reckon on that.

Delagi was soothing in his reply: "I shouldn't say Arthur'll make much trouble. He won't shoot. Not if you give him the wink."

Vitale was irritable. "How can I do that? It means it's all got to come out."

"I don't see that."

"It's long odds but it will."

"Well, Cito won't stop it now. I don't reckon he could. And I'll bet Johnson'll sit still. That is, if there's half a dozen guns out at the start. Cito promised that."

"I expect you're right. But I don't like it.... You'd better start. They're getting to look as though they've all been bit by the same flea."

The guests, nearly half of whom had had a whispered word that there was a mock hold-up to come, were looking curiously at those who headed the table.

Delagi rose. For ten minutes his soft Italian voice was eloquent in praise of their eminent, noble-natured friend, whose heart was in the welfare of the Bronx, and particularly (he implied, though he did not bluntly say) in that of its citizens who were of his own original nationality.

He sat down, and Vitale rose to reply, amid loud cries of applause. But they had scarcely died when four men entered the room from the stairs at Mr. Jellipot's back. As they moved round the table, someone hazarded a guess that they were an entertainment troupe. At the same time three others came in from the top end of the room. As they ranged themselves round it, their guns came out. One, who had two, and a white silk handkerchief round his face, called out in a hard, menacing voice: "Will everyone keep still and put their hands on the tables before them."

Mr. Jellipot was peeling a pear. Did that operation sufficiently fulfil the required condition? He did not know, but he went on, and the bandits showed no interest in what he did.

He saw Burke look round sharply. There was a moment of hesitation—a mere second—but he was too experienced in such matters not to know that the guests—even he—would have contended against hopeless odds. He saw a gun levelled at his back, and his hands flattened on the table with more celerity than was shown by others who were less experienced in the deadly game.

One of the men called out: "Better frisk them for guns." The man behind Burke stepped forward and took two from him. That, at least, was a thorough search.

Detective Johnson lost his gun also. He had made one or two spasmodic efforts to reach it, which had ceased abruptly at a threatening motion from the nearest bandit. Vitale's eyes had been fixed upon him in wide entreaty not to start shooting it out, which he had not failed to understand. He gave evidence afterwards that "he clenched his teeth and his eyes stared out, and he shook his head at me."

Vitale did not resent this description of his facial gestures. In fact, he corroborated it in very similar words. But he persisted that it had been a genuine hold-up, as much a surprise to him as to any other victim there. His idea had been that, when ladies are present, hold-ups should proceed in a civilised manner and violence and bloodshed should not occur.

But even to some of those present who had had no warning of what to expect there was an air of unreality about the affair.

It was not only that the appearance of seven men was probably unprecedented in such events. Two—three—even four there might be. They would be enough to overawe a social gathering, and why should there be others to share the spoil? It was not done.

But apart from that there was a lack of business purpose, a curious indecision, about some of the men. It was as though they were acting in a play they had not rehearsed, and waited for cues which were slow to come. Some of the guests were not "frisked" at all.

The man with the handkerchief round his face called out: "What's the matter with you? Are you losing your nerve? Take their pins and watches."

He went himself to detective Johnson, and pulled off his watch and chain.

Johnson cried out: "Don't take that. My wife gave me that. My wife's dead."

The man snapped off the police whistle and handed it back. He went on down the room.

The bandits were now busy in all directions. Watches and chains, tiepins, wads of notes, and some feminine jewellery were passing into their pockets, amid a clamour of protests and pleadings from those they robbed.

One man, Bravate—the one among them, whether by chance or arrangement, to be thoroughly identified afterwards—had taken watches and money from the chairman and the guest of honour. He came down the room and paused behind Mr. Jellipot's chair.

Mr. Jellipot was not greatly concerned. His watch was of moderate value. He did not wear a chain, such as was popular with that Italian community. He had not more than thirty dollars in his wallet. He would have said that the experience would be worth the price had he lost them all. His conscious reaction was a desire to discuss the matter with the invaders.

"I am afraid," he said smoothly, "that I have not much that would be of any value to you, but I have been wondering—"

Taking no notice of this, the man's hand was reaching for his breast-pocket when someone cried: "He's English. You won't get much from him." And another, to better effect: "He's Tozer, Battle & Young."

The man growled: "Why didn't you say that?" He drew his hand back as sharply as though he had been stung. Mr. Jellipot observed that there are advantages in being a criminal lawyers' clerk.

The man returned to the top of the table, where an argument between the chairman and another bandit was proceeding. There were watches on the table, apparently being returned. Dr. Martoccio called: "Can't I have mine back?"

Vitale found it and passed it down the table.

The chairman, Delagi, appealed for a chain, and one was thrown to him. The men were now withdrawing. Dr. Martoccio observed that Bravate, as he passed him, had a good-humoured expression; it was as though he were concluding a successful joke rather than a serious crime. His expression inspired the doctor to appeal: "Can't I have my chain too?"

Bravate said: "Sure you can."

As it was handed back, Delagi called down the room: "Here, you haven't given me mine. This is Magistrate Vitale's chain."

But they would not stay longer. One of them called back, "We'll mail it to you," but whether in earnest or derision Mr. Jellipot could not tell.

CHAPTER LV.

Dinner in New York II

THE bandits withdrew, the last one standing at the door with a gun pointed toward the guests till his companions were down the stairs, and their car doubtless ready for instant movement when he should join them.

As they left, babel broke out again. It was not every guest who had been fortunate enough to have anything returned. Almost all of them had lost money. Much jewellery had been taken. Delagi complained of a loss of over sixty dollars. Dr. Martoccio confided to Mr. Jellipot that his loss was only a few dollars less.

Detective Johnson had risen. He looked, and doubtless felt, a much-worried man.

Vitale called to him: "Don't do anything in a hurry, Arthur. We'd better talk this over."

Johnson took no notice. He ran down the stairs. In a few minutes he was back.

Vitale came up to him. He had made a short speech in Italian to the other guests during his absence, which appeared to have had a soothing effect. He asked: "You haven't made any report?"

"Not yet. But I must. It's dreadful for me. Losing my gun and all."

"There might be ways of getting it back. Did you see anything of them?"

"No. There was the sound of a car down Southern Boulevard. Everything was quiet besides that."

That was not wonderful. It was 1:10 A.M. on Sunday morning. The cars for the guests were not due till a later hour.

Vitale said: "Well, come and talk it over, and we'll see what can be done."

Johnson went to the top of the room. He went into a huddle with Vitale and Delagi. When a detective is in such a position, are not a magistrate and an ex-magistrate men on whose advice he may wisely rely?

As they sat down together two shots sounded from the street; but everyone was too much occupied with his own affairs to take much notice of them.

Mr. Jellipot saw that Burke had left his place and was engaged in an angry altercation with Terranova, who appeared to be replying in soothing words. He could not guess what it meant, having no clue to what had occurred.

Actually, the mock hold-up had succeeded in its object. The wallet containing the murder contract had been removed from Burke's pocket. Terranova had not lost fifteen grand because he had not brought money with him which he had no intention of paying.

Now he was saying that the document would be recovered—*must* be recovered in the interests of *both* of them, because it gave both away. He was ready—even anxious—to pay as soon as that recovery could be made. But, for the moment, document and money alike were gone. So far Burke did not suspect the truth. He cursed himself that his vigilance had relaxed. If he had had one extra second to bring out his gun— But who would have thought of a hold-up being attempted on such an occasion, at an assembly half of whom were gangsters or gangsters' friends, and who had met to honour a magistrate on whose good-will any of them might depend on the next day?

Mr. Jellipot knew nothing of this, nor could he guess what effect the hold-up would have had in Cassidy's contemplated transaction, but the weirdness of the event was beyond anything that he had hoped to be privileged to see.

"I have imagined," he said to Dr. Martoccio, "what a hold-up would be like, but it was something different from this. It shows how different reality may be from that which appears plausible to our own minds. If a hold-up should be so represented upon the stage, I suppose it would be received with hilarity and regarded as clever farce."

"It's a queer business," the doctor agreed, "but it's cost me more than fifty dollars, which I'm not likely to see again. There's not much farce about that."

He knew more than Mr. Jellipot, having understood Vitale's Italian oration. He knew why the plundered guests were sitting patiently round the tables. They had been told that efforts—probably successful efforts—would be made to recover what they had lost. He was bewildered by guesses which went wide of incredible fact.

Terranova had finished his talk with Burke and gone back to his place. The face of the professional killer was black with anger, but fear and uncertainty were also there. He supposed that Johnson, when he left the room, had summoned the cops, and they were gentlemen who, for several reasons, he was not anxious to meet. Particularly not in bulk. If he must deal with cops at all, he preferred them one or two at a time. He was inclined to go.

But it would be dangerous, for his bodyguard would not have arrived. He had a natural doubt of what Terranova might have prepared for him in the street below, on the assumption that he would leave with fifteen grand in his pocket which the Artichoke King had shown no willingness to pay. And his guns were gone. Yet, even so, it seemed the less risk to take. He left his place and moved quietly toward the door.

Meanwhile the discussion between magistrate and detective proceeded. Johnson urged, with prophetic truth, that he was jeopardising his position by delaying to report the hold-up. Vitale argued that it would be better not to report it at all. In the end they compromised for an hour's delay.

After that the police came. There was much enquiry. Lists were taken of the guests. Assurances (of less than doubtful accuracy) were given that none had left since the hold-up occurred. Schedules of missing property were made. The police estimated that cash and jewellery to a total value of five thousand dollars had been removed.

It was said (and afterwards denied) that three of the guests—Joe the Baker, Savino of the doubtful wife, and Daniel Iamascio—had been sent to bring back the missing jewellery. However that may have been, it is a fact that much of it was returned before morning came.

Vitale also had the pleasure of handing back the detective's gun. He said that it had been found lying at the street door. Could he be expected to explain that?

It was a night with which Terranova had most reason to be content. Burke had gone off without suspecting that the hold-up had been other than a genuine catastrophe for both of them. The murder contract had been recovered without payment of ransom and had become ashes before the arrival of the police.

The true nature or the event would be revealed to an astonished public in a few days (as Terranova did not foresee), but it was to mean little to him.

Burke would read it, but his fury would have no effect. Back in Michigan he would kill a cop who lacked discretion to leave him alone, and, after that, he being wealthy, and America being large, he would be a fugitive, avoiding arrest for two years, during which he would have his face altered by an unscrupulous surgeon; but in the end he would be caught, tried, and sentenced to life imprisonment, that being the severest penalty which is known to Michigan law.

Terranova would be arrested, but the police would find they must let him go. The damning paper was burned, and he could laugh at so wild a tale. He would suddenly become unknown to his fellow-members of the club. Even the restaurant proprietor would be baffled. "I no see this man," de Somma would testify, with the emphasis to be expected from one of his Latin blood.

Terranova would explain to the eager reporters that he was being made the goat of a quarrel within the Democratic Party ranks. Jimmie Walker, the Mayor, and Al Smith, the former Governor of New York, had fallen out, and this trouble had fallen upon a peaceable man. "Boys, I only want to be left alone." What could be fairer than that?

Mr. Jellipot's name was not among those which the police so competently compiled. The fact was that he had left a scene which he had been fascinated to observe because, perhaps for the first time in his life, he had been overcome by extreme fear.

He still knew little of American law, but he had learned that, while a criminal can get bail, a witness to his offence is liable to be kept in jail till the day of the trial comes. There is a fair-sounding reason for this in the fact that a criminal who passes into another state may (in some cases) be brought back, where a witness cannot. But if a witness cannot be compelled to return from another state, there must be even less hope of recovering him from a foreign land! If he should await the arrival of the police, would he be "held" till the bandits' trial?

The thought brought a further fear, logical in itself, though it went beyond any probable danger in which he lay.

He had heard that a man had lain for several months in jail awaiting trial for the murders at the Hotsy-Totsy Club, because Jack Diamond, also accused, could not be found. He wondered whether the trial of the seven bandits, if one or two should be caught, would be delayed until there should be a full bag.

He imagined himself being "held" while the years passed, and young Whalen coming cheerfully to see him at the intervals of the changing seasons to see him that the two had become three, or the four five, and to assure him that it could not be many months before the seven would be lined up to face the indignant law.

He was aware that his knowledge of American judicial procedure was neither exact nor complete, but he was not sure that he wanted to know more. He imagined his London practice ruined by long neglect while he would be confined in a New York jail.... His eyes went to the door, and his feet soon took the same direction.

It was cold in the empty street. The frosty pavement had a thin sprinkle of snow. An east wind blew from the sea. It was better to walk on than to stand. In the New York of that day a taxi was never distant to find.... One was coming now at slow cruising speed.

He stepped to the edge of the pavement to signal it, if it should be disengaged, and, as he did so, was aware of a man who came unsteadily from a shadowed doorway, and was a few yards before him with the same intention. He was not near enough to see his face in that uncertain light as the car drew up, but he heard distinctly in the clear, silent air the direction he gave the driver, "58, Bevis Street," which was easy to bear in mind. As the car turned away and he moved forward again, he saw that there were dark stains on the snow where the man had crossed the pavement. If he were not wrong, they were blood. The car had picked up a wounded man.

When he was able to stop another car, he directed it to take him to the Hotel Atlantis. Queerly, he had a feeling that he would be safer there than he was now in the open street.

CHAPTER LVI.

PAUL MAKES A GOOD GUESS

IF you've got plans," Moll said, "I'd like to know what they are."

"I wouldn't say I've got plans," Paul answered cautiously, "but I've thought of a place I know."

"Place for stopping the car? You've got to think they'll be going fast."

"And we can't wreck it. I know that."

"What's the place like?"

"The road dips to a hollow, and there's a little creek to splash through at the foot—it'd be frozen now—and a sharp rise beyond. I've told you it isn't a good road. They couldn't go fast there."

"It isn't only that we can't wreck the car. I don't want a rough-house. Lady Crowe might be the first to get something not meant for her."

"Or it might be meant.... You don't think you can talk soft to Slinker or any other rat that Maloon'd send on a job like this?"

"I'm not loony. But we might make them sit up when they've stopped the car. They'll have to put up somewhere."

"They haven't done much putting up yet. They must have done like we. Slept in the car."

"They have to stop for eats. Where'd they do that?"

Paul looked doubtful. "I haven't been this way for a bit. Roads soon change. There'd be Beddoes'. They'd pull up there, it's a good guess."

"Then we'll stop at Beddoes'. Could you find out when they'll be near?"

"I could that."

After this conversation Moll sat silent while they left behind several miles of the flying road. They were three to two, even if Lady Crowe should be unable to help. There was satisfaction in that.

She knew that she herself could take a straight aim, though she would never have the lightning quickness that such occasions required. If they had to shoot it out, she had little doubt of what the issue would be. But she wanted something different from that. She neither wanted to stop a bullet herself, nor for Lady Crowe to get one which might not be intended for her. And, besides, there was the bother of the cops. However necessary your act might be, or whatever kind of rat you might have good reason for knocking off, you could never rely upon them to let it alone. Here was a position which, if fully explained, would justify almost any violence in rescuing an abducted girl, but was the publicity which it would entail what those concerned would desire? She did not know what deal her friends—particularly Tim—might have made by this time with Capone. Publicity might, or might not, be an upsetting factor. But it was a risk to avoid. She asked: "You know Beddoes?"

"I wouldn't say he'd know me."

"What sort is he?"

"I wouldn't call him a crook."

"He wouldn't join in with them?"

"Not with kidnappers. There's few would."

"Is Beddoes' near that dip?"

"No. It's way beyond that."

"What did you mean to do there?"

"Hold them up at the top of the rise. They couldn't get past us, and they wouldn't have room to turn. They'd come up too slow for a smash, and they'd be surprised."

"I'd say they would.... I thought we'd be at Beddoes', waiting for them to walk in."

"Well, we can't do both."

"I know that. We'd have to put Beddoes wise."

"Yep. He might muscle in on the wrong side if he didn't know.... My creek wouldn't be a bad spot. There's a few trees lying round. There aren't many of them as you go west."

"I know that. I'd say it's good. But we'll have Beddoes'."

"It's you to say."

"How far is it?"

"Beddoes'? We're on the right road about twelve miles from here, and then it's way back, maybe twenty more."

The two cars, which would soon be approaching one another, were now less than two hundred miles apart....

Evelyn, still scarcely recovered from the drug which had been injected into her arm by the combined efforts of Slinker and the car driver after a moment of frantic struggle, when they had stopped under a deserted archway in a New Jersey back street, sat alone in the back of the car, Slinker being beside the driver.

She had not been badly treated since she had recovered consciousness, which she rightly attributed to the orders under which the men were acting, rather than to their proclivities; and she had come to a bargain with them which had made the journey more tolerable than it could otherwise have been. She was to be left undoped and to have the exclusive use of the back of the car, on condition that she would make no disturbance nor attempt escape when they should pull in, as at times they must, for food or gas, at filling stations beside the way.

She had been warned that any attempt on her part to create disturbance or flee would be dealt with by an instant bullet. The laws against kidnapping were so severe, and were now so sternly enforced, that it would be mere prudence to make certain that she should not be alive to identify them, if they themselves should be in flight in consequence of her having broken away.

If she made no trouble for them, she was assured that there was no evil, beyond a time of detention, intended for her, which she saw to be a very probable thing. She had no intention of submitting quietly to a programme which, she had no doubt, aimed at the blackmailing of her husband, but she had some confidence in his ability to deal with the position successfully, and she saw that her chance might come. "Reggie," she thought comfortably, always comes out on top in the end, and I'm not going to spoil everything by giving these beasts an excuse for using their guns. But if I get half a chance—"

Neither this attitude of prudent wariness, nor the terms of truce she had made, reduced the extremity of her hatred of Slinker, against whom, since that moment of struggle which had ended in the prick of a needle in her left arm, she had felt a murderous impulse such as she would not have thought it possible that any human being would rouse in a generous mind.

On his side, there may have been little less than equal hate, for which he had the excuse of a bandaged hand. Her teeth had met under his thumb when he had covered her mouth to stifle her call for help, and the wound had become so inflamed during the last day that the hand would be of little use to lift or to aim a gun, which, even with a reputation for using both hands for such purposes, was a disadvantage which would put any gunman into a savage mood.

Now she sat back, watching a bare, almost treeless country, through which they ran fast for many miles on an empty road. It was an undulating land that rose higher and higher towards the foothills of the Rockies. It sparkled with a thin coating of powdered snow.

Her eyes fell casually upon Slinker's bandaged hand, and were lit with unholy joy. And she had teased Reggie with talk of being drawn to this loathsome toad! The thought brought another—that she had come to the New World against his wish and advice. If he had to pay a big ransom to get her free, or if it cramped his deal with Capone, how long would it be before she would hear the last of what she had done? But no, the question wasn't exactly that. Thank Heaven Reggie didn't nag. What would matter would be that she'd be so mad with herself.... She must contrive some device to get free. There was no other way out of this ghastly mess. If Slinker had been alone, she would have leant forward to strangle him with her hands Or would she? As he was not alone we shall never know.

The man at the wheel, whom Slinker sometimes addressed as Porky and sometimes as Chink, was twice his size and had an aspect of heavy brutality. He was grossly formed rather than fat, and had the look of a Swede of the worst type, with discordantly repulsive oriental eyes. Robbery with violence was the offence for which he had served two terms in a Michigan penitentiary. Murder, of which he had been more than once suspected, had not been proved against him.

Frank Gill had engaged him from a Detroit slum for the purpose of this abduction. He had received five hundred dollars in advance, and was to receive an equal payment on arrival at the Montana cabin, where he had been told that he would leave Slinker in charge. He would have sold his soul for a smaller fee. Neither he nor Slinker could betray Maloon, for his name had not been mentioned to them....

"We'll pull in?" Porky enquired, as they saw a white shack blotting the whiter snow at the roadside a short distance ahead. The run had been long, and he was getting both tired and hungry.

"Nope," Slinker said. "I've heard tell there's a better joint way on. There's a back room there."

With more forethought than his duller companion, he had made enquiries concerning the facilities of the road. "It won't be that far," he added, seeing the discontent on the face of a hungry man.

So they ran on to Beddoes', as Paul had guessed that they would, and as a bending road brought it to view they saw a car standing before it, not as though turned across the road to block their way, but somewhat aslant, and with one of its off doors swinging open.

Slinker looked at it with wary eyes. It did not look like a trap. It was certainly not how the cops would have closed the way. But it indicated that others might have stopped at a place where he would have preferred their absence, even if nothing further than that.

"We'll go slow," he said. "You stay here and keep your hand on the wheel. We'd get past with a squeeze."

He got out, with his sound hand in his jacket pocket, and walked round the standing car.

Finding it to be empty, he pushed open the door of the refreshment room. He saw it to be empty of visitors, and the bar was vacant. He called: "Bring her along." Evelyn, as hungry as the men, cramped with sitting, was glad to get out. She followed Slinker in, Porky coming behind.

Slinker knocked on the counter and got no response. "If there's no one in that back room," he said, "we'll just help ourselves. Guess we'll have a look-see."

He pushed open the door and went in. He would have drawn back next second, but Evelyn and the bulkier Porky blocked his retreat.

CHAPTER LVII.

Fatal Results

REDHEAD had what she thought to be a good plan. She remained of that opinion, which is beyond proof, and it would be waste of time to discuss, for the opportunity to operate it did not occur.

Things went uncontrollably wrong, with results which were bad enough and might have been worse.

They reached Beddoes' about ten or fifteen minutes before Slinker's car could arrive. They would have been sooner, but the road for the last ten miles had been deplorably bad. Still, it seemed enough.

Redhead went into the bar with Paul, leaving Cæsar in the car. She had a reasonable expectation that they would make a better impression if the gunman were not to be an immediate exhibit. But it was a needless precaution, for the room was vacant. Seeing this, and having lost some minutes in knocking without response, they looked into the back room. Finding it also to be unoccupied, Paul went out to find the proprietor. He went round the back of the garage, and some further minutes passed during which he did not return.

Meanwhile Redhead called Cæsar in. "We'd better wait in the back room till Paul finds Beddoes," she said. "They may be here any minute now."

Cæsar had what he thought to be a better idea. He would leave the door of the car open, and hide within it. One of the kidnappers would, he said, be sure to look in, when he could tell him to stick them up. If his gun were ready he would be sure to secure that result or to get the first shot.

Redhead said: "That's plain silly. We don't want gunning. Not one at a time, anyhow. You'll do what I say."

He gave way sullenly. It was his instinct to lie in hiding on such occasions—an inclination that became stronger as the event neared. But he had left the door of the car open, and so it remained.

Redhead had her way, but was not easy in mind. Where was Paul? Without his aid, and that of Beddoes if it could be secured, her plan would be of no avail, and any second now there might be the sound of the coming car.

Paul had found Beddoes, who was repairing a water-pump at the rear of the garage. It was work he could not easily leave, and he was a man slow alike of movement and thought and speech.

He excused the deserted bar by the urgency of what he did, and added that few came along that road in the winter months. They would be snowed up any day now—perhaps till the spring.

He heard Paul's tale with no visible emotion, and then said: "You'd better call up the cops. You can use the phone for that. But I don't want a rumpus here."

"We don't want the cops on this. We're not that sure what these men might try if they knew they were being tracked."

"You reckon they don't know that?"

"We have no reason to think they do."

Beddoes looked up from his work with doubtful eyes. "They'd count you'd do something to get her back. How'd I know—?"

He broke off at the sound of a shot, quickly followed by a second, and then, at a second's interval, by a third, after which there was silence. Paul was already running toward the refreshment room, his gun in his hand. Beddoes, without haste or delay, stolidly followed....

The door opened inwards. It had a panel of frosted glass. Slinker pushed it open and faced Cæsar and Redhead with lifted guns. Cæsar said sharply: "Put them up, Cito. Quick, or you're a dead guy."

Slinker lifted his bandaged hand. "Don't shoot, Cæsar," he said. "I've had a knock. There'll be no harm from me."

He would have withdrawn, but that Evelyn and Porky were so close behind. He moved so that Evelyn partly sheltered him as he spoke, and at the same moment he shot from the jacket pocket with his left hand.

Cæsar fired as the bullet struck. He sank to the floor, and his shot went wide. It shattered the glass of the door.

Porky jumped back, pulling Evelyn roughly with him, and at that instant Redhead fired. She might tell herself that she was slow at such crises, and not be wrong. Had Slinker had the use of his two hands, it is likely that her moment would not have come. But she was certain in what she did. The doorway was now blocked by a dying man, over whom she had no scruple to tread.

She went resolutely to the outer door, her anxiety for Evelyn's rescue being tempered by a natural wish not to increase the casualties through her own decease. She knew nothing of the man who had dragged Evelyn away, or of how combative his disposition might be.

Porky was not actually in a fighting mood. A splinter of glass had cut his cheek. The wound was deep, and he was a sanguine man. It bled freely, and, as he ran, he thought that he was more hurt than he was. He blamed the bullet for that which the glass had done.

Fearing that other shots would pursue him, he ran to the further side of the car, dragging Evelyn, who could only struggle vainly in the grip of hand's which seemed to her to be of a monstrous size. He had confused thoughts, in a dull mind, that there were still five hundred dollars to be secured, and that she would be a hostage for him.

He opened the back door of the car and threw her in so roughly that her head struck the door-handle on the further side, dazing her for a time, though causing no serious injury. He jumped into the front seat and drove through the narrow road-space left by the other car.

There was a noise of splintering wood and of cracking glass as it struck and shattered the swinging door, but it got through, and, as it did so, Redhead fired twice at the tyres, which she did not hit.

The brisk skirmish had been so rapid that Paul only came in view as the car was moving away.

"I've shot Slinker," she said, listing events in the order in which they were impressed on her own mind. "The other man's got away. He's got Evelyn. Cæsar's shot. We'd better follow at once."

Paul was cooler. He said: "Sure we will. But we'll have to sort things out here."

He saw that, if they should dash away leaving two dead or injured men lying about, they would not be likely to go far before the cops would be interfering, with resultant delay, if nothing much worse than that.

Beddoes was coming up behind. He may have heard what was said. Saying nothing himself, he led the way back to the scene of conflict. He looked at two dead men and a broken door.

Neither of the men had been lovely in life, and they were unattractive now. He said, "They're just swine," and looked at Redhead with considering eyes.

"Reckon," he said, "they shot each other."

"I shot Slinker," Moll answered boldly. "It was just him or me, and half a second to decide which." She added: "You'd be put to to find one who needed a bullet more."

Beddoes said slowly: "You've no call to say that, ma'am. I'd say they shot each other if you ask me. It'll be for the cops to say.

"Of course, you'll have to let them know what's happened," Moll assented. "But if there's no need to say it's me—"

"I can't say what I don't see. When I'm down mending the pump—

"Then we can go now?"

"Reckon you'd better if there's someone you want to catch.... You might be no worse for another gun."

To the surprise of those to whom he spoke, he pulled open a drawer under the counter and dropped a gun into his coat pocket. He got into the car with them, and Paul drove it forward at a speed he had not used even in the height of the chase of the last two days, while Beddoes struggled to fix the hinge of the broken door, and Moll turned her thoughts to the conflict which she supposed to be still ahead.

For five miles, or six, they drove on at a pace which may have made the silent Beddoes regret the impulse which had led him to where he sat, and then he was thrown forward with a jerk which brought his head into hard contact with the windscreen frame, as Paul braked and swerved to avoid a head-on collision with a car which came toward them at a pace not greatly inferior to their own.

"You needn't shoot him unless you want to particularly," Evelyn said happily, as the car came to a standstill beside them. "He's got one gun poking into the back of his neck

Paul said: "Chink, you'd better put your hands up and get out of the car."

The man stood with raised hands, while Paul took from him the two guns that his pockets held. The blood had dried on the fleshy face and had made black streaks down his coat. He looked as miserable as he felt.

"You'd better scram," Paul said. "You'll have no more use for the car."

The man stared at the emptiness of the snow-covered, desolate country. He said: "You're not going to leave me here?"

"We're not staying, and we don't mean taking you along."

"I can't walk that far."

"That's just too bad."

Paul turned away. He took the gun from Evelyn's hand. He asked: "How'd you get this?"

"It was pushed under the cushion. I knew before, but I didn't dare to use it while there were two of them to deal with."

"I'd say not.... You know there's no bullets here?"

"I had some doubt about that, but while it was poked into the back of his neck neither of us wanted to find out."

"No.... You'd have been back in his hands, or have wrecked the car."

Beddoes said: "Likely you'll want to talk. I'll bring this one along." The three of them got into the one car, and he took the wheel of the other. So they went back to his garage.

On arrival there he showed that, though he might be slow, he was thorough in what he did.

"I've got to ring up the cops about this," he said, "and you'd better clear. I'll give you five minutes to get fed, if you'll help yourselves. If you're gone by then, and go west, I wouldn't say I'll know much when the cops come. There's been two gunmen shooting it out in my shack while I was mending the pump, and I don't see how they'll make more of it than that." He added to Moll: "But there's something you'll need to do."

He led her back to the room where the dead men lay, and picked up Cæsar's gun. "It's not as dainty as yours," he said, "but you've got to change. You wouldn't want them to find that the bullet in that dead wop by the door came from one in your bag."

He took hers and wiped it carefully. Then, with a cloth round the barrel, he pressed the butt into Cæsar's hand. "I don't rightly know," he said, "if you get much prints from a dead hand, but it's the best we can do." He dropped the gun on the ground.

"You've been a real friend," she said gratefully, as she tried to fit Cæsar's gun into a bulging bag.

He looked at her steadily, as though puzzled by what she was, until she grew restless under that silent scrutiny.

"Maybe," he said, "you've had trouble enough. You'll be wise if you see that."

"This hasn't been trouble for me," she replied. "I was glad to help. You'd understand if you knew more."

"Maybe I should.... But you'd better clear.... There's those that learns when it's too late."

"You've got us wrong," she said. "But I'll say you're a white man."

She went back to the others, for she saw he was impatient for them to be gone. They joined their thanks to hers, and offered money he would not take.

When they had driven off, Paul at the wheel of one car and the two girls in the other, Beddoes rang up the police, and then, with a careful thoroughness, removed all traces of their presence and of the hurried meal they had had.

He still thought it was a queer business, the status and character of the Englishwoman puzzling him most of all. The other two he thought he could place, though he was less than sure. Cæsar, who had been of the party, he judged to be one of the meanest rats he had seen, dead or alive.

But he was not sorry for what he had done. He told himself that he didn't hold with kidnapping women, and, let the truth of that be what it might, he reckoned there'd been trouble enough. It was a view of the matter which Sir Reginald, through whose perverse generalisation it may be said that (more or less) all the trouble began, could not have failed to approve.

CHAPTER LVIII.

So Evelyn Gets the Wood

IT was early on Sunday afternoon when Mr. Jellipot returned to Chicago and drove straight to Capone's home, where he supposed that Sir Reginald would still be.

There was some formality and a little delay before he was admitted, for he had not arranged to return, and even guests of a previous day were not accepted at that steel-shuttered stronghold without the master's explicit order therefore.

But after that short delay his welcome was cordial enough, and it was a very few minutes before he was served with a good meal and then invited to Capone's private room, where Sir Reginald and Clancy were with their host, waiting to hear what the event might be which had led to that prompt return.

He gave the narrative of his experience to attentive ears. Sir Reginald knew him too well to doubt the accuracy of what he heard, which was no weirder to him than had been other happenings of the short weeks since they had landed from the docks of the Hudson river, But the two other auditors heard with expressions of astonishment in which the note of incredulity was not hard to hear. Yet there were qualities of lucidity and precision in the account they heard which impressed their minds, and details of authenticity which could not have been invented by one as inexperienced as Mr, Jellipot clearly was in the ways of the world they knew. When it concluded they looked at one another with puzzled eyes.

"I'd not have said," Capone commented, "they'd have had a hold-up at that dinner. It has me beat."

Clancy nodded. With all the night clubs, all the speak-easies, all the social gatherings of a Saturday night in New York to choose from, to pick on a ceremonial dinner to a magistrate whom the underworld had no occasion to dislike, and whom it would be the worst folly to offend!

Clancy added: "And seven men!"

That was where astonishment faltered and incredulity had its way.

Yet there were still details they could not doubt. There was the presence of Burke. That was not a name only. Mr. Jellipot described the man. There was cause for wonder in the mere fact of his presence there. And where Burke was, trouble was not likely to be far off. Yet he appeared to have had no part in the matter. He had been meekly robbed, and had then risen and gone his way.... And before the hold-up Terranova had approached him, and they had talked in a friendly style?

Mr. Jellipot must surely be mistaken there. It was too well known that Terranova was one against whom Burke had a deadly grudge. Mr. Jellipot agreed that the aspects of the two men gave some support to that. Burke had looked angry at times, and Terranova anxious to placate. Beyond that he could only tell what he had seen.

Capone began to calculate time. "You didn't lose much getting back," he said, and there was renewed scepticism in his voice.

"I didn't mean to lose any," Mr. Jellipot replied. "I thought at first I'd get back to the Hotel Atlantis, and I drove to Central Station, because I'd left baggage there. But by then I'd made up my mind to come on by the next train and get a berth on that if I could. I thought, if I could get over the state border before morning, it might be better for me."

"The *Baltic's* sailing again on Saturday," Sir Reginald said. "The first minute we know Evelyn's safe we'll book on it for home. We can board it at Boston if it looks as though you'd better not go back to New York."

Mr. Jellipot looked disturbed. "If," he said, "the cause of justice should require my return, I should be ashamed if I were not there. But it is another matter to be held in a foreign jail, which I would do much to avoid. But I may have run from that which I need not have feared."

Mr. Clancy said that, in his estimation, he had been a wise guy.

As he made this remark, Miles entered to say respectfully that the telephone had been ringing for some time in Sir Reginald's room.

The banker leapt up quickly. Was it news of Evelyn at last? But when he reached his room the ringing had ceased. He could learn no more than that there had been a long-distance call from South Dakota, which had just been cancelled.

Wroth and anxious, he returned to Capone's room, after arranging that he should be summoned at once if the phone should ring again, in time to hear Mr. Jellipot saying: "The name was certainly Bevis Street, and I am almost sure the number was fifty-eight. That it was Cassidy was an idea which had naturally occurred to my own mind, and I was disposed to connect this condition with the two shots which I had heard half an hour before. But in that I may have been wrong."

So he may. De Somma afterwards swore that two shots had been fired by him. The restaurant proprietor who could not recognise Terranova had been so anxious to call in the police that he had run into the street and fired two shots in the air to attract their notice. We must believe what we will.

Capone said: "There's something you might put the cops on to there, if you're so keen."

Sir Reginald said it should be done.

"You wouldn't know how," Clancy said. "You can leave that to me."

It was a few hours later that the New York Police got a message from a call-box that they might find a wounded man needing help at 58 Bevis Street, Bronx. They made instant efforts to trace the caller, but he had gone too quickly. What was he but a voice out of the night?

Clancy had rung up Larry Fay, who had told one of his men to give a street loafer a dollar to phone the message, with a promise of another if it should be proved by the event that it had been promptly given.

The police found, at least, that they had a straight tip. Cassidy lay fully dressed on a bed where he had bled to death from a bullet wound which, had he had proper attention, would have been little danger to him. The numbered shield on his gun made identification easy. Beyond that the police faced a blank wall.

But the newspapers were so full of other matters concerning police administration during the following weeks that it passed almost unnoticed, and they had no desire themselves to turn the spotlight upon another murder they could not solve....

The telephone rang again. Capone took it up. "No, Sir Reginald, it's not for you this time. It's for Clancy." He passed it over, and Tim said: "That you, Moll? Everything panned out right?"

"I'd say it has. But is Sir Crowe there? Evelyn's tried to get him on his line till she was fair sick."

"Yes. He's here. You've got her safe?"

"Well, she's here. She did the last act. Say, Tim, Slinker's dead, and Cæsar."

"That all? They're no loss. Knocked anyone off besides them?"

"I haven't knocked anyone off. Not in this state, anyway. But I can't go on talking to you. Ask Sir Cr—Sir Reginald to come on."

Next moment the banker heard his wife's voice: "That you, Reggie? I thought you must be having an afternoon sleep.... Yes, I'm all right. I wouldn't say it's much thanks to you, but we'll say no more about that if I get the wood.... Yes, *of course* I'm all right, only I've been putting on weight, and I don't see why I should forgive you for that.... I'd walk back only Moll won't agree. See you tomorrow, more likely than not."

Abruptly she rang off, leaving explanations for the next day.

It was at a later hour that Sir Reginald, digesting this conversation, wondered why it had not occurred to him to say that it was not he to whom forgiveness was due, and to remind her that it was against his will she had come. But that, he reflected, is what women are.

These short conversations left the question to be answered: Had the condition of Maloon's release been fulfilled? Capone said that he did not see that it had. The fact that two men were dead suggested a violent rescue, for which Maloon could have no credit at all. Sir Reginald did not dispute that. But he said that the bargain with Maloon stood so long as Evelyn came safely back.

Capone hesitated. He had still much at stake, and he had a curious unwillingness to show his worst side to his English guests. All the same, the bumping-off of Maloon, now that Evelyn's safety was sure, was such an obvious thing to do!

In the end he said that Clancy should decide, and Clancy said that when Lady Crowe actually returned he'd let the yellow dirt go. It was a way of putting it which was fortunate for Maloon, for it would give him six midday hours of safety, which he could use better than those of the closing day. It made little difference to him in the end, but that is another tale.

We must call this one done, as the *Baltic* casts loose the hawsers on Boston pier, though we may believe that the Crowes did not fail to follow the surprising course of Police Commissioner Whalen's enquiry into the events of the Vitale dinner as they were reported at fullest length in the New York press. Nor to notice reports of the exceptionally numerous bumpings-off of the next three months, such as that of Fred Gill, who was found shot through the head on a Dearborn road, as the Detroit press duly chronicled, during the first week of the New Year. And there was satisfaction of a negative kind in the fact that, of the Clancys, they read nothing at all....

Sir Reginald stood at the rail, with Evelyn at his side, as they watched the fading line of the bleak midwinter New England coast. "I wouldn't have missed it," he said, "if it had cost me that five million grand that I reckon now will be withdrawn in a way that will be no more trouble for us. And what a country it is!"

"I just love it," Evelyn answered. "We'll have to come again when we haven't got quite the same visiting list to get through.... But what I'd like to know is what's going to be done about Brook Meadow Wood?"

"You've lost the bet. You know that as well as I do. It's no use opening your eyes till they almost fall out. But I've told Jellipot he can buy it if it's not too dear.... I'm thinking," he added inconsequently, "Grice'll be an angry man by about now."